A

Dark

Tyranny

# OTHER BOOKS BY C.M. PENDLETON

Of Darkness & the Light:

*A Dark Tyranny*

*Ruins of the West*

# A

# Dark

# Tyranny

*~ Book One ~*

Of Darkness & the Light

C. M. Pendleton

© 2014 by C. M. Pendleton.

Copyright protected by the Copyright Office of the United States of America - TXu 1-911-550.

All rights reserved. No portion of this book may be reproduced, stored in a retrieval system, or transmitted in any form or by any means---electronic, mechanical, photocopy, recording, scanning, or other---except for brief quotations in critical reviews or articles, without the prior written permission of the publisher.

Publisher's Note: This novel is a work of fiction. Names, characters, places, and incidents are either products of the author's imagination or used fictitiously. All characters are fictional, and any similarity to people living or dead is purely coincidental.

*For Heather, Hudson, Lucas, Isabella and Remy.*

*A special thank you to my editor Amanda Siegel.*

## ~ CONTENTS ~

| | | |
|---|---|---|
| | Acknowledgments | i |
| 1 | Prologue: The Child Monger | 1 |
| 1 | The Cold Red | 5 |
| 2 | The Shoreline | 12 |
| 3 | Illusions | 15 |
| 4 | The Coming Storm | 28 |
| 5 | Out of the Shadows | 38 |
| 6 | Of Monsters and Curses | 46 |
| 7 | Servant to Slave | 52 |
| 8 | A Messenger in the Night | 59 |
| 9 | A Nighteye No More | 70 |
| 10 | The Long Road | 77 |
| 11 | Slavers | 84 |
| 12 | The Meeting at Kor | 97 |
| 13 | The King's Devil | 102 |
| 14 | An Encounter Along the Road | 111 |
| 15 | The Greenling Woods | 117 |
| 16 | A Council of Brothers | 131 |
| 17 | An Ancient Ally | 139 |

| | | |
|---|---|---|
| 18 | A Struggling Village | 147 |
| 19 | The Beginning of Isolation | 164 |
| 20 | A Difficult Decision | 174 |
| 21 | A Visitor in the Night | 183 |
| 22 | Night at Lake Lune | 189 |
| 23 | Let One Live to Kill Them All | 200 |
| 24 | The Face of the North | 216 |
| 25 | The Gorgon Caravan | 227 |
| 26 | A Midnight Meeting | 232 |
| 27 | The Land of Karth | 249 |
| 28 | The Realm of the North | 264 |
| 29 | The Acolytes | 271 |
| 30 | The White Ruins | 282 |
| 31 | An Entrance at Dawn | 285 |
| 32 | The Battle of the White Ruins | 296 |
| 33 | Dark Tyranny | 304 |
| 34 | A Dark Council | 317 |
| 35 | Fury | 323 |
| 36 | The War Begins | 329 |
| | Epilogue: The Lisbeth | 336 |
| | List of Names | 339 |

## A DARK TYRANNY

Map of Altaris — 348

About the Author — 350

## Prologue

### The Child Monger

The hooves of the horses beat against the dry ground leaving a stagnant cloud of dust in their wake. The riders were five strong, clad in tarnished bronze mail; their spears upright in hand. They forced those spilling from the markets and taverns to clear the road or be run down. The lead rider wore the mark of the Noble. To the townsfolk, he was the child monger, the baby stealer; some simply referred to him as the monster.

Wyndale was the smallest village in the Western Realm. It was surrounded by deep forests on all sides. It was said that there were more thieves in the forest than trees. The straw shacks in the village were pushed together so close that there were no secrets amongst those with ears. It was not long before the whispers of the Noble's arrival in the village that mothers began to call to their children and lock them indoors. It was a futile attempt at safety, but an attempt none the less.

His mother and father frantically ran through the

hut pulling what belongings they could grasp into a woven sack. The child monger was coming. It was all they could think of.

"We'll not make it. They'll see us," tears were beginning to run down her cheeks.

"We have to try, Mary," he said, almost in a whisper. "I don't understand. It's too soon. He's not even a year yet."

"We should have left sooner ... at half year's end. He's going to take him," those words opened her eyes to a waterfall of tears. She could no longer stay brave. She knew it was over. "He will take our child, Henri. We have lost him ..."

His father picked up the trunk in both hands. The woven branches cut through his hands. It was too heavy. He stopped for a brief moment.

*Think, Henri. You need to calm your senses.*

"I hear them. The horses ...," she picked up the child and held him tight. His breath was warm against her neck. He was so small and fragile, a babe yet. Soldiers on horseback carrying away her child, it was too much. He was too innocent.

"I need to think," said Henri.

"They're coming," replied Mary.

"My father's coin," said Henri.

"What?" asked Mary.

"They may take the child ... but the man we will know."

Henri threw the trunk on the dusty floor scattering its contents until he found the leather pouch.

*This is all I can do. Deal in truths now.*

"My child," she understood. She rummaged through her cupboard until she found them. Elder sap, thin leaf, root burn, and some thresh moss for the pain.

*Forgive me.*

The father took the child and laid him upon the table. He revealed the coin from the pouch. It was

# A DARK TYRANNY

tarnished gold in color with the insignia of the First Kingdom, a broadsword encased in the sun.

"This coin is from my father and his father before him. It was found off the Black Coast in the gullet of a sandfish. They're bottom dwellers; he must have swallowed it before my grandfather fished him to the surface," he spoke to the child as much to himself.

"I hear them," she handed him a bowl with ingredients mixed to a thick paste. The smell burned the eyes. The child began to cry.

"This coin is of the First Kingdom. If any other has one in all the realms, I have not heard of it. I had hoped to bestow it to you later in life," he carefully held the coin with the tips of his fingers; a cloth between skin and coin. He put the coin in the dark paste.

"I could have tried to sell this relic. They would have simply taken it, as they now come to take you. Instead, we keep it. Evidence of a history once great. A time we've strayed from."

He opened the child's robes and gently placed the coin upon his chest. The babe cried and his mother cried with him.

"This mark will stay with you. It will be a mark to know you by when you return; a symbol to keep you steadfast in your years," his father could no longer hold his tears at bay.

"They are here," she said. He removed the coin. Before replacing the child's robes, the mother sprinkled thresh moss on the image of the coin that now marked her son.

"We will leave soon. We should be gone before they return to the hold. They will see the mark and come back for it," he began to pack the trunk again. "We will return when our age hides our image. They will be done with him by then ... and long forgotten about us."

There was a thud at the door.

"Open!" bellowed one of the soldiers.

Henri opened the door while his wife held the babe one last time. She breathed deeply to remember his scent. She felt his hair upon her cheek. Her lips kissed the soft rolls of his neck. A tear rolled from her eye and onto his head.

*I love you. I will never forget you.*

"I am here by the divine rights of King Uthan of the Western Realm. The King lays claim to harvest all boys born during his own season of birth." The words dryly rolled off the Noble's tongue; a speech said too many times. His thin nose would have slanted to a sharp point but it had been broken causing a notch to rise from the soft bone. It gave his voice a nasal hiss. Sweat dripped down his head causing his thin black hair to spread and lay limp over his scalp. It was hot out and the child monger had grown tired of herding the little runts to the keep.

"Please. Our first child died in the belly," Henri pleaded, knowing it would lead to nothing.

"Well then, you should have thought of that before you put your cock in her," he said, disinterest dripped from his voice. "If you must blame, then hold yourself into account. The king's season of birth has not changed since the day he was born. I have other rats to gather. Give him to the guards or give yourself to their sword."

The mother cried while gently whispering in her son's ear. The child touched her face with his soft hands. She brought the boy to the smallest of the guards. She told herself all the lies that would make it easier. The guard would see the innocence in her son and see to him while he grew. He would keep him from harm. He took the child but not once looked at him.

"The king has this child by divine rights. He will be returned to you in death or after he is of no more service to the realm ... whichever is first."

## Chapter 1

The Cold Red

Snow drifted down around the horse and rider. The forest itself was deep in slumber; it was frozen under a blanket of ice and snow. The barren trees pointed to the cloudy heavens. Their foliage was long since dead. The horse slowly crunched through snow with each step, packing more ice to the earth. The rider was bundled in a patchwork of bear furs. A coarse yellow beard grew about the rider's face. His thick hair drifted out of his hood. It blew like the tip of a flag in the wind. It was longer than his chin but did not reach his shoulders. The horse was easily fifteen hands, but the rider's bulky frame kept the steed from dwarfing him. Albeit, the rider and his steed were like insects when compared to the thick trees of the forest. The trunks of the Wielder trees alone were as thick as a house or tavern.

Had it not been for the breath of the horses and their riders, he would not have seen them in the distance. He knew that running in this cold was not an option. It would kill his horse and get him no further from them. His black mare had been good to him. He would not freeze its lungs for what could not be avoided. Instead, he kept moving forward towards them. The riders brought their horses to a trot. There were four of them. They wore fur cloaks but he could see the glint of steel under them.

*They have not been in these woods long. They are kingsmen or hunting a bounty ... perhaps both.*

The forest still slept as the riders drew close. The snow continued to console the wind.

"You there," the second rider called. A sheathed long sword was attached to his saddle. "Speak your name."

"I am drifting snow ..."

"Your head can drift from your shoulders. We'll take it to the next village, maybe someone will recognize you. Although, you could just tell us," said the bald rider atop a pale grey horse. His face was dusted with dirt and snow; his blackish teeth were scattered within his mouth.

"Come now, let's not play this game," said the center rider. He pulled back the hood of his cloak. His face was thin and chiseled. A scar led from the top of his scalp and, erratically, flowed down his face to rest under his chin. The crystal blue of his eyes had the look of violence. "We know it's you, Matthias."

"Denthas. They have you tracking me in this frozen hell?" said Matthias.

"Orders ... orders lined with gold, but orders still."

"Soldiers collecting bounties ... is this the way of it then?"

"Some things have changed since you left, my friend."

"Let's just take him and be on with it," crowed the bald rider. He removed the axe strapped to his back. Matthias saw that he had deep scars along his neck.

"Easy, Jarren," warned Denthas. "This is no common brigand."

"You should just let me through, Denthas," said Matthias. "This will only end in blood. We've shed enough."

"You shed your own blood a long time ago," replied Denthas.

"You'd have done the same."

"A whore and her runt mean nothing to me," said Denthas. "Worth all this, are they?" asked Denthas, as he looked around. "The running ... the killing. Yes, we've seen your wake of bodies."

"Bounty hunters and brigands alike. Their blood is on the realm's hands, not mine. Your man there has marks of a rapist along his neck. Is this the type you now keep among the ranks?"

"I'm not bothered by blood, Matthias ... or stolen cunt. I do, however, care about gold," Denthas motioned with his hand.

One of the riders let loose an arrow. It thudded into the throat of Matthias' horse. The great beast reared back throwing him off. Another arrow pierced its fleshy stomach. It let out a guttural cry as it fell on its side. Matthias pulled a sword from his saddle. The dying horse shook with fear; its blood warming the air around it in a bellow of soft steam. Matthias pulled another sword that was sheathed on his back. He let his bulky cloak fall to the snowy earth.

*I am tired. Wasn't paying attention to the other riders. It was a green mistake.*

Another arrow let loose. He could feel it fly past his head.

*The trees. Make them come around to fight on my terms.*

Matthias ran to one of the large Wielder trees.

The other riders moved in. Their horses fought through the snow at a forced run. Jarren was the first to round the large tree. His horse clumsily pushed through the frozen terrain. He heard the panic of his horse as Matthias's blade cut through its neck. It didn't rear; it just seemed to fall, almost lifelessly to the snow. Jarren fell with his horse. He heard one of his legs snap from the weight of the dead beast. Matthias was upon him before he could even make sense of the pain in his leg. In one motion, Matthias put his sword through the top of Jarren's chest plate and into his heart. The other two soldiers rounded the tree with swords in hand. Matthias swung his sword as he turned to them. He was able to deflect one blow from taking his head. Instead, he felt the blade bite deep into his shoulder. His blood was warm. He could feel his woolen tunic and leather cuirass grow damp. The other rider's swing was off. His horse was unsteady in the snow. Matthias simply backed away from the blow. He swung one blade at the horse's hind leg. It fell with a shriek. The other blade hit the soldier in the back of the neck; he fell with his crippled horse. He let out a gasp of pain as he laid twisted upon the snow. His horse tried to stand back up, but fell again. Matthias followed through with another strike to the soldier's neck.

The other rider turned his horse for another run at Matthias. Matthias raised both swords, bracing himself for the attack. The soldier rode at him. His swing was steady and placed. It sliced through the falling snow. Matthias crossed his blades to deflect the blow. Steel rang out casting bits of spark and metal. Matthias turned as the horse passed him. Suddenly, he felt his body lurch forward.

*Denthas ... another green mistake.*

He felt the arrow pound into his back. It sent a searing pain down his right arm and leg. He lost feeling in his arm; it was numb. His sword grew heavy.

*Concentrate. Strike with my left and throw with my right. Move from Denthas.*

He felt another arrow catch the side of his right leg. It buried deep into the muscles of his thigh.

# A DARK TYRANNY

*I need to take this rider down. Move from sight.*

The rider was on him. Matthias fell to one knee feeling the soldier's swing barely miss his head. Matthias sent his sword into the belly of the horse. It reared and fell. He swung his blade again before the horse hit the ground. He cut through helm and cloak, as his sword bit hard into the falling soldier's head. A third arrow grazed Matthias's neck sending him falling sideways to the ground. Pools of crimson blood were scattered throughout the snow.

Matthias stumbled back to his feet. He heard Denthas' horse moving towards him. It was a fast walk. He had underestimated him.

*I should have killed him first.*

The sword in Matthias's left hand fell. He was slowly losing control of his leg as well. He could no longer feel the arrow in his back, only the ache of the one buried in his thigh.

*I should let him kill me. I will die quick now or slow after.*

The thought of slowly freezing to death did not welcome him. Denthas was at him now with an arrow notched.

"Drop your sword, Matthias," ordered Denthas. "Your day is here. Embrace it."

"The thought had occurred to me," Matthias dropped to one knee. His leg began to give. His mouth had the taste of metal and blood. "Yet, I don't think I will let go so easy today."

Matthias tried to stand, but his leg would not have it. He fell to the ground snapping the arrow lodged in his back. The snow fell slowly down around him; he looked skyward. He thought of Mara and Wylin.

*I will see you shortly, my loves.*

He was tired. This is when he first caught a glimpse of it, soaring down like a sword of light from the heavens.

Denthas pulled back on his bow.

"Don't move. I need your head recognizable for the bounty."

The heat started to rise around Denthas before he could aim his shot. He looked up in shock. His horse reared, throwing him to the ground. He felt his arrow sink into his knee. Denthas looked to the sky in terror. The beast cast a piercing cry that cut through the silence of the forest. It was the size of three warhorses. Its thick wings pushed it through the cold air and made a sound like a ship's sails filling with wind with each stroke. It almost appeared as a winged lion, however, it was made up of fire; a pure radiating heat that seared throughout its form. Burning feathers with a whitish blue hue coated the beast like coals in a fire. It was made of raw heat and flame. The great beast arched its back and threw its hind legs forward. A searing white heat radiated from its talons. Denthas scrambled to notch another arrow as he staggered to his feet. He turned his bow to it, but the shot was too hastened. The arrow flew to the sky far from its target. He dropped his bow to run. Denthas felt his knee lock. The arrow had pierced the top of the knee and protruded out the bottom. He fell to the earth biting his lip. It was too late. A white searing light was all around him. His eyes burned. The snow began to melt. The burning light around him suddenly turned to darkness. He never saw the claws of the beast or felt them slice through him like warm butter. In an instant, the life in his eyes became clouded with death. Denthas was no more, only pieces of him lay lifeless in the snow.

Matthias stared at the beast in astonishment. Its body breathed in heavily. The enormous creature moved with grace. The bodies of soldiers and horses were strewn about. Matthias was all that remained. It turned its fiery head to him. The eyes of the fiery lion cast down upon him. The heat warmed his skin, but did not burn.

*I am dying anyway. I will take this heat like a warm blanket.*

Matthias closed his eyes.

*So tired.*

He felt claws grip his body, but there was no pain.

"Sleep now," Matthias heard the words in his head like a distance voice. In a gentle motion, the beast wrapped its talons around Matthias. The fiery creature lifted its wings. A gust of wind blew snow and shook the branches of the Wielder trees, as the great beast ascended into the expanse of sky above.

## Chapter 2

### The Shoreline

It was close to morning. The first hints of light would soon wake the horizon. A light fog spread over the coastline. Lewdale was a small fishing village with its wooden homes resting along the shore of the Southern Realm. It was only a day's walk to the Eastern Realm, so the village thrived on trading its catch to its neighbors. However, Lewdale was part of the Southern Realm. This fact was no longer in dispute. The villagers did not care which realm they served. Taxes and homage would come from either side so they no longer carried to whom they gave it. They spent their days fishing the waters, instead of worrying about kings and land.

Molt and his brothers always woke early. They were all in their early thirties and each one had a wife, and at least one child. Molt had four children. As they stood on the shore by their boats, Molt and Cravis untangled a net, while Desmond put oars and the main sail in the hull of their small boat. It was a sloop with a centerboard; perfect for getting in and out amongst the small neighboring islands. A breeze blew over the shoreline. It was wet and cold.

"It will be cold today," said Molt.

"Let the sun come up," replied Desmond.

"It's cloudy. You cannot see the sky. It will be a cold day," said Molt.

"Do you see something out there?" said Cravis. He pointed towards the water.

"Yes. Stars reflecting on the water?" asked Desmond.

"It's too cloudy. It's not stars. I see it too," said Molt.

Cravis put down the net and walked to the edge of the water. He wrapped his arms around his chest to stay warm. He looked out into the water. Small lights flickered in the distance. More of them continued to appear. They steadily rose up and down. There was a yellow hue about them. Desmond approached Cravis. He stood beside him looking at the lights.

"Look," said Desmond.

"They're moving," said Cravis.

"They're not lights. They're torches. They are all moving together with the water. God and kings. We need to leave," said Molt.

"You're right! They're torches," said Cravis.

"They keep appearing. There must hundreds," said Desmond.

"Hurry!" said Molt. "We need to warn the village!"

A fiery arrow escaped the darkness. It hissed through the air and thudded into Desmond's chest. Desmond fell hard to the sand. His clothes slowly caught fire. The steel tip of the arrow pierced through his chest and out his back. Desmond's body laid lifeless upon the sand.

"Desmond!" yelled Cravis, as he ran towards him.

Another arrow caught Cravis in the neck. It knocked him sideways. He grabbed at the arrow, as blood streamed down his neck. He choked and coughed. Cravis fell to his knees gasping for air. Molt ran. He heard two arrows hiss past him. One of his legs flew to one side, as a searing pain burned above his knee. He tripped. Looking down, he saw another arrow jutting from his leg. He started to stand but another caught him in the back, while another thudded into this waist. Molt laid to one side. He felt his blood pool around him. The fire on the arrows slowly spread. He looked out at the water, while he struggled to breathe. Torches illuminated the black hulls of the vessels. They glided through the water like shadows. A fleet of warships slowly descended upon the shores of Lewdale.

## Chapter 3

## Illusions

The hawk was a short-winged bird. It soared high above the forest in tight circles. Finn had decided upon the goshawk for that day. Its short wings made it ideal for quick bursts of speed and darting between the trees. The trees kept the forest shaded. Sunlight cascaded between them in thick beams. Finn could hear the faint ring of the gauntlet that wrapped its talon. Finn and the bird had already caught two small hares and a squirrel. They were close to being done for the day. Finn enjoyed hunting. He did his best to prolong his time away from Castle Red.

It was not long before he whistled to the bird for its return. He tethered it to his wrist and began the walk back to the castle. He gave the goshawk small bits of a field mouse as they walked. Finn knew what it was like to be a servant to someone. Unlike the hawk, Finn would not be released at the end of the year.

*If I could fly like you ... I would never return.*

Nylah sat at the table with her aunt and cousin. She looked at her bowl of stewed beef and potatoes. The oil from the beef pooled atop the broth. She missed the buttered fish, olives, and ripe tomatoes of the isles. Things in the realms were different. Her hair was usually curly and fell in dark ringlets, but the climate of the Southern Realm caused her hair to feel dry and brittle, and made her skin feel tight and coarse. Perhaps, it was the water or the air. She felt like a stranger; she was a stranger.

"Eat your food, Nylah. They do not have their evening meal here until much later," said Lady Tanda.

Lady Tanda's hair was braided and pulled back. She sat with perfect posture. She looked like a stern version of Nylah's mother. Her pale skin did not look as delicate as it did on Nylah's mother. Lady Tanda's demeanor caused any delicateness of skin tone to look waifish and sickly. She was not a mean person and could be kind at times. She was an orderly woman that respected rank and designation.

"Yes, Aunt Tanda," said Nylah. She reached for the basket of bread at the center of the table.

"The stew as well," said Lady Tanda, as she straightened her dress and regained her posture.

"You really shouldn't ask so many questions this time," said Lilith. Nylah's cousin had the same pale skin as her mother, Lady Tanda. She did not look sickly like her mother, instead her pale skin and off-putting demeanor gave her an arrogant rudeness. Her brown hair was pulled back tightly into a bun. Nylah had trouble looking at her without smiling. Lilith's eyebrows seemed to stretch upward from the stress of her hair tugging her scalp.

"I was curious about the mill," replied Nylah.

"Lilith, leave her be," said Lady Tanda. "She has not been exposed to this."

"Why would your father not move from the isles?" asked Lilith.

"Because there are no ships inland or fish for that matter," replied Nylah.

"Her mother made her choice," said Lady Tanda.

"But why?" asked Lilith.

"She loves my father and he builds ships," said Nylah.

"Ask as many questions as you like, Nylah. I only ask that you be respectful. The Baron is a powerful man in this realm. He does business with our family, your family," said Lady Tanda.

"Of course, Aunt," said Nylah.

"We will be meeting with Lord Hartley and the Baron later. I'm sure you will have plenty of opportunity for questions," said Lady Tanda.

"You can always ask me your questions," said Lilith. "I've seen a lot in my twenty-three years."

"I've a question then," said Nylah.

"Do ask," said Lilith.

"How do you get your hair so tight?" said Nylah, smiling.

Lilith felt her hair. Nylah could no longer hide her laughter. She tried to conceal it with a cough but it was no use. Lady Tanda looked sternly at both Nylah and Lilith. She put down her glass and laid her hands upon the table.

"You are practically the same age. You should be friends not bickering nuisances to each other," said Lady Tanda.

She looked at Lilith.

"God and kings, Lilith. Loosen your hair," said Lady Tanda, smiling.

The three of them had a moment of laughter. It felt good to Nylah. It felt like home.

"You should pull your hair back some, Nylah. You have charming eyes. You should let others see them," said Lady Tanda.

"They are very green," said Lilith.

"They are your father's, no doubt," said Lady Tanda.

"I would like to meet your father," said Lilith.

"You are always welcome. It would be nice," said Nylah.

"Come now, finish your food. Lord Hartley wants to see the Baron's falcon or some such thing," said Lady Tanda.

---

The mew was behind Castle Red. It was originally near the stables, but the hawks and falcons could not relax close to the horses. Finn put the goshawk into the mew and left for the kitchen. He would give the hares to the butcher for cleaning and dressing. He had other plans for the squirrel. He put it in a small sack. Finn could see the stone tower attached to the castle. The stones of the tower were older than Castle Red itself. The Baron had ceased using the tower a long time ago. The guards had not slept there in years. There was only one occupant now, and it was kept in a cage. This was the perfect time for Finn to visit the great bird.

This was his favorite time of the day. It was one of the only times he felt a semblance of freedom. His was a life of servitude to the king. He and a host of others were given to the Baron as a gift. Finn had grown up in Castle Red. He was a falconer, which entailed his hunting the Baron's land for small game. Falconers also keep the smaller predators like fox and feral dogs at bay. The Baron's mew was full of many different birds for hunting. Bow and bird, the villagers called it. However, Finn had no bird like the Red Falcon. He

## A DARK TYRANNY

often wished he could release it. Let it soar again, though it would mean his death. The Blood Falcon of Castle Red was worth more than the life of one servant. The least Finn could do was feed it more than simple grain and insects. He tried to feed the bird at least twice a week. It depended on each day's hunt, but he was normally able to catch and conceal at least one small animal each week for the great bird.

---

The Baron and his party ascended the stairs of the tower. They wound up and around in tight circles. The tower of Castle Red was the largest tower in the Southern Realm. The stairs wound for what seemed like an eternity. The stairs were no longer safe for one person, much less a large party. There were no railings along the cracking stone walls. One slip of the foot meant certain death.  Two guards led the way; two more followed behind. Large slits in the walls let dusty light cascade into the tower. They crisscrossed the entire way down, like a spider web cast by the sun.

"Careful now," the lead guard spoke with a rasp. His mustache twisted down around his dry lips. "These stairs ain't seen this many boots in at least a hundred years."

"They certainly ain't seen the likes of maidens or lil' ones," a thin faced guard chimed in. He looked terrified that one of the highborn families would fall to their death. It would certainly mean the dungeons for him, or worse.

"I was bequeathed this beast. The least I can do is show it to some that would take interest," said the Baron of Moor, a portly man with a constantly flush face. There was too much walking and riding in this world; his large frame had grown tired of it by the age of nine. Now in middle age, he was quite sick of overexerting himself. However, he'd let his wine and his boasting get the better of him during the midday meal. The wine was gone now. He had sweated it through his shirt and pants before the twentieth stone step. His thin mustache was now soaked. It limply hung against his fleshy lips.

"Is it truly the last of its kind?" asked Lady Tanda.

"If there is another, I have yet to lay eyes upon it. One may hear the tale of a forester catching sight of one, but it's nothing more than that, a tale." The Baron leaned against the wall. He willed himself to take another step, then another, then another.

"Have you heard it scream," asked a boy clutching to Lady Tanda's dress for safety.

"Alas, I have not, nor would I want to," said the Baron as he paused to catch his breath.

"They say it can drive a man to madness," spoke Lord Hartley. He carried the ends of his cloak like a woman clinging to her dress as she jumps a puddle. His very presence sent bile up the Baron's throat. The Hartleys were only made highborn after the last war. They had no real noble blood. "I must admit that I am quite intrigued by the stories of these beasts."

"If we could ever get to the end of these bloody stairs," sighed Lady Tanda.

---

Finn had not been in the cell long before he began to hear voices outside the room.

*No one ever comes to the tower's cell.*

He could hear sounds of women and children. It was strange to hear such voices filling the emptiness of the tower. The cell was usually quiet, except for the sounds of feeding the great falcon. He was holding the squirrel he had brought for the bird.

The door to the tower cell opened. Finn saw the

large group stagger in. They were breathing heavy with sweat on their flush faces. Finn stood straighter as they entered. He quickly put the squirrel back into the sack. Finn began to think of what to say to the Baron. He was always anxious around him. He had been this way since they brought him here as a child.

"God and kings!" exclaimed Lord Hartley. He looked in awe of the great bird in the cage before him. The thick steel cage took up the entire room. There was just enough space for the group to spread out around the flat bars. The bird itself took up most of the cage. It was nearly the size of a stag or large pony. Its claws wrapped tightly around a bar crossing just above the floor. "It's enormous ... and the color."

"A deep red," spoke the Baron, "the color of blood."

"A Blood Falcon," the little boy spoke to himself. "They're real."

"Indeed, but he is the last of his kind. When he leaves this world, the only red falcons left will be the ones that adorn the castle's banners," spoke the Baron.

"And shields," replied the child.

"Aye. You there," the Baron motioned to Finn. "What business are you carrying on with?"

"I was ensuring the bird had water and grain, sire."

"One of your falconers, sire," spoke a guard.

"Why is the bird blindfolded?" Lady Tanda seemed none too impressed.

"For our safety madam. The bird has a scream that will bleed your ears," said the Baron.

"Lack of vision keeps this bird from using its voice? How pathetic for such a renowned beast. When do you take it off?" asked Lord Hartley.

"Why, never," replied the Baron. Did the bloody fool want the bird to shake the tower to the ground?

"This beast has been blindfolded since the days of your father's fathers?" questioned Lady Tanda.

"We won't be feeding the bird just now. Not with

guests in its presence," the Baron spoke to Finn, as he ignored the question.

"Aye, sire," Finn backed up from the cage. This was the moment he first saw her. The waves of her thick dark hair cascaded around her shoulders in tight ringlets. She had eyes of emerald seas that caught Finn unaware. He stood for a moment, lost. She looked to be from the isles, as her skin was a soft brown and she had high cheeks that were rounded instead of sharp. They made her eyes seem larger and kind. She smiled at him. Finn felt his face go flush. One of the other girls giggled and said something. Finn stood motionless. He was lost in the woman before him.

"Hello," Finn said quietly to her.

She smiled at Finn and began to speak.

"That will be all," ordered Lady Tanda.

"Yes, my Lady." Finn turned to leave them with the great winged falcon. It was a bird that had lived for over one hundred years. It would outlive them all. It was thing of myth and legend, but all Finn thought of was a pair of green eyes that had stared back at him, even if for a brief moment.

"How many falcons do you have, Baron?" asked Nylah.

"There are many different birds in the mew," replied the Baron.

"I have never seen a mew," said Nylah.

"This can easily be remedied," said the Baron. "I can ensure you see the mew before you depart."

"I believe we are traveling to Nedding tomorrow. Are we not, Aunt Tanda?" asked Nylah.

"We plan to see their fabrics," Lady Tanda said to the Baron.

"You can see the mew tonight if you like," said the Baron, "if it is agreed upon by your aunt."

"May I?" Nylah asked Lady Tanda.

"See that you are back soon. We are dining with

Lord Hartley," said Lady Tanda.

"Of course, Aunt," said Nylah, smiling.

"See that she sees the mew," the Baron said to Finn. "See that she is safely and expediently returned to her quarters after she has seen the birds."

"Yes, sire," replied Finn. His heart pounded in his chest.

"Enjoy the mew, cousin," Lilith said with a grin.

"Shall I follow you then?" Nylah said to Finn.

---

There was a chill to the air when Finn and Nylah left the tower. The sun was slowly setting; its warmth was being tucked away beyond the horizon. They made their way across the courtyard. Farmers led oxen and wagons through the dusty streets, carrying turnips and potatoes. Villagers bustled across the courtyard and through the castle grounds. Glenshire Village lay directly beside Castle Red. The villagers sold their goods to all those passing through. Finn could hear the distant sounds of lutes and pipes drifting through the village. He pulled his cloak over his shoulders. His hair fell just below his chin. He pulled a leather strap from his pocket to keep it from blowing over his eyes. There was an unusual breeze, an almost warm air laced with streaks of cold. Nylah walked with her arms across her chest. She did not raise the hood of her cloak. The breeze blew the ringlets of her hair back and Finn could see the contours of her face. He tried not to stare at her. She walked beside him in silence. Neither seemed to know what to say. Finn felt he should say something. Anything. They both began to speak at once.

"I'm sorry. Go ahead," said Finn.

"No, it's ok. What were you going to say?" said Nylah.

"I was just going to ask about falconry in the isles.

You're from the isles, are you not? I mean, you're not from here. I guess they do not know falconry there," said Finn.

"No. No falconry and, no, I'm not from here. And ... yes, I am from the isles."

"You look different than them ... your aunt and the others."

"I favor my father."

"He is from the isles?"

"Yes, much to the chagrin of the others."

"I would love to see the isles someday."

"You should then."

*She doesn't know I'm in servitude.*

"Do you like birds?" asked Nylah.

"Some of them. I was assigned to clean the mew. I ended up being an apprentice to one of the falconers. I'm now one myself. The birds have grown on me."

"You've no say in your work then?"

"No."

"I'm sorry. I've been speaking as if you did."

"It's quite alright. It is a nice change."

"Will you ever return?"

"Home? To my parents?"

"Yes."

"Someday, I suppose. They are in the Western Realm though."

"Why are you in the Southern Realm, then?"

"In the Western Realm, children born in the month of the king's birth are claimed for servitude. It is the same in the Southern Realm. They sometimes exchange the children to prevent their parents from seeing them."

"To keep them from taking their children back?"

"Wouldn't you?"

"I suppose I would. That is very sad."

"I didn't mean to upset you. It will not last forever. At least I have a task I prefer. I could be peeling onions or cleaning bedpans," said Finn. He grinned at Nylah to lighten the mood.

The sun had almost completely set before they arrived at the mew. A soft glow of yellow surrounded it. Lanterns hung from the outside rafters of the wooden building. The mew was round and tall. There were no corners. It was a circular building with a roof that should have come to a point, but the very top of the roof was cut flat. A plate of blown glass laid flat over the opening of the roof, allowing the sun and moon to shine into the heart of the mew. Finn took two lanterns from the door. He lit both and gave one to Nylah. The rich smell of straw, dust, and wildlife drifted from the mew. Nylah could hear the movement and the flapping of wings.

"Don't worry. They're in cages," said Finn, as he opened the door to the mew.

The ceiling of the mew seemed much higher from inside. The glass at the top let the first hint of stars drip down into the mew. The lanterns cast a soft glow against the varnished wooden walls and straw floor. Dust drifted up through the light, while steel cages littered the round walls. They stacked upon each other. The top of the mew was one large cage to itself. Branches were stuck into the walls for perching.

"The cages are so small," said Nylah.

"We rotate the birds. Each one has time in the larger cage to stretch its wings and move around for a while," said Finn. "The others are small though. I agree."

"How many falcons are there?" asked Nylah.

"They are not all falcons. It's called falconry but different types of birds are used. This one is a goshawk. A hawk. I took her out today. She has shorter wings so she is good for the forest ... quickly catching hares. This one is a Gyrfalcon. She is much larger and better for distance."

"Her patterns are beautiful."

"Mist is one of my favorites. We're not supposed to name them but she's different. The white and black patterns are so crisp and sharp. I prefer her to the others, but don't tell them," said Finn with a smile.

Nylah stared at Finn and smiled back.

"Are all of them females?"

"Most of them are. The females are usually larger and stronger."

"I guess you need both for breeding," said Nylah.

"Actually, we don't breed them."

"You catch them?" asked Nylah.

"Yes. We train and hunt with them. We release some each year. Mist will be released at the end of the season. It's my favorite time."

"But you work so hard to train them."

"Nothing deserves to live in a cage," said Finn. "We keep them here and train them. They are fed, but not too much. They must think that we are their main source of feeding, so they are kept just above hunger. They could fly away at any time during the hunt, but they return for food."

"But, they are hunting food."

"It's an illusion. They are only as captive as they choose to be."

"That is sad."

"It is why the best part of my year is releasing them."

"Do they ever stay?" asked Nylah.

"Would you or I?"

"No," Nylah replied. She looked at Finn. She could see he was a good person. He had a gentle way about him that made her feel at ease.

"Once they hunt and get to keep the spoils, the illusion is gone. They realize they are free."

Nylah stared at Finn. His brown hair was pulled back with a leather strap. However, some of it escaped and lay over his high cheekbones and down around his chin. He had the frame of a woodsman. He was neither thin nor heavily muscled. Nylah supposed his hands were rough and calloused. His face was brown from the sun. He spent most days outdoors. She could tell. His cage was much larger than the birds, but a cage none-the-less.

"Will you return home to the isles?" asked Finn.

"Yes. My mother and father thought it would be a learning experience to see the realms."

"Do you like the realms?"

"They are different."

"That's a pleasant way of saying you're ready to leave."

"I miss home. You understand," Nylah said. She realized that Finn had no home the moment she spoke.

"Unfortunately, no. However, I imagine that I would."

Finn and Nylah stared at each other in an awkward silence.

"My name is Nylah."

"I'm Finn."

"It is a pleasure to meet you, Finn."

## Chapter 4

### The Coming Storm

Finn passed through the crowds towards the castle's bake house. His mind raced with thoughts of Nylah. He thought of so many things he should have said to her. He wished he could relive their time at the mew. Finn hoped to rise early enough the next day to see her off. He would find a reason to be nearby. Finn was excited. He wanted to tell someone about it. His excitement quickly turned to hunger when he realized he had not eaten since the early afternoon. His stomach made a hollow moan.

*Margery is working the ovens today. Biscuits with honey and bacon.*

The smell of the bake house always warmed his spirit. The bake house was made of thick slabs of wood. They made the building itself seem small. The wood was oiled a deep golden brown. There was a soft glow from the windows. The bake house had two large doors in front. They bore the red falcon crest of Castle Red.

"And just exactly what would you be wanting?" said

a middle-aged woman, as Finn entered. She was comely for her age, but quite tired. Dough was stained on her shirt and apron. Her blonde hair was pulled back in a knot. She had hazel eyes that were quite kind.

"Don't be coy, Margery. I'm here for your famous breads ... and pleasant conversation," said Finn, as he grabbed a roll from the counter.

The bake house was one large room with a loft above. The ovens were always on and the smells of honey filled the room and drifted out into village. The floor was made from wide stones that had been sanded flat. A thin layer of flour blew across the stones with each footstep. Ingredients and utensils were strewn about but never lost. There was an odd sense of comfort and order in the bake house. It was, in large part, due to Margery.

"Flattery will get you food from me anytime," said Margery. She was actually pleased to have a visitor. She quite enjoyed Finn. She tossed some strips of pork and a small vanilla bun at him. He hopped onto the counter and began to eat.

"It may storm later," said Finn.

"Good. We could use a rain."

"Almost a warm chill to the air," said Finn.

"Perhaps we will be having a dry rain," she smiled at him. "What has you so set this evening? You almost look happy ... excited."

"The Baron has visitors it seems," said Finn.

"The Baron always has visitors. What is it to you, though?" she asked.

She knew before he even spoke. Margery had known him for far too long to have to guess at his thoughts. He wasn't her son, but he would do.

"I met a woman. She's from the isles. I didn't ask but probably the coast of Hythor," said Finn.

"And ..."

"Her name is Nylah. She has beautiful green eyes.

I've never seen such green," Finn said to Margery, as much as to himself.

"Ah ... go on," Margery filled two wooden cups with apple wine for them.

"She wanted to see the mew. We ended up talking about much more. It's strange.  She's the first free person to speak to me as a person, an equal." The wine had a light sprinkling of cinnamon. It warmed Finn's face.

"So you saw a highborn woman with beautiful green eyes, did you? She was smitten with you, Finn. No highborn woman wants to see birds squawking about. She wanted to talk with you. At least it seems you made the most of the encounter" Margery said, as she laughed and tossed a piece of dough at him.

"Ha. Maybe you're right. I never even considered it. I'm in servitude to a king I've never met and smitten with a highborn who leaves tomorrow," Finn said, as he drank the last of his wine.

"I didn't mean it like that, Finn. It was a jest is all," Margery said. She drew him close putting both her warm hands against his face. Finn looked down. "Look at my eyes, boy." He looked up. "I serve just as you. I haven't a husband nor a child."

"The fault isn't of your own," Finn felt shame creep up his throat.

"This is true. The king is at fault, but I am as much at fault. I have taken what I was given," she said.

"You had no choice," replied Finn.

"I'm here. I could have left. There are places beyond the reach of a king," she whispered.

"Please, Margery. I'm sorry," said Finn. He looked around to ensure no one had heard her. Tongues were removed for far less.

"You deserve more," her eyes became moist, "you deserve a young lady with green eyes and a home with children."

# A DARK TYRANNY

"I have you," said Finn. He felt his face go flush.

"That you do, love," she said, kissing his forehead. Margery's heart felt heavy with regret for them both. Perhaps, in another life she would be his mother and he her son. They could see the realms in all their glory as free folk, however, not in this life. This life was different ... much different. "Come, forgive me ... let's have more wine. I want to hear more about this highborn woman."

Finn smiled at her. He hoisted himself up on the thick wooden counter. It caused a cloud of dough and flour to lift into the air. Margery turned to get what remained of the apple wine.

"We haven't met the king," he whispered coyly, "*but we can drink his wine.*"

"Ah, that we can," said Margery.

Suddenly the room lit up in white light. Margery dropped the bottle. It crashed against the stone floor.

"Was that lightning?" said Finn.

His eyes slowly adjusted back to the dimness of the cabin. Thunder began to shake the earth. It was as if they were in the thundercloud themselves. The noise echoed and rang out so loud it caused their eyes to squint. The thunder continued to rumble like a starving beast deep within the ground.

"Do you hear that?" asked Margery. "Something in the thunder ..."

Finn could hear it too. It was raining now. However, the thunder still persisted. It was as if a beast with its long tail was scraping the earth in its wake. The constant rumble filled the night. What kind of thunder never stops? Finn felt a cold fear creep into his mind.

*It isn't just thunder.*

"Finn, what is it?" asked Margery.

"Douse your oven!" said Finn, as he grabbed her by the arm.

"What?" asked Margery.

"Kill the flame!" yelled Finn.

Finn ran to the window and looked out into the courtyard.

*Riders ... an army.*

He could make out the shapes of horses and figures riding atop them. The shadows of spears and long axes.

*What army rides with a storm at its feet?*

He had never fought for the King nor rode to war. He hunted the king's forests for deer and boar. He was a falconer. He had never killed a man and didn't know if he could.

"What is it?" Margery whispered. There was a palpable fear in her voice.

"Riders. I can only see their shadows," said Finn. He knew he had to keep her calm.

"What do we do?" asked Margery.

"We stay inside and be quiet. They will worry about the castle guard and the village militia. We can wait to see how."

Suddenly, thunder clasped the night sky once again. For a brief moment all was lit.

*This is no army.*

Margery was now at the window with Finn. She gasped at the sight of them. Finn grabbed her, covering her cries with his hand.

"Ssssh. Margery, you must stay quiet!" he whispered, looking directly at her eyes. She was like a wounded animal. She had to run or scream. There was no understanding of her surroundings.

*She will get us both killed.*

"Gorgons! They are gorgons. Gorgons, Finn!" she cried.

"We must stay quiet. They will still have others to worry about. We must remain still and quiet," said Finn, as he gently let go of her. "I need to look once more." He needed to know if they were truly safe for the moment.

# A DARK TYRANNY

*Gorgons will take this castle, the village, and all with it.*

"No. They might see," she whimpered.

Finn crouched down on his knees; he made his way to the window. The thunder continued to rumble and wake the night.

*Gorgons ... walking snakes.*

He looked through the corner of the window.

*It's dark inside. They cannot see. They will not see.*

Lightning lit the sky. He saw them. An army of gorgons clad in shadow mail and soaked leather. Some had axes but most had spears and shields. Their thickly scaled skin was a deep black with a pale gray underbelly. The scales pulled tightly over their hulking frame. He could not see their eyes. They were too black. The gorgons were larger than men. Their bodies were like knotted ropes of thick muscle. The gorgon's heads were round, almost like an ape and their mouths were full of jagged yellowish teeth. A tail extended from the back of their tunics and wrapped tightly around one of their legs. It was rough with dirt and wear. Small spikes coated it like a blanket of nails.

*Gorgons ... walking snakes.*

It was all Finn could think of. This was not supposed to happen. Gorgons had been gone for centuries.

*Cleary, they are back.*

In a brief flash, the lightning was gone and the darkness coated the intruders once again. Finn sank down against the wall.

"We must leave here at once," said Finn.

Death had descended upon the castle and all around it. Finn was certain that the cabin walls could not keep it out. Margery nodded with tears welling in her eyes.

"Pack what food is here but be silent about it," he ordered.

"Please don't let them in, Finn," said Margery. She was losing her nerve. He knew they had to hurry.

"I won't. Hurry now. I will watch the door," whispered Finn.

*If they enter what will I do? I will die. We will both die.*

There were screams in the distance. The sounds of arms clashing mixed with moans of death. The darkness began to harbor some light. The flickering of flames could be seen.

*The village is burning.*

Smoke began to layer the air around them. The kindling of flames could be heard on the roof. It was like someone slowly crunching a scroll or parchment into a ball. The window crashed. An arrow landed against the far wall. It was greased with oil and burning. Fire fell in drips.

*They are burning the village.*

Margery let out a startled gasp.

"Hurry, they are burning the grounds. We need to go," said Finn.

"Do they see us?" asked Margery.

"I don't know. I don't think so. I think they're firing arrows to burn everything. Still, we must hurry. The cabin will burn quickly," said Finn.

"They will see us," she said, frozen with fear.

"We will burn in here," said Finn. He grabbed her and the satchel of food she had packed. "At least we will have a chance, but we'll have to run. Do you understand?"

"Yes," said answered.

"Ok. Stay close," Finn said, as he slowly opened the door. "Don't shout, just follow."

The smell of smoke and burning flesh permeated the air. He grabbed Margery's arm and began to run south, away from the castle and the village.

*We need to get to the woods. Clear of the chaos.*

Shadows were in the distance, but Finn couldn't make out if they were friend or foe. The thunder continued to shake the earth. They stayed close to the sides of the buildings to keep concealed. Air suddenly whistled passed Finn. It almost burned his cheeks. He didn't know they were arrows until they thudded into an adjacent building.

*They see us.*

Margery's arm went limp in Finn's hand. She fell hard to the ground. Her dress was soaked with dirt and blood; it poured from two arrows lodged in her chest. She got to her knees. She was in shock, but strangely calm. For a brief moment, she took in all around her. She felt the arrows jutting from her chest. A slow stream of blood dripped from their steel tips that protruded from her back.

"Margery!" yelled Finn.

"Finn, go ... it's ok. Go ... please," she said.

Another arrow passed through her neck forcing her to the ground. She lay dead on the wet ground. Rain fell around her. She was face down with her hair twisted. It almost seemed a dream.

*This can't be real.*

Finn heard more arrows bite into the wooden building behind him. One arrow hit the ground and slid another twenty yards. It disappeared into the night. He ran. Finn heard arrows and cries behind him. He couldn't tell if it was the sound of horses or more thunder. His heart raced while his head pulsed. Finn didn't look around him. He just ran.

*I have to make it to the woods.*

A frightened mare barreled towards him from out of the darkness. It was wild-eyed and panicked. Finn lunged to one side, but he was not quick enough. Suddenly, his world went black. He was on the ground, laying on his side. His vision came and went. It was like struggling to wake from a dream. For a brief moment, Finn could see the riderless horse running in the distance, its saddle flopping loosely on its back.

*They're coming for me. I have to go.*

His eyes wouldn't focus. He heard the rain, the thunder, and screams. The sound of people crying out and animals dying filled his head. More arrows flew through the night but they seemed random. Perhaps, they were volleys or stray shots. There was no way for him to take in what was actually happening. Things were moving in a haze.

*The falcon.*

Finn had no idea why he had thought it.

*They will kill it.*

It had lived longer than any of them.

*He is a prisoner as much I. Where will I go?*

He made a decision without the question of why. It brought him staggering to his feet. His soaked clothes clung to him. He ran west back towards Castle Red. The ground shook with the crashing of thunder. Horses beat the ground while running through the night. Finn had trouble staying on his feet. His legs were flailing faster than his balance. He would fall and not know whether it was from his coordination or an arrow. It took him no time to reach the tower, but it felt an eternity. He opened the door to the tower. The hinges moaned. Then, there was yelling. Finn didn't understand the guttural bellows of their language, but two gorgons ran towards him. One stopped and let loose a bolt from a crossbow. It hit hard into the stone wall of the tower and broke. A fragment of wood whipped into Finn's face. It burned and stung. He ran into the tower and began the ascent.

*I will die here. I die today.*

The gorgons' massive frames made them turn sideways to enter the tower. The larger of the two was more gray than black. His face looked to have been burned. One eye had turned a putrid yellow while the other stayed a soulless black. He wore boiled leather with tarnished steel greaves. His arms seemed to almost bust from his skin. The gorgon was a beast but moved with cautious agility. He yelled at Finn from the bottom of the stairs. Finn couldn't tell if it was anger or a mocking laughter. He ran up the broken stone steps as fast as his legs would take him. His lungs burned; his heart felt as if it was going to explode. Finn began to smell smoke. The higher he went, the thicker it became.

*The tower is on fire.*

He could hear the steel cage rattling and thumping against the wall.

Smoke bellowed from beneath the door. It rolled out in choking waves. There was sporadic clanging against the door that echoed throughout the tower. Finn didn't have time to think about what lay behind it. He simply lunged into the door, pushing it open. One of the iron hinges burned his shoulder, as he stumbled through the door and onto the floor. The wind was knocked out of him. Finn kicked the door from the floor, knocking it shut. He took in a deep breath, but then coughed until he gagged and vomited a thin, smoky bile. The gorgons were near the top of the tower. He could hear their weapons scratching against the stone walls. He pulled himself to his feet. The massive falcon kicked at the cage trying to spread its wings.

"Easy now," said Finn. He didn't know if he spoke to the bird or himself.

The massive Blood Falcon thrashed against the cage.

"Be calm. I'm going to get you out. I'm opening the gate," said Finn, as he slowly opened the thick steel cage. The bird paused. The leather mask was still clasped tight to its head. There was a crash at the door. The falcon twisted its head towards the noise. In one motion, Finn pulled the leather from atop the massive beast. He felt the cold hands of a gorgon clasp to the back of his neck. Its fingers dug into his skin causing his neck to twist. Then there was a noise ... a scream. His eardrums felt as if they exploded. Darkness took his vision as he fell to the floor.

## Chapter 5

### Out of the Shadows

The nails on his spiny fingers smoothed out the edges of the wooden flower. It was a rain flower with a long curved stem and drooping petals, each one would be painted white with a maroon center. He rolled the stem in his fingers. It worked just as intended. The drooping petals rose up and slowly brought the flower out of his hands, as it floated briefly into the air and landed on its side. If teacher Carolyn poured some water on it first, Mirkus was sure it would sprinkle and twist through the air. Rain flowers only bloomed in the Green Lands. This one was made of wood, but would be magical to the school children. If the paint dried quickly enough, he could leave it by the door. He knew their instructor would be teaching them about it. What a surprise to have one waiting for them that morning!

Mirkus shuffled through the hollowed trunk of the mallop tree. Mallop trees used to cover the southern realm like weeds in a fields, however, they were rare these days. Hundreds of years ago, King Tiersus had gathered all the trees in the four realms to build fleets of ships for the Sea Guard. The remaining mallops were but a few and scattered across the land. Their ancestors were now long rotted leagues below the surface of the water, remnants of a long ago battle. Mirkus had lived there for a few seasons so far. He was leery of being too close to the village and its school, however, the mallop tree was quite large and made a suitable home. In time, Mirkus had grown quite fond of the children, with their distant laughter and youthful innocence. The sounds filled the old tree with life. He had also taken an interest in his letters, as it was one of teacher Carolyn's favorite subjects. He would listen to her teaching the kids and then practice carving his letters into a thin sliver of wood. What would the class think if they knew a Nighteye listened intently to their lessons? The thought of a cursed creature learning with the children of men. He had decided early on to only go outdoors at night while remaining safely hidden during the daylight hours. A Nighteye was a bad omen to most villagers. They wouldn't take kindly to a cursed race living among them. It made no difference. Nighteyes were beasts of fairy tales now anyway. In fact, Mirkus often wondered how many villagers still believed in Nighteyes at all. Everyone knew the story of the collapse of Grimhaven, however, with enough time, the world can forget even the worst of its history. The past is quick to take to story. According to folklore, Nighteyes' were now just a smarter version of a goblin that tricks knights and kings out of gold and maidens; a thing of times past, make believe. Mirkus was very real though. He might slightly resemble a kind of goblin, one with soft yellow eyes and moss colored skin. However, he was no goblin. As far as he knew, goblins were not real, as he had never seen one nor overheard a tale about one that sounded authentic. It made no difference; this was all of no consequence to Mirkus. For that night, he was only thinking of painting a toy rain flower.

The morning would soon rise with a thick coat of mist covering the grass. The dim light of the hour would give the village and adjourning school a hazy and tired demeanor. Smoke would begin to drizzle from chimneys, as the villagers prepared for another day. The smell of apples and sweet rolls would drift into the schoolyard filling the mallop tree with fresh scents of breakfast. Mirkus lay in his large tree dreaming of the smells. He had a hard time during these hours of dawn breaking. They were peaceful and calm, but lonely. Mirkus would lay there listening to the world once again come to life. Those hazy hours of the morning were for the common and rich alike. It was a time held by no man, but each found a pleasure in it. However, Mirkus would find himself at his lowest when the sun began to wake. Isolation and solitude never hurt as hard as when a new day arose to all but him. He was a Nighteye and the curse of those before him had stolen all that could have lain ahead. There was no new day for Mirkus. Instead, he laid there dreaming of the smell of sweet rolls and honey. The rain flower would be waiting at the school. What new contraption would he leave the children tomorrow?

Mirkus sat up in a start. Something wasn't right. He could smell it. There was a thickness to the air. Those last hours of darkness seemed to harbor a dread. There was a sense of fear that crept up his neck causing a cloud of anxiety to grip him like an iron vise.

*I must do something. What? Something's wrong.*

Thoughts poured through his head. The ground began to tremble. He heard the mallop tree cry out like a great ship turning hard at sea. Wood twisted slightly and then settled back in place. The ground moved and swelled. Dust fell to the floor; it filled the air. The ground continued to move. It was a slow stirring, like the earth itself was waking from a deep slumber. A large echoing grind pulled through the bowels of the dirt below. Then ... it stopped. There was silence.

Mirkus left his tree. The normal chill was gone. There was a musky stench of decay rising from the ground. It was nauseating. Worms and other creatures scurried from the safety of the soil. They toiled blindly on the loose dirt. Mirkus could hear stirring in the village.

*I'm not the only one that heard this.*

A howl pierced the night. It was neither dog nor wolf. It had the sound of human agony layered with a bestial moan. The ground moved once again. Mirkus shifted to keep his balance. There were screams.

*It's coming from the village.*

He ran towards it. Suddenly, roots began to snap and burst. Patches of earth ripped open and gave birth to beasts that clawed their way into the night. The creatures ran with the swiftness of wild horses. The black mass of their frame was hulking; it lifted with each breath. Steam rose from matted fur. They were darker than the night that surrounded them. The wolves' eyes did not glow red, but rather had the dark lingering tint of blood. The night hid them. However, Mirkus could see them all. His eyes were attuned with the night. He could see the screaming wolven beasts descend upon the town. The villagers did not see them until it was too late.

*Do something! I can't just stand and watch!*

Mirkus paced outside the village. What could be done? He had no idea how long he could fight, even if he tried. It was forbidden. He could only think of the children from the school. What was happening to them at that very moment? They would wake to the sound of a true monster at their door. The beasts would crash through their windows and walls.

*No, this is not right!*

He could stand it no longer. His heart felt as if it would burst from his chest.

*They are only children!*

He ran.

Rain began to fall to the ground. Mirkus' legs moved faster than he thought possible. He was quiet and agile by instinct. Every moment seemed to flow together. The village stank of death and blood. Mirkus entered the turmoil of the village. Villagers ran only to be engulfed by hungry beasts. Their screams lasted only until claws and teeth ripped the life from them. Their bodies were pulled and twisted in many directions, as the soulless creatures fought for food. Mirkus grabbed the first object he passed. It was a dulled pitch fork leaning against a stable. He felt heat grow beneath his skin. Two fires kindled within him. One was a controlled rage, while the other was the burn of a curse on his kind. He tightened his grip on the handle. He had no idea how long he would live.

*I will take as many with me as I can.*

One of the hulking creatures stood in the middle of the road. It growled, as it feasted on a lump of flesh. Mirkus could not tell who or what it had been. The beast stared up at him. Mirkus ran with the pitch fork. He was amazed at how easy it was; time seemed to slow for him. He knew when to dodge and strike. It was as if he had battled his entire life. It felt so natural. With one motion, he thrust the dull metal rods of the pitch fork into the chest of the beast. They tore through muscle and bit into bone. He drove the creature into the ground. It howled with fright as it struggled. Mirkus then twisted the weapon to pull it free. He heard flesh tear and bone snap. He then threw the pitch fork into another beast. It thudded into its skull with the grace of a javelin. The beast made no sound. It simply fell to the wet earth, as if it had been long dead. Mirkus continued to run towards the screams. He began to feel as if he were sweating boiling oil. His hands felt like melting wax. However, the fire of rage kept him moving. He saw it, a sword, lying in the hand of a corpse. The lower torso had been clawed off and a line of entrails littered the earth. It was a sword. It was tarnished and old, but an actual weapon none-the-less. Mirkus took it with an agile grace while continuing to run in the chaos.

Mirkus cut and slashed his way through the beasts. He pivoted his frame from the onslaught of attacks. When he was clawed, he instinctively twisted with the motion. The wolves could not claw him to the ground. It was all too natural for him.

*This is who I am.*

He could not keep track of the dead creatures that lay in his wake. He simply killed all that he saw.

*The sun will be up shortly. They will leave. I must live till the sun rises.*

It was an eternity until the first ray of light crawled from the darkness. The rain began to carry the sun like falling prisms. The pack of wolves began to thin. Some clawed back into the earth, while others ran to shadowy patches of the forest. Others stayed. They were blood thirsty for the Nighteye that had cut through them. Blood leaked from his body; it dripped down his legs and off his fingers. He clutched the blade with a fury. Mirkus didn't feel the wounds from battle. The burning of his skin was far too potent. The last of the vile creatures caught Mirkus' blade in its skull. The sword bit down deep pushing its jaw from its socket. The blade would not dislodge, or Mirkus was simply too weak. It didn't matter. The beast fell to the wet soil. Blood and rain mixed throughout the road. Mirkus fell to his knees. Rain washed the blood from his face and hair. He could see some of the villagers and some of the children. They looked at him with wonder. Some villagers pointed while others cried holding loved ones.

*Some live.*

They were not all dead.
*I saved some.*
He looked at his hands. They cast a dull red glow. The pain was immense. It spread to his limbs. He felt it crawl up his neck.
*I raised weapons but I do not regret it. I do not regret this death.*
He looked at the morning sky. He could hear the rain gently land upon the roofs of the village. A trough was filling with water. There was a dog barking in the distance. The clouds were a soft white against the light purple sky of morning. The heat overtook him. He fell back, as the last bit of life left him.
*Today will be a good day.*
Blackness.
The purple sky had turned into a light maroon with clouds scattered throughout. The villagers had gathered around the Nighteye to look. None had seen one and some children were too young to even hear tales about them. They did not look to the sky but rather the ground. No one saw the white light that descended down from the great expanse above. The water on the earth around them began to be pushed back. Something was repelling it. This is when they first noticed her. She was not a true color but almost a pure light. Some would say silver while others called it a flame. The light was a translucent blue that was brighter than anything they had seen. A great wave of heat blew against them. Her wings slowly beat with the pulse of the world. The villagers backed away in awe.
"A Grandeur," some said, while others fell to their knees.
The Grandeur's slender frame towered over them. Her wings draped over her like a cloak, as her feet touched the earth.
"Do not be afraid," her voice was a thousand voices at once. It was calming, yet powerful, an ancient power

that had lingered since creation. "I am here for this one."

"Please," a crying woman clutched her dead child. "They killed my Marilynn. They've killed her." Her child was cradled in her arms like an ivory doll.

The Granduer had a look of sadness. She approached the crying woman. A hand of light caressed her face.

"All that is wrong will be turned right," said the Grandeur.

"Bring her back! Please!" pleaded the woman.

"Bring my boys back as well!" a voice cried out. Slowly, chaos began to erupt. Shouts and pleas for the dead to again live rang out. Crowds of the remaining villagers surrounded the Grandeur.

The Grandeur turned and took the dead Nighteye into her arms. Her light radiated over him. Her wings opened with the sound of a great ship's sails filling with wind. She rose from the earth hovering above the masses.

"Don't leave us! Please!" they shouted as she ascended into the sky.

Suddenly, a great light in the sky rivaled the sun and a thousand voices echoed at once, "Do not lose yourselves in despair. The time will soon be at hand. Look above, the sun has risen."

The Grandeur disappeared like a star shooting back into the heavens. The sun had overtaken the morning.

## Chapter 6

## Of Monsters and Curses

**B**lackness. There was no light or color. Matthias couldn't tell if it was dark or if he was blind or dead. It was simply nothing, a void. He wrestled with the utter lack of awareness. He could smell the musky scent of earth, moss on rock.

*I can hear. The sounds of water dripping ... slowly. A stream? No. A leak. The ground is hard ... more rock than dirt.*

He moved his hand along the ground.

*Damp but not wet ... a cave or crevice of some type.*

The great beast breathed out slowly. Matthias felt its warmth.

*I am not alone.*

"You are in Kor," Matthias heard, though it did not speak. The words seemed to move into his mind like a drifting wind.

"Am I dead? Dying?" he asked.

"You are alive, Matthias," it said.

"So, you are some winged beast that speaks

Altarian? If you plan to kill me, spare me your words."

"That was Ryoch. He does our bidding, as we do the bidding of another. He took you here for me. I have no intention of killing you, Matthias."

"Stop calling me by that name," Matthias spoke in a whisper. Bile burned his throat at the sound of the name.

"It is just a word. It represents your person," replied the voice.

"That person is no more," Matthias said.

"Those of this world do not have that power. You alone cannot change the person you are," the words lingered in his mind.

"Then I live only long enough to die," he replied.

*I will see them in death. They wait for me.*

"You ... the feared warrior? Hunting those that did not bow to your king? You were the killer of those that would not worship the throne. Were you not?" asked the voice.

"No longer. Kill me if you wish to punish me for past actions," he said, as he sat up on his knees. "But do not speak to me as a servant of the king ... any king."

"Too much death is already at hand. These are times above those of murderous kings. A storm has come and mortal rulers will fall. These four small realms of Altaris will crumble with the rest of Ehlür."

"I care not for the four realms or the mad kings that rule them," said Matthias.

"This is one of the reasons you are here. Someone will come for you soon."

"You leave me here blind? I cannot see. Is this my penance ... to slowly die in the rocks of Kor ... food for the carrions of the mountains?"

*My death is deserved ... why do I still fight it?*

"There is need for you yet in this world, Matthias."

He heard the great beast rise. Its wings beat down like a herd of wild horses. It pushed itself from the ground with a leap. The stone ground almost shook from it taking flight. The fiery creature flew from the cave. The cave opened from the side of a mountain that crashed into the sky like the curving blade of an axe. Matthias lay upon the damp rocks. He wanted to weep, but like so much else in his life ... he was unable. Instead, he listened to the water drip into the cave like a slow bleeding wound.

---

Mirkus woke. His head was pounding. His muscles were sore and aching. His ribs felt bruised. He was cold. A light snow had begun to fall around him, but was too warm yet for it to stick. The leaves from the great field of mallop trees held the snow just long enough to make the light reflect soft silver. Mirkus lay on a small pile of leaves and broken twigs. A lake rested solemnly in the center of the field. A stone jetted from the center. It had been pounded into the shape of an enormous great sword. Its hilt rising from the water. The hilt was fashioned as a winged lion and the sword's cross-guard were the outstretched wings of the lion. Its clawed feet wrapped tightly around pommel, which was a water onyx carved like the sun. The water onyx seemed to pull light into its orb and cast it down the stone blade of the sword. Melted snow carried the light, as it dripped down the statue into the water below. Mirkus could hear the water caressing the moss around the lake's edges.

*Am I dead? I am still in pain.*

He rose slowly so his body could adjust to the agony of moving. He couldn't tell if the snapping sound were the twigs from his bed or his bones.

Mirkus bent down by the lake filling his hands with the cold water. He drank deep and poured what was left onto his face and hair. Something was different. He felt his face once more. He then saw his hands and arms. Without a thought of his pain, he leaned over the water to glimpse his reflection. He saw it in small ripples. His leathered skin was no more. The fingers that were once crooked and narrow were straight and fleshy ... and his face. His skin was now light with high set cheekbones. His matted, dry hair was now the color of deep silver, almost pewter. It fell around his neck. It was soft to the touch. By all human standards, Mirkus was quite striking.

"I don't understand," he spoke aloud.

"Your curse is no more," said the Grandeur behind him. Her wings wrapped around her body like a cloak of radiant feathers.

Mirkus fell to his knees. It was the Grandeurs that cast the curse upon the Bournes.

"I don't understand ... I broke the vow. I raised a weapon," Mirkus looked upon her from his knees.

"You broke the vow of your people out of honor for another tribe. Sacrifice is not without honor," her voice was the sound of one and yet a thousand voices at once.

"Am I dead?" asked Mirkus.

"Do you see a path to the Great Halls of Ehlür? No, you are not dead. You are very much alive. You are at the seat of your people. This is where your kind started ... where you began. The High Woods. The covenant with your people was at this very lake."

"I didn't know this place was real," said Mirkus.

"And yet, now you are here," she said, as she walked closer.

"I don't understand this," said Mirkus. He looked around.

"A time of war is at hand," she said, gently caressing his face. He could feel a warmth move through his limbs. His pain was leaving. His body felt new ... stronger.

"Stand," said the Granduer.

Mirkus stood. He could see the Grandeur's face in a way that he could not before. She was beautiful. Her features were soft and overlaid with an aura of comforting light. Something was different. Mirkus looked at the lake. Light was crisper. He could see the individual rays as they gathered around the water onyx.

"What's happening?" he asked. He rubbed his eyes.

"Your curse is no more. You are no longer Mirkus or an omen of foreboding. You are not a monster. You are a Nighteye no longer. You are a Bourne again.

"I never knew life as a Bourne. The first war ended before I was alive."

"Mirkus is a name for a Nighteye, but not a Bourne. You will be Luras," said the Granduer.

"Why? What do you want from me," asked Luras in a whisper.

"You have been chosen. You are an Acolyte. You will stand with the others against the coming storm. They will need one of your kind."

"An Acolyte?" said Luras. His eyes reflected a hue of bluish silver light.

"Darkness again descends upon the world. Kingdoms will fall. The petty battles between kings are over."

"Can't you stop them? The Granduers ... the Creator. Can't you all stop it?" asked Luras.

"It was not the hands of the Great One that let evil back upon this world," replied the Grandeur.

"You could help stop it."

"Make no mistake, the forces of evil may swell, but they will not drown this world. However, will this generation cast darkness back into the shadows, or will it be the next? This is the question for you and all others," said the Grandeur.

"Why did you save me, then?" asked Luras.

"Acolytes will keep evil at bay until the world of men and their great armies decide to rise up ... or fall. The world is not alone."

"But why not just strike it down yourselves?"

"The hearts of men are best refined by fire."

"What am I to do?" asked Luras, almost to himself.

"You are to meet another in the Mountains of Kor. Travel there at once. Remember, Luras, this world has not seen your kind for hundreds of years. They will hate you."

"How will I know the person I am to meet?" asked Luras.

"The same way he will know you. By the eyes of the Acolyte."

## Chapter 7

### Servant to Slave

Finn woke from a daze along the road from Castle Red. There was a pounding ache in his head. His legs slowly moved with the rest of the captives. He had no idea he was even walking. His body must have taken over while his senses slept. Finn was caked in mud. It had dried to his clothes; he could feel it inside his boots. Blood was dried from a cut above his brow. He could feel it wanting to open if he moved his eyebrows. He did not recognize the man that was yoked beside him. They were like a herd of cattle. A small oxen yoke was strapped over each person's shoulders. A rope wrapped around their necks and went down around their waist before leading to the next in line. There were two lines of captives. A leather harness attached each person's foot to the person walking next to him. They were slaves.

*Where are they taking us?*

The gorgons walked with their captives. Finn could see them more clearly in the light. The creatures were more menacing when not cloaked in darkness. It looked as if beasts from a violent nightmare had been pulled into the living world. They looked much stronger than the night before. The gorgon's upper body looked more like a hairless ape. Their teeth were stained yellow and jagged. The creatures walked erect with their hardened tails wrapped around one of their legs. It tightened and slithered like a snake on its prey. Scales wrapped tightly around their bulky frame. Their dark scales swelled and slid over each other as they marched. Some of their scales had a deep red outlining, while others had yellow. They appeared like beasts dressed in armor, but they were not simple-minded.

*These beasts will burn through the realms.*

One of them wrapped himself in leather jerkin dyed red over a black tunic and pants. The handle of his whip was in his right hand. Its corded leather lash dragged in the dirt beside him like a second tail. His scaled left hand was missing three fingers. His eyes were black but full of violence. He enjoyed running the slaves. Finn made sure to not stare at him, although, he studied the creature in protected glances. The other gorgons did not utter their slithered black speech to him.

*He is below them somehow. They look down on him.*

Finn made a mental note. He had no idea why.

A portly man up the line slipped down to one knee and then fell to his side.

*Waltur the butcher.*

Waltur tried to rise, but he was large and soft.

*Get up, Waltur.*

The gorgon in red yelled a deep language that Finn couldn't understand. He lashed out with the whip. It struck Waltur across the face and down his chest. His skin opened almost immediately. Blood began to steadily drip, as Waltur cried out. He tried to stand but fell again. This time he pulled the men down beside and in front of him. The rope that connected them all pulled tightly. The man in front of Waltur began to grasp at the rope around his own neck, as Waltur's full weight pulled the rope tightly. He gasped for air; his finger nails dug into his neck as he fumbled with the rope. The whip lashed out again and then again. It hit Waltur and others around him. The gorgon approached Waltur.

*Get up, Waltur. Get up!*

It pulled a short sword from its belt.

"No! Please!" Waltur cried out, but his last words were just gurgles of blood. The gorgon's blade tore easily through his neck. His body hit the ground in a lump. The gorgon held his head in his two-fingered hand. He forcefully said something to the captives. They did not need to understand his speech to know what he said. The gorgon dropped the butcher's head to the ground. Finn had to walk over the body as they kept marching forward.

Finn began to make mental notes of all those around him. He had to know some of them. They were all from Castle Red. He studied both lines of captors in front of him. Everyone seemed so different. Fear and exhaustion caused them to appear like strangers. He had to recognize someone's face whether stranger or not. Finn saw the stable boy. He had aged twenty years since the day before. His eyes dripped heavy black shadows. There were clean streaks down his face from tears. He limped slightly. Finn began to make out familiar faces but he could not remember some of their names.

*Am I tired or wounded inside. What are their names?*

Then, he saw her ... Nylah.

*She's alive!*

The night and morning had pulled her from his

thoughts. A sudden rush of excitement ran through his heart. She was more beautiful than he had remembered. His excitement turned to a surge of guilt. He thought of Margery and how her body was probably still lying along the road outside of the bake house. He was thinking of himself and no one else. Nylah was deathly frightened. Finn had seen the look on her face before, but from men on the gallows. It was as if she could die at any moment, so all her senses were heightened from fear. She too was exhausted. Finn wanted to weep. Margery was dead. Now, Nylah would most likely die, along with him and the rest of the village. He had never even had a life, at least the life of a free man. He was a forced servant that was now a captive. Death was very near.

An odd thought came to Finn. It was clear and obvious. He knew it was right. He could achieve one last thing. One thing that would be his own decision and not that of a master or beast. He thought of Margery lying dead. He wasn't able to help her. Finn thought of Nylah. She was all he had left. Everyone else was a stranger. I can help her. There was no decision to make. He would try and help Nylah escape, whether it cost him his life or not.

*I will help her ... the choice of a free man.*

The captives marched steadily northwest throughout the majority of the night. More had fallen along the way and were left to the scavenging beasts and carrions that had begun to follow them. They left a stink of blood and fear in their wake. The gorgons did not let them rest until a few hours before dawn. The gorgon in the red jerkin yelled out something, as he pointed to the ground. The captives' ropes were removed. The villagers knew immediately and fell to the earth. Some passed out from exhaustion the moment they were off their feet. A few women began to breastfeed their babies, while others pulled their kids to them for comfort. Finn noticed an older plump woman looking around. She was like a trapped deer.

*She is going to run.*

The gorgon in red must have seen the same thing. He grasped the fleshy woman by her hair and dragged her away. She flapped like a fish and cried out. It was too dark to see what happened, but her screams became gurgles. Then, there was silence. Finn heard the sounds of cutting and hoisting.

*They are dressing her. They are going to eat her.*

Finn wasn't the only one that realized this. A deathly silence came over the prisoners. Another gorgon came to the group and grabbed a man by his foot. He tried to resist but the creature pulled him like a doll. The rest of the group huddled together. Shouts were heard, as some villagers were being crushed in the middle of the group. No one wanted to be on the outside. Sounds of crying and sobbing erupted. The man the gorgon had taken let out a shriek. A snapping sound was heard and then nothing.

"Stay calm," some of the prisoners whispered. "Back up ... back up! Stay calm."

Finn knew this was his chance to move closer to Nylah. They would be roped again in a few hours. If he was beside her, they might tie them together. He could also speak to her, plan an escape. He looked her way hoping they would meet eyes but she kept staring at the ground. One of the Baron's guardsmen was in front of her, but kept trying to move behind. He needed to move from the outside row and away from the gorgons' grasp. He was pushing Nylah and cursing for her to move.

"Wake up. Move your arse," he said. He was middle-aged with a thick mustache. Finn knew him. He had seen him kill a dog once with a knife, as the other guards laughed. His name was Timmons.

Timmons pushed himself behind her causing Nylah

to snap out of her trance. She tried to move back, but he buttressed himself behind her. She was on the outer rim of the group now, fresh for gorgon pickings. Finn was five to six prisoners deep inside the group. He began to crawl toward the outside. Others filled in behind him like water. Once he made it out, it was easier to breathe. The air was clean. He wiped his hands on his pants. He must have crawled through blood, urine, and all manner of things. He moved along the outer edge of the group slowly so not gain attention from the gorgons. She saw him as he got closer. There was a sense of relief on her face, as if she had been waiting for him. It was the look he would sometimes give Margery after a long hunt with the Baron. He was a familiar face in the midst of strangers.

"Are you ok?" Finn whispered. He felt his heart beat a little faster. She was beautiful even in the present horror they found themselves in. She had a grace to her motions like Finn had never seen. Her green eyes burned in the darkness; her black hair still hung in ringlets. Her high cheeks led down to a straight jaw. Finn had never seen a woman whose face was soft and yet sturdy.

"Finn," she said.

*She remembers.*

"Are you hurt?" asked Finn.

"I don't think so. What are these things?" she whispered.

"Gorgons ... walking snakes. I've only heard about them, though. I didn't think they were real."

"They killed my aunt," she whispered.

"I'm sorry. They killed a friend of mine as well."

"I don't know if my cousin survived," she said. "Do you know where they are taking us?"

"I haven't any idea. We are going northeast though. Don't worry, I plan on getting you out of here," said Finn.

"How?" Nylah asked.

"Shut your mouths, the both of you," Timmons hissed from behind her. "If you draw their ire, by god and kings, I will slit your throats before they take me." He had a dagger in his hand.

"Who will you hide behind then?" said Finn. His words struck out like a snake. The rules of kingdoms no longer mattered. Timmons was just another captive.

"Watch yourself, boy," warned Timmons.

*He's right. Trapped men will soon become animals.*

Finn leaned close to Nylah to whisper in her ear. He could smell her hair. Her skin was warm and healthy.

"Try to stay by me at all times. I have no idea when our moment will come but it will. We have to be ready," whispered Finn.

"You just met me. You could get killed," she whispered.

"If anyone deserves to live ... it's you. I'd rather die trying ... than not at all. We have to be ready, though."

She shook her head that she understood. They sat in silence for the next three hours. The time laid hard on Finn. He began to doubt himself. He was one person amongst an army of gorgons. Would there even be a chance? He feared they would both die knowing he failed. The sun began to hint at rising and light trickled in through the trees. The gorgon in red cracked his whip and everyone rose to their feet.

"Stay by me," Finn grabbed Nylah's arm.

## Chapter 8

A Messenger in the Night

The horse was not bred for war; it was lean and agile. The gelding was dark gray. It caught a slight glimmer from the moon. The horse's hooves threw dirt and mud, as it pounded through the path. A boy rider carried a sealed note for the king. The lightest of boys and swiftest of horses were picked to be a bringer of the King's Seal. This royal messenger carried a dire message to Easton Welthorn, King of the Eastern Realm. The horse and rider however still had to make it through to the forest's edge.

The Seat of the Eastern King was safely tucked in the mountain city of Horos. Horos was more of a fortress than a city. One had to make their way through the surrounding forests only to reach the mountains. Horos was nestled within a valley of almost impenetrable mountains. Protective walls encircled the city. They were made of granite and quartz. The city of Horos acted as a barrier to the castle. Castle Horos was primarily quartz with thick wooden beams from the forest trees. The mountains pulled rain and water down into the valley. The grass was thick and the soil ripe for growing. The valley itself stretched for hundreds of miles. The Eastern Realm was the smallest of the four realms but its seat was highly sought after. Its forests were rich and the mountains full of fine stones and jewels. However, getting to Horos was another matter entirely. Rumors of forest creatures were dwarfed by the rumors of rock beasts within the mountaintops. One road led through the forest, up the mountain, and into the valley. The older villagers said that the road was guarded by more than just men. Beasts of forest and rock still roamed at night. Most dismissed these as stories to frighten wayward children. However, the road was still best traveled in daylight.

The gray horse galloped through the night; its rider not caring of the noise he stirred in the depths of the darkness. The speed of his ride would be his best defense. They trampled down the path towards the opening of the forest. A slight rain began to fall. The rider pulled his cloak tight, and steadfastly gripped the reins. The horse charged through the rain.

---

"Do you see that? There ...," a thin tower guard named Dowery pulled his cloak from his head to get a better look. He had a long mustache that dripped over his mouth. The rain caused it to splinter out over his bottom lip. He was thin, bedraggled, and wind burnt.

"I can't see nothing in this mess but rain," the older guard didn't even bother to look.

"I believe it's a rider."

"Notch a bow then," the old guard grumbled. "Make 'em stop if he gets too close."

Dowery pulled a bow from the stone wall and gave arrow to string. He did not release but kept the arrow on the shadowy figure riding towards the gate.

"That's strange ...," said Dowery.

"What?"

"It's just a horse," Dowery said, almost to himself.

"What do you mean just a horse?"

The old guard moved to look down at the road.

"It's a horse. There's no rider," Dowery said again. It was true. A pale grey mare ran wildly through the sleeping village and towards the castle walls. An empty saddle flapped upon its back.

"Turn the gate!" the old guard yelled down from their perch on the tower.

Four men came out of a stone hut built against the interior wall of the castle. They pulled their cloaks around them, as they left their fire. A large wooden wheel with six handles was close to the iron gate. They each grabbed a handle and began to walk the wheel in circles. The gate screeched and ground, as metal scraped against metal. The gate rose showing its spikey teeth, as they left the muddy earth.

"Keep your arrow on her," the old guard instructed Dowery.

The gray mare was frightened and wide-eyed. Her eyes rolled back, as the guards approached. She breathed heavily. The guards slowly approached the horse. It sidestepped, snorting and frothing.

"Easy there, girl," one man called out.

Another man took hold of the bridle. He was able to grasp one of the loose reins before the horse reared and tried to run again. He was pulled down through the mud and into a wall. His collar bone cracked against the stone.

"Release," the old guard told Dowery. The arrow sliced through the rain and caught the horse in the neck. It reared back with a startled yelp. The horse fell to the ground. Another soldier removed his sword and put the horse out of its misery.

"Any sign of the rider," one of the men called out.

# A DARK TYRANNY

"No," yelled Dowery, "there's no rider that I can see."

"I suspect we will happen upon him in daylight," said the old guard.

"There's a satchel here with a royal seal," said another guard, as he untied the wet leather satchel. It had an emblem of the Great Tree with swords for branches. It was made of ivory. The guard wiped mud from the satchel and took off one glove to open it. He then realized it wasn't dirt or mud at all. "Blood," he called to the others.

---

Malvern hurried up the stairs with the satchel. His old and frail frame reminded him of his age with each step. His head was bald with the exception of a few strands of gray hair littering his scalp. Malvern's beard was long but patchy. His small face did not suit a beard. It seemed to pull his skin and face downward, making him appear even more exhausted than he actually was. His woolen robe was wet at the bottom. It stuck to his sandals and pulled against the cold stones of the castle. He could hear Easton's heavy breathing before he reached the thick wooden door to the king's quarters. The steady hum of women moaning lightly echoed down the stairwell. Malvern approached the door. He stood a moment to gather himself; he needed to regain his breathing. He stood, wiped his lips, and pulled down on his beard. Malvern lightly knocked on the door.

"Your grace ... I'm sorry to disturb you," he tried to whisper, but it came out more like a rasp.

Malvern stood quietly, trying to listen for the sounds of movement. He heard nothing so he lightly tapped on the door again. He knew the king would be upset.

"Leave us, you wretch. Whatever it is can wait

until morning," a voice belted out from the room.

"I am sorry, your grace. An urgent message has arrived."

"You are defying an order from the king."

"I beg your mercy, your grace. It bears the mark of the four realms."

There was silence. Malvern stood not quite knowing how the king would react. He rubbed his lower lip with his teeth. Suddenly, the door opened and the king stood in front of him. He was naked. Easton Welthorn had a stocky frame. What was once muscle had long since turned to flabby pale flesh. The king was in his mid-thirties, but he had the look of an older man with a tired body. His hair was brown with a slight curl. He kept it closely cropped. His eyebrows were thick with wild, stray hairs darting up. The king's chest was a mass of hair that curled down past his belly to his groin like an unruly overgrowth of thick black weeds. Malvern saw two naked women sprawled across the king's bed. One looked directly at him, while the other poured more wine into cups. She was already drunk and spilled most of it onto the silken sheets. Malvern pretended not to notice. Easton scratched the curly hairs amassed around his cock, as he stared at Malvern suspiciously.

"Have you never seen two whores, Malvern? Where is this rider bearing a note?" said Easton. His breath stank of wine and sex.

"There was no rider, just a horse. The guards say that there was blood and pieces of scalp and hair on the horse's saddle. The satchel was soaked in blood. It has been cleaned to not dirty your grace's hands." Malvern held the satchel up for Easton to see. Easton opened the satchel pulling out a tightly coiled scroll. He let the stained bag fall to the ground, as he turned to read the message.

"Summon my regency."

# A DARK TYRANNY

"At once, your grace ... and what of Ellison?"

"Leave my brother be. This is a regent matter."

"Of course, your grace. At once," Malvern scurried from the room.

The court regents were comprised of the Royal Treasurer, Captain of the Guard, Minister of Land, and two of the king's Council Elect. The Council Elect were two men the village elected to give voice for the people during times of major decisions. Both men were in need of a bath. They reeked of old mead and vomit. King Easton was yet to find a Council Elect that did not want the luxury and comfort befitting the office and, of course, the women. There was always the women. The position was a joke, which was why Easton had allowed it. It would quell the village into submission and make him appear the better man.

The rest of his regency was handpicked by the king himself. Jon Leland was the Royal Treasurer. His leather tunic was finely oiled with an expensively dyed red linen shirt underneath. His boots and pants were always clean. His beard was always trimmed into a fine point at the chin. Jon Leland's hair was thinning and gray at the sides. Riley Moore was the Minister of Land and dealt with many offices of the realm. He was responsible for the sheriffs, bankers, and other officials of each region of the Eastern Kingdom. Riley Moore kept a pensive look about him. He was thin and astute. Haurice Marlon was the Captain of the Guard. His frame was stocky and well-muscled. Age had given Haurice a thin layer of fat over his muscles. He kept the kingdom defended and ready for war. Malvern was not part of the regency, but was always present by the king in times of counsel. Easton now wore pants with an unbuttoned tunic. He drank wine directly from the bottle.

"They say the Red Castle has fallen," said Haurice. He was not one to mince words. "Beasts and gorgons are raiding villages along the southern borders."

"They say that the skin clan is openly crossing borders," said Jon.

"Vile bastards."

"Did they take the castle? What are they taking from these villagers?" asked Easton.

"We have not seen any of this first hand," said Jon.

"The castle was sacked but not taken. The beasts kill the villagers, while the snakes seem to take them," said Haurice.

"Take the villagers? For what?" Easton smirked.

"Food most likely."

"The snakes will use some of them for weapons," said Haurice.

"Weapons?" one of the Council Elect was taken aback.

"They will sacrifice them," Haurice spoke very matter-of-fact.

"This is all superstitious conjecture. The truth is that all we know is that Castle Red has fallen. We have reports and gossip about the other. Nothing more," Riley Moore begin to pace.

"We should begin to fortify immediately," said Haurice.

"I agree," spoke Riley.

"Your majesty, if I may," Malvern spoke directly to Easton. He spoke in a manner that led others to think of his point before he actually said it. He had learned long ago that men will move on their own ideas at a much brisker pace. He would plant the seed; they would water his point.

"We are convening, Malvern," Easton retorted sarcastically, "this is the point. Speak."

"We are all learned men. History is known to us. If the supernatural are again at war ...," spoke Malvern. He made efforts to contain his enthusiasm.

"We have no reason to believe this," interrupted Jon

Leland.

"Indeed. But if they are ... history will tell us what the future brings," spoke Malvern.

"Decimation," uttered Haurice.

"A kingdom broken into four parts ... four rulers. It was just one before the first war," Malvern wanted them to put the pieces together for themselves.

"What are you suggesting?" Riley Moore stated very bluntly.

Easton gulped down another mouth full of wine. It left his thick beard damp. Malvern could see he already knew; he had already agreed. Malvern need only continue to frame the idea.

"We supply the castle and surrounding grounds with provisions for many months of barricade," instructed Malvern.

"Hide? This is your idea," retorted Jon Leland.

"He means to weather the coming storm," Easton finally spoke.

"We move food, armaments, soldiers, nobles, tradesman, pertinent supplies and people into the grounds. Let the principalities war amongst themselves," suggested Malvern.

"And reap the spoils of what is left," Easton said, almost to himself.

"What of your people? The outlying territories?" asked Jon Leland.

"We cannot possibly hold them all within our walls" said Haurice, again bluntly.

"Nor do we have enough provisions. It would take all the crops and livestock under your rule to simply feed an army for months on end," stated Riley Moore.

"We could requisition all the crops and livestock in the name of the king," claimed a grinning Malvern.

"You ask the people of the realm to hand you their life, Malvern," retorted Jon Leland.

"Not me. The king ... King Welthorn asks them.

Their king, your king, Jon Leland," said Malvern. He did not like to be questioned but tried to maintain his composure.

"How will you make them?" asked Haurice. "They die by spear, starvation, or worse. You will be asking a man to choose his manner of death. This will be no easy task. It is one thing to threaten a man with death, but to threaten a dead man ... this is another matter completely."

"Or ... of course, we do nothing and wait for not just their death, but that of the entire kingdom and its king," Malvern's words dripped of malice.

"Since you are not our ruler, nor will ever be, I ask the king," replied Haurice.

"Indeed," muttered Jon Leland.

"I am the king," spoke Easton. He looked at his regency. "Malvern is right in his thinking but his methods are flawed. The people will not choose death. We could make them but it would take time, of which we have very little," his mind raced.

*This moment is destined. This plan ... my plan. It is right.*

"These are dark times. The people would welcome a distraction, a celebration. This midnight message ... it was nothing more than a response regarding my impending marriage," said the king.

"Ah. Excellent, your grace," said Malvern. He knew immediately.

"We tell the people I am to be married. It's been long enough. I'm sure they would welcome another queen," spoke Easton.

"And who is this queen, your majesty?" asked Jon Leland.

"There is no queen," Riley Moore said plainly.

"It will not matter. There will be no celebration. It will not come to that," said Malvern.

Jon Leland looked at the king paying no attention to

# A DARK TYRANNY

Malvern. He knew his king was ridden with faults, but this?

"I have no intention to marry. We begin placing large orders of supplies. We instruct the people to harvest early and surrender a portion of their yields to the crown. This, of course, due to the approaching marriage, festivities, and all that comes with it. They can more than regain the loss by selling to merchants, dignitaries, and other revelers staying within the realm for the ceremony and ongoing festivities."

"Of which, will never occur," Jon Leland could not meet eyes with his king.

"You now follow, Jon," said the king, as he drank more wine. "The castle walls will be long shut before any truth is discovered."

"There will be women and children, your grace ... standing by these gates. We are to watch them starve or be murdered by these enemies ... of which, Malvern is so keen to believe are ravaging the kingdom?" asked Jon Leland.

"They die so others may live. Such is the way of war, Jon," replied Malvern.

"Your grace ... is there no other way?" whispered Jon Leland.

"What do you say, Haurice?" asked the king.

"I am a soldier," said Haurice, looking at the king. "I do as my king commands, as always."

Malvern was relieved. There was now only Jon Leland. The Council Elect made no difference. They were a token gesture by the king and their silence underscored that they knew their place.

"Good," spoke the king.

"And your brother," asked Riley Moore.

"He is to know nothing about this. I am to get married. This is all he should be told. His sickness has made his steel weak in these matters."

"As you wish, your grace," replied Riley Moore.

"Your grace," Malvern motioned to the two naked women asleep on the bed. "What of these two?"

"Yes. Haurice please dispose of them," the king said. He drank more wine.

"As you wish," replied Haurice.

The rest of the regency left the room to begin putting plans to action. Haurice pulled a dagger from his belt.

"I will also need you to dispose of the Council Elect," said the king, putting down the empty bottle. "Men of that ilk cannot be trusted in times like these."

"Yes, your grace," said Haurice. He approached the sleeping women. The steel blade glinted in the light.

"And Haurice ... Jon Leland as well."

## Chapter 9

### A Nighteye No More

Luras went southeast towards Kor. It had been two days since he left the High Woods. He had already passed the village of Breft and the small farming lands of Wellington. Luras reveled walking in daylight. He was able to see the large trees of the southeast. Their green leaves and heavy branches sprouted yellow and gold buds of the alchemist flower. They were quick to bloom and slowly broke away from the trees. Their petals carried in the breeze like a golden wind. Large rocks were scattered throughout the landscape. They were covered with the deep maroon leaves of the Evening Vine. Luras would eat the berries that grew along the vines. There were sweet and tart. The rocks would only get larger as he traveled closer to Kor. Soon the rocks would turn into mountains. For now, they lay scattered throughout the forest and fields. Luras would occasionally rest his legs by lying upon them. He would stare up towards the expanse of blue sky. The falling alchemist flowers would drift by like golden butterflies dancing in blue. Daylight was more beautiful than he had ever imagined.

Although Luras was no longer in the decrepit form of a Nighteye, he still stayed off the main roads to avoid contact with villagers. Instead, he journeyed primarily on small pathways used by hunters, shepherds, and others wishing to avoid the towns, villages, or any other unwanted surprises. The realms had not seen a Nigheye in generations. There were only tales from hunters seeing one briefly, which were easily dismissed. However, he knew that no one had seen one a Bourne, ever. The Bourne had long since passed due to the curse. They were Nighteyes now. Luras was the only Bourne in a thousand years. He was the first and only to walk upon the realms in true form since the youngest days of Ehlür. Luras took every opportunity to look upon his reflection in small pools of water along the path.

His face and body were not that different than an ordinary man of narrow build. The only difference was his silver hair and an overall hue to his skin. His pallor was the same as a man, but there almost seemed to be a slight radiance about him. It was subtle, but others would surely recognize that something was different about him, even if they could not place it at first. The one aspect of his appearance that was directly noticeable was the soft blue glow from his eyes. It may take a villager a moment to see the slight radiance of his skin, but they would have no trouble seeing he was an Acolyte. His eyes exuded a soft glow that would be even more prevalent at night. He had the eyes of the Acolyte. There was no hiding it.

Luras kept the hood of his cloak pulled over his head. A few white hairs draped across his face and below his chin. He tucked them behind his ears but they refused to stay. He wore a wool shirt and cloth pants with some worn leather boots. He was neither

# A DARK TYRANNY

dressed nor armed for confrontation. He would need to remedy this prior to entering the rocky lands of Kor. He had no idea how he would get these provisions, as he had no money. However, he did have food growing around him and a small canteen of water. He also had daylight and this was his favorite provision of all.

It was the last hours of the afternoon. Evening would soon pull the sun below the horizon. This was when Luras first began to notice steady trails of smoke. They bellowed upwards into a sky of deep red and purple. He began to look for high ground. He saw a massive rock in the distance. He ran to it and used the Evening Vines to climb up. He could feel its berries crushing under his grasp. The rock was just big enough for him to see over the trees. He saw thick wooden beams smoldering in the distance. They were what remained of the thatched roofed houses that made up a small village. It had been burned to the ground. He did not see any movement. The village seemed empty. However, if this was so, it was only recently abandoned or worse. Luras began to wonder if the same beasts had brought their carnage upon this village. He began to think of the school and the children being pulled from the dark of night by nightmarish beasts. He slid from the rock and quickly ran to the village.

It was obvious that this village was at one time a charming place tucked safely in the woods. Forestry and carpentry tools were outside some of the smoking buildings. The villagers most likely traveled a few times a year to neighboring townships to sell their goods. He would have liked to have seen this village and smelled the sawdust and cider mixing in the air. The homes were of white clay and wood. Their thatched roofs would have hung over the sides dripping straw and branches. There were three large apples trees growing in the center of town. The children probably played around them and then ate the fruit, while looking at the clouds. Two of them were charred while one was untouched by flame. This was a close knit village. They all would have known each other, families joining through marriage. Weddings and festivals were most likely a quaint but charming event. The village coming together to celebrate. However, all that was gone now. The village was in shambles. It had been burned to the ground. Luras saw debris in the road. It was charred black. He assumed it was furniture or people's bags. They probably tried to run. Perhaps, a village watchman was able to give word to them beforehand. Some might have gotten away, but it was obvious that others did not. Bodies lay upon the dirt roads. Some were whole bodies contorted from the flames, others were simply pieces or chunks of flesh. They were riddled throughout the smoking village. Luras examined some of the bodies.

*This is not from the same beasts.*

The random pieces of flesh were not torn or ripped by claws. The cuts were straight and sharp.

*Steel did this ... an army with weapons.*

Luras saw a somewhat intact building further down the road. It was the jailor's house. The steel cage inside had kept the whole place from crumbling. The roof was not thatched like the others. There was an underlining of wood with metal joints. It was made to keep people in, but it also was able to keep the majority of the fire out. Some of building was gone but it would make a good place for Luras to shelter for the night. The scent of death lingering in the village could attract scavengers once the moon was up. He decided to look for supplies in the village and then he would sleep in the prisoner's cell. It was not a key lock door but he could knot a rope around the bars to keep wolves or other beasts from getting in. It was safer than sleeping outdoors when a nearby village had cooked flesh littering the streets. No, it made sense for him to sleep at the jailor's house. He would bury the bodies in the morning. He had no time for that at present. The sun was almost down.

Luras rummaged through the village for supplies. It did not matter, but he still went to lengths to not destroy any more of the village. It had seen its horror and deserved rest. The forest would eventually overtake what was left. It would give it refuge under blankets of green vines and grass. In ten or more years only the one apple tree would remain. The rest would be long covered in vines and shrubs. Luras had never been there before but he missed it all the same.

One of the dilapidated buildings had a large frame to it. Luras thought it might have been a town hall or inn of some sort. He walked over the foundation to see if any supplies might have survived the flames. This is where he found the corpses of the remaining villagers. There was at least thirty or more dead. They were in a heap behind the building. Their captors had little regard for the living or the dead. The fire had long gone out. They were charred but Luras could see immediately that the fire was not what killed them. They had clearly experienced terror in their final breaths.

*They were skinned.*

The villagers had been skinned and by hands clearly skilled at performing such actions.

*Skin Slavers.*

Luras quickly left to finish searching the rest of the village. The sun was going down. He did not think they would be back after sacking the village, but he would feel better in the safety of the jailor's house all the same. He needed a weapon and thicker clothes. He had to find something ... anything. Before he got back to the jailor's house, Luras was able to find some leather riding boots. They were of a much better quality than the ones he had. He also found a tightly woven cloak. It was such a deep green that it almost looked black. He did not find any better pants, but there was a leather vest that he took from a blacksmith's hut. It was slightly large for his narrow frame, but wearing it over his wool shirt took away some of its bulk. He then tied a strip of leather around it to pull it snug to his body.

Luras had not thought to look through the jailor's house until he returned. There were two crates with steel wrappings. They were key locked. He searched the house pulling out drawers and opening cabinets. They were all charred and burned. He rummaged through a desk and wall closet before finding a ring of keys. He fumbled through them but none of the keys worked. Instead, he began to chip away at the side of the wood with the largest key. The wood had been severely burned. Luras then tore two of the steel wrappings off. It was much easier than he had imagined. This made him momentarily worry about sleeping in the jailor's house at all. Perhaps, it wasn't as sturdy as he thought. The contents of both crates were bound in a rugged piece of boiled leather. He unrolled them upon the blackened floor. Luras felt a moment of relief. He should have searched here first. He found two sheathed swords, a hooked dagger, and a leather satchel. Inside the satchel was a worn leather bracer that had begun to crack. Luras thought it was probably used for archery. He also found a pair of padded gloves, and two strings for a bow. He was unable to find a bow. It must have burned in the fire. He packed the items in the satchel and carried the rest to the metal cage.

Luras used the boiled leather that the swords were in to secure the door to the cage. He knotted one to the top of the cage door and one to the bottom. Scavengers feeding on the dead villagers would not be able to reach him. It would take a person to untie the knots or something very strong to pull the door from its hinges. Luras felt confident that only mindless beasts feeding at night would venture into a village riddled with charred corpses. He sat with his back to a far corner of the cell and pulled the hood of his cloak down. A thin breeze blew through the village and between the bars of the cage. Luras kept his weapons within reach. However, he fell asleep almost immediately. He did not hear the wolves or their fighting over flesh. Sleep overtook him.

## Chapter 10

The Long Road

The gorgons had marched the prisoners for days. A trail of dust, sweat, and blood flowed behind them like a wake. The only food the prisoners received was at night and it was a gruelish white paste that tasted more of dirt than anything else. Some of the prisoners were unable to eat it. They were quickly overcome with starvation. The captives that fell from exhaustion or had finally given in to their wounds were trampled over by the herd of prisoners. The gorgons tossed the bodies into a large wheeled wagon like fallen debris. It was pulled by two gray, long haired oxen with matted fur. Finn and Nylah stayed close together. The prisoners were no longer bound. There was simply too many of them to rope together. Brigands of gorgons continually joined the larger mass with more prisoners. These gorgons were probably outriders raiding smaller villages. Finn decided that he and the others would be used as slave laborers or worse. It was getting more difficult for Finn to find a way of escaping with Nylah.

# A DARK TYRANNY

There were too many gorgons. They were directly in the middle of a moving host of snake walkers. If they were able to leave the group of prisoners, Finn knew they would have no way of blending in with them. They would stick out in any situation. Finn's head ached, as he constantly scanned his surroundings. He did not want their chance of escape to pass them by.

The last three days were like a muddled dream to Finn. If it was a dream, he was unsure whether to wake or stay a sleeping captive. Even in the midst of what seemed hopeless, Finn treasured each moment he had with Nylah. Things as simple as the way she spoke and moved fascinated him. She had a wit about her as well. He had never seen anyone or anything that possessed his thoughts like she did. If he had to die, he knew of no other way he would rather approach his death. Her skin was the color of almond and vanilla. It was soft to the touch. Her skin retained its glow, even while they trekked through the dust and dirt. The bright green of her eyes radiated like an emerald on fire. She was simply the most elegantly beautiful person that Finn had ever seen. He could not have imagined a more intelligent or beautiful woman. He would die to save her. Finn felt his life inconsequential to the magnitude of hers.

Finn was taken by how she persevered. They had been walking for so long. She was surrounded by creatures that could kill her at any moment, yet she concentrated on Finn. They would talk to each other in whispers. Their conversations had been random at best. She told him about the Emerald Coast where she grew up. She had two sisters; Marigold was the oldest while Lily was the youngest. They would play in the shallows together along the beach. When the tide was low, small pools of clear water would form in the dunes. Small fish would swim there and become stuck waiting for the tide to come back in. The girls would look at them and wade through the pools. Finn had never known that type of free life and he envied it. He would love to see the pools. Her family lived in a large stone house that overlooked the shoreline. She would fall asleep listening to the waves; the ocean would sing at night. Nylah had a pleasantness to her that calmed Finn. She had her wits about her at all times and he enjoyed talking with her.

"How much further must we walk?" asked Nylah.

"Well, we don't want to arrive where they are taking us. The longer we walk, the more chances we have," Finn replied.

"How could we ever escape this," Nylah spoke almost to herself.

"I don't know, but we will. Sometimes a few are better at watching than many. I'm starting to think that everyone here will most likely assume someone else is watching us. It is odd, but I think we might stand a better chance with a large group that is occupied with other things ... than a small group that is only occupied with us."

Finn did not know how they would escape. He could not find the opening they needed. He knew they were intended for some type of slave labor. Why else would they take them? He knew that some of them were for food, as did the others. They had a foreboding look about them. They seemed nervous to be on the outside of the captives. Instead, they stayed in the center and did not look at the gorgons. They were nothing more than a herd of cattle being moved along by the gorgons to their own slaughter. Some would work; some would be eaten. Finn had seen the gorgons pluck men and women alike out of the ranks in the evening hours. They would never return but the gorgons remained strong and of good stamina.

"I wonder where they are taking us?" said Nylah.

"White Rock," a rough voice uttered from behind

them. "They're taking us to the ruins."

The man was in his late forties. His skin wrapped loosely around his head. It was beginning to crack from the sun. Finn knew immediately that he was a former prisoner. The penal code for rape was burned into both his cheeks. They were long scarred over but the image remained. The stumbled skin of his neck had the number IX inked across it. He had raped nine women. His head had been shaved, but traces of hair now grew in patches across his scalp. His teeth were framed in black and purple gums. The man's body was clearly malnourished, but it seemed to have grown accustomed to years of neglect and abuse. He looked at Nylah like a hungry wolf.

"Before it was ruins, White Rock was a temple," said the man. His voice was scratchy and gruff. He eyed Nylah with a grin.

"What kind of temple?" asked Nylah.

"Nylah, this man is a convict. Leave us be," Finn said to him.

"A dark temple ... and we're all convicts now," he said, keeping his eyes on Nylah.

"How do you know this?" she asked.

"My grandmum would tell tales about gorgons at White Rock. They would take you to an altar and open you from crotch to neck with a jagged blade. As your life came pouring out, they'd steal your soul," he said, looking into her eyes.

"Enough," warned Finn.

"Some say they put the souls into weapons ... jewelry," he spoke to Nylah.

"Don't listen to him Nylah. He is trying to scare you," said Finn.

"Of course, they'd say that gorgons were just fireside tales as well. However, here we walk among them. Could be that I'm wrong, *Nylah*. After me grandmum told me those stories, she and the rest would get drunk off forest ale. Then, they'd beat me until my teeth cracked ... sometimes worse," he said. The man smiled exposing his gnarled teeth and black gums.

Nylah began to sob. Finn kicked one of the man's legs causing him to fall. The rest of the captives kept moving. The man had trouble getting back up. By the time he was up, Finn and Nylah were further up in the crowd of prisoners.

"Don't listen to that man. We will survive this ... we will," Finn said. He took her hand.

"How are you so sure?"

"Because we've only just met," Finn said, as he smiled at her. She smiled back.

Finn wiped her eyes with the sleeve of his shirt.

"You are very kind, Finn."

It was not until late in the evening that the prisoners were allowed to rest. They all fell to the ground immediately. Nylah sat close to Finn. His presence was a comfort to her. She had no idea how she would have dealt with this nightmare alone. She leaned in against Finn, resting her weight on him. She laid her head against his shoulder. Finn could smell her hair, feel it caress his face. He put his arm around her. The dust had dissipated with the lack of walking. A cool breeze wandered through the camp. Finn breathed in the clean air. He looked at Nylah leaning into his arm. The night was perfect if not for the evil dwelling within it.

"Finn," Nylah whispered. She spoke almost to herself. "I don't want to die."

"You won't. You won't die ... not from this," Finn whispered. He turned her head to him and lightly kissed her forehead. Her skin was sweet and soft to the touch. "Imagine the campfire tale this will make someday. Nylah taken by the walking snakes only to escape her captures with wile and cunning. No one will believe it, yet here you sit ... and there you will be."

"Truly ... aren't we beyond escape?" she asked.

# A DARK TYRANNY

"I don't think so. I think we will have a chance."

"My cousin is probably dead."

"Perhaps ... but you don't know that."

"She's not here."

"We can go look once we're gone from here."

"I just want to go home. I want to be with my family. I should never have come."

Finn felt a pang of guilt for being glad she was here.

"Well, we're here. We just need to escape and get you back home."

"I'm tired."

"Sleep. You will need your strength."

"What if we're asleep and miss our only chance?"

"I will stay awake for both of us. Sleep. It's ok," Finn said.

Nylah closed her eyes.

"I was thinking about the birds. The mew," whispered Nylah. "You said they could have flown away anytime while you were hunting with them."

"Yes," said Finn.

"Why didn't you?" Nylah asked in a soft whisper.

"Why did I not leave?"

"You could have just left ... just like the birds."

"Some cages are bigger than others. The Southern Realm is one large cage for me ... or it was."

"I should never have left the isles and you should have run while you could. Now look," said Nylah.

"Had I left, I would never have met you."

"Finn, you are kind. I am not worth all of this, though," Nylah whispered. Finn could feel her breath on his face.

"I'm sorry you are here, but I am happy I'm here with you. I would like to be somewhere else with you ... but if it must be here, so be it. I've been in a cage my whole life. If I can free you of yours ... well, it will be a good thing."

"I wish I could show you the isles."

*I want to see the isles.*

"We are still very much alive, Nylah. The isles are still there."

Finn felt Nylah drift into sleep. Her weight was fully against him. He could feel her breath on his neck.

Finn stared at the night sky. The stars pulsed with light in the expanse of blackness around them.

*They burn so brightly in such a dark void.*

"You rival the stars in this darkness," he thought aloud. He breathed in the air and pretended to himself that he and Nylah were not captives. Rather, they were a couple finding refuge in the open land and solitude of the night sky. He wished it were true.

*I have to get us out.*

It was not long until sleep crept over Finn as well.

## Chapter 11

## Slavers

No one felt rested when the sun crept over the horizon. It cast a soft orange glow that slowly became a deep maroon. Exhaustion and hopelessness had spread like a plague in the night. The ground was littered with blood, urine, and other filth that mixed with the damp earth. The gorgon in the red tunic cracked his whip to wake the prisoners. Some continued to lay unshaken despite the commands of the gorgon in red. They had died during the night or were at the cusp of death. Gorgons pulled them by their feet, as they dragged them to the wagon. The dead and dying were tossed on top of the other corpses. There was a slight movement from the bodies in the wagon. Those that refused to die easily gave the pile of bodies a slight movement. It was as if one giant creature was slowly dying.

Finn stood with Nylah. She held his hand and waited for what the day would bring them. Finn could tell she was more apprehensive than the previous days. He also noticed that the camp was busier than it had been. There was a different atmosphere to it all together.

"We should make sure to stay close today," Finn whispered.

"Ok. What's happening?"

"I don't know. Something doesn't seem right though. Something's different. We might get our opportunity. We have to be ready."

The gorgons slowly got the camp moving. Blood and filth stayed behind in shallow pools. They made no attempt to hide their presence. Finn studied the gorgons. There was a structure to their units. Most of the gorgon foot soldiers wore tunics the color of coal and kept their thick tails coiled around one leg like a pulsing vine. The gorgons in red tunics ran the prisoners and had small units of foot soldiers keeping watch. Finn had seen a few gorgons dressed in light chain mail over yellow and black tunics. Their tails were uncoiled; they walked with an air of superiority. They were most likely generals of some sort. They had groups of gorgons under them. Finn thought they were perhaps the same as barons or nobles with land and army under them. The one thing he knew was that they were superior to the others in the camp. Finn could hear the generals giving instructions in their black tongue. The foot soldiers donned their weapons. Some carried banners of black and yellow with serpents embroidered in red.

"The camp is going to have visitors," said Finn.

"How do you know? What if today we arrive at our destination?"

"No. We are still in familiar lands. They are taking us somewhere further than here. I think we are somewhere between the Southern and Eastern Realms. No, someone's coming to us," said Finn.

"Maybe the realms are uniting. An army perhaps ...," said Nylah. She had a hopeful tone to her voice.

## A DARK TYRANNY

"Perhaps," Finn replied. He did not want to soil her hopes. "We should be prepared though. Whatever it is could be our chance to get out of here."

Finn took Nylah by the hand. They walked slowly with the rest of the pack. Finn took care to keep them close to the outside of the crowd of prisoners, but kept one or two between them and the gorgons. They could easily get to the center of the group if the gorgons began picking prisoners for food.

"Look up," said Nylah, pointing above them. A large flock of long necked birds had taken to circling the caravan.

"They look like mud vultures. They've taken to the scent of blood we're leaving behind," said Finn.

*And the scraps of flesh and bone. A black cloud is hovering over us ... waiting for someone to lose their way.*

"Will they hurt us?" she asked. She then looked around and revealed a small smile. "Surrounded by armed snakes and I'm worried about birds."

She laughed quietly.

Finn smiled at her.

"Don't worry. They won't attack."

They continued to walk for most of the day. The sun beat down on them, although a slight breeze blew in from the east. It kept the thoughts of the heat at bay. However, when the captives finally felt the effects of the sun, it was too late. The heat had already enveloped them in its grip. Finn and Nylah kept pace with the other prisoners but made sure to not overexert themselves. Those that fell to the heat ended up in the wagon or were left behind for the birds to strip to the bone. The heat broke in the late afternoon. The sun had moved behind the clouds causing the sky to turn a deep red and purple. It outlined the contours of the clouds making them appear heavy. The sound of a war horn echoed over the prisoners. It was not a sustained noise,

but a short burst of raspy staccato blows.
"Something's happening," said Finn.
"What?"
"I don't know."
Finn clasped tightly to Nylah's hand. He pulled her forward to get a glimpse of what was happening.

A large host came from the west. They brought with them wagons and carts pulled by long haired oxen that appeared malnourished. Most of the host was on foot, while some rode on enormous jackals. Others walked these beasts with collars and thick steel chains. They were led like dogs on a lease.   The jackals were long-legged and had thick girths with matted black hair. Their eyes were black and void of life. There was only a thin strip of yellow iris that outlined their dead pupils. They snapped at each other when too close. There was not a pack mentality between them. They were lone hunters forced together. This was evident by the large scars that some of them had. Others had freshly bleeding claw or bite marks. Finn had only seen scavenging wild dogs or coyotes before. He had never seen this type of creature and felt sure that the others had not either. They seemed more sinister than wild dogs and much larger. Saliva and spittle dripped from their teeth and around the corners of their black mouths. They didn't lick their face like an ordinary animal would. Instead, they just let the spittle drip off their jagged teeth. They only had one concern: killing and eating. It was like they were from some dark land full of shadows and death.

Finn immediately saw that the host was not made up of ordinary men. They appeared distorted, almost deformed.

"What's wrong with them," Finn thought but spoke the words aloud.

"Skin Slavers," a voice said from beside Nylah.

It was an elderly woman. She had dirt outlining her

wrinkles, which made her look almost ancient. She wore a tattered dress that revealed her bone thin legs. Blue veins wrapped around them like a tightly coiled vine. Finn could see her sagging breasts through the frayed material of her dress. She seemed to already have the look of resignation. She had decided that she would die a slave or worse. Regardless, it would be soon. Finn felt a burning hatred for the gorgons. This wasn't the end that this woman deserved. This wasn't the end that Nylah or he deserved. He hated the gorgons. He hated being a servant of the king. He hated everything else in the world that led up to that very moment. Finn had met Nylah and was unable to have one normal interaction with her. He would die a slave next to a woman that he found captivating. He was once again in a cage. Finn saw that Nylah felt a great deal of compassion for the older woman. She had taken her arm to help her stand.

"Skin Slavers?" asked Nylah.

"People call them by different names ... Skin Slavers, Flesh Dreamers, or Spirit Thieves. It depends on where you were raised and if you're old enough to have even heard of them," the woman said.

"What do they want?" asked Nylah.

"Us," replied the woman.

"What is your name?" asked Nylah.

"I'm Tilda."

"I am Nylah. This is Finn."

"Where do I know you from?" asked Finn.

"I sold quilts in the market," replied Tilda.

"You have seen them before? Where?" asked Nylah.

"I've only seen them once before now. It was not a large group like this. It was just one of them ... a single man. I was just a child. We lived on the southern shores in a small village. Everyone was raised and grew up together. So, the week some boys began to disappear, we knew something was wrong. The elders knew that a stranger was in our midst."

"What did you do?" asked Nylah.

"Ah. I did nothing. I was just a child. The elders though ... they set out to look for the boys. They ended up at a set of caves along the shoreline. The ocean had carved them out, smoothed their edges. It seemed like quite a magical place to play."

"Did they find them there?"

"They did. The boys were dead but he was not."

"Was he deformed like these other men?" asked Finn.

"Oh ... they are not deformed. They look that way but make no mistake ... they are quite human," said Tilda.

"What is wrong with them?" asked Nylah.

"You just cannot see them up close. Pray you don't have to. They are members of the occult. You see, they found the man and boys. The boys were dead," Tilda said. Her eyes began to gather tears. "They had been skinned. Their flesh ... it was flayed off them. He was wearing it. This man was wearing their skin."

"No," Nylah let out a small gasp. Tears welled up in her eyes.

"They said that he was in such a trance by the fire that he did not hear them enter the cave. He mumbled some type of incoherent speech ... some black speech."

"What did they do?" asked Finn.

"They took the skins and buried them with their bodies. They buried them in one grave to be together."

"This man, he was a Skin Slaver?" asked Finn.

"What did they do with him?" asked Nylah.

"They tethered him to a stake over the grave and burned him alive. They said it would release their souls in the afterlife. You see, the man, the Skin Slaver, he wore their skin, stealing their souls and making them slaves to him in the afterlife. It is said that Skin Slavers can travel between life and death. They burned him to free the boys. I remember, he never screamed as the flames took him ... not once."

"Why would these Skin Slavers be dealing with gorgons?" Finn asked, almost to himself.

"I don't know ... I don't know. I fear, though, that our world is over. The world we have lived in up to now ... it's over," Tilda said, sighing.

"Nothing is over yet," said Finn. He had to remain calm and positive.

*We will escape this.*

The army of Skin Slavers forked out as they approached the captives. They rode and walked along side of the prisoners staring at them. No one would look them in the eyes. The tension was palpable. All eyes stared at the ground or another captive in front of them.

"Move closer to the center," Finn said. "But move slowly."

"Come with us," Nylah whispered to Tilda.

They began to make their way into the center of the group. The situation had gotten much worse. Finn looked at the Skin Slavers when he thought no one would see him. Nylah and the woman kept their heads down. Finn saw them. They were indeed human. However, the woman was right. They wore layers of skin on their bodies like armor. One of them had the lower half of someone's face tied to him like a partial mask. Another wore a tunic made of human flesh. Finn could see what looked like legs and feet wrapped tightly around the slaver's waist. Finn felt a shiver of pure fear for the first time. The gorgons were an evil that acted upon brutality and force. However, these Skin Slavers were evil that manifested itself with cruelty.

*She cannot be taken by them.*

Nylah was beautiful. They would take her the moment they saw her. She needed to stay hidden within the group.

A large slaver rode alongside of the captives. He was much bigger than the others and had an air of superiority. He was a leader of these men in some fashion. Finn could tell right away. He straddled an equally huge jackal. It was brown with patches of black fur. The beast had bare patches of scar tissue behind its ears and along its neck. It snarled at the captives, as its rider kicked it along and pulled at the reins. The man was completely shaven. He did not have eyebrows or hair along his arms. He wore a thick black vest made from human flesh that was heavily tanned. His leather shoulder armor was adorned with the flesh from human heads on either side. One face was black, while the other was white. They were each pulled tightly over the leather armor. Hair was still attached and draped over his arms. The faces were like death shrouds. No eyes or teeth were left. It was just a face with gaping holes. The man had a large sword strapped to his back. The hilt was made of bone. Finn could only imagine that it was sheathed in some hideous manner.

The man rode to one of the gorgons in a yellow and black tunic. The two leaders discussed the captives. Finn could see the Skin Slaver motioning with his hands over the prisoners. The gorgon was not overly concerned with the Skin Slaver's gestures. Two other gorgons wearing a yellow and black tunic joined them. Finn thought the discussion was becoming angry, due to the gestures of the Skin Slaver. Still, there were now three gorgons and only one slaver. The slaver was either overly confident or completely ignorant of his situation.

One of the gorgons made a nodding gesture and then walked away, as if nothing had happened. The Skin Slaver rode back towards the captives. He spoke to other slavers in a tongue that Finn did not recognize. It was a harsh guttural language. One of the slavers whipped the oxen pulling his wagon. It was covered in hard wood. A large trunk the size of a horse was in the back. It too was made of wood, but it had thick metal strips pulled tightly over it. There was a key lock securing the lid. The slaver rode the wagons to a nearby group of gorgons. The gorgons grunted with effort as they took the trunk from the wagon. The trunk hit the ground with a thud, pushing dirt and dust from under it. The wagon lifted up when the trunk was removed. The slaver slapped the oxen a last time with the whip. They began to move again. This time the wagon was directed towards the captives.

The lead Skin Slaver yelled to the others, as he turned his reins on the jackal. The other slavers began to gather around the captives. They stared at them without emotion. The slavers began to separate the men from the women, and children from the adults. The captives were like cattle at an auction. The slavers inspected their skin, mouth, and hair. Captives that passed the initial examination were put in a line to be inspected by an older slaver. The top of his dirty scalp was visible. He had long matted hair dangling from the sides of his head. He wore skins that were dark, most likely from the Claw Archipelagos. The old slavers teeth had a thick crust of yellow coating them. A stench of decay emanated from him.

Finn saw the captives being separated into groups. He grabbed Nylah's hand and held it tightly. This would be their only chance. He knew, if they were separated, they would never see each other again.

"Finn," Nylah whispered.

"Stay with me. We have to leave. We are going to run."

Finn looked around frantically. A forest was to their northwest. However, they were fully surrounded.

"We are going to run," Finn said again.

"We will never make it."

"North and then west to those trees," said Finn. He

began to walk in that direction. He led Nylah by the hand.

"They will kill us," said Nylah. The fear in her voice was palpable.

"They will kill us here or later. This is our only chance. They will split us up now."

Finn turned and put both hands on Nylah's arms. They were soft. He longed to have them around him. He looked directly into her eyes.

"If we don't try now, we will be split up. I don't see that we will have any other chance, Nylah. Now, you must listen."

"Finn ..."

"Listen, I will cause a distraction. I will get their attention. You must run to the forest. No matter what happens. Don't look back, Nylah. Run as fast as you can. Do you understand?"

"What about you?"

"Don't worry about me. I will try to meet you, but you must run and not look back."

"You are lying. They will take you, Finn."

"If only one of us can leave, it has to be you. Now, tell me you understand. Tell me you will run."

Nylah paused. She looked at Finn with tears in her eyes.

"I understand," whispered Nylah. She looked down and then back into his eyes. She leaned into his arms and kissed him. Finn felt her lips softly press into his. He felt her tongue gently caress his open mouth.

Finn wanted that moment to last forever. It was the one moment he was not a slave.

"You have my heart," Nylah whispered.

"More reason you must live," Finn said. He felt her arms around him. He smelled her hair. Her skin was soft. Finn's heart ached.

"We have to go," Finn said. He felt anger building inside him with the thought of not feeling her lips again or feeling her touch.

They moved to the outlying edge of the captives. One more step and they would be away from the pack.

"The forest there ... do you see it?" asked Finn.

"I do."

Finn paused.

"This isn't fair," whispered Nylah.

Finn had no words. He pulled her to him and kissed her one last time. Nylah's arms wrapped tightly around him. He felt her breasts against his chest. Her breath was warm against his face. Finn pulled her from him.

"You have to run."

"Ok."

"Ready. Go! Now!"

Nylah began to run, but she fell immediately to the ground. Her ankle seared with pain. She had been tripped. She could taste dirt in her mouth. Blood dripped from her bottom lip.

"Where are you going, ma lady?" said the rapist prisoner from days earlier. He looked gaunter and his clothes were dirtier. He stared at Nylah laughing.

"You bastard!" Finn screamed.

He tackled the man, knocking him to the ground. The man was caught off guard. He had not expected Finn to be so brazen.

"Nylah run!" yelled Finn.

Nylah got to her feet. Her ankle wanted to buckle. It burned. She began to run the best she could. The trees were so far away. She could hear Finn yelling behind her. She kept hearing his voice in her head.

*Run. Don't look back. Run as fast as you can.*

She ran.

Finn felt his fists begin to ache, as he pummeled the man below him. Anger burned within him. Finn felt a slaver's foot slam against his face knocking him to the ground. He was momentarily jarred from the impact. Another blow landed in his stomach. He felt his breath shoot out. He gasped for air. Nylah was yelling in the distance. Finn tried to stand and look for her.

*Run.*

He felt the bluntness of a club rack against his back. He fell to one knee. Blood had begun to pool in his mouth. His vision was blurry. The captives moved into groups to isolate themselves from Finn and the bloodied prisoner on the ground beside him. They wanted to stay unnoticed. This allowed Finn to catch a quick glimpse of Nylah. She was being carried by a large gorgon. The beast was bringing her back to the group. Nylah tried to pull away from him but instead just flung in his arms like a ragdoll.

*No!*

Two slavers now stood over Finn. One had four faces hanging around his neck like a gruesome necklace. His teeth had almost rotted out. The other hid behind a mask of skin. He was enormous. His arms bulged causing them to stick out from his wide chest. His belly protruded heavily from a belt made of scalped hair. Finn saw that he had dull green eyes. The smaller one with the necklace of faces followed Finn's eyes to Nylah.

"A nice morsel we have over here, eh?" he said. His voice was high and his lack of teeth made his words smack together. His English was harsh.

"No," Finn whispered to himself.

The small slaver kicked Finn to the ground.

"Let's see what's here ... you there," he said motioning to the gorgon carrying Nylah. The two slavers began to walk towards the gorgon.

Panic seared through Finn. Fear and anger brought him back to his feet. He shot like lighting towards the slaver. He slammed into the back of the small slaver causing him to crash to the ground. The slaver coughed, as the wind was knocked from him. Finn grabbed both sides of his face and began pounding his head into the hard earth. The slaver was wide eyed with a look of fear and bewilderment. He was completely taken off guard by Finn's attack. Blood started to trickle from both his ears and nose. The necklace of faces tore off, as a cracking sound came from the man's skull.

Finn felt a much harder kick against the back of his head. He fell from the man instantly. He ears rang; he had trouble focusing. He barely made out the masked slaver. He towered above Finn. The slaver stooped down grasping Finn with both hands. He picked him up. One hand had Finn by the shoulder and the other by his neck. Finn dangled in his grasp. Finn kicked at the man but it did no good. The slaver was a mass of muscle. Finn felt his shirt tear open. He could feel his life slipping to blackness. He struggled to breathe. The slaver's hand squeezed tighter around Finn's neck. The head slaver yelled to the one holding Finn. He dropped him to the ground like a sack of rocks. Finn felt his throat open back up and air rush in. He gasped for breath. A sword cut through the rest of Finn's shirt, as he laid face up on the ground. He could see the lead slaver looking down upon him.

The lead slaver looked down staring at the large markings on Finn's chest. It was an imprint of a coin from the ancient kingdom. The slaver smiled revealing his teeth. They had been sharpened to points. Finn felt himself being lifted up and tied to the back of the slaver's jackal. He was being taken by the slavers along with some of the other prisoners. Before Finn passed out, he saw Nylah being put back into the crowd of prisoners that the gorgons were keeping. Tears fell from her eyes. She looked directly at Finn. He was full of rage and anger but couldn't keep conscious.

*It can't end this way ... Nylah.*

Finn passed out into darkness.

## Chapter 12

## The Meeting at Kor

Matthias sat in the cave with his back against its rocky wall. It had been days since the grandeur had spoken to him. Water seeped from cracks that splintered like veins throughout the stone walls. It dripped down onto his head, neck, and back. Matthias could not see, but he had become accustomed to the noises of the cave. He knew when a scavenger bird flapped down inside the cave or when a headstrong rodent was exploring. It also did not take sight for Matthias to know he was both exhausted and starving. His body hurt from hunger and thirst. He drank water from the cave when he could no longer take the pang of dehydration. Without sight, he had no idea if the water was tainted. It had an earthy taste of dirt and minerals, but it had not made him sick.

*I should have let Denthas kill me. I envy death, yet I still rage against it.*

Matthias heard a distinctly different sound than he was accustomed. It was not an animal or the wind blowing rocks and pebbles. He was certain it was a person. The steps came in two and there was a small time between each one. Someone was walking. Matthias was not sure whether to speak or remain silent. He could not see. Remaining silent felt futile.

"Who is here?" Matthias did not expect his voice to be so hoarse and raspy.

"You're here," Luras said, "I have been looking for you all over these mountains."

"I haven't moved from this one."

"Yes. I'm sorry. I was told you would be in these mountains, but I didn't think to ask which one."

"Well ... you have rescued me. The adventure is over. Now, if you will, please give me some food."

"Yes. I have some fruit," Luras said. He removed his cloak and began looking through his leather satchel.

"Fruit? I suppose I will have to make do."

"Here."

"I can't see."

"It's here," Luras put a small cloth sack of fruit in Matthias' hand.

He ate it quickly. The sugar and juice woke his sense of taste. His stomach began to growl.

"My name is Luras."

Luras felt odd saying his new name aloud.

"I am just a dying blind man."

"Surely, you have a name. Here is some water," said Luras. He put his canteen into Matthias' hand.

"Thank you."

Matthias paused for a moment in thought. There was no harm in a name.

"My name is Matthias. I do not want to go any further into it."

"I understand."

"How long have you been looking?" asked Matthias.

"Two days. I saw the carrion birds flying over here at sunset yesterday."

"Yes. They've been patiently waiting for me to die."

"I'm glad to find you well ... more or less. Please eat and drink. I will try to gather some wood for a fire."

"Aye. Thank you."

The sky was turning gray, as the sun slowly set on the mountains. Luras gathered sticks and branches and put them in a broken hollowed out log. The Kor Mountains were rock but some small trees and shrubs sprouted out. The mountains were mostly lifeless. Birds and rodents were the only residents that stayed, everything else just passed through. All the same, Luras felt it safer to stay in the seclusion of the cave rather than sleep at the foot of the mountains. He would take his chances with the birds and rats rather than the darker creatures rampaging through the realms.

The fire crackled inside the cave. It cast a yellow hue to the walls. Luras and Matthias sat by the fire, while their shadows did the same on the walls of the cave. A breeze caused the fire to flicker momentarily interrupting the shadows. Luras had stumbled upon a carrion with an injured wing while rummaging for wood. It was now hanging over the fire sizzling. Matthias had already eaten a good portion of it. The meat was thin and rough, but it was the only food he had eaten besides fruit in days. Luras tried some but he had not acclimated to the taste of meat. Nighteyes lived off fruit and vegetables so he had never tasted meat until then. A scavenger bird does not make a suitable first experience for roasted bird.

"I never thought something that tastes so bad could taste so good," Matthias said, as he took a large bite of meat.

"You've been hungry."

"Have you eaten some? I don't want to eat it all."

"Please do. It does not seem to agree with me. I am more of a farm eater ... fruits and vegetables."

"Well, a plump farm turkey is what you need ... as do I."

"We will have to look into that," said Luras.

"So, you have seen the Grandeur ... or one of them? I only saw some beast," said Matthias.

"Yes. She sent me after you."

"Why you?"

"I do not know. Why you?"

"That's a very good question. I do not favor any king or god. I want nothing from the lot of them."

"I believe we are to be Acolytes. I was told that I would be or ... well, I am one now, I believe," said Luras.

"An Acolyte? The world must have fallen apart while I was a blind prisoner here," Matthias said, mockingly.

"I suppose you are to be one as well."

"Rubbish. I am no Acolyte. Are your eyes glowing?"

"They are."

"Well, I am blind. I would prefer to die blind in this cave than help a king or a god."

"Why do you say that?" asked Luras.

"Gods and kings take what they will ... leaving all else to die," Matthias said in low tone.

"Which king did you serve?"

"The butcher king in the north."

Luras felt it better to leave this alone.

"May I," Luras asked, as he moved closer to Matthias. "I would like to see what is wrong with your eyes."

"If you were going to kill me, you would not have fed me."

"Well, it is a carrion so you could still die yet."

Matthias let out a small laugh.

"Take a look if you must."

Luras gently opened the lids of Matthias' eyes. He lightly touched the side and base of each eye. They were hard and cold to the touch.

"Do they hurt?" asked Luras.

"Not particularly."

Luras leaned back and put his canteen close to the fire.

"Your eyes are coated in clay and some type of small scales ... the size of fish scales."

"I don't feel them."

Luras took the canteen and poured some water onto his hands.

"Lean your head to the side. You are going to feel some warm water."

Matthias felt the water slowly pour onto his head and close to his eyes. The water was warm and cascaded under his eyelids. Luras held Matthias' eyes open and poured more water. This time it was directly onto each eye. Matthias felt clumps soften and wash away. He could feel his eyes growing lighter. Then, actual light slowly began to seep in. Matthias felt his eyes begin to move again. If was like they were awakening from a great sleep. He rubbed them with his palms. Clay and scales broke apart and fell to the ground. Matthais took the canteen and poured more water into his eyes. Blurred vision gradually focused into a dark cave. The dark cave slowly became occupied with light from the fire. Matthias looked up and saw that Luras was not a human. He was a Bourne.

"A Bourne?"

"It was the Grandeur. I was a Nighteye before."

"Your eyes," Matthias stammered, "they glow. You are a bloody Acolyte."

"Yes," Luras answered, "and you are as well."

Matthias looked down into a pool of water that had gathered by him. His eyes shimmered with a soft translucent hue of blue. He kicked the water splashing it into the fire with a hiss.

"No! I will not do this!" yelled Matthias, "I am no Acolyte!"

## Chapter 13

The King's Devil

The village of Timball lay just outside the walls of Castle Horos. The sun had set causing the crafters and merchants to move indoors. It was full of homes made from stone. They had thick wooden logs split in half for their rooftops. The village had both the resources and safety of the mountains and forest. It was obvious in the materials the crafters used and the merchants sold. There was a high quality to everything. The mountains provided rich minerals, while the forest provided sturdy timber. The village itself was largely built around a statue that stood in the center of Timball. It was an exact replica of Castle Horos. It did not have the tower on the north side because it was carved before the tower was built, however, the statue was very much the image of the current castle. It was a statue of exquisite craftsmanship. The stonework was painstakingly accurate to the smallest of details.

Many years ago, an invading force from the west had marched towards Castle Horos. The ruler at that time was King Peltor. He had the statue built to mock the invaders. King Peltor announced that should they reach the village, the statue was the only castle they would take. He had the craftsmen carve a stone man dressed in the royal garb of the castle steward. The figure was placed in the front of the gate of the statue. It was a stone man surrendering the stone castle. It would only have further enraged the invaders. However, they never reached the village. They retreated back to the west, due to disease running rampant among their ranks. It is said they lost more men to sickness than fighting. The western invaders and King Peltor were now long dead and gone, but the statue still stood. Over time, it had become the center of the village.

The Greenwood Tavern stood not far from the statue. It was a two-story building built from massive rock. They had swirls of minerals in them that cast off a copper color. The minerals infused in the rocks seemed to give off a flickering or twinkle with the rising and setting of the sun. A stone on the top wall of each side of the tavern had a sun carved into it. The roof was wood and painted a deep forest green. It was constructed well after the time of King Peltor, but it had been there long enough to be considered a mainstay of the village. The tavern saw many villagers come and go. It had stayed in the same family line since it was erected. The current owner was Camille Greenwood. She was a large woman with ample breasts, stomach, and appetite. Her face was hard, but she had a jolly smile when she let it show. She was married to Cyrus Tulling. She had kept her maiden name of Greenwood to insure the tavern was always owned by a Greenwood. It was not a normal act, but the villagers understood. They also knew that Camille had a fiery temper. The sun had recently set causing the tavern to come alive with villagers. There was a steady stream of them coming and going. The tavern was a good place for people to learn what was going on in the realm. It was also, of course, a good place for drinking. The residents of Timball needed both.

An enormous open fireplace stood in the center of the tavern. A pot full of chestnuts hung from a pole over the flames and their aroma drifted from the fireplace mixing with the smell of ale, smoke, and sweat. The walls were adorned with various paintings and heads of large elk, deer, and moose. A mounted owl stood perched in a corner. A few wooden carvings stood in various places. One was a bear rearing on its hind legs. Directly below the bear was a carving of a field mouse rearing on its hind legs. Tables and chairs were in no specific places. They were strewn about in whatever formation the current patrons wanted. In one corner, a group of men huddled together rolling dice. Some of them cheered with each roll, while others grimaced with defeat.

A group of merchants and crafters sat at two tables that had been pushed together. Jared Horn was doing the majority of the talking. He was a large man with thick forearms, a soft belly, and a mustache that was twisted upwards. He took short puffs on his pipe while continuing to talk.

"I've not received one word from Warren Town. No orders. No supplies. With the king's wedding, you would think the lack of correspondence queer."

"My brother lives close to those parts ... in Graywood. I've not heard from him, either," said an older woman with coarse gray hair.

"Some hunters passed through heading northeast ... towards the coastline. There's stories of bandits freely roaming just west of here," said Jon Lince, a tall fellow with sunken eyes. He was the village's copier of books, scrolls, and letters.

"I brought some carving stones to Doghead. They spoke about gorgons sacking Castle Red," said a tightly muscled quarry worker.

"Stories ... no facts. Do you think the king would wed during an invasion? They are just stories. Don't get people working for naught," said Jared Horn.

"If there's to be a wedding, where is everyone?" retorted Cal Mossy. He was a logger with a broad back and chest. "I ain't seen nobody here ... coming or going. And where are the councilmen? Something ain't right I tell you."

"Calm down, Cal," said Jared Horn.

"The wedding is still weeks away," said the older woman.

"The farmers are still reaping their crops for the donation. People will come and money will be made," said Jared.

"They are lying. Don't you see? Something is not right. Nobles are being moved inside the castle walls. Why?"

"Calm down, Cal. Lower your voice," warned Jon Lince, as he looked around the tavern.

"Why? The ears of the king might hear? I ain't seen the king in months ... only his tabulate collecting the realm's unearned share," quipped Cal Mossy. He stood with his fists against the table.

"Cal, sit down," warned Jared.

"There is a plot afoot and it is as thick as thieves. Don't no one else see!" yelled Cal.

"Come now, Cal Mossy," said one of the men that was rolling dice. His hood was pulled low. "I can assure you that there's not a plot afoot ... and no thieves thickening."

"And you would know this how, sir," said Cal.

"Because my brother told me himself. There will be a wedding in a matter of weeks."

"The king's brother," whispered Jon Lince.

"He meant no offense, sir," said Jared Horn.

"I'm no king or sir. Please, call me Ellison or you or

bugger ... just not sir ... and, thank the Creator, not king."

At this, a small rumble of laugher was heard across the tavern. It rubbed Cal Mossy sorely. He turned red.

"I am to believe there's no plot by the word of the king's devil brother," Cal spoke very loudly.

"Come now, Cal," yelled Jared, "show the man his deserved respect."

The tavern grew silent.

"It's ok," said Ellison, "it's true ... I do appear quite devilish."

He pushed his hood back revealing his white skin and hair. His red eyes were the only color to his pale face. He grinned at Cal and those looking at him. Most were accustomed to seeing him with his hood up. Ellison was lanky with chin length white hair tucked behind his ears. He was handsome by normal standards but his lack of pigment distracted the eye.

"I can, however, assure you that my father did not sack a witch ... nor did my dear mom roll with a warlock," said Ellison.

A wave of laughter filled the tavern.

"In truth, no one knows why I am this way ... but a devil, I am not. Besides, aren't devils handsome ... and kings," Ellison spoke with a grin.

Laughter ensued. This time even Call Mossy let a fleeting grin pass his lips.

"I beg your pardon," said Cal.

"Think nothing of it. Please have a drink with me. I've rolled enough coin away for one night. Talk of devils, it's this jolly lot of ruffians here," Ellison pointed to the men rolling dice. They laughed and sneered in jest.

"Bring more coin to roll away tomorrow, devil," laughed one of them.

Ellison laughed and threw a wooden spoon towards the table. The group laughed and waved him off.

It was well past the midnight hour when Ellison fumbled his way into the living quarters of the castle. He hummed a tune and continually walked over his own feet. The living quarters of Castle Horos were attached to the northern tower. It housed the king's council and other visitors of noble heritage. It was quaint and comfortable. There was always a fire going in the main room and with various dignitaries talking politics in its great leather chairs. However, at this hour, all had long gone to sleep. It was only the fire and Ellison. He sank down into a chair and stared at the fire. It was common for the morning kitchen workers to wake him in that chair with a cup of coffee, some bacon, and sweet bread.

"Another night at the Greenwood I take it."

"Malvern, you are awake at this hour?"

"It is hard to sleep with all the noise ... humming and fumbling about."

"I hope you gave a fiery rebuke to whichever scoundrel that was," said Ellison.

"Ah. Well, I know it's not my place but it's not proper for the king's brother to drink and carry on in the village. It ... it sets a poor image for the king," Malvern spoke in a dry tone.

"I assure you that your words have sunk into my thoughts. I will change my ways."

Malvern remained silent, as he scratched at his patchy beard.

*The arrogant bastard.*

"Tell me, Malvern, I am hearing lots of talk about this wedding. Some of the townsfolk are worried. They have not seen visitors, nor have any orders been placed for various things."

"Who are these people?"

"No one particular. These are things heard out and about Timball. Perhaps, you could have someone transcribe a copy of the acceptance letter from her father. It would do the village well to have the reassurance."

"Ah, this is a good suggestion. I will take it up with the king."

"Do you have the letter? I would love to read it."

"Where is this concern coming from regarding the wedding?" questioned Malvern.

"Nowhere ... I would just like to read it."

"I don't have it. I imagine it has been sent to the archivist. I will try to find it for you when time allows. Will this meet your needs?"

"Yes, of course."

"If you will excuse me."

"Yes. Good night."

Malvern scurried out of the room in the direction of the kitchen. His sandals slapped against his feet with each step. Ellison winced. His head was already beginning to feel what the morning had in store for him. He stared at the fire feeling his eyelids grow heavy. It felt as if his eyes had only shut briefly, but Ellison could tell that he had been asleep for a while. It was still dark. Morning would not arrive for a few hours yet. Ellison pulled himself up from the chair. He awkwardly walked toward the door.

The briskness of the night air helped to wake him. He walked to the visitor stables by the living quarters. Fumbling with his pants, he unlaced his crotch just enough to pull himself out and begin to piss onto the straw. He stared up at the sky while relieving himself. He thought of his discussion with Malvern and how peculiar he had acted.

*Why would it be archived so soon?*

There was noise coming from the stable. It was not a horse; it was the sound of a muffled cry. It was rhythmic. Ellison thought he could make out loud breathing as well. He finished and laced himself again. He grinned, as he pictured a guard naked from the waist down with his wife bent over a stable rail. It was not uncommon for them to visit their husbands during a stretch of night patrols. Ellison turned to leave but the muffled cry continued to peek his curiosity. Something about it was quite odd. He pulled open the door to the stables to see a boy of roughly fourteen years leaned over a stable rail. Ellison recognized him as one of the boys that worked in the kennels. He was whimpering, as Malvern stood behind him with his robe pulled up over his waist. Malvern had sweat dripping from his brow. He was breathing heavily and grunting with each thrust of his waist. Ellison rushed towards Malvern pushing him to the ground. Malvern looked up with shock. His robes were twisted revealing his thin bowed legs and erect cock. Ellison kicked the old man.

"Are you ok?" Ellison asked the boy.

The boy pulled up his woolen pants and ran.

"He is just a boy!" Ellison yelled, as he kicked Malvern again.

"You bastard," Malvern yelled. Blood dripped from his mouth.

Malvern stood to get up but Ellison punched him back to the ground.

"I should have let your father kill you! Devil bastard!"

Malvern lay on the ground spitting blood. His eyes were wild with rage. He pulled himself to his knees. He kept one arm against his stomach.

"You will pay for this," said Ellison.

"You mean from the king that sticks his cock in two or three whores a night! No, you misjudge your brother."

"I will tell him you said that."

"Do. He will boast of it. You are nothing but a curse upon this castle."

"I do not prey upon young boys."

# A DARK TYRANNY

"You're a drunk ... a gambler and debtor. You would be long dead by now if you were of any other house," Malvern said, as he breathed heavily. "Dark times are coming to these walls, boy. Solid council will come before cursed blood when such dark times beat against these castle walls."

"What are you saying?"

"You will be surprised to find how your precious villagers will turn to folklore in desperate times. It will not be hard to convince them of your deviled curse. They would burn you without forethought."

"You raped a boy. I will tell the king. You are done here, Malvern. Your threats are just threats. Go near that boy again, or any other, and I will tear your lungs out."

## Chapter 14

An Encounter along the Road

Finn pulled at the rope around his neck. It had caused his skin to become chapped and raw. He alternated between putting his fingers between the rope and one side of his neck. It was a momentary relief but also caused the twine on the other side to dig deeper into his skin. He guessed that they had walked for at least a day. Finn did not know how long he had been unconscious, but he knew that only a day had passed since he had awakened.

The slavers were fewer in number but still moved much slower than the gorgons. They stopped frequently. Finn had no idea why. He would lie down and stare into the sky. He thought of Nylah. He wondered where she was and if she was alive. Some of the slavers would occasionally pull at his shirt to look at the coin marking. They discussed it in a language that Finn did not understand. It was a crude guttural language. The head slaver would always show up yelling and scolding the men. He was protective of Finn

## A DARK TYRANNY

like a thief to his treasure. Finn could tell though that the slaver's authority was waning, at best. It was obvious to him that they all wanted his marking. They wanted his skin.

The last glimmers of light hung over the horizon before the slavers stopped to setup camp for the night. The party had turned sharply west during the day. This put them close to the Norberry Woodlands. These were hardly woodlands since they consisted mostly of large plains of grass with only random patches of small trees. The grass was covered in small Norberry flowers. They grow like weeds. Their petals are a deep purple. The slavers picked a small formation of rocks nestled beside some thin trees. The skinny trees slowly moved in the breeze. Their large maroon leaves gave them an appearance of adolescence, like a child wearing his father's gloves.

The slavers built a fire along the wall of the rock formation. The rocks blocked the wind. The prisoners were tied together in a lump away from the fire, but within eyesight of their captors. The rope around Finn's neck was removed. It was now around one of his ankles. The other end was tied to a stake just outside the larger group of prisoners. He could hear them whisper amongst themselves. Finn pulled at the rope. He had not lost the desire to escape. Although, he had no idea which direction to run. He didn't know where he was. He would try to find Nylah, but he had no idea where the gorgons had gone. Finn would have to simply backtrack and hope to find their trail. There were too many questions and thoughts racing through his head.

*Concentrate on breaking free.*

"They are brewing something over the fire," one of the prisoners whispered to the others.

"No," another said in a whispered panic.

A deep blue smoke slowly rose from the slavers' fire.

They laid plants and flowers over the burning wood. It caught fire in a puff and bellowed more layered smoke. The slavers sat around the fire chanting in their garbled tongue. Their eyes were closed while they continued to breathe the smoke in deeply.

There were more whispers.

"What are they doing?"

"I believe they are preparing for the spirit world. I think they mean to kill us."

"They are burning mince root and sea plant. I can smell it."

"Sailors use sea plant to numb rope burns. Why breathe it in?"

"We need to break these ropes. We need to run. They are going to kill us."

Finn heard their whispers. He could smell the fire as well. It had a putrid stench about it. The mince root crackled in the fire and glowed a deep red. The sea plant burned quickly and drifted in the air. Finn pulled at the rope with all the strength he could muster.

*I won't die this way.*

"One of them is coming!" cried one of the prisoners.

A slaver approached the prisoners. He had a dagger with a handle made from stained bone. He had pelts of skin hanging from two belts that crossed his chest. They swung as he walked. The prisoners squirmed with fear. The slaver grabbed one by the foot and cut deeply above the ankle. The prisoner flailed about like a fish and screamed out in pain. The slaver grabbed his other leg with a strong grip. He sank his dagger into it as well. The other prisoners screamed out in fear or sat in shock. The slaver then cut the rope that held the man. He dragged the man by one of his legs towards the fire. The prisoner clawed at the dirt to stop but it was no use. His legs burned in agony. His strength and determination had all been taken from him. When the slaver reached the others at the fire, he grabbed the man's hair and pulled him into a sitting position. The prisoner sobbed grabbing the wound on his legs. The slaver did not hesitate. He slipped the dagger between the man's shoulder blades. He pulled the knife down his back. The prisoner's eyes widened. He yelled like a wounded animal.

Finn did not look. Instead, he pulled at the rope. He could hear the man crying out and the other prisoners screaming. He could feel the stake move slightly. The ground around it cracked. He pulled feverishly at the rope. He kicked at the stake. It moved slightly giving Finn more hope. He kicked and pulled like a trapped fox.

"Two are coming back!" yelled a prisoner.

Finn turned to look at the slavers approaching. He caught a quick glimpse of a slaver at the fire putting on fresh skin. The two slavers were discussing something as they walked. They looked at the prisoners. Suddenly, Finn saw them point at him. He saw one of the slavers pull a dagger from his belt. The other one looked back. The head slaver was not with them. He motioned towards Finn.

"They're coming for you," yelled a prisoner.

"You need to run!"

Finn pulled at the stake pushing it back and forward. He frantically kicked it and pulled at the rope. He yelled out as he pulled. He felt all his muscles straining and aching. The two slavers stood over Finn and watched. One said something to the other. He grunted or laughed. Finn stood and backed up as far as the rope let him. One of the slavers grabbed the rope and began to pull. Finn's leg went from under him. He hit the ground with a thud. The wind knocked out of him. The other slaver grabbed his leg. Finn kicked with both legs at the man. He had a grip like a giant. He raised his knife. Suddenly, he got a queer look upon his face. He jerked forward slightly. Blood dripped from his mouth. He turned to look behind him. Finn saw that a long spear was sticking from his back. The slaver fell. The other slaver held his dagger out. He did not see where the spear had come from. He yelled out a challenge. Finn rose to his feet grabbing the spear jutting from the dead man's back. He had to put one of his feet on the man's back before it pulled free. The other slaver did not even notice him. He was busy looking behind him for whoever had thrown the spear. The other slavers at the fire began to turn to see what was happening. Finn tried to loosen the stake with the spear. He kept one eye on the slaver. The slaver turned towards Finn. He began to lunge at him, but a sword cut him from shoulder to stomach. He fell like a stone. The head slaver stood over the dead man and looked at Finn. He yelled something to him and pointed at the spear. The other slavers were at Finn now. They looked at the dead man and at the head slaver. He yelled and scolded them in their black speech. The head slaver again looked at Finn. He yelled and looked at the spear in Finn's hands. Finn knew he was being ordered to drop the weapon.

*This is my only chance at freedom. I can at least die with honor.*

He raised the spear, pointing it towards the slavers.
"No."
The head slaver raised his sword. He spoke to the other slavers and pointed to Finn's chest.

*He is telling them not to strike my marking. I will strike it myself before they take me.*

Finn heard the whoosh of a dagger fly through the air. He moved but the blade crossed his shoulder before it bounced off landing on the ground. He saw another slaver raise his dagger. He took his time to aim.

*They will slowly bleed me to death.*

Finn heard another whoosh, but this one was deeper and came from above. Wind blew down from above them. Everyone felt it. The slavers, prisoners, and Finn looked into the night sky. The slavers ran to their wagons to get larger weapons. Others lit torches from the fire. The head slaver held his sword tightly, as he looked into the darkness above. Finn saw a quick glimpse of a shadowy beast swoop from the sky.

*It has talons.*

The head slaver was lifted into the darkness with a startled scream. He disappeared up into night. Finn heard his screams abruptly stop. The other slavers looked up. Legs, arms, and the head of the slaver fell back down. Finn then heard a familiar sound. It was deafening. His ears rang with it. His eyes lost focus. He fell to knees. Before passing out, Finn saw the giant falcon swoop down again. It sliced through four slavers with its talons.

*The Blood Falcon.*

## Chapter 15

### The Greenling Woods

Matthias' strength had slowly begun to return by the time they reached the end of the mountains. The rocky ground had given way to a soft green moss. It covered the ground and most of the trees. It had a fresh smell of evergreen and pine. The trees themselves were tall and shaded the forest from the rays of the sun. Even in the brightest part of the day, the forest was dimly lit like the early morning or late afternoon. It was calming. Matthias had even found it easier to breathe.

"Do these woods have a name?" asked Luras.

"I believe they are the Greenling Woods, but I'm not certain."

"The Greenling Woods ... it is a fitting name."

"There should be a main road just north of these woods. I will go east from there."

"You will not continue north?"

"Luras, go north if you must. I plan to go east and board a ship from there."

"You're truly leaving?"

"There is nothing here. Let gods and kings fight against themselves. I will take no hand in it."

"But a hand has already taken you. You have been selected by the Creator of the world. Where will you go where you do not have the eyes of an Acolyte?" asked Luras.

"I am no Acolyte," Matthias spoke, incredulously.

"Matthias, I don't know you. I do not presume to. But what has made you so hungry for death and isolation? Others would find this to be a great honor."

"You were a cursed beast until only days ago. Your curse was removed and your honor restored," Matthias had a mocking tone. "You are happy with things. I understand. But we do not share the same life. We are not brothers in war. So continue to pick your berries and feel honored to have a curse removed from you ... that was bestowed upon you for reasons that weren't even your own. It's convenient how some Creator can curse you and then remove it whenever it befits him."

"You do not know me," Luras replied. He continued to walk in a somber mood as he gathered his thoughts. "You are not the only one with hardships. I was cursed. I saw dark beasts claw their way through my village ... pulling children from their beds ... killing their parents. I watched the children go to school, learn to read and to write. I made them toys. These beasts slaughtered the village."

"Your village?" asked Matthias. "They knew you lived there? I doubt it. Why, I always thought a Nighteye an ill omen for any village. A village was destroyed. Lots of villages burn. It is tragic, but it happens."

"Well, at least I know my life was lost protecting them. I did not run away into the snow to hide or run to the sea."

"You mistake my morality. I would gladly burn every village in the four realms to their very foundations to have back what I lost," said Matthias. His face turned red with anger.

"Is this what deadens you?" asked Luras.

"You will not speak of this," answered Matthias. He had violence in his eyes.

"I'll speak of it no more. Know this though. Many men like you are losing their families and their homes. They are losing the same things that could deaden any man inside. It is true that I've never had a wife or a family, but that does not mean that I have not wished it so. When we reach the road, feel free to go wherever you like. I am certainly not keeping you."

The two men walked in silence. The wind blew through the forest causing the moss to slowly swell like a sea of green. Luras picked berries when he saw them. They grew mostly on vines that coiled around fallen trees. He wrapped them in a cloth that he kept in his bag. He offered some to Matthias who accepted each time. The forest had a life to it that was calming. It was not long until the two were speaking again. This time it was about the forest or the food they liked to eat.

"You've never had ale?" asked Matthias.

"No. I have seen them make it ... filling up barrels with wheat and such."

"Well, it is decided. Before we part company, we will have a drink."

"I am not sure a village is ready to see a Bourne quite yet."

"They will sooner or later. More so, you'll be the center of some drunkard's story. He will swear to the four realms that a Bourne entered a tavern and had a mug of ale ... right there beside him."

They laughed at the thought.

"No one will believe him," laughed Matthias.

"Well then," laughed Luras, "we will give it a try."

"Yes, indeed. No one will believe the poor fool."

Matthias continued to laugh. He laughed so hard

that he almost began to cry. The sounds of laughter filled the forest.

They made camp by two fallen trees. One had most likely fallen and hit the other causing it to fall as well. They were both rotten but were covered in moss, which made them soft to lean back against. Luras and Matthias had cleared a spot for the fire by pulling back the moss from the ground. The trees blocked out the breeze and allowed the fire to stay healthy. It gave off smells of pine and evergreen. The site made a comfortable spot for them to sleep. Luras had prepared a dinner of berries, apples, and some dried meat from the bird they ate in the mountains. It wasn't much, but it calmed their bellies.

"I haven't had ale but I did find a Boar root. Have you ever had that? It's quite good warm with berries, which I have in abundance at the moment," said Luras.

"There's a first time for all things."

Luras took a mangled black root from his bag. He began to cut it with his dagger and crush berries over it. He added some dried leaves he had found and tossed them in a metal cup. He added water and put it beside the fire to warm.

"Your weapons there ... where did you find them?" asked Matthias.

"I passed through a village on the way to Kor. It had been burned. The villagers had been skinned and thrown into piles. I found these in a jail," replied Luras.

"Let me look."

Luras gave Matthias the two swords he had found.

"They are very old and quite dirty," Matthias said, as he felt the blade of the sword. "But, I suppose it will still cut through skin and muscle. It might break on the way out though ... if it lodges in bone."

"These were all I could find."

"It was good to look. The villagers were skinned you said?"

"Yes. Their skin was taken. I did not see it happen, but it seemed like the occult."

"Skin Slavers. I didn't think they were real. People call them by so many names and have so many different stories about them. They seemed like fireside tales."

"I haven't seen them either, but I too heard stories. I look at the stories differently though. Nighteyes and Bournes ... they are fireside stories as well. Yet, here I am. If I am real ...why not them?"

"After all that has happened in the past few days, I would wager they are real too."

"Yes. They are also horribly cruel judging from the village."

"Cruelness is commonplace in the four realms. You will find this out quickly."

Luras took the metal cup from the fire with his cloth. He smelled it and took a sip.

"It is ready. Here," Luras said, as he handed over the cup.

"To the mighty Boar root," Matthias said, as he took a drink.

Matthias puckered his face and coughed. He hacked once and spit.

"God and kings!"

"Is it not to your liking?" asked Luras.

"I've had nothing like it before. It tastes sweet and harsh all at once."

Matthias drank more. This time he his face was only half as puckered.

"I think I like it. It's not ale, but it's not bad. Here."

Luras drank slowly. He spit some out into the fire. Small green flames quickly burst and disappeared.

"Now, I like it even better," laughed Matthias.

The two drank into the night. The Boar root slowly overtook them. Matthias yawned and stretched out against one of the fallen trees. Luras continued to look

# A DARK TYRANNY

at the fire.

"One thing, Luras. This is my first time in this forest ... but I have heard tales of wisps. I doubted their existence as well. But now, who knows?"

"Wisps? Wood fairies?"

"Wisps, tiny creatures that can't keep their dirty grubby hands off travelers' things. I would hate to wake tomorrow and find all your rusty swords gone," said Matthias.

"What would a wisp do with a sword?"

"Hoard it away ... sell it. I'm not a wisp."

Luras pulled his bag and swords closer to the fire. He leaned back against the other log and closed his eyes. It was not long until sleep crept over them both.

---

The embers of the fire slowly pulsed with a sedated glow. They were all that remained awake. Matthias and Luras had long been asleep. If they were awake, they would have seen tiny lumps of moss moving cautiously to their campsite. There was a noise coming from it that sounded almost like complaining. The moving stopped and the complaining grew louder. Then, a small line of smoke began to slowly trail upward from the lump of moss. The grumbling would start and stop in tandem with the smoke.

It was not long until two more lumps approached the smoking lump of moss. The two new moss lumps began to shake. It was then that two tiny heads popped out and looked around. They pulled the moss down beside them like stepping out of a net or like a child taking off his shirt by pulling the collar down over his arms and leggings. The two little men were plump, bearded, and wore tiny leather tunics and pants that were stitched with twine. Their clothes had plants and moss attached to help them blend into the forest. Their skin was very pale and their beards were very long. They were both no larger than a hand. The first lump stayed in the moss. It was still smoking and still complaining.

"Come out of there, Watsy ... and put your blimey pipe away," whispered Locke. He was slightly taller than the other and wore round glasses made from glass, twine, and wood.

"Knock it off, Watsy. You'll wake them," said Hermie, who was particularly plumper than Locke.

The smoke continued. However, the moss was pulled down revealing a testy little man. He was bearded, as well, and held a wooden pipe between his teeth.

"Ah, you've arrived I see," said Watsy a bit irritated.

"We're here," said Hermie.

"Yes. So, I sent word of travelers with no response. I followed them. I hung around in the dark watching them eat and drink. I sent word again. Now, you're here. Thank you for your expedience," said Watsy, as he took another deep toke from his pipe. "Further, I don't care anymore. I will smoke my pipe and worry of thick and thin some other day."

"We're sorry, Watsy," said Hermie.

"Poor Nickel was snatched up by an eagle. It took the greater part of the day to sort that out," said Locke.

"It weren't easy getting him back neither," said Hermie.

Watsy stared at them puffing away.

"We said our apologies. It's done. Let's see what we've got here, Hermie," said Locke, as he moved closer to the camp.

"Very well, let's see," said Watsy.

The three little men began to sneak around Luras and Matthias. They appeared like sleeping giants to the little men. Watsy and Locke looked in Luras' bag. Hermie gracefully pulled Luras' dagger, in one fluid motion, right from his belt ... sheath and all.

"I've some berries here ... oh, and Boar root," said Watsy.

"God and kings!" said Locke.

"Something good?" asked Hermie.

"Tell me I'm wrong ... but blimey if I ain't looking at a Bourne," said Locke.

"A Bourne?" said Watsy. He dropped the berries and went to the have a better look.

"Is that truly a Bourne?" asked Hermie.

"I ain't seen a Bourne before, but I'd wager a thimble of rice ale that it is," said Watsy.

"It is a Bourne," said Locke. "I seen drawings in the mapper's books."

"Well, what do we do?" asked Hermie.

"That muscled one there is as human as any, but this one ain't. I agree with Locke," said Watsy.

"There weren't nothing nice in their bags. Wouldn't a Bourne have treasure or something?" asked Hermie.

"Yes, Bournes carry chests of diamonds and gold with them. Wake up, Hermie," mocked Watsy.

"Do you see their eyes?" asked Locke.

"What about them," asked Hermie.

"No, I see it too," said Watsy.

"There's some light under them ... like their eyes are glowing behind their lids," said Locke.

"This is a queer bunch," said Watsy.

"We should go tell Weyton," said Locke.

"They could be gone before we got back," said Watsy. "One of us should stay ... or one of us should go."

"Hermie, go tell Weyton about all this. Watsy and I will stay here and keep an eye on them."

"I'll be back in a thumper," said Hermie.

Hermie disappeared under the moss. He was again a lump of moss running through the forest floor. Watsy and Locke sat down by a tree. They watched the two sleeping travelers. Watsy lit up his pipe once again. He took a deep drag. He stretched out with his back to the tree making himself comfortable. Smoke slowly twirled and danced from his pipe.

"Again, Watsy? Your pipe will give us away."

"Give us away? Ah, poppycock. They are sleeping by a smoldering fire and you're worried about a tiny bit of smoke from me?"

"Always for yourself."

"For myself? I'll have you know that *myself* would rather be sleeping in my own bed ... so, don't you go on about what *myself* wants."

"Pipe-down, you angry bugger."

"Pipe-up!"

"Ssh, you'll wake them," said Locke.

"You're the one going on talking and making nonsense."

Luras woke suddenly. He did not know if he had been dreaming, but he woke with the feeling of not being alone. He looked around seeing that their belongings were strewn about the camp. His berries were spilled on the mossy ground. Some of them looked as if a bite had been taken like a half-eaten apple.

"Matthias, wake up. Someone was here."

Luras stood to his feet.

"What?" asked Matthias, half asleep.

"Someone was here. Look at our things."

Matthias slowly left sleep behind, as he rolled to one side and sat up. He rubbed his eyes.

"I thought I heard something. Now this," said Luras.

"It does look like someone or something was here."

"Wisps perhaps?"

"Perhaps. I'm sure you scared them off. I doubt they return."

Matthias leaned back against the fallen tree. He was still tired and his eyes burned from sleep.

# A DARK TYRANNY

"I'm not so sure. I heard something right before I woke. No, I think they are still here ... hiding."

Luras walked around the fire peering into the darkness and the mossy ground below. He saw a small light on the moss. It was faint but it stood out in the darkness.

"There ... do you see it?"

"Ha. I do," said Matthias.

Luras walked to the small patch of light. He bent down and grinned, as he picked up a tiny sliver of wood.

"It's a pipe."

"A small one to say the least," said Matthias, who was now standing beside Luras.

"It's still burning. They are hiding."

"From the size of that pipe, I don't think we'll see them unless it's their choice. I'm going to rekindle the fire," said Matthias.

Luras and Matthias began to walk back to the fire.

"Alrighty then, hand over my pipe!" said Watsy.

"I said to stay down!" Locke yelled to Watsy.

"They already know we're here. My grandfather give me that pipe and I'm not about to lose it over your fear of giants," retorted Watsy.

"And who are you?" asked Matthias.

"I'm the bloody owner of that pipe," said Watsy.

"Come here," said Luras. "No one is going to hurt you."

"There will be some hurt, if you don't release my pipe this moment. And, don't speak to me like I'm some frightened child. I'm fully grown. I might be small but I fight like a badger. A wild badger too ... not some tamed fat badger that fetches fish."

"Watsy, stop it. You are going to anger them," said Locke.

"Watsy is it?" asked Matthias.

"Come here. I'll give you your pipe. I have no cause

to keep it," said Luras.

"Although, you both seem freely open to rummage through our possessions," said Matthais.

"Very sorry. We do apologize for that," said Locke.

Locke slowly walked to the camp. Watsy followed behind him. Luras tried not to stare but he was amazed at their tiny stature.

"These is our woods. We have the right to inspect whichever travelers we want," said Watsy.

"Your woods? This is a big forest for such a small man," said Matthias.

"Did your grandfather make this pipe," asked Luras. "The craftsmanship is quite nice," said Luras.

"Why do you want to know? Gonna sell it? You'll get nothing outta me," retorted Watsy.

"He is being gracious, you bloody nitwit," said Locke.

"He smoked it. I know that," said Watsy.

"Well, it is fine craftsmanship. Here, take it. I did not plan on leaving with it," said Luras.

Watsy walked to Luras, who had bent down to hand over the pipe. Watsy snatched the pipe from his hands. He looked over the pipe begrudgingly.

"You didn't smoke from it did you? You can't smoke from another's pipe ... just tell me if you did so I can burn it in your fire ... here and now."

"No one smoked from your damn pipe," said Matthias. "Take it and leave us alone. We have no cause with you and, frankly, I am sick of hearing you moan like an old woman."

"I beg your pardon!" said Watsy.

"Enough, Watsy. These men are being gracious and you're making a damned fool of yourself ... again," said another voice from behind him.

Two more little men appeared behind Watsy. It was Hermie and he had brought with him a much older man with soft blue eyes, gray hair, and a long gray beard that was twisted and tied at the end. He did not wear a leather tunic like the rest. Instead, he wore a cloth robe that was a deep faded green and a pair of worn-in leather breeches.

"Weyton," said Locke.

"I brought him back just like you said," spoke Hermie with a smile on his face.

"It appears that we arrived not a moment too soon," said Weyton. "I apologize for any lack of etiquette on their part."

"No. It is quite alright," said Luras.

"We were just being told that you own these woods and that you have a right to inspect and take our belongings," said Matthias. He looked at Watsy when he spoke.

"Well, I'm sure that was Watsy speaking off again. I will say that we do live in these woods. We have for hundreds of years. Given our ... well, for lack of better words, our stature ... it is a cautious thing to make sure those that travel here are straight and narrow," said Weyton.

"We have had bandits and other rogue bunches pass through from time to time," said Locke.

"My word, I didn't quite believe Hermie but now that I've seen you up close ... you are indeed a Bourne," said Weyton.

"Yes," said Luras.

"And your eyes ... I've seen eyes like those before but only in drawings. You are Acolytes are you not?" asked Weyton.

"We are," answered Luras.

"Blimey. Real and true Acolytes right here in our woods," said Locke.

"He is an Acolyte," said Matthias.

"Your eyes glow as well," said Weyton.

"My arse could glow too, but it doesn't mean I accept it," replied Matthias.

"Well, I would wager that when the great Creator selects you for such a duty ... it's hardly within your power to deny it ... glowing arse or no," said Weyton.

"What is an Acolyte? Are they soldiers?" asked Hermie.

"No. Acolytes are selected by the great Creator to keep evil and its dark passions at bay," said Locke.

"When dark creatures invade, the Acolytes are formed by the Creator. They keep evil from enslaving the world. They give the rest of us time to decide our fate. Will we follow our dark lusts or will we fight against the horde," said Weyton.

"This is talk suitable for mindless men that babble in the streets," said Matthias. "A Creator of the world could simply vanquish all evil at any time. There's no need for Acolytes. It is stage play."

"No, that's not how it works," said Weyton. "If we are to stand for good than it is logical that standing for evil is available. You cannot have good without evil or evil without good ... otherwise, you would just have what is and what isn't. The Creator has laid an alternative to evil. When men sit upon their laurels, evil gains a foothold. There is a choice. During such dark times, the Acolytes give us time to make it."

"You're tellin' an Acolyte about Acolytes? This whole lot is queer. That Bourne could be an Acolyte," said Watsy, "but this bugger just seems like a foul-mouthed bully with blue eyes. I wouldn't ..."

"Enough with this," said Weyton.

"It's alright," said Matthias.

"Have you seen anything strange in these woods? South of here two villages were destroyed. Wolves larger than men. They could run on two legs or walk upright. They seemed to come from the ground," said Luras.

"I have not seen those beasts," said Weyton.

"Nor have we," said Locke.

"But, there is a gloom over these woods. I have ordered our scouts to stay together," said Weyton.

"Tavishar is north of here along the road, so is Reddington. Travelers find food and lodging there. You would learn more news regarding the four realms there," said Weyton.

"Although, and no offense given sir, they might not take lightly to your being there," Locke said to Luras.

"Thank you for your caution," said Luras. "May I ask, are you wisps?"

"Ah, there it is! Wisps!" retorted Watsy.

"We've been called wisps, fairies, or groundlings, but these are mostly the names given to us by his kind," said Weyton, as he gestured to Matthias.

"We are Woodlanders," said Hermie.

"The common name is Woodlanders. We were once called the Garriadune," said Weyton.

"They say that you steal from travelers," said Luras.

"They do," said Matthias, pointing to Luras' bag.

"I will not deny this. However, we don't take it for thrill or overall vice. We are quite defenseless against even the smallest of brigands. We have rumor and fireside tales. People stay away from these woods because of what they hear. Yes, we stoke the fire to keep it warm, but it is in the interest of survival," said Weyton.

"What do you do with it ... the things you take?" asked Matthias.

"Some things we use ... food, cloth, and other materials. Larger items we store," said Locke.

"They are in the Den," said Hermie.

"Blimey, Hermie. Will you draw them a map next?" said Watsy.

"Are these all the provisions you have?" asked Weyton.

"Yes. I was able to find these in a village I went through."

"If the Great Creator sends his Acolytes through our woods, the least we can do is outfit them as best we can," Weyton said to Locke.

"It's not prudent to give our stores to those passing through ... whatever their cause," said Watsy.

"We do not use it," said Locke.

"Gather your belongings and follow us," said Weyton.

## Chapter 16

### A Council of Brothers

The king's chamber was much more lavish than Ellison's living quarters. Ellison had always felt uncomfortable around the grandiose parts of Castle Horos. Even as a child, he had preferred the more moderate accommodations set aside for guests. Easton told him time and again that the king and his kin should always maintain their higher place. He eventually relented, allowing Ellison to live permanently in the castles' living quarters. The king would always summon him to talk of the mundane and, at times, Ellison thought it on purpose, as some sort of retaliation for living below his heritage. Ellison was fine with the walk to the castle, especially since he had requested this meeting days ago.

Easton's chamber had two empty wine bottles on the floor beside the bed. The bed was disheveled, as was Easton himself. The room had a stale odor to it. There was a desk in one corner, an insignia of the castle carved into a wooden shield that hung from one wall.

The wooden insignia was painted a deep orange and brown with a helm in the middle. It was to represent the impregnable fortress that was Castle Horos. The door to the balcony was open causing a light wind to swell the maroon curtains. Ellison found it odd that the breeze did not clear the foul air from the room. Easton was wearing a finely woven robe of blue silk. He was tired in the eyes. He rummaged through the room looking for another bottle. His search proved futile.

"Wine!" Easton yelled to the door.

Ellison could hear scrambling in the hallway. He wore a fine leather tunic that had faded. His hood was back showing his pale features. Easton was used to his appearance and had long ago learned to accept it.

"When do they clean your quarters?" asked Ellison.

"Daily, but it is still early. Excuse this mess. Here I thought I was the king."

"You are the king and it is almost midday," said Ellison

"Will you be feeding me later as well ... wiping my arse, perhaps?"

"Ha. No, I will have to leave that to your servants."

"And they thank you."

"What of Jon Leland? Any news about his demise?" asked Ellison.

"I have Haurice personally handling this. A member of the king's regent is protected like the king himself."

"Yet, his throat was slit to the bone. I am only glad the same guards are not watching you."

"It is tragic and I plan to carry out justice to the perpetrators and those that let him down in their efforts."

"Do you think the same fate has befallen your Council Elect? What word of them?" asked Ellison.

"They are not mine but that of the people. We are looking for them as well. Since when were you so interested in the workings of the realm? You were always more interested in drink and gambling."

"I worry for you is all. Your regent grows thin and the village is full of rumors."

"Is this the cause of the meeting that you have been hounding me about? I'm here. Although, I do know what this is all about."

"Have you thought more about Malvern?" said Ellison. He spoke in a serious tone.

"I told him that if I ever heard tell of these acts again, I would personally remove his temptation from between his stick legs. Does that work for you?"

"So, he still remains at the castle ... in his current work?" asked Ellison.

"Ellison, if I castoff every member of my regent for indiscretions, I would have no regent."

"Raping a boy is hardly an indiscretion. Also, your regent thins on its own. Why?"

"You think Malvern killed Jon Leland and the Council Elect? Then, he had a congratulatory raping of the stable boy. Is that your assumption, brother?"

"I think he raped a young boy, and that is enough. We were both boys once before. We would not deserve that nor would anyone else."

"I do feel for the boy, but it is not enough to cast him off. When I replace Jon Leland, I will have the treasurer compensate the boy for his suffering. Does this suffice to your idea of justice and morality?"

"Three members of your regent are gone. One is confirmed dead and the other two are most likely the same. I find this very alarming. I don't trust Malvern. He should not be part of the council meetings to uncover this plot."

"Fine. I will keep Malvern, but exile him from those meetings. Will this be to your satisfactory or would you just prefer to wear the crown for a few days?"

"The crown is much too heavy for me, dear brother," said Ellison.

"It is a great deal easier to make decisions out from under it. Although, I wear it none-the-less. There are times I wish it had gone to you. I envy your dicing, drinking, and whoring at will," said Easton.

"Our father thought better than to give the crown to a red-eyed boy. No kingdom would allow a demon to rule," said Ellison.

"He was correct, Ellison. If anything, it would have united the other realms against us. Kingdoms love a common enemy and a demon would have made them froth at the mouth. You would have made a wonderful tyrant, brother."

"Well ... of course, I am no demon. But, yes I understand."

There was knock on the door.

"Wine, your majesty," spoke a nervous voice from the behind the thick wooden door.

"Well then, my breakfast has arrived," said the king.

"Yes. I will leave you."

"Come in," said the king.

A young woman came in with a jug of wine and a basket of bread. She put them on the king's desk. Ellison moved past her. She stared at his eyes and face, as he wore his hood up on most occasions.

"Oh, one last thing," said Ellison.

"Now what?" asked the king, as he poured wine into a glass.

"The village is growing leery about this wedding. It is in a few days but no one has arrived. They are worried about their harvests and all the preparations they have had to supply."

"They voice their grievances to you and not the king?"

"No, I hear words in passing."

"You can tell your passing words that they need not worry. A wedding requires guests does it not?"

"It does," replied Ellison.

"Then, there will be guests ... because there is indeed a wedding."

"Splendid. Will I get to meet her?"

"My bride ... of course."

"Before the wedding. I would like to meet her and offer my congratulations before the wedding."

"Right. We will see. It is a busy time. Will that be all?" asked Easton, mockingly.

"Yes, your majesty," said Ellison.

Ellison bowed and left the room. The king drank his wine. The servant girl bowed to the king, as she walked to the door. She did not look him in the eyes. There was a nervous haste to her walk.

"Wait," said the king, shutting the large door. It creaked and thudded to a close. Easton looked at her with a great appetite.

"Your majesty, I must attend to the wedding preparations," she said in a nervous tone.

"Of course, however, I have more pressing concerns for you at the moment."

---

Malvern scurried through the courtyard. His talk with the king had wounded his pride. He now knew the king regarded his council of great value. Otherwise, he would have killed him at the request of his demon brother. However, the talk also angered Malvern. He did not like to be spoken to like a child. He was there when Ellison and Easton were born into the world.

*Who are they to question me?*

King or not, Malvern did not take kindly to being questioned or reproached. He had decided that he would do whatever must be done to see Ellison dead. This would be no hard task with the rumors of the occult marching again. Ellison was a demon in the eyes of the people. There would only need to be a little motivation to ignite the people against him. If the whoring king got in his way, then he would deal with that as well. Malvern was too old and wise to take orders from children. It did not matter whose belly they came out of.

He entered the living quarters. No one was in the main room. Malvern was relieved at not seeing Ellison and his smug face. He poured a glass of water and continued to his room. The door was shut. He opened it with little thought. His room smelled of dust and moldy leather. There were wooden shelves built into the stone walls. They were adorned with books. His desk had a map on top of it with a candle on one corner and a book on the other to keep it straight. Malvern entered the room. The door immediately shut behind him. Malvern turned but Ellison had the upper hand. He hit Malvern's brow with the handle of his dagger. It erupted with blood. Malvern was so caught off guard that he had no idea how to react. Ellison slammed him against the wall causing books to crash down. He held him there with his forearm against Malvern's neck. He placed the tip of his dagger to the man's throat. Malvern came to his senses. His eyes went wild with rage. He tried to grab at the dagger and pull himself away, but Ellison was stronger and wrangled him back.

"I will kill you if you try to move again. Do you understand?"

Malvern just stared at him.

"Tell me you understand," said Ellison, as he allowed the dagger to draw blood.

"I understand, you bastard!"

"You will tell me what is afoot."

"I don't know what you are talking about."

"What is going on in Castle Horos. No wedding is going to happen. Jon Leland is dead. Tell me what you know."

"Why don't you ask your brother," Malvern yelled

# A DARK TYRANNY

with spit dripping from the corner of his mouth. Blood from his brow began to cover his eyes.

"I am asking you," said Ellison. He raked the blade of the dagger across Malvern's arm. It went white before the blood welled up.

"Ah! You will pay for this with your life!"

"Tell me or the next cut will ruin your odds with any stable boys."

"You truly are a demon. A curse upon this castle!" said Malvern. He spoke almost to himself. He was in shock.

"Your raping days are over," said Ellison. He began to move the blade towards Malvern's manhood.

"Wait! Wait!"

"Why should I?"

"There will be no wedding."

"Continue."

"Preparations are underway to stock the castle for a barricade. Gorgons and the occult are moving north. They destroyed Castle Red. We will weather this storm from inside the walls," said Malvern.

"And the people?"

"They provide the provisions."

"But stay outside the walls? They will die," said Ellison.

"People die in such times. You will see this for yourself. Being the brother of a drunken king will not save you forever. A different time is afoot."

"And Jon Leland?"

"He did not agree."

"Does my brother know about this?"

Malvern began to laugh. The blood that had dripped into his mouth began to spray out in laughter.

"Does he know? You are truly daft."

It dawned on Ellison that this was truly a daft question. His brother knew about it. He had probably designed it. It was now Ellison that grew full of rage.

He hit Malvern again with the handle of his dagger. This time it was the side of his head. Malvern fell backwards. The wall kept him upright. He let out a groan. Ellison brought his knee up, crashing it into his stomach. Malvern gagged. Ellison followed with his elbow to the man's jaw. Malvern fell to the floor in one motion. His breathing was shallow but steady. Ellison looked at this dagger. He would love nothing more than to kill this man. He sheathed it and left the room.

*I need to find Cal Mossy.*

## Chapter 17

### An Ancient Ally

Finn woke with a pounding headache. His mouth was dry and full of dirt. The wound on his shoulder was no longer bleeding and there was a throbbing that hummed under his skin. He rolled to one side and slowly stood up. His head spun and it took him a moment to get his bearings. He staggered to one of the wagons and leaned against it. He looked around for any of the slavers. They were gone. How many had actually lived long enough to run?

*I hope they died ... all of them.*

He could tell the night had been full of slaughter. Blood, bones, and bits of flesh were strewn about. Finn could not tell if it was from the slavers, the slaves, or both. The group of slaves was gone. Finn hoped they had escaped during the commotion. He looked around for water but found none. The only thing intact was the kettle that was over the fire the night before. He dared not touch it. However, he did find a set of flint and steel by the fire. He was hungry and thirsty. Finn needed to find a village. He needed clothes, weapons ... anything. He had to get to Nylah before the gorgons reached their destination.

*I have to save her.*

He kept thinking of her walking alone with the other prisoners. Finn scanned the camp to look for weapons. He found a chipped dagger with a bone hilt and a sword. They both had dried blood along the blade and hilts. He would keep them until he found something more suitable. Finn was about to leave the camp when he felt the same gusts of wind from the night before. Feathers ruffled against themselves. He heard what sounded like daggers being driven into stone. Deep breathes were being taken behind him. The sounds of clicks and low guttural whistles rumbled behind him. He slowly turned. He knew it was the falcon.

The great bird was perched atop the small formation of rocks by the camp. It was the first time Finn had seen it outside the cage. It was much larger than he remembered. The bird's body was the size of a small horse or pony. Its wings wrapped its sides but, judging by its body, Finn imagined its wingspan was enormous. The falcon's feathers were a deep maroon with brown strips layering its chest and stomach. Its almond-shaped eyes were like large black disks.  A patch of bright red skin encased them. Its beak was faded black and curved down to a point in the front. The great bird had massive claws that latched onto the rock, digging into the stone. The talons were razor sharp. Finn could see the sun reflect brightly from them, like the steel of a highly polished blade. The slavers stood no chance against the falcon. It had sliced through them like a sword to melted wax.

"Easy," Finn said to the bird.

The falcon tilted its head, as it looked Finn in the eyes.

"I'm not going to hurt you," said Finn.

He felt the bird had no fear of him. It clicked in a deep tone and scratched one of its talons against its beak.

"You probably have no idea what I'm saying. Thank you, though. You saved my life."

Finn turned to leave. He had to find Nylah. However, he turned back to the bird once more.

"I'm truly glad you are free. Go somewhere that you will never be bothered or caught again."

Finn turned back around and walked towards the path. He put the dagger under his belt and carried the sword. He had no real idea what he would do or how he planned to free Nylah, but he could not just leave her. Finn felt a deep connection to her.

*She is a part of me now.*

Finn heard the beating of the great bird's wings. He turned long enough to see the Blood Falcon effortlessly lift itself into the air. The bird let the wind do its work and was lifted like a kite high into the clouds. Its wings only beat for minor readjustments. It let out a deep cry, as it flew between the clouds. It was one of the most graceful things Finn had ever seen.

"Goodbye, friend."

Finn began to backtrack the best he could. He went south staying off the roads. However, he stayed close enough to be aware of any travelers. He did not want to risk passing Nylah if she was split from the other prisoners as he had been. Finn walked for two days and did not see a single traveler. He thought people were either hiding, caught, making their way to safer lands, or dead. Finn did not know what lands would be safer. Was this strictly an attack on the Southern Realm or was it all of Altaris? He decided to concentrate on freeing Nylah. He would worry about where to go once they were safely away from the gorgons. In truth, he had no real idea how to rescue her. She was traveling with an entire battalion of gorgons, snake walkers, so he knew that, whatever plan he might devise, it would have to happen at night. He had to find them without them finding him first. Finn knew from when he was a prisoner that gorgon scouting parties kept joining the others. He had to make sure he did not wander into a small gorgon raiding party.

Hunger and exhaustion began to set in. Finn started to feel pangs of frustration and despair. How could he think of freeing Nylah when he could barely move? His throat felt swollen from thirst and there was a throbbing in his head from hunger. Finn had eaten what berries he could find but they were scarce. He had no bow, spear, or any real means of hunting. He had seen a few squirrels and rabbits, but was unable to catch them.

*If I do not eat soon, I will die.*

Finn made his camp in a dense part of the forest. There were two wide trees whose trunks broke off into larger roots. The roots jutted out into the ground like thick fingers pressed into sand. They would block any fire from being seen on the road. A fallen tree laid on the ground with underbrush and plants growing over it. Finn had planned to make a fire, but he was too tired. The moment he sat down with his back to one of the large trees, he had no desire to move. They were Dower trees so the bark was not hard like other trees. Instead, they were quite soft to the touch. Some called them Sleep trees for this reason. Finn laid back and closed his eyes. He felt so weak. He knew he was falling asleep; he hoped he would be able to awaken.

Finn did not remember falling asleep, but it couldn't have been for long. There was still the hint of the evening sun glimmering sleepily on the gray and maroon horizon. Finn was startled. He woke from his sleep in an instant. He heard the rumbling of the great falcon overhead. Its wings swirled the air around it and he felt wind being forced down with each flap of the bird's wings. Finn put his hands to his ears. He was too weak to deal with another high pitched shriek. For a moment, Finn wondered if the Blood Falcon had planned on killing him. There was not much in the way of food that he had seen. An object fell from the sky cracking branches on the way down. Finn jumped to his feet; his heart pounded in his chest. The object hit the ground with a dull thud. The falcon made a low noise and landed softly on a fallen tree. It buckled and snapped under the bird's weight. Finn could see blood dripping from the falcon's beak.. One of its claws clutched a mass of fur and meat. It looked like part of a bear or large goat. Finn quickly glanced at the ground to see what had fallen. It was the hind quarter of a deer or, judging by the size of it, a stag. It was as if the rump and one leg were cut with a butcher's blade. The cuts were made by something sharp and precise. The deer had probably never even known the falcon had killed it. It was alive one moment and simply dead the next. Finn felt his stomach begin to ache for food.

"Is this for me? You have been busy haven't you?"

The bird lifted its claw and pulled at the meat with its beak. Finn slowly pulled the deer's leg to him. He did not want to misjudge the falcon. He was not sure if this was truly meant for him. However, to Finn's astonishment, the great falcon continued to rip strips of flesh and meat from what it had in its claw.

*You did bring this for me.*

Finn quickly removed his chipped dagger from his belt and began to dress the deer leg. It was not long until deer meat crackled above the fire. Finn could not wait for it to fully cook. He kept cutting small strips of meat that looked ready. He cut them as quickly as could to keep from burning his fingers. He ate all there was to eat of the deer. Finn slept more soundly that night than he had in a long while.

Finn walked a much greater distance the next three

days. His stride had returned somewhat. The wound on his shoulder had not festered and was healing nicely with only a slight bruising. He was relieved because he had heard of others dying from infected wounds that were much smaller. Finn had still not seen a single traveler along the road. There was only one other that he continued to see. The Blood Falcon. It never strayed too far from him. He could see it in the sky. It would leave him for a few hours but would always return. The falcon brought him a boar the next night, which Finn had eaten greedily. He did not know what connection the great beast had made with him, but it seemed to be watching over him. He had secretly fed the falcon mice and squirrels while at the castle. He had also freed the bird from its cage. However, Finn would never have thought the Blood Falcon would actually know or remember him. Finn enjoyed the bird's watchfulness. It made him feel a little less alone. The bird could also prove useful when he caught up the gorgon horde. One shriek from the falcon could drop hundreds to their knees. Finn knew this firsthand.

It was the early afternoon when Finn heard someone else. It was a scream, a woman's scream. It did not sound like someone startled. It was a scream full of distress and panic. Finn looked towards the direction of the sound, but only saw the forest. It was like the voice of haunted souls calling out from under the trees. It rang out again! Finn looked but saw nothing. Then, a shadowy glimpse shot across the corner of Finn's sight. He turned looking harder. Finn began to run in that direction. The scream came again, but this time he heard more than a woman's voice. Finn slowed his running. It would be no use running into a group of gorgons or Skin Slavers. He heard the sounds of a struggle.

Finn could see three figures in the forest, two men and a woman. The men were not Skin Slavers or gorgons. A heavy set man was holding the woman down. He was behind her with his knees on her arms. His flesh was pale and a bulge of stomach dripped over his leather britches. His hair was red. He wore a full beard with a scar across his left cheek that did not allow any hair to grow. The other man was thinner and dirty. He had dull green eyes that sunk-in deeply. His pants hung below his buttocks. He laughed while thrusting deeply into the shaking woman. Her screaming had turned to sobs and sudden fits of anger.

"Easy there. The more you fight ... the longer I go."

The other man laughed.

"Hurry up, Bromley. I need a turn at this lass," said the other man.

"They'll be nothing left but a soggy tear when I'm done."

Both men laughed, as the woman tried to move one of her legs to kick Bromley. He stopped thrusting and hit her. It was a hard hit. The woman let out a grunt. She quit fighting. Finn felt anger rising in his body. It was like back at the gorgon camp. He was angry. Finn had no real training with a sword. He was a hunter, a falconer. He gripped tightly to the bone hilt of his dagger. The blade pointed down from his hand rather than up. He had seen soldier's holding it this way. Finn held his sword in his other hand. He had to do this fast. There was no room for a mistake. He could not fight two men. He did not like how the men were distracted, but distracted nonetheless.

Bromley's body stiffened with satisfaction and froze. Finn seized the opportunity. He thrust his sword into Bromley's back. It hit bone but slide between and sank deeply into his body. The man yelled in agony. The portly man released the woman and began to rise to his feet. The woman rolled away kicking him. Finn quickly ran to the man. He had already risen to his feet. He saw Finn and turned to run. However, Finn drove the dagger into the man's back. The dagger was sharper than the sword. If it hit bone, Finn could not feel it. The man did not yell but rather let out a cough. He turned before Finn could pull the dagger out. The man looked bewildered. He coughed again. This time blood spat from his mouth. He put his hand to his mouth and then looked at the blood. He turned and tried to run. The man fell twice but continued to move forward in a clumsy manner. There was sudden rush of wind. Finn saw the falcon swoop down and rake one claw against the man. It did not pick him up, but rather dragged one of its talons across the man. Finn saw one of the man's arms fall before the rest of his body. The man fell and did not rise. The falcon was already back in the sky over the forest.

The woman looked around. She felt her face. Her woolen dress was still pushed up over her waist. The hair between her legs was dark and abundant. Finn could see blood smeared on her thighs. He turned his head but realized the woman might need help standing.

"I'm not going to hurt you," said Finn.

He moved to her holding out his hands. She pulled down her dress and began to sob.

"Do you live near here?"

"Yes. He ... he spilt his seed," she said crying. She wiped herself with her dress.

Finn gently knelt down and picked the woman up. She was not heavy at all. He could tell up close that she was not much older than he. She had olive skin and brown eyes. Her black hair had been braided and twisted up before the men attacked. Finn did not know what to say to the woman. He felt regret for not finding her sooner or killing Bromley quicker.

"Show me where you live."

## Chapter 18

A Struggling Village

The morning was very gray and a slight breeze brought a chill to the air. The sun was hidden behind dark clouds; a storm lingered on the horizon. Matthias and Luras had only been up for a while. They looked like shadowy figures moving through a deserted forest. The Woodlanders had outfitted them well. Luras wore a well-oiled black leather tunic with metal ringlets along the chest, deep brown leather pants and a pair of finely crafted riding boots that fit him perfectly. He wore a dark green cloak made of thick wool. Luras now had two thin sabers that had been intricately smithed. Their blades were thin but incredibly sharp. The sabers' sheaths were not made to lay at the waist but rather crossed Luras' back. Each sabers' hilt jutted out from under his cloak. Matthias could tell that the blades were not made in the four realms. They were most likely crafted in the lower archipelagos south of the realms. They must have been brought north by traders. Of course, this was before the Woodlanders took them.

Matthias was astonished at the hoard of items the Woodlanders had amassed. Their storehouse of treasure was in a cave that was a day's walk from their camp. It was overflowing with weapons, jewelry, coins, cooking supplies, and anything else they could carry. The Woodlanders had given them a small bag of coins to use on their way. Matthias had found a vest made of leather with metal strips on the front and back. He wore it over a woolen tunic that had been dyed a deep maroon. He too wore a cloak, but his was made of thin leather with a woolen lining. It was a dark brown. Matthias had a large greatsword strapped to his back. Its hilt was made to look like a horse rearing on its hind legs. The sheath was leather with a picture of a herd of wild horses etched across it. Matthias almost did not take the sword because it was too distinguishable. The owner would recognize it off hand. However, Weyton told him that it had been in their storehouse for quite some time. The owner was mostly dead. Matthias found the sword too balanced to leave behind. He also took an axe and a dagger, which he slid under this belt.

"We should be out of the Greenling by the day's end. The road should lay just beyond the forest," said Matthias.

"How far is the village from there?"

"Not far. We should be eating a warm meal by midday," said Matthias.

"You should continue north with me, Matthias. There will be others like us."

"I will leave the fighting to god and kings."

Luras did not press the issue. Instead, he pulled his cloak tightly around his shoulders to keep warm.

"It will storm today," said Luras.

"It seems so. The sky is darkening."

The sky had grown much darker by the time they reached the road. It still had not rained, but there was a low rumble announcing its impending arrival. The road was little more than a wagon trail. It was overgrown with weeds, but there were two thin dirt wheel paths that had been worn down. Matthias and Luras had not followed the road long before they could see small trails of chimney smoke drifting up like twisting vines into the expanse of dark sky.

"We're close," said Matthias.

"Should I let you go in first?" asked Luras.

"You can't hide forever."

"My kind has hidden for a thousand years."

"You are the only Bourne in the four realms ... probably, the only in the world. You are no longer *your kind*. It's just *you*. Anyway, I think people will be more interested than scared."

"We will soon see," said Luras.

"Besides, we have to eat."

The village was small. By appearance, it was mostly made up of farmers and craftsmen. The homes were no larger than one or two rooms at most. Their walls were a mix of mud and clay with wooden beams for foundation and support. They had thatched roofs that were strapped down with leather and rope. Many of the homes had a small pen for pigs and a chicken coop. The road that went through the village was much wider than the trail that led to the village. It was lined with limestone. The road itself had a faint glimmer due to granite stones being pounded into the dirt and the stones kept it from washing away. The road circled through the village and led back to the main road. There was a small tavern in the center of the village and beside it sat what was either a church or a small meeting hall. Empty craft booths and merchant tables were setup in the center of the town. A skinny dog wandered through the outskirts of the village. It stopped to look at Luras and Matthias as they approached the village. It tilted its head slightly and studied the new arrivals. However, it lost interest and continued on its way.

"Where is everyone?" asked Luras.

"Inside, perhaps? The tavern is there. We can eat and get rooms for the night. The storm will bear down hard," said Matthias.

The two walked down the road. A light rain began to fall; it was almost a heavy mist. A rumbling of thunder shook the ground, causing the pigs and chickens to stir uneasily in their pens.

"Something is not right," said Luras.

"State your business," said a gruff voice behind them.

The two turned to see a large man approaching. He carried a poorly-crafted spear and wooden shield. His boots were dirty and caked with mud.

"It's ok. He's not a fighter. He looks like a farmer," Matthias said to Luras.

"State your business," the man repeated.

"State *your* business," said Matthias. "Where is everyone?"

"I am an alderman of this village. We are not taking kindly to strangers these days. I suggest you keep on your way."

Matthias heard the draw of a bowstring. Another man was standing behind a wagon with a notched arrow ready for release. A third man appeared on the road in front of them. He was a heavy set man with a wide jaw and thick eyebrows. He held a large two-handed axe meant for trees.

"You're an alderman. Where's your townspeople? I don't see any villagers. Are these the two men that voted for you?" said Matthias.

Luras started to intervene but he could see that Matthias was comfortable in these situations. He looked as if he could kill each man there at any time.

"Leave us be. It's not that we do not trust you. We do not trust *anyone* right now," said the large man with the axe.

"Look at their eyes," said the man with bow, "and look at that one there. God and kings …"

"It's ok," said Luras.

"Their eyes are glowing," said the bowmen.

"What is he …," said the man with the axe.

"We are Acolytes," said Luras.

"He is an Acolyte," said Matthias, "and a Bourne, so I suggest you lower that bow."

"A Bourne?" asked the bowmen. He looked at the alderman.

"A Nighteye," said the alderman.

"He don't look like a goblin," said the man with the axe. "Their eyes are glowing."

"He is not a *Nighteye*," said Matthias.

"I was, but now I am an Acolyte," said Luras.

"He is a Bourne. Personally, I would like you to keep your weapons up because I want to see a Bourne fight. I've yet to see him swing a blade, but if the stories are true, it would be quite a sight. You have heard the stories, I'm sure," said Matthias.

"I am not going to hurt you," said Luras. He gave a puzzling look to Matthias.

"Skin Slavers raided our village a few days back. They killed most and took some others with them," said the heavyset man with the axe. "They took women and children. The survivors took what arms we had and left to get what was theirs."

"And you stayed here?" asked Matthias.

"There are others still here," said the alderman. "We are all staying together in the tavern."

"There's smoke coming from these homes," said Luras.

"To give the impression that more are here," replied the alderman.

"A scouting party from the Northern Realm came shortly after. They took a good deal of our supplies," said the man with the axe.

"A scouting party? From the Northern Realm?" asked Matthias.

"Yes. They said the Southern Realm is almost completely fallen, only small unorganized bands of men remain," said the alderman.

"What else did they say?" asked Matthias. "How long ago did they leave?"

"They mentioned some of what we experienced here ... Skin Slavers raiding the four realms," said the alderman. "I'm not sure they will return. There's nothing left for them to take."

"And gorgons sacking the Southern Realm," said the man with the bow.

"Gorgons?" asked Luras.

"Yes," said the alderman.

"Have you seen them?" asked Luras.

"No," said the alderman.

"They also talked about wolves," said the bowman.

The rain began to pick up. The sky rumbled and shook the ground.

"What village is this?" asked Matthias.

"Reddington," answered the alderman.

"We should get inside," said the man with the axe.

"We mean no threat to you. We can leave at first light," said Luras.

The alderman paused to think. He looked at them one last time.

"I don't suppose I can deny two Acolytes shelter ... a Bourne at that. Norris, go stoke some of the fires and get back to the tavern" said the alderman.

The large man with the axe left to do as the alderman instructed. The rest left for the tavern.

The tavern was much larger on the inside. The tables had been moved to make room for sleeping. There were thick beams of exposed wood across the ceiling. The mud and clay walls revealed the occasional wooden support beam. The windows were shut tight and each one had a wooden panel on the inside that was closed and latched. A twelve-point set of antlers was mounted above the door. The bar had quilts and blankets laid over it to dry. Eight or so children sat on blankets and pillows listening to a woman tell them a story about a lost pony that met a wisp knight. She looked up at the men as they entered but continued reading. Two older men played a game of Ricklot at a corner table. The rest of the villagers were mostly women and boys too young to fight. The tavern was lit with lanterns and candles. There were two large fireplaces that glowed red. When Luras removed his hood there was a hush to the room. The children looked at him in wonder and whispered to themselves. One of the men playing Ricklot put down his wooden pieces.

"It is alright," said the alderman.

"Who are they?" asked a bone thin woman. She had a narrow face and bags around her eyes.

"They are leaving at first light," reassured the alderman, "they are passing through. It's starting to storm."

"They could be more slavers. You don't know, Thorson," said the woman. Some others began to look as if they felt the same. They began to gather around the woman.

"Calm yourself, Lindy. Look, they are Acolytes," said the alderman.

"That one ain't human," said a plump woman behind Lindy.

"No, he is not," said the alderman.

"He is a Bourne," said Matthias. "We are only passing through. Some food and ale would be nice."

"I am Luras and this is Matthias. Thorson is right. We are Acolytes. We're going north. We plan to leave in the morning," said Luras.

"Well, I suppose you are here now," said Lindy.

"Take off your weapons and put them there. We are having stewed beef. Dedra will bring you some ale."

"Many thanks," said Matthias.

"Yes, thank you," said Luras.

The men sat at one of the larger tables. Candles were strewn about it for light. Luras, Matthias, Thorson, and the bowmen ate stew from wooden bowls. A pitcher of ale was at the center of the table. Luras' cup remained full.

"This is Wreth," Thorson gestured towards the bowman.

"Hello," said Luras.

Matthias nodded his head as he ate.

"Pardon, but ... can you see better ... with your eyes like that and all?" asked Wreth.

"Some. Things seem ... crisper than they did," answered Luras.

"You are asking the wrong person. He seems to glow regardless," said Matthias.

"You do," said Wreth. "You have a slight glow to your skin. It is almost blue or silver."

"I suppose. I don't feel it. It does not do anything really."

"How did you stop being a Nighteye?" asked Thorson.

"A Grandeur," answered Luras.

"You saw a Grandeur?" asked Wreth.

"Yes. I was hurt or ... killed. I'm not sure. She brought me back from my wounds. When I awoke I was a Bourne ... and an Acolyte."

"And you?" Thorson looked at Matthias.

"Similar ... but I am not an Acolyte. Tomorrow, he will go one way and I another," said Matthias.

"You look to be an Acolyte," said Wreth.

"He is but refuses," said Luras.

"I didn't think there was a choice," said Thorson.

"There is always a choice," said Matthias.

"The stories of the Acolytes ... weapons smithed by Grandeurs ... golden armor and the lot," said Wreth. "Is this true?"

"I don't know," said Luras.

"Perhaps we met the wrong Grandeur," said Luras.

Luras held his cup of ale to his nose. He smelled and took a drink.

"Well, what do you think?" asked Matthias.

"Interesting ... bitter," said Luras.

"It gets better," Matthias said with a grin.

The men laughed.

"Excuse me," said a boy. He tugged at Luras' arm. He was not more than four years old and had large brown eyes with sandy blonde hair.

"Yes?" said Luras.

*This is the first child that has ever spoken to me.*

"They say that you are a Nighteye," said the boy. The other kids looked on.

"I was."

"Don't Nighteyes make toys?" asked the boy. The other children giggled and whispered.

"Well, I did ... yes," answered Luras. "What is your name?"

"Robert."

"Robert, I happen to be very good at carving spinning rain flowers," said Luras.

Robert's eyes widened and the other children whispered excitedly.

"I can make a rain flower that you can spin with your hand and it will float into the air. If you put water on it, it will spin off like a real rain flower. Would you like one?"

"Yes, please," answered Robert, grinning.

"Perhaps, then, I will make some for you all," said Luras.

The children cheered, Robert grasped Luras by the hand and pulled him to his feet.

"We have some wood here," said Robert, as he led Luras away. The other children gathered around and followed them to a pile of wood stacked by one of the fireplaces.

"Are you a cobbler elf now?" asked Matthias. "I thought you were going to finish your drink?"

"Save it for me," said Luras, as he sat by the fire looking for the right piece of wood.

"He is a strange lot," said Matthias to the other men. They grinned and laughed under their breath.

"Tell me, did this northern scouting party have information about what caused this or why we seem to find ourselves at war?" asked Matthias.

"They were a tight lipped group," answered Wreth.

Matthias nodded. He knew a northern scouting party south of their land meant that the realms were fracturing.

"That is until they helped themselves to our stores. Once the men had a belly of food and ale, their tongues were not so imprisoned," said Thorson.

"What did you learn?" asked Matthias.

"Mostly rumor ... conjecture. Some of the men talk of a sorceress in the Dargan Highlands," said Thorson.

"The Dark Realm," muttered Wreth under his breath.

"So this sorceress is leading an invasion with Skin Slavers and gorgons?" asked Matthias, incredulously.

"That might have been her plan. They said that worse things came about," said Wreth.

"What do you mean?" asked Matthias.

"You can open a door for evil .... but you cannot control it. She might have learned the hard way about that one. You can't corral the dark powers of the world like cattle to your bidding. It is like a weed. You cannot manage it. Probably thought she could ... but weeds grow in cracks and crevices ... under the ground. Suddenly, they sprout up from the hidden places in the world," said Thorson.

"A dark army comes at us from the Dargan Highlands. They are far north of the Northern Realm. It's no wonder they are looking for secure spots further south," said Matthias.

"Keep in mind this is just rumors from soldiers. There is no fact there. No one truly knows ... you would have to travel to the Dargan Highlands itself to know for sure," said Thorson.

"The Northern Realm will not travel there. They are already scouting south of their realm," said Matthias. "They are looking for footholds to fall back on, if needed."

"Then all the realms of Altaris are again fractured ... probably all of Ehlür," said Thorson.

"This is why the Acolytes have risen again," said Wreth. "You're to give us time to organize and stand against the enemy."

Matthias took a drink of ale.

"Your friend there ... his kind brought evil to the realms a thousand years ago. Now some other group tries to do the same ... to use evil for their own means," said Thorson.

"I will be far from it," said Matthias.

"Yes. I am only an alderman from a small village, but tell me ... where will you run that evil is not under your foot or grabbing at your ankles?" asked Thorson.

"I seem to have a great talent for finding old men that think they know what's best for me ... regardless of having just met them," said Matthias.

"No ... no, I am just talking. I do understand though," said Thorson.

"Understand what?" asked Matthias.

"Your hostility about all this ... Acolytes, war, and whatnot. I am not overly traveled, but I think I know which Matthias you are," said Thorson.

"Careful," Matthias spoke deliberately.

"Where is Norris?" interrupted Lindy.

"He should be here. I thought he was with you," said Wreth.

"No. I ain't seen him since you all left." She was now more nervous than angry.

"Your man with the axe?" asked Matthias.

"Yes. He went to stoke the fires in some of the homes," answered Thorson. "He should have been back."

The men rose and went to the door. Wreth started to open the large wooden door that was barred from the inside.

"No. Leave it," ordered Matthias.

Luras put the partially finished rain flower on the brick mantel of the fireplace. He went to the others to see what was happening. Matthias and Thorson unlatched the wooden panel to a window and looked out. They studied the center of the village. It was empty. The rain was coming down in heavy sheets. It was very dark. The only time they could see clearly was with each crack of lightning that struck across the darkened clouds. The thunder echoed like a waking giant.

"Do you see anything?" asked Luras.

"It's dark. The rain is blocking out everything," answered Matthias.

The sky lit up once more like veins of gold splintering out across the sky. Thunder shook the tavern, causing the children to run to the woman that had been reading to them.

"There!" said Matthias.

"God and kings," muttered Thorson.

Norris was in the center of the road looking at the tavern. He stumbled and moved slowly.

*I just have to make it to the tavern. There are Acolytes in the tavern.*

His right leg was not listening to him. It kept

buckling from his weight. The bone protruded just above the knee. The ligaments and muscles in his leg had been ravaged. It seared with pain. He walked holding onto his leg with one hand, while holding his other arm around his chest. His torso throbbed and bled with each breath. The beast had raked its claws across his chest. They had felt like hot knives stripping meat from bone. Each time he breathed or moved, he could feel his blood seep from his wounds. It happened so fast. Norris was not even sure what had occurred. Was it a bear? He had seen teeth and claws.

*It ran on four legs but stood on two ... like a person. How did I get away?*

It had thrown him around like a child's doll.

*I just need to make it to the others ... to the tavern.*

Thunder shook the ground. Lightning lit the sky. There was no longer a delay between lightning and thunder. They were coming at once. Norris could see the tavern clearly when the lightning ripped through the dark sky.

"There is something behind him," muttered Thorson.

The hulking beast was on all fours. It slowly walked behind him in the rain. Its eyes glowed a reddish yellow. It was big. Its frame was the size of a fully grown Tundra bear and had thick muscles coiled around it. Its fur was black and prickled up. The beast moved its head looking around the village, while it stalked Norris.

"A Storm Wolf," whispered Matthias.

"Teams of these wolves destroyed my village. There must be more," said Luras.

"You should arm yourselves," said Matthias, as he began to secure his weapons and armor.

Luras tightened his tunic and again donned the thin sabers given to him from the wisps.

"What is it doing?" said Wreth.

"It's a scout," said Matthias.

"We have to help him," said Wreth, grabbing his bow from the wall.

"No," ordered Matthias, "stay inside."

"He's right," said Thorson in a hushed tone. "Put out the candles and fires ... make sure the windows are boarded."

"We can't leave him there," said Wreth.

"No! You can't leave him there to die!" yelled Lindy.

"Lindy, *quiet*. Everyone, get the children and go to the cellar, *move*," said Thorson.

"He is alive, yet we leave him to die," said Wreth.

"I am very sorry, Wreth. But your friend is already dead. That is a scout out there. It wants to lure us out. There are children here," said Matthias.

Norris screamed. The wolf snarled and pounced on him. He fell like a sack to the muddy ground. The Storm Wolf snarled into the night, as it circled its prey. Norris began to pull himself towards the tavern with what strength he could muster. He was too weak to move. His body stayed. His hands only pulled mud in his direction. The beast stood over him. Norris did not see the wolf move. He only felt its teeth sink into his neck. There was muffled gurgle of blood and then a snapping sound. Norris was dead. The beast stood on two legs above him. It let out a low rumbling howl, as blood mixed with rain and dirt.

Lindy yelled out, while Wreth tried to comfort her.

"He is gone, Lindy. You need to get below with the children," said Wreth.

The wolf scout circled the corpse. It looked around the village, as it lifted its wet and bloody snout into the air. The sky rumbled and cracked; shards of light splintered across the sky. The ground began to moan like the hull of a great ship twisting at sea. There was the sound of a beating against the earth like a herd of wild horses.

"Do you hear that?" asked Thorson.

"Brace yourselves. They're here," said Luras.

The ground shook underneath the village. The men steadied themselves to keep from falling. The ground and road in the village vibrated. There was a great rupture like an explosion. The ground fractured with jagged fragments of roots and loose rock exploding from the earth. Storm Wolves bolted at great speeds from the large tears in the ground. It was as if the dirt and mud was giving birth to foul beasts. Storm Wolves ran from the muddy ground on two legs. Other wolves raced through the village on all fours. They roared and howled like beasts mad with rage. Some of the wolves stopped to tear at flesh from the corpse in the road. Others smelled the dead man and then lifted their snouts to the air. The scout from earlier continued to circle Norris. It howled into the night.

"Do they know we're here?" asked Wreth.

"I don't know. They know enough. Stay away from the windows and door," ordered Matthias.

"The children and others are locked in the cellar below," said Luras.

"Perhaps, they will find nothing and continue on their way?" asked Thorson.

"I do not think so," said Luras.

"Thorson, you should arm yourself," said Matthias.

"Oh, yes," replied Thorson.

Thorson took hold of a sword. He looked at it with resignation.

"We are not dead yet," said Matthias.

The men stood in the tavern listening to the wolves. The storm continued with shocking bursts of light and great thundering bellows. They could hear the wolves run past the tavern, hitting against its walls. Suddenly, the door slammed against the wood that latched it shut. There was another thud against the door and then it stopped.

"Calm yourselves," whispered Matthias.

A thud was heard on the roof of the tavern. Dust fell from the ceiling. Wreth looked up and then at the door. A scrambling could be heard on top of the roof.

"That roof will cave," whispered Thorson.

Luras reached back and drew both his sabers. Matthias already had his greatsword drawn. There was another bang against the door.

"Prepare yourselves," Matthias whispered.

Wreth looked around. He did not know where to aim his bow.

"They are coming in. Stay together. If we fight apart, we will die," said Matthias.

"Wreth, breathe. Look at what you shoot ... if I die today, I do not want it to be from one of your arrows," said Luras, grinning.

There was another bang at the door. Wreth aimed his bow at the door. He held the string lightly between his fingers. Suddenly, a wolf barreled through a window breaking both the glass and the wooden panel. Wreth twisted but his arrow slipped and lodged in the wall beside the door. Wreth tripped and let out a scream. The wolf snarled and lunged towards him. Wreth instinctively covered his face. Matthias threw his greatsword with both hands. It caught the wolf in the belly and sent it rolling. It grabbed at the greatsword jutting out of its belly, as it stood. Its snarl was gone; it was replaced with a high pitched howl. Luras swung both sabers down into its chest. They sliced through easily. He brought one blade back up removing the wolf's arm. It fell to the floor. Matthias removed his greatsword from its opened belly.

"We need you in this, Wreth," said Matthias.

Luras helped him up.

"Go stand behind the bar and shoot anything with fur," said Matthias.

"There are no windows there," whispered Thorson.

# A DARK TYRANNY

"I think the time for whispering is over," said Matthias.

There was more banging on the door. This time it was much louder and with more force. The banging was constant. They wanted in. Another wolf burst through the window. Two more followed. A fourth wolf broke through another window. The wolves stood two legged and lunged towards the men. Matthias kicked a table towards one wolf causing it to stumble. He sliced down with his greatsword catching another wolf in the shoulder. The blade dug deeply through its torso, almost cleaving it in two. The wolf that stumbled threw the table over. An arrow hissed through the air lodging in its neck. The beast snarled and ran towards Wreth. Another arrow hit just below its neck. It took one step back but kept coming. Luras twisted and dragged one of his blades across its stomach. Its insides spilled from the cut. Luras gracefully twisted in the other direction letting his other blade strike into the beast's heart. It fell. Matthias swung at another wolf taking off its arm and cutting into its chest. The beast fell to its knees and he kicked it to the floor. Luras saw Thorson on the floor holding his chest. Blood spilled out from between his fingers. Luras ran to him. A wolf stood over him. It turned to strike at Luras, but it was too late. Luras' blades struck through the neck and cleaved its head. Luras helped Thorson to his feet.

"We will put you behind the bar. Stay calm. Panic will cause your blood to flow more rapidly," said Luras.

The door to the tavern split down the middle and broke off its hinges. Wolves began to flow in like water.

"Wreth!" yelled Matthias.

Wreth let loose arrow after arrow. Matthias was able to cut at the wolves as they barreled through the opening. Luras sank his blades into every wolf he saw. He remembered his village. He remembered the other children that had been slain. Luras and Matthais' eyes grew brighter. The darkness no longer mattered. They could see clearly, as if it was day.

"I am out of arrows!" yelled Wreth.

"Take Thorson to the cellar," ordered Matthias.

"I can help," said Wreth.

"Help by bringing him the cellar. Go!" yelled Matthias.

Matthias swung in large arches, hitting wolves in all directions. They lunged at him scratching through parts of his armor. He felt pain in his arms but continued. Luras watched as Wreth opened the cellar and helped Thorson. Once they were down, Luras locked it from above.

"They are safe," yelled Luras.

A wolf slammed into Luras knocking him off his feet. He turned before the wolf could pounce down on top of him. Matthias cleaved the wolf above the waist. Blood and bone erupted from the beast.

"We need to get them away from here," said Luras.

Luras stood and barreled out the door and into the rain. He stood in front of the tavern, close to Norris' ravaged corpse. The wolves ran after him. Luras stood in the road with both blades drawn. Blood and rain dripped along their edges and off their tips. The wolves circled him, snarling. Matthias pulled his sword from a wolf and ran to the door. He knew that Luras always had a slight glow but, he had never seen him like this. The Bourne radiated a hue of red. His skin was not red, but the silver hue was gone. It had been replaced. Matthias looked in astonishment. The anger of the Bourne was of legend. However, Matthias now saw it with his own eyes.

The wolves circled Luras. There were at least fifteen of them. They snarled and gnashed their teeth. One would start to move towards him but then fall back in the circle. The blades of Luras' sabers reflected the lightning and the hue of his skin. A wolf charged at him. Luras evaded the wolf's pounce with grace. He brought down one of his blades. It caught the wolf at the top of its skull. Luras did this in one motion. His eyes were back on the other wolves before the corpse hit the muddy road. The other wolves were enraged. They continued to snarl and howl into the night. Two more lunged forward. Then three more charged with them. Luras moved with fluidity. He dodged one wolf, while sinking his sabers into two others. He pulled them out, while slashing two others across their chest and belly. A wolf grabbed Luras by the arm and neck. It lifted him off the ground. Another wolf raked its claws at his chest. Luras brought down a saber cleaving the arm of the wolf holding him. It dropped him. Luras fell to the ground and rolled back to his feet before the other wolf could sink its claws into him. Luras felt blood drip down his arm and into his tunic. The wolf that missed him reached out flailing its claws in a frenzy. Luras twisted to one side, as he cut the wolf's right leg. It fell to the ground, still trying grasp at him. He sank a sword into its heart. Luras felt a gust of air fly past his head. An arrow hissed and caught a wolf through the eye. Its tip cracked through the back of the skull. Two more arrows flew by him, landing into more wolves. Luras looked back to see Matthias. He had Wreth's bow.

*He removed the arrows from the wolves in the tavern.*

The remaining wolves began to disperse. They fell to all fours and ran into the surrounding forest, disappearing into the night. Matthias shot arrows as they scurried into the darkness. Luras fell to one knee. He breathed heavily. It was still raining, but the lightning was no longer constant.

"That was quite a show," said Matthias.
"I didn't want them to enter the cellar."
"Well, they did not."

Matthias helped Luras to his feet.

"That was impressive for never having had any weapon training in your entire life," said Matthias.

"It just ... seems natural."

"We need to have someone look at those wounds. You're bleeding."

Luras' arm and chest seared with pain.

"Matthias."

"Yes."

"You are not leaving tomorrow."

## Chapter 19

### The Beginning of Isolation

The boy ran through the streets of the Timball. The king's soldiers walked in squadrons, while others rode the village streets on horseback. The villagers scurried like mice through the roads, trying to make it to their homes or businesses for shelter. Soldiers burst open the doors to storehouses and began to carry out bags of provisions. They loaded wagons with wheat, corn, beans and salted meats. Any villager or merchant that shouted at them met the tips of their spears. The fortunate ones were only kicked and beaten. Timball was falling into utter chaos. The boy was able to dart in between all the horses and wagons. Confusion and pandemonium allowed him enough stealth to navigate through the streets. His size benefited him as well.

"As was declared by King Welthorn of the Eastern Realm, all provisions and items of value, for the longevity of the realm, are hereby claimed in the name of the king. The requisitioned provisions will be dispersed to the people of the realm as need determines. This was enacted in order to thwart the current tyrannical bandits that seek to wreak havoc within the realm for personal gain," bellowed a captain on horseback. He read from a parchment. He rode the village surrounded by four other flag bearers and soldiers. He continued to recite the proclamation throughout Timball.

The boy had made it to the edge of the village. He could see the wood mill in the distance. He hoped that the others would be there. He ran from the village towards the mill as fast as his legs would take him. He breathed heavily knowing that he was almost there. He could rest once he made it. The king's proclamation still echoed behind him and throughout the village. He could still hear the screams and shouts of villagers. The boy dared not look behind him. His legs were moving too fast to keep up. He stumbled and fell, causing his lip to bleed and his mouth fill with dirt. He stood feeling his mouth, spitting blood and earth. This only made him run faster. His heart pounded.

Ellison, Cal Mossy, Jared Horn and Jon Lince sat a table made of thick wood that had been heavily stained. It was a simple round design. Its legs still wore a light coating of bark under the finish. The round table top revealed many tree rings. A map was spread across the table. A jug of water kept it from moving. Saws and other woodsmen tools hung against the walls. There was no woodwork being done inside or outside of the mill.

"If we were to gather as much supplies as we could, we could form a caravan. Head north. We could ask King Tellos for refuge," said Jon Lince.

"My brother would never allow that," said Ellison.

"We would leave in the late hours of the night," said Jon.

"It would take planning. Could the village keep such a secret from the king?" asked Jared.

"Given the circumstances, I think so," replied Jon. "We've slowly taken what we can from the realm to store. The villagers have been largely quiet so far. They understand what is at stake."

"I agree. We cannot wait here. But we don't know what awaits us on the road. It would be a large caravan ... they are not easily concealed," said Cal.

"So we take our chances here or on the road north," said Ellison.

"At least we have a chance going north. We know what awaits us here," said Jon. "This is not a perfect plan but I do not see any other way. We cannot simply take Castle Horos or overthrow your brother."

"We should float this idea to the others," said Ellison. "It is dangerous. We should all be aware of the risks."

"I can talk to ...," started Cal.

The door burst open. Cal Mossy and Jon Lince jumped to their feet. The boy stood in the door frame. He was breathing rapidly. He tried to catch his breathe.

"Ethan? What is it?" asked Cal Mossy.

"They are sacking the village," he said between breathes.

"Who is?" asked Ellison.

"Your brother. He is raiding Timball."

"Come in. Shut the door," said Jared Horn.

"I saw riders behind me," said Ethan, shutting the door.

Jon Lince brought him a cup of water.

"Thank you, sir."

"Please sit," said Jared. He went to the window.

"They are taking storehouses ... killing or beating those that resist," said Ethan.

"Put the map away," said Jared. "He is right. There are riders."

"Then our plan to go north is too late," said Jon.

"It seems so," said Cal. He pulled the table to one

side. A cellar door appeared below it.

"I think those days are done, my friend," said Ellison.

"Soldiers are here," said Ethan.

Four men on horseback approached the mill. They wore leather tunics that were dyed a deep reddish brown. Plated armor was on their chests, shoulders, and forearms. Two men dismounted and drew their swords. One more remained on his horse and carried a spear. The fourth was a captain. He did not wear the same armor as the others. He wore a leather tunic that was dyed green. He was a heavyset man with long sideburns that almost met at his chin. The hair on his head was a dull red and patchy. He was very pale, which made the hair on his neck and forearms seem thick and abundant. The sun was turning his fleshy skin a pinkish red. His horse was swaybacked; it snorted loudly.

"Come out," said the captain in a dry tone.

There was silence from within the mill.

"If this were the first place we started today perhaps, hiding would work. However, this is most definitely not the first place we have been today. If you do not come out from this mill, these soldiers will come in and drag your fresh corpses out by their ankles. The boy will be no exception. He will find no quarter here. He will be with you among the dead here today. So, I will not ask again," said the captain.

There was silence. The captain's horse snorted and hacked.

"Go," the captain ordered, as he nodded towards the two dismounted soldiers.

The door opened before they could enter. Cal Mossy and Jon Lince walked out from the mill. The boy, Ethan, was between them.

"Show us your hands," said the captain.

The men opened their arms out revealing they had

no weapons.

"Good choice," said the captain.

"Which one of you is Calvin Mossy," asked the captain.

"I am he," said Cal.

"Em. There you are. I suppose I should know you, but I don't bother myself with the comings and goings of this filthy village. You are all much too *high-minded* for your own good," said the captain.

"Where is your wagon?" asked Cal.

The captain looked at Cal with contempt.

"I was told the king is taking storehouses for the realm. You are here at my wood mill but I do not see any wagons. Your soldiers seem to have strong backs, but I don't think they will be able to manage," said Cal.

"The wagons ... they will be along shortly. I would not concern myself with them. Bring them closer," said the captain.

The two dismounted soldiers motioned at the men. They walked further away from the mill towards the captain. Ethan looked around nervously. The day had been too much for him.

"I was informed that you may know the location of someone we are looking for," said the captain.

"Who is this?" asked Cal.

The captain motioned to one of the soldiers. He immediately slammed the hilt of his sword into Cal's abdomen. Cal coughed and fell to one knee.

"Let's try this again. Where is the king's brother? I was told you had spoken to him on occasion. He is a wanted man and giving shelter to a wanted man is an immediate sentence of death. So, I will ask a final time," said captain.

"There is no need for you to keep talking," coughed Cal, as he stood up. "He is inside with one other."

The captain motioned to the dismounted soldiers. They turned and entered the mill with swords in hand.

The captain looked down at Cal Mossy.

"You could have spared us this entire ...,"

His words were cut short, as Cal pulled a dagger from inside his waistband. The captain's horse spooked and jumped to the side. Cal sank his dagger deeply into the horse's neck and pulled. The animal screeched and staggered. The captain jerked on the reins but it did no good. The horse was dead before it fell to the ground. The captain's leg twisted and snapped loudly. He rolled on the ground in pain, but his leg was pinned under the weight of the dead horse. Jon Lince grabbed Ethan by the arm. They began to run. The mounted soldier looked at his captain with surprise. He pulled hard on his reins. His horse snorted and turned towards Jon and Ethan. Cal grabbed an axe from a wood pile. He rushed and swung blindly at the horse. The axe missed the body but came down hard on its back hoof. The horse jerked, reared, and stumbled. The rider fell from the saddle. Cal buried his axe into the soldier, hitting him in the collar and neck. Behind him, one soldier walked out of the mill. He was no longer holding his sword. Blood trickled down his arm and off his fingers. He looked around once before falling to the dirt. A dagger stuck from his neck.

"Ellison! Jared!" yelled Cal. He pulled the axe from the soldier and walked to the mill.

Ellison appeared in the doorway.

"Ellison!" said Cal.

"Hurry. Help me with Jared," said Ellison.

Jared was lying by the large wooden table. He held his arms tightly around his stomach and chest. The other soldier lay dead beside him.

"Cal," said Jared, in almost a whisper.

"Let's get you out of here," said Cal. "We can get you to a healing table."

Cal bent down putting his hand on Jared's cheek.

"We need something to carry him on," said Ellison.

# A DARK TYRANNY

"No ... you can't move me. I was cut too deeply. I'm holding everything in. You need to," Jared's eyes slowly fell to one side. The tension in his arms was gone.

"Jared," said Cal.

Ellison looked down at them.

"He's dead," said Cal.

The captain no longer tried to free his leg from under the horse. Instead, he laid on his side moaning in agony. Cal and Ellison left the mill. Ellison carried one of the soldier's swords. Cal still had his axe.

"We gather whatever supplies we can muster. We head north tonight. I will go tell everyone I can," said Ellison.

"What if someone sees you? You don't exactly blend in," said Cal.

"They will kill you, but not me," said Ellison. "Besides ... I won't get caught."

"I'll finish up here and load my wagon with what I have," said Cal.

"I will tell everyone to meet at dusk by the lake," said Ellison.

"At least we'll not want for thirst at the beginning of the journey," said Cal.

"How so?"

"Look, a storm is coming," said Cal.

"Dusk ... the lake," said Ellison. He pulled down the hood of his cloak and ran towards Timball.

Cal walked to the captain.

"You cannot do this. I am a captain of the Royal Army," hissed the captain.

"This filthy village of Timball. The one that you do not concern yourself with ... and, therefore, do not know my face. We are leaving your king tonight. But you, you, will be staying here ... and this image of my face ... the one you did not know before ... it is the last thing you will see in this life."

"You will die for this!" yelled the captain, as he tried

frantically to pull his leg from the horse.
Cal swung his axe.

## Chapter 20

A Difficult Decision

The caravan continued to push north. The gorgons marched the prisoners at an intolerable pace. If a prisoner fell from exhaustion or dehydration, they were thrown into a massive wooden wagon, as if they were already dead. Some of the prisoners were left where they fell. The carrion birds and other scavengers made quick use of them. The gorgon army continued to grow. Scouting parties would join the larger army with more captives each day.

Nylah was exhausted. Her lips were dry and cracking and her throat burned from thirst. Each step she took felt like it could be her last. The soles of her feet ached; blisters had long rubbed off leaving raw skin. Her forehead had started to peel from exposure. Nylah's stomach ached from eating the pasty gruel the gorgons gave them. She walked arm-in-arm with Tilda, the elderly woman that had seen a skin slaver as a child. They leaned against each other as they walked. Nylah would occasionally turn to look at the forest's edge. She searched the tree line for any movement.

"Are you looking for him?" asked Tilda.

"Yes. I don't know why ... but yes."

"Look all you want," said Tilda, smiling.

"I am so thirsty," said Nylah. She felt her lips as she spoke.

"You can't think about it. We have to keep walking."

They walked slowly with the other prisoners. It was a large group that was pushed tightly together. The look of resignation and fear spread throughout the captives. The group itself moved like a large beast that was slowly dying.

"I don't understand," said Nylah, almost to herself. "If they are invaders, why are we walking north ... towards their lands?"

"I do not know the mind of a gorgon. Perhaps, they are bringing captives back," replied Tilda.

"This is no invasion," said a man behind him. He was a middle-aged man that wore a soldier's tunic. It was now torn and tattered. His hair was thick and had been cut close to the skin. It had since grown enough to reveal graying along his temples.

"You were a soldier," said Nylah.

"I was," he said in a low voice.

"I'm Nylah. This is Tilda."

"Douglas Ramsey. I was lieutenant before all of this ... at Castle Red," said Douglas.

"Quiet. You will draw their attention," another man scolded them.

"We are walking to our deaths anyway ... or worse," responded Douglas.

"You don't think this is an invasion?" asked Nylah.

"No. They are not claiming lands. They had Castle Red, but chose to burn it to the ground. I have been in an invasion and you do not burn castles that you have sacked."

"If they are not invading then what are they doing?"

asked Nylah.

"I believe they will invade. But this ... I think they are raiders. They are here only to take things back with them. Back to their lands. They're taking *us* ... not our lands or castles or gold. They are taking *us* and scorching all in their wake," answered Douglas.

"What will be left," said Nylah, quietly.

"That I do not know. I doubt they care," replied Douglas.

"There must be more to it than that. You might be right about taking us. I mean, we find ourselves walking north. But there is more to this ... this plan. There are other lands than just the four realms. Altaris is small compared to all the lands of Ehlür," said Tilda.

"Well then, we will have to ask our Maker about this plan because we will sooner see Him than hear it from a gorgon or skin slaver. We will leave this world not knowing any reason for our leaving. This is if we even die ... all this talk of the White Ruins and taking of souls," said Douglas.

"They will not take anyone's soul at the ruins. Stop talking nonsense. You are scaring others with your fireside tales," Tilda retorted sharply at the soldier.

"Fireside tales, eh. I thought gorgons to be fireside tales. Yet, here we find ourselves," smiled Douglas.

Nylah turned again to the forest's edge to look for any movement. Nothing.

---

Finn woke to the smells of warm bread and honeyed tea. He stretched his arms out and felt his back crack and pop. Finn rubbed his eyes. His shoulders and arms were sore from carrying the woman to her home. He realized that he was not wearing any boots. He looked over to see her standing in front of the cupboards. She was splashing butter over bread and tasting the tea to make sure it was sweet enough. She wore different clothes. Her black hair was braided in a long ponytail. The sun shone through the window. It brought out the golden hue to her skin. Flour floated in the rays like tiny fairies.

"I apologize if I woke you," she said.

"No. It's fine," Finn replied, as he looked around the cabin.

"You fell asleep in that chair. I tried to wake you. You could have slept in my brother's bed, but you wouldn't stir."

"I'm sorry. I was very tired, I suppose. This is the first time I have slept inside in days. I guess I took full advantage."

Finn looked around the cabin. It was small but homely. The walls were made from thick maple trees. There was a large fire pit on one side. Herbs and spices sat atop the mantle, while leaves dried over the fire. The smells of the cabin made Finn heartsick for Margery and the bake house. There were a few books on a table by the chair he sat in. A large deer skin was spread over the straw floor. There were two bedrooms off from the main room. Finn stood and walked over to them. One was obviously for her parents. There was a straw bed with quilts over it and a wooden bureau. The other room had three smaller straw beds, one bureau, and a small wardrobe. One of the straw beds had a white and violet quilt over top and a stuffed doll that was faded and worn.

"Where are your brothers?" asked Finn.

"They left with my father," said the girl.

"Where did they go?"

"Skin Slavers raided Winthorp ... a village near here. They left with the others to help those that were taken."

"They left you here?"

"My father said it was safer than taking me with them," she said. Her eyes begin to well with tears.

"I'm sorry. Are you okay, from yesterday?" Finn asked. He felt strange mentioning it.

"I do not want to speak of it right now," she said, sheepishly.

"I'm sorry."

"It's alright. My name is Imeldris."

"Oh ... yes, my name is Finn. It is a pleasure to meet you, Imeldris."

"I made you some bread. There is tea as well."

"Thank you."

The bread was on a large wooden plate. Finn took it and his cup of tea. The bread was soft and sweet. Finn tried to slow down but he ate two pieces of bread before he sat at the table. He put the plate of bread and tea in front of him. He could not stop himself from eating.

"I'm sorry. This is so good," he said, smiling.

"It's quite all right. I can make more," said Imeldris.

"What of your mother? Is she somewhere?" asked Finn with a mouth full of bread.

"She died when I was little. It's just me for the moment," she said. Imeldris smiled at Finn to not make things awkward.

"I'm sorry about your mother."

"No need to apologize or be sorry."

"I ... I keep saying I'm sorry. It must be strange; it's strange for me. I ... I would say I'm sorry for it, but I don't feel I should say that again ... at least not for a while," Finn said with a confused look.

Imeldris grinned and laughed.

"There is a water basin in the bedroom. You should clean up after you are finished. You're quite dirty," said Imeldris.

"Yes. I would love to wash this dirt off me."

"You were going to apologize weren't you?" Imeldris smiled.

"Yes. I was," Finn sighed.

Imledris laughed and began to knead more dough.

"I have eaten all of the bread. Had you already eaten?" asked Finn.

"I did. I am making more now."

"Then I will wash this dirt off."

"I took out some of my brother's clothes. You look close to Morris' size. They should fit," said Imeldris.

"You don't to have do that."

"You are wearing rags, Finn. Clean yourself and put on those clothes. Go on."

Finn cleaned himself and put on the clothes. The pants and shirt were slightly long. He had to twist up the sleeve of his wool shirt. He tucked the pants into a pair of worn leather boots. The boots fit perfectly, which was important since he would be doing quite a bit of walking. He slipped on a leather tunic that buttoned in the front. There was also a leather cowl with a woolen lining, an archer's glove and forearm guard for a right handed bowmen. The leather on them was old and faded. They appeared to have been painted green once, but time and wear had begun to chip away at the color. They were not decorative.

"You brother used these for hunting. Are you sure it's ok for me to take them?" Finn said, as he walked back into the main room. His put his hands through his wet hair pushing it back.

"Yes. I am sure he would have given them to you if he were here. There is an extra pair of woolen pants there as well. I also have an extra bow and quiver I can give you. It's not the only one here, so don't feel bad taking it."

"Thank you, Imeldris."

"You are welcome. Do you feel better being clean and out of those rags?"

"Yes. In fact, it's made me quite tired. I guess I didn't realize how tired I was."

"You can stay if you like. Sleep," Imeldris said, smiling.

"I would like to but I mustn't. I have to get going. I have a long way to go yet."

Imeldris looked solemn at Finn's mention of leaving. She walked to the table and sat down. She did not cry, but tears welled in her eyes.

"Please sit, Finn. I ... there is something I have to say."

Finn sat at the table. He put a hand on her shoulder.

"Are you all right? I know you don't want to speak of yesterday, but ..."

"I would like to speak with you about yesterday," said Imeldris. She looked down at the table while she spoke. She then looked up at Finn. Her soft brown eyes filled with tears. She stared directly at him. Her voice was not quiet or meek, but instead was confident in what she had to say. Her voice was in contrast to her eyes, which showed the sadness of lost innocence.

"I see," replied Finn.

"I ask that you listen before making a judgment. Those men in the forest. They took me against my will. I didn't want that nor make them, nor want you to think I did. They accosted me for no reason."

"Of course."

"They were filthy rogues that deserved the death that came to them. I now find myself at a strange crossroads of sorts."

"Imeldris, none of this was your fault."

"I know that."

"Well, I suppose I don't understand."

"My belly was ripe for a child when they raped me, Finn. They took me and now there is a great chance that I will have a child. I will be a mother to any child that I bring into the world. I will love it, fully and completely. Finn, there is one thing I would ask of you though."

"What?"

"Lay with me. Let there always be a thought in my

head ... a chance ... that my child was not born of rape, but by a man that saved me in the forest. Give me this thought," said Imeldris, as a tear slowly moved over the contours of her cheek and chin.

"You may not even be with child. You do not know this yet. I might only raise your chances. I ...," Finn broke off into silence.

"It is a lot to ask. I understand. You will never see me again, Finn. You will go your own way. What does it matter? Am I not attractive to you?" asked Imeldris.

"No. You are very pretty, Imeldris. It's just ... my heart is not in this. I promised someone that I would help them. She is out there and I am here. I ... it would not be right."

"Your heart is with another. I understand. I am not asking for you to stay. Go to her. I only ask for you to give me the thought ... this idea to live with. Let me pass on your story to my child in place of yesterday. Finn, you must believe me, when I say I am with child. Lay with me and then go to her."

Finn sat in thought. He put his fingers through his hair.

"I understand. You must believe me when I say that part of me wants to do this for you. Another part of me would not be able to look at Nylah without feeling I betrayed her."

"Her name is Nylah."

"Yes. I want to do this Imeldris, but I cannot. However, you can still tell your child that I am the father. Tell him or her ... my name is Finn and I was falconer at Castle Red. I do not have a surname, but I do have these markings," said Finn. He unbuttoned his tunic and pulled open his shirt.

"What is that?"

"I have had it as long I can remember. A religious man at the castle once saw it when I had the red fever. He said it was some kind of seal. He said to not show it to anyone."

"Who gave it to you?"

"Perhaps, my parents ... I don't know. Tell this to your child. If for any reason I ever meet him or her, I will claim them as my own. You have my word."

"What is the difference, Finn? You would claim them, as if we did lay together. Everyone would think we laid together. Your Nylah would think it. Yet, you will not actually do it. What is the difference?"

"The difference is that I will know."

Imeldris nodded her head. She looked at Finn with teary eyes. He felt a wave of guilt wash over him. She stood and began to unbraid her hair. It cascaded over her shoulders.

"I was attacked and raped. You saved me. I have fed and clothed you. You are welcome to stay as long as you like. I am only asking you one thing before you leave. I do understand your heart is with another and I have respect for your honor. I only ask you one thing before we part ways. We will never see one another again. I only ask ... I ask that you give me hope, a small sliver of hope to rest my heart. Allow me to not build the story of my child's father on a rape or a lie. Allow me to truthfully tell my child who their father is ... or could be. Give me this one thing, Finn. I know it is a lot but ..."

Imeldris unbuttoned her dress. It fell to the floor. Her dark hair fell past her shoulders in thick waves. Her skin was the color of almonds.

Finn looked at her. There were bruises and swelling around her arms and neck. The corner of her mouth still bore a cut. The rest of her was smooth and soft. He felt both shameful and guilt ridden at once.

"Surely, you would find some pleasure in this," said Imeldris.

Finn stood. He continued to look at Imeldris. He stared into her eyes searching for the right answer or the right words. When Finn finally spoke his words seemed incredibly loud, as they filled the silence in the cabin. He made a decision. It was the first one he made as a free man. He prayed that it was the right one.

## Chapter 21

### A Visitor in the Night

The carcasses of the slain wolves had been gathered together and burned. They were now no more than ash and bones. The alderman laid in a fresh grave beside the tavern. The name Thorson was etched upon a wooden gravestone. The remaining villagers had boarded the parts of the tavern where the wolves had broken in. They used what materials they could find to fortify the tavern until they could leave. It was decided shortly after Thorson's death that they would gather what supplies they could muster and journey as far west as possible. They would not wait for the wolves to return.

Night had fallen over the village. The tavern was full of sleeping bodies. They laid on the straw and blankets. The children laid huddled together in a small lump. Luras slept close to the fire with his back against the wall. His wounds had been well bandaged and they were beginning to heal. Three wooden rain flowers sat beside him. Another partially carved one was still in his hand. Matthias sat in a chair in the corner of the room. He had one foot propped up on another chair in front of him. He was restless and unable to sleep. The wolves would return. He was sure of it.

Matthias stared at the fire. It cast warm and deep hues of red and orange. The last remnants of the flame cracked and threw shadows against the walls and floor. Matthias blinked and looked again at the fire.

*What was that?*

A shadow flickered from the firelight. However, the shadow was not rooted. It moved. It glided over the wall and cascaded down, blanketing over the sleeping children. The shadow moved like a ghost across the room. It was a shapeless cloud devoid of any light or color, a moving cloak of darkness that floated over sleeping bodies. It continued across the room and slid under the front door of the tavern, like cold breath disappearing into the night air. Matthias jumped to his feet and reached out for his sword. It was leaning against the wall beside him. His hand did not reach the weapon. Matthias was shocked. He was no longer in the tavern at all.

*I am outside.*

The night was dark. There were no stars in the sky. There was only the low light of the moon reflecting down from between clouds. They roamed like lost animals in the night sky. Matthias felt a wave of coldness descend around him. His skin prickled, causing the hair on his neck to rise.

*I am not alone.*

"Reveal yourself," Matthias said into the night.

Matthias turned in circles, watching the darkness around him. He looked for any movement.

"Reveal?" a low guttural voice hissed. "I have revealed myself. You are here are you not?"

"Show yourself."

"Such strong words for one with no weapon or

means of order," the voice rumbled. "How does one even strike out at a shadow?"

"This is sorcery," said Matthias.

"Sorcery? Sorcery is for the weak and feeble minded," hissed the voice. A shadow attached itself to the voice. It flickered in shape. It appeared human, but drifted in and out of form. It would take the shape of a human, only to dissipate back to a mass of darkness. There were no eyes, only the contours of a face could be seen in short glimpses.

"Who are you?" Matthias asked.

"Why are you here, Matthias?" the voice rasped.

"How do you know my name?"

"Your questions and orders are tiresome. What will you get out of this?"

"Out of what?"

"You are no Acolyte," it spoke with disdain.

"Why am I of concern?"

"You are all of concern ... but our concern is with you, at present," it said. The shadow broke into two versions of a human and then drifted back to one.

"Leave me," ordered Matthias.

"We would gladly leave you ... should you leave them."

"I plan to," Matthias spoke, almost to himself.

"Or ... come with us."

"Come with you where?"

"You preyed upon this rabble ... now you are chosen ... for this? He laughs at you," the voice hissed with disgust.

"I am done with war," said Matthias.

"He took your family and now gave you this ... servitude. Your family taken and you a slave. He takes with one hand and then takes more with the other. Go north, Matthias ... to us. Finish off this rabble you are with. Kill this cursed Bourne and the rest."

"I want no part in any of this."

"It will happen to you or for you. Make no mistake ... he will enslave you. Come to us, Matthias ... for your family," the voice hissed.

"My wife and son ... they are long dead."

"Are they?" the voice gargled.

"If you know my name, then you know of the north."

"Let us help you take your revenge. First, kill the Bourne ... then, you unleash your revenge. Your realms deserve no mercy. You, of all people, know this. First, kill the Bourne," it hissed.

"No."

"Kill the Bourne. Kill him ... kill him ... kill him. Kill the Bourne," the shadow yelled. It split into two shadowy figures, then three and kept morphing into more dark forms. A mass of dark figures stood around Matthias.

"I will not kill these people!" declared Matthias.

"Kill the Bourne! KILL THEM ALL," the sound of a thousand voices echoed into the night. The forms shook and twisted with rage. They moved into one formless dark void and then back into many. They flickered and yelled. Suddenly, the shadows dissolved into the night like mist. Matthias could still hear the echo of their voices in his ears.

*Kill the Bourne.*

"Matthias," a familiar voice spoke. "Matthias, wake up. Everyone is leaving."

Matthias opened his eyes. He was back inside the tavern sitting in the chair. The earliest rays of the sun passed through the cracks in the boarded up windows. Luras stood over him.

"Everyone is leaving," said Luras.

Matthias nodded. He rubbed his eyes and stood looking around the room. He picked up his greatsword and began to strap the sheath to his back.

"Are you all right?" asked Luras.

"Yes ... yes," replied Matthias.

## A DARK TYRANNY

"They are packed. Everyone will be leaving soon. They are going west, just as you. It seems you will have company after all."

Matthias watched as a villager began to etch letters into the outside of the tavern door. He was a weathered old man with piercing blue eyes. It took what strength he had to chip away at the wood.

"Letting the others know where we've gone ... in case they return. We have others' wives and children here," said the old man.

"Let us hope those wolves cannot read," said Matthias, as he walked past the man and into the daylight.

"Do you think they will come back?" asked the elderly man.

"The wolves? Yes, I'm sure of it," replied Matthias.

"The others ... the other villagers," the man said. He stared directly into Matthias' eyes looking for some type of hope.

"That ... I cannot answer," replied Matthias.

"Well, I will leave this message in hopes they do," the man replied. A sadness was in his eyes. He continued to etch and chip away at the door with all his strength.

The villagers had put what supplies they had in one wagon. Two more wagons held the children and those too old to walk a great distance. The wagons were hitched to two gangly oxen and one was hitched to a mule. The remaining villagers stood by the wagons, waiting for the start of a long journey on foot.

"Keep them safe," Luras spoke to Matthias.

"I have decided to go north," said Matthias.

"North?"

"That is what I said."

"What has changed?"

"I don't know, Luras. I do not claim to be an Acolyte or part of some grand scheme or plan ... but going north seems to make sense to me ... at least for now."

"For whatever reason, I am glad to hear it," said Luras.

"Besides, I think I've grown fond of seeing you glow red and kill things," replied Matthias.

Wreth walked along the wagons checking the harnesses of the animals. He ensured the hitching was done properly. The children watched him as he walked past. Some of them held wooden rain flowers, others held wooden swords. Wreth winked at them as he passed.

"Are you ready for an adventure?" Wreth said. He smiled at the children.

"Wreth," Matthias called out. He approached with Luras.

"Matthias, you will be coming along then?" asked Wreth.

"I am going north with Luras."

"I thought you were traveling west," said Wreth.

"As did I. I'm sorry."

"Someone needs to keep this Bourne from jumping into a pack of wolves," said Matthias.

"Do you have enough supplies for the journey?" asked Luras.

"If all goes well, yes. I hope to catch a deer or boar along the way as well," replied Wreth.

"Use your arrows sparingly," warned Matthias.

"Aye," Wreth nodded.

"Trust no one along the road. No fires at night. Pull the wagon from the road when you make camp. Don't be in sight of any other travelers ... or worse," said Luras.

"You have precious cargo in these wagons. Do not hesitate to use that bow when needed. It's better to question a dead person's motives than to find out while dying," said Matthias.

"I understand," replied Wreth.

"It is a dark road that awaits ... north ... west ... makes no difference," warned Luras.

"Safe travels, my friend," said Matthias.

"And to you both," replied Wreth.

## Chapter 22

### Night at Lake Lune

It was late in Timball. A thin layer of fog had gathered around the village. A light wind and sprinkling of rain kept it at bay. A dim light from the moon lit the village. Clouds slowly migrated across the sky. The village was no longer vibrant. It was quite empty. The only movement was of feral cats and stray dogs rummaging for food. The villagers that remained stayed locked securely in their homes. The city guards no longer patrolled the streets. The village was left to its occupants. The chaos of martial law had dissipated. Castle Horos seemed like another realm entirely. Provisions, supplies, and those individuals deemed of value by the king now safely resided within the walls of the castle. Looting had not yet begun, but the villagers were left with little stores for winter. Those that stayed in the village felt that the time would come soon enough. However, the majority of villagers had packed their remaining supplies and left for the lake. Word had traveled fast that a caravan would leave that night.

# A DARK TYRANNY

They would go north hoping to find refuge with King Tellos in the Northern Realm.

Ellison stood looking at Lake Lune. On a normal night, the glassy surface of the lake would reflect the moon. He remembered swimming in it. As a child, Ellison had more freedom at night. The sun had always been especially harsh on his white skin. There were also less eyes at the lake at night. He remembered how he would slowly sink into the water, as to not make ripples or waves. The moon's reflection would lay over the still lake. Ellison swam into the moon and lay on his back floating in the water. He would stare up at it, as he drifted in its image. It was one of the happier memories he had. On a dark night, the stars would always be in the water. It was a stunning sight. However, this night was different. The lake's surface caught the falling rain, causing small circles to form and grow outward. It was like an unplanned series of patterns playing out over top of each other. Ellison watched the rain hit the lake. There was no moon, just a black void of water that pulled in the rain and devoured it. There was a wooden deck that had been built. Small boats were tied to its posts. There was a wooden canoe sitting face down atop the deck. It was old and chipped. Ellison pulled his cloak tighter to keep out the rain. The hood of his cloak stopped just above his dull red eyes.

Villagers were already there and more continued to arrive. They came with their arms and backs full of possessions. Some had wheelbarrows full of items they did not want to leave behind. There were also those that only carried their children and the clothes on their backs. The villagers looked worried and confused. No one quite knew who was leading them or where they should stand. The only thing they were sure of was that they did not want to be left behind.

"We were able to get three wagons. Jon believes that he can get another one. That will give us four, a half dead horse, and three old cows. It will be a slow journey, at best," said Cal Mossy, as he approached. He wore a large cloak that barely fit over his bulky frame. His faded boots were muddy. A simple forester axe was strapped to his back.

Ellison nodded and continued to study the lake.

"We will announce our presence wherever we go ... slow and loud. I've walked through the crowd. Some of them are very frail ... others are already sick," said Cal.

"Where else do they have to go? There is no medicine or a healing table in Timball ... not anymore," replied Ellison.

Ellison turned and began to walk towards the growing caravan.

"What's troubling you, Ellison?" asked Cal.

"The world is falling apart. We will move from one danger likely to only find another. We are like fish jumping from a boiling pot ... only to land on the plate," said Ellison.

"Do you no longer agree to go north?" asked Cal.

"There is nothing here. It doesn't matter where we go ... just that we go. North is as best an option as any," replied Ellison.

"Each person here comes on their own. We are strength in numbers, but no one was forced. No one's fate is in your hands," said Cal.

"No ... but it should have been," Ellison spoke, almost to himself.

"You would have done better ... been better ... but this is a different time. We live out what we're given" said Cal.

Ellison tightened his cloak again. He looked over the caravan.

"When Jon returns, we should leave at once. The children should ride in one wagon. Their parents can walk beside it, if need be. Supplies in one wagon and the other for the sick. If supplies are with those that are

## A DARK TYRANNY

sick ... make sure it's not food. We don't want everyone getting sick at once," said Ellison.

"Aye. We need to leave before this storm arrives," Cal said, as he looked to the sky. "Also, before your brother catches wind of our departure."

"My brother has what he wanted. I doubt he cares any longer," said Ellison.

The rain began to grow. It was no longer a light sprinkling. Thunder rumbled in the distance causing the cows to grow restless. The wagons were hitched. The children sat together in the back of one wagon. An old gray mare with a sloping back stood ready to pull them. The thunder made the children huddle together tightly. Animal skins and spare cloaks had been given to them to fight off the rain. The villagers stood by the wagons. They were both anxious and frightened for the journey. Cal Mossy walked the line of the caravan. Ellison stood at the front.

"No word from Jon," Cal called out to Ellison, as he made his way to the front of the caravan. "He should be here."

"The storm is growing. We need to leave while we can," answered Ellison.

"What about Jon ....the other wagon?" asked Cal.

"You said yourself ... we will travel slowly. He will be able to catch up to us."

Cal looked into the distance for any sign of Jon or the wagon.

"Something doesn't seem right," said Cal.

"All the more reason that we should leave ... *now*."

"You are right. We should leave," Cal said. He continued to look into the distance.

"Everyone! Listen!" announced Ellison. "We are leaving. Try to stay together. It will be a wet start, but this will not last. Stay together and try not to fall behind. If you grow tired or ill, we have a wagon here to allow time to rest."

The caravan slowly began to move. The wheels of the wagons splashed through puddles as they rolled to life. The villagers were glad to start moving.

"Are you armed?" asked Cal.

"No. I have only what you see," answered Ellison.

"Take this," said Cal, as he handed a dagger to Ellison. "It's for hunting but it's better than nothing at all."

"Where are the swords from the soldiers?" asked Ellison.

"Jon has one. I gave the other to Sam Hemling. He is walking last man in the caravan," answered Cal.

"This storm will be on top of us soon," said Ellison.

"At least people will know what lays ahead. It's a long journey ... best to remove any delusions now," answered Cal.

Cal turned and looked into the night. The forest was dense and black compared to the lake behind them.

"Did you see that?" asked Cal.

"What?"

Ellison put one hand over his brow to block the rain.

"I thought I saw movement."

"Jon?" asked Ellison.

"I don't know. I don't see it now. It ... there!" Cal yelled, as he pointed.

"What was it? I saw it for a moment. It was moving too fast. It couldn't have been a wagon. We'd still see it," said Ellison.

"Something is not right. We need to move faster."

"He could be on a horse."

"If that were true, why would he be coming from there instead of the road?" asked Ellison. "Since when does a horse run in and out of shadows?"

"There is something out there. It's Jon ... being pursued, perhaps ... or not Jon at all," said Cal.

"Let's not find out," said Ellison.

"We need to move faster!" Cal yelled to the caravan.

# A DARK TYRANNY

The rain picked up. Ellison watched as the caravan moved past him.

"We are not moving fast enough. I am going to check on the wagons. Keep your eyes on whatever that is," said Ellison.

"Aye. Tell Sam to not let anyone fall behind. Perhaps, they're just scouts ... your brother keeping his eyes on us," said Cal.

"I don't think he cares that much. I ... God and kings," Ellison muttered.

There was a rumble and lightning splintered across the sky. For a brief moment, the world around them was full of light. Darkness was lifted and everything was exposed.

"My God," muttered Cal, "there are hundreds of them. Run!"

"Run! Everyone go! Leave whatever you have! Run!" yelled Ellison.

Ellison ran to the caravan. Suddenly, the supply wagon ripped apart. Supplies and wood flew to the air knocking back everyone around it. Wood fragments ripped through flesh. People fell screaming. An enormous beast stood over the wagon. It stood on two legs and howled into the night. It stood beside a massive rip in the ground. Jagged roots and rock twisted from the hole like severed veins. Other beasts followed from the open gash in the earth. Villagers ran. Storm Wolves came from all directions. Some ran on all fours while others stood upright. Their eyes gleamed red and their matted fur stood up from their muscled frames. They were enormous compared to the frail villagers. Very few people had weapons and they were all tired. They stood no chance. The wolves barreled into them easily knocking them to the ground. Others grabbed the villagers while continuing to run. Their teeth sank into flesh with ease. Ellison stood watching the chaos.

*What do I do?*

"Ellison!" yelled Cal.

Cal was swinging his axe at anything that came near him. He sliced through the wolves as they ran. They howled and rolled to the ground.

"The children! We need to get them to the castle!" yelled Cal.

*My God ... the children.*

Ellison turned and ran to the wagon with the children. They were laying down flat in the wagon.

*The wolves had not seen them yet ... or they will wait until everyone else is dead.*

Ellison ran through the wolves and villagers. Wounded villagers yelled out while they hobbled or laid on the wet earth. Others lay dead with wolves tearing muscles from bone. A wolf ran past Ellison. Its shoulder slammed into his leg causing him to fall. He hit the earth hard. The wind flew out of his lungs. Ellison put one of his arms up to block the wolf and the other scavenged for the dagger at his hip. However, the wolf never stopped. Ellison turned to get up. The ground was wet with rain and blood. His heart raced.

*I will die tonight.*

He saw Cal swinging his axe in a bloodied frenzy. Cal was not a warrior, but he was no stranger to the axe. His blows were strong. The blade did not lodge in bone, each swing ate through the wolf leaving a trail of blood, meat, and chips of bone in its wake. Ellison stood.

*I have to get to the wagon.*

The old nag in front of the wagon shook nervously. It pulled at the reins and chewed at its bit. Ellison could hear the children crying. He ran to the wagon. The harnesses seemed in place. There was no time to check. He jumped to the seat of the wagon.

"It's all right. We're getting out of here. Stay down," he told the children.

Ellison slapped down hard on the reins. The horse yelled out. The wagon jerked forward faster than Ellison had expected. The horse was panicked. It ran. The wood moaned as the wheels began to move. Ellison slapped the reins down again. The horse jumped and the wagon began to pick up speed. Bodies littered the grounds. The wheels rolled over flesh and rock causing the wagon to bounce. Wolves ran by the wagon, as they ravaged the fleeing villagers. Some villagers grabbed onto the wagon screaming, but were ripped away while others lacked the strength to hold on. Ellison could still see Cal. He swung his axe wildly. Cal saw that Ellison was in the wagon. The brief moment their eyes locked was all it took. A wolf charged at Cal. It was in the air before he was able to face it. Cal fell to the ground. Ellison lost sight of him. The wagon kept moving.

Ellison charged the wagon towards the village. The chaos behind him was spreading out past the dying caravan. He heard panting and growls but did not look around him. He was focused on the castle. The horse breathed heavily. It was too old.

*Stay alive ... don't die yet.*

The wagon rocked to one side. A wolf slammed into it but the wagon kept moving. The horse yelled out in fear. The children huddled together in the back crying.

"We are close now. Hold onto to something. Keep low!" Ellison instructed them.

Ellison slapped the reins but it did no good. The horse was already galloping as fast as it could. It had a deep guttural rasp to its breathing. Ellison could see the village.

*Not long now ... stay with me.*

The wagon made it to the main road. The wheels rolled smoother now. Three wolves had caught up to the wagon. A fourth wolf ran alongside it. It leapt and grasped onto the wagon. The wagon leaned on two wheels and was about the flip. The beast snarled and dug its claws into the wood. It started to pull its back legs onto the wagon. The children screamed. Ellison swung his dagger at the wolf. The blade opened a gash on one side of its mouth. The beast cried out. It bit at Ellison's arm, as it fell to the ground. The wagon bounced, as it pommeled over the fallen wolf. Ellison looked at his arm. It was bleeding. Its teeth must have grazed it. It was bleeding but Ellison didn't have time to do anything about it. He slapped down hard on the reins.

They were in the village. The wagon barreled through the street. It was moving too fast. Each turn caused the wagon to slam into the wall or a storefront. The wolves ran just as fast. Ellison turned the wagon down an alley. It raked across a stone wall. Wood cracked and splintered as the wagon turned. One wolf tripped and rolled, while another ran on top of it to make the turn. The third did the same.

"Open the gates!" yelled Ellison.

The gates to Castle Horos were to the right of the alley. Once they made the turn, the gates would be visible. Ellison had no idea if anyone was manning them.

"Open the gates! I have children!" Ellison screamed.

There was a stone wall at the end of the alley. The road turned right or left. Ellison did not slow the horse down. He doubted he could anyway.

"Hold on!" he yelled.

Ellison pulled right on the reins as hard as he could. The horse slid to the right losing balance. The wagon moved sideways; it hit the wall hard in the turn. The lead shafts of the wagon cracked. One of them broke and dragged along the ground beside the horse. The horse jumped and kicked as it ran. The spokes of the wheels that hit the wall splintered. One wheel was almost cracked in half.

*This won't last much longer.*

# A DARK TYRANNY

The gates were just ahead. Ellison could see three torches behind the gate.

"I have children! Open the gate!"

"What's out there?" yelled a voice from behind the gate.

"Open the bloody gates!" ordered Ellison.

The wolves turned the corner. One jumped up and pushed off the stone wall.

The horse tried to stop at the gates but it couldn't. It tripped over the broken shaft and fell to the ground. The other shaft snapped and dug into its hind quarter. The wagon slid to one side. It stopped with a jolt against the stone walls and the gate. Ellison flew forward, hitting his head on the rail guard of the wagon. Blood began to pour from a cut over his left eye. The world seemed to spin around him.

"I have children. Please let them in. I am ... I am the king's brother. Let them in," muttered Ellison.

"It's the king's brother," said a soldier behind the gate.

"Quickly, crack the gate. Let in the children," said a voice behind the three soldiers.

"Yes, sir. Right away."

The soldiers cracked the gate open. The children climbed over the wagon. One of the soldiers hurried them through the gate.

"This one is too hurt to move," a soldier pointed at Ellison.

"Hurry and bring the children to the castle. Go! Tell the king that I will try to save his brother."

"Yes, Malvern," said a soldier.

The soldiers moved the children away from the gate towards the castle.

The wolves were close. They slowed growling at the wagon. Their prey was cornered and they knew it.

"Malvern," Ellison muttered. There was a ringing in his ears; he was still spinning from the crash.

"Seems you find yourself on the outside."

"Help me," whispered Ellison.

"Come. Hurry," ordered Malvern.

Ellison slowly stood moving to the gate. He wiped the blood from his eyes. His legs shook under his weight. His arm felt as if it were on fire.

"Hurry now," said Malvern.

Ellison leaned against the gate.

"Open it," whispered Ellison.

Malvern leaned forward. Ellison felt a sharp pain just above his stomach. It burned deeply. He looked down. A dagger jutted from his body. He looked at it and then at Malvern.

"Why in all the four realms do you think I would help you? You made your choice ... now die in it," hissed Malvern.

Malvern scurried off towards the castle. Ellison tried to move but he couldn't. He leaned against a stone wall by the gate. His legs gave and he slid down. He sat on the ground with his back to the wall. He looked at the dagger, the wagon, and the slowly dying horse in front of him.

*Where would I go anyway?*

He heard heavy breathing and the stench of blood. The snarling of a wolf drew close. Ellison closed his eyes.

*I will not fight this.*

The wolf growled as it approached. Its hair stood. Its red eyes gleamed at Ellison. Saliva mixed with blood; it dripped from its mouth. Its massive frame looked down at Ellison. It lunged at him with its razor teeth. However, it stopped and stared at him. Ellison could feel saliva dripping onto his face and neck. He could smell the putrid breath of the beast. It roared at him and then howled up to the night sky. It turned and ran. The others followed.

Ellison opened his eyes. He was alone. Blood pooled

around him and mixed with the rain. His breathing was shallow. He wanted to pull the dagger from his stomach but was too weak. He felt the blade with each breath. It hurt. However, his arm began to feel strangely warm. The burning in it had stopped. There was just a warmth that seemed to radiate up his arm to his shoulder and neck. The feeling continued. Ellison did not work so hard to breathe.

*What is happening?*

## Chapter 23

### Let One Live to Kill Them All

Finn felt better to be moving again. He walked fast and, at times, ran. He had lost two days in his search for the gorgon caravan. He stayed close to the road but out of sight. There had been no other travelers, just a corpse with two arrows sticking from its chest. Birds and rodents had already had their way with it. Gorgons and Skin Slavers were no longer the only threat. Thieves and bandits thrived in times of chaos. Imeldris had witnessed this firsthand.

Finn's new clothes made him feel less of a prisoner. He now had a bow, a quiver full of arrows, and a small sword at his hip.

*I'm no longer escaping. I am now tracking them.*

He had a satchel on his back that had supplies, such as a blanket, flint and steel to start a fire, a water skin, and a few days' worth of food. It was not too heavy. Finn was still light enough to travel fast. The falcon did not venture far from Finn's sight. It would occasionally disappear into the clouds, but Finn knew it was keeping

# A DARK TYRANNY

a watchful eye on him. It gave Finn a sense of comfort and safety.

Finn traveled for three more days without seeing anyone. He tried his best to conserve his supplies. He ate salted meat and drank cider. The wineskin still had spiced ale in it from beforehand. The cider had a slight bitterness to it and an aftertaste of cinnamon and sugar. Finn managed to kill a forest hare. He only used one arrow, which didn't break or chip. He liked the feeling of being able to return the arrow to the quiver. Finn knew that once the arrows were gone, he might not be able to obtain any more – or at least arrows that were well crafted. He cooked the hare over a spit and gave what he did not eat to the falcon. The great beast had taken to perching close to his camp at night. Finn would wake each morning to the sound of beating wings and wind bellowing down against him, as the great bird ascended to the sky again. It had also begun to lessen the distance it flew during the day. It was keeping a closer watch on him.

*Are we getting closer to danger? Are we catching up with them?*

The sun was out on the fourth day. The sky was mostly clear allowing the heat to blanket the earth. Finn had woken early. He was moving quickly through the forest. It was warm, but a light breeze cooled his skin. It made him cool in the shadows under the trees and very hot in the open. There were two thin clouds in the open sky. The falcon was gliding just under them. Finn watched it as he moved. He began to hear it crying out more than normal. In fact, he thought it might be gliding in a circle.

*Have you found something? Is someone coming?*

This gave Finn a rush of energy. He began to run in the direction of the great bird. He stayed in the forest as much as possible. He did not want to run headfirst into a gorgon scouting party or more Skin Slavers. Finn moved cautiously. He began to hear something in the distance, a clanging mixed with muffled yells.

*Swords? Someone is fighting ...*

Finn was close to the edge of a large clearing. He put his satchel of supplies down beside a tree. He covered it with leaves and sticks. Finn took the bow that Imeldris had given him. He held it firmly and notched an arrow. Slowly, Finn moved to the edge of clearing. The noises grew louder. It was the deafening sound of metal on metal. He could see them.

*Gorgons. A scouting party. God and kings! Who are they fighting!*

It was a gorgon scouting party. They had one ox-drawn wagon. The ox had an enormous arrow jutting from its jaw and was sliced through the belly by a large blade. The beast was a lump of hair and blood on the ground. The wagon was on its side. There was a line of arrows in the ground waiting to be fired. However, the gorgons must have been surprised. Their attackers were too close now for arrows. Five gorgons laid dead on the ground like heaps of scaled flesh. Blood pooled around them. The remaining gorgons numbered between ten and fifteen. Finn could not be sure because everyone was moving so quickly. Some of the gorgons had swords, while others gripped spears. Finn had forgotten how big they were. The gorgons were enormous. Finn thought the leader was dead because the captains were the only ones with uncoiled tails. He had never seen them like this – they were scared!

They were the largest men that Finn had ever seen. They wore thick leather tunics that were lined with animal skins and fur. Steel ringlets and thin metal plates were woven into the leather. One man carried an axe in each hand. The others wielded swords and shields that were painted a faded green and gold. Their hair was long and braided in places, as were their beards. These men did not fight like trained soldiers;

they were brawlers. They fought with a harshness. There was no mercy to be found.

They slashed at the gorgons in a focused rage. Their strength was massive. One of the men slammed his shield into two gorgons. Finn saw blood and teeth fly, as the gorgons shot backwards landing on the ground.

*They bleed black blood.*

The man with the axes chopped and sliced at the gorgons. He kicked one to the ground. Another man brought his shield down hard on the fallen gorgon's neck. It stayed lifeless on the dirt. One gorgon jabbed wildly with his spear at the man with the axes. He swung his axe to block the spear, but instead he missed the blade and hit the wood below it causing it to split in two. The spear tip hit a metal plate on his tunic and slid off his chest. It cut into the man's shoulder and arm. The giant man roared out in pain. He lurched forward and slammed the top of the axe into the gorgon's face. Bone and skin pushed inward. He followed by swinging his other axe. It bit deeply into the gorgon, cutting through his arm and burying itself in its chest.

Finn was amazed at how the men fought. They did not fight in formations like the trained soldiers he had seen at Castle Red. Instead, they worked together with the sense that each man knew the other was capable of destroying his adversary. They helped each other, but not out of training. These men were warriors; they fought with anger and veracity. Finn found great pleasure in seeing the gorgons die in battle. He loved the look of fear in their eyes. He thought of the caravan. He thought of Nylah.

*They are scared of these men. Gorgons die just like us.*

The last two gorgons turned to flee. The men stood their ground but did not give chase.

*This is my chance.*

Finn stood raising his bow. He looked straight down

the arrow. There was a light breeze so he aimed slightly high. He knew the arrow would hit the mark. It would bite just below the neck of the gorgon. He lightened his grip on the bowstring. Everything he had ever learned about the bow ran through his mind.

*Don't pluck the string. Let the string slip through my fingers. Let the bow do the work.*

Suddenly, a large arrow whooshed past the men. It hit the back of the gorgon. The thick steel tip burst from its chest. Finn's arrow was still notched.

*There must be another man in the woods. One of them was watching with his bow the entire time.*

Finn quickly turned his aim at the remaining gorgon. He quickly raised the arrow from its mark. He let the bowstring slip through his fingers. The string snapped forward. However, before the arrow sailed out, a thick piece of dark wood hit the arrow causing it to slide along the ground and bounce off a tree. Finn looked up and saw another man staring down at him. He held a large bow.

*He hit my arrow with his bow. He made me miss.*

"We need him to live," the man said.

Finn stared up at the man. He was wide chested. His vest exposed his muscled arms. His hair was gray and pulled into a ponytail. The man's beard was braided at his chin and hung down over his neck. He wore faded leather pants and boots. These men were even larger up close. Finn felt his rage building again. Giant or not, he had caused Finn to miss.

"I had him. I wouldn't have missed," said Finn.

"Indeed, boy. There lays the problem. We need him to live," replied the man.

"Why?" asked Finn.

"I found a human here," the man yelled to the others and laughed.

"Bring him out. We haven't much time," replied the man with the two axes.

"Come. Grab your things," said the man. Finn grabbed his satchel from under the leaves. They walked to the others. Finn felt like a child standing with them. They were at least three hands taller than the largest man at Castle Red. There were five of them. The three that fought the gorgons and the two bowmen that were watching from the forest. Finn looked down at the dead gorgons. Their black blood was drying in the dirt. Finn thought of dead snakes still being able to bite.

"They are quite dead, boy," said the man that had found him.

"Who are you?" asked Finn.

"Are you still mad? Did that one gorgon mean that much to you?" replied the man.

"I wanted to kill him. I want to kill all of them," said Finn.

"Our actions do not need an answer, especially to some young human. He needs to move. They will be here soon," said the man with the axes.

"We let him live because there are two scouting parties. We just killed the small one. The gorgon will bring the others to us," said the gray haired bowmen.

"Let one live to kill them all," said one of the men with a shield.

"There will be fighting here. Leave. We cannot account for a boy," said the man with the axes.

"My friend is being held by them. I'm not a boy," said Finn.

"All humans are young. Go north if you must," said the man with the axes. "Do not stay here, though."

"I can fight them," said Finn. He felt his anger rising up again.

*Why am I forcing this? I just want Nylah.*

"His aim was right. He would have hit the gorgon," said the bowman.

"We do not need this," said the man with the axes. Finn could tell he was growing tired of the discussion.

The man began to wrap a cloth over his wounded shoulder.

"What's your name?" asked the bowman.

"Finn."

"Finn who? What's your family name?" asked one of the men with a shield.

"I haven't a family name. I was born in servitude to the king," replied Finn.

"I am Borman Thyn of the Stone Water clan," said the bowman with gray hair.

"Gilnor Kynd," said one of men holding a shield. He had hair the color of straw that went to his shoulders. His beard was coarse and pulled down. A braided leather strap wrapped the center of it. "And this is my brother Dord Kynd," Gilnor pointed to the other bowman.

"This is Hemlor Nyman. He is the Earl of the Stone Water clan," said Borman. He pointed at the other man with a shield. He was older than the other men but just as strong. His hair was long and appeared to be thinning. However, Finn saw that his hair was not thinning at all. He had a large scar that twisted down the side of his head. Hair did not grow on the scar, but it was thick all around it. Helmor kept his beard trimmed not too far below his chin.

"Your valor is honorable, Finn. However, a fight is coming. We cannot be distracted by you," said the Earl of Stone Water.

"Leave now ... or you will be buried here," said the man with the axes. He looked at Finn with great disdain. His skin was browned from the sun. His hair and beard were brown, but had also been lighted from exposure. The blood on his arm had dried. The cloth over his wound was now covered in dried blood.

"Calm yourself, Torin," said Helmor.

Finn was hot with anger. He did not know why he had to stay and fight. He could just pass them and track

# A DARK TYRANNY

the caravan. However, he was tired of being told what to do. He was no longer a servant; he was no longer a slave to gorgons. He was a grown man that was free. Most of all, he carried a deep hatred for the black snakes that had taken Nylah.

*I will stay. Let these men kill me if they must, but I will at least make one of them bleed. I am no longer a servant to anyone.*

Suddenly, there was a shadow overhead. Finn looked up to see the falcon with its wings outspread. It soared down quickly with a graceful speed. It turned its legs down opening its razor talons. It beat its wings to come to a stop, as it landed on the overturned wagon. The men were large but the falcon was larger. The wagon cracked and splintered under its weight. It eyed the men fiercely. There was no hesitation.

*It will fight these men if I do. It is with me.*

Finn walked and stood in front of the great falcon. Its wings were outstretched. The great bird's size and wingspan towered over Finn.

"I will stay and fight."

The men looked at Finn and the enormous falcon.

"Stay and fight," said the Earl of Stone Water.

"And bring your bird," said Borman Thyn, causing the other men to laugh.

---

The sun was beginning to set. A deep red and orange hue laid over the horizon before the second scouting party approached the wagon. This scouting party was larger than the first. Finn was able to count at least fifteen of them. The gorgons were cautious in their approach to the overturned wagon. They looked it over while standing over the corpses of the slain gorgons. One of them pulled a large arrow from a corpse. It showed it to the others. Finn could not hear what they said. However, there was an agreement among them. These gorgons carried spears and shields. The black tunics they wore had long ago faded. Some were torn in places. Their tails were all coiled around one leg.

*These gorgons have seen battle. They are footmen. Where is their captain?*

Finn and Borman Thyn were both far from the wagon. Their bows were aimed at the gorgons. They aimed high to adjust for the wind.

"Something is wrong. Who is leading them? There is no leader among them," whispered Finn.

"This is not the entire scouting party," replied Borman.

"Where are the rest?" asked Finn.

"I don't know but we are about to strike them. We either give them enough time to discover our positions and fight exposed, or we kill these and prepare for the onslaught," replied Borman.

Finn breathed in deeply, as he looked to the gorgons.

*Are the others watching us, as we watch them?*

"Steady yourself," whispered Borman.

"I am steady," replied Finn.

*Calm yourself. They make much larger targets than quail or pheasants.*

"Remember, we all leave this world. You will die one day ... either some future time or this moment. If it is today, I am eager to take as much of these vile snakes with me as I can.   Together though ... we might be able to take them all," whispered Borman.

Finn set his aim on a gorgon. He aimed slightly high. The arrow would hit just below the neck. He pulled back on the bowstring and looked to Borman.

"I have my mark. We will try to kill them all," said Finn, as he continued to keep his eyes on the gorgon.

Borman drew a thick wooden arrow and notched it. The bowstring stretched as he pulled. He looked the gorgons over and took a target. The one holding the arrow. He aimed. The string and bow groaned and stretched. Suddenly, the arrow sang as it shot towards the gorgons. It ripped through the air and caught the gorgon in the neck, just below the chin. The gorgon flew backwards into the wagon. Black blood poured on the wagon. The other gorgons raised their shields, but it was too late. Finn's arrow whistled through the air. The target had started to turn, but it still dug deeply into the gorgons back. The gorgon twisted and fell to one knee, as it reached for the arrow. Blood dripped from its nose and mouth. It cried out in a guttural rasp and fell to the ground.

"You killed your gorgon. Nicely aimed," said Borman. "Now, continue and remember ... don't hit us."

Finn notched another arrow and picked a gorgon. However, another larger arrow ripped through its waist and abdomen. Finn could see Dord Kynd notching another arrow. He was positioned just north of Finn. The gorgons held their shields up. They didn't know which direction the next arrow would come. Finn released another arrow. It soared towards the gorgons catching one in the arm. It tore through muscle and tendon. Finn heard a rush through the woods. He saw Gilnor Kynd, Hemlor Nyman, and Torin running to the gorgons. Gilnor and Hemlor ran with their shields out front. They crashed into the gorgons like rolling mountains. Finn saw chips of bone and teeth explode from the shields. Torin hacked and chopped through the dazed gorgons. Another arrow sailed passed Gilnor Kynd and dug into a gorgon's skull. Finn watched the carnage.

*It should not be this easy.*

Finn felt the ground rumble. He heard the sounds of a horn behind him. It was the hollow sound of a war horn. It echoed three bursts in short succession. Finn quickly turned to look.

*God and kings!*

The rest of the scouting party charged towards them. There were more than twenty of them. They were a mass of hulking muscle and scales. Two gorgons carried their standards of war. A black and yellow banner with a coiled snake poised to strike. One gorgon held a war horn carved from the tusk of some beast Finn had never seen. He continued to sound the horn in three rapid bursts. Enormous wolves, of the like Finn had never seen, ran alongside the gorgons. Some of them seemed to spring from the very ground itself. The land moaned and crevices ripped open with sounds of splitting wood. The wolves jumped from the gaping holes in a full run. A man rode atop one of the wolves. Two other men charged with the gorgons.

*Skin Slavers!*

Finn turned and ran towards Borman Thyn and the others. He held tightly to his bow.

"Behind me!" Finn yelled.

The men had already heard the horn blasts. Finn felt one of Borman's massive arrows whisk by his head. He heard the yelp of a wolf, as it cried out and rolled to the ground. He did not turn to look; he kept running. Gilnor and Hemlor still battled three gorgons at the wagon. Finn notched an arrow and fired. His arrow strayed from its mark, but diverted the gorgon's attention long enough for Hemlor to strike it down with his sword. Dord shot an arrow past Finn, towards the approaching army. Finn did not turn but he could hear that it found its target.

"Find cover and use every arrow you have," Borman said to Finn.

Finn ran past the men and the wagon. He stood behind a tree with massive roots that twisted into the ground. He leaned into the tree and notched an arrow. The gorgon army was close. A wolf charged away from the pack towards Dord Kynd. Saliva dripped from its jaws, as it growled and leapt at Dord. Its red eyes were wild with a snarling rage. Borman grabbed the wolf with one hand around its throat. It snapped and wrestled in Borman's grasp, as it ferociously bit in every direction. Borman threw it to the ground. The wolf tried to regain its footing, but it was too late. Dord stabbed down with one of his thick arrows. It cracked through the wolf's skull leaving it writhing on the dirt. Dord put one foot on the wolf and pulled the arrow free. He notched it and sent it sailing back towards the gorgons.

Finn aimed towards the skin slaver riding the wolf. The slaver was thin with tightly wound muscles, like a knotted rope. He wore another man's face as a mask. Finn's arrow whistled over wolves and gorgons until it found its mark. The skin slaver twisted back as the arrow lodged into his collarbone. He slumped to one side and tried to regain control over the wolf. He momentarily met eyes with Finn. He yelled and kicked at the wolf causing it to charge towards Finn. Finn quickly notched another arrow. This one hit the slaver in the stomach causing him to fall from the wolf. However, his hand was tangled in the leather strap that he used to rein the wolf. The wolf continued to charge at Finn. The skin slaver twisted and flapped beside the wolf like a doll. When his hand fell loose, the slaver simply rolled to a stop in a clump of flesh and broken bone. Finn reached for another arrow, but kept his eyes on the wolf. It was enormous. Finn fumbled with the first arrow he took. It fell to the ground. He grabbed another and quickly notched it. However, it was too late. The wolf had leapt at him. Finn could smell the dank odor of its fur. He could feel the heat from its breath. The teeth of the wolf were stained yellow and jagged in places. The arrow shot out into the ground. Finn tried to jump away from the wolf, but it was too late. Finn felt a gust of wind as the falcon swooped down. It knocked Finn to one side, while snatching the wolf up into its talons. The wolf cried out and convulsed in the falcon's grasp. The great bird ascended up, as it sliced through the wolf with its razor sharp talons. The wolf fell in two pieces over the gorgon army.

*I am alive.*

The gorgons and men met clashing together. Borman had dropped his bow. He held a sword in each hand and hacked wildly at the gorgons. The men fought closely together with their backs to the overturned wagon and each other. The gorgons poured into them like river water wrapping around a stone. Finn had less than ten arrows remaining. He carefully aimed each one. He shot wide of the men and hit the gorgons on the outside of the cluster of battle. The falcon circled close to Finn. It swooped down raking its talons across the gorgons. Finn heard screams and saw blood spurt from the group. The great bird would always return to Finn to ensure his safety.

Gilnor Kynd pushed forward with his shield knocking gorgons back. Torin swung ferociously at the enemy, severing limbs and cracking spears. The last remaining wolf charged the men. Its jaws sank into Torin's arm. He stumbled and then slammed the hilt of his axes into the wolf's back. It snarled and pulled at his arm. Hemlor sliced through the wolf's neck with his sword. Its head separated from its body and both fell to the ground, which was now littered with corpses. As Hemlor turned back to the gorgons, a spear sank into his chest. He grabbed at it, but another followed into his stomach. He coughed and labored to breath. His lips grew wet with blood.

"No!" yelled Torin.

Torin swung his axes in a rage. Hemlor's heavy frame fell to the ground. Torin reached out for him, but a gorgon thrust his spear at him. Torin cut through the spear but the bladed tip cut deeply across his waist. He cried out with anger. Borman drove both his blades into the gorgon's chest and kicked it to the ground. Torin held his waist and leaned against the wagon. Gilnor, Dord, and Borman stood in front of him, as they battled the remaining gorgons. They were covered in the dark blood of the gorgons.

Finn spotted the last of the Skin Slavers. His donned skins were bloody. It made them curl and hang strangely from the slaver. It was as if he was molting. The slaver was turning to run from the fight. Finn notched an arrow and sent it sailing towards him. It struck the skin slaver in the back. He twisted and fell forward. Finn fired another arrow where the man fell. Suddenly, Finn felt a heavy blow to the back of his head and neck. He stumbled and turned. The gorgon swung again with the base of a broken spear. Finn dodged to one side causing the gorgon to only hit his shoulder and arm. Finn thought his arm would sink into the earth. He stabbed the beast in the neck with an arrow. It yelled in a garbled tone. Finn reached for another, as the gorgon grabbed him by the neck and jawline. He brought him close up to his face. The blood spilled from the arrow jutting from its neck. Finn buried another arrow into its gut. It squeezed Finn's throat. He struggled to breathe. The gorgon suddenly straightened and released its grip. Finn saw the falcon's talons emerge from the gorgon's chest. It rose up taking the gorgon with it. The falcon closed its sharp claws slicing through the gorgon's bones and crushing its chest. Finn grabbed for his bow on the ground. He found it and turned back towards the fight. Borman Thyn stood in front of him. He was coated in sweat and wet with blood.

"The gorgons are dead or retreating," said Borman.
"We've won," said Finn.

"It seems. But our Earl is dead and Torin is gravely wounded," replied Borman.

Finn stood. His legs felt weak. He saw Gilnor and Dord standing at the overturned wagon. Torin sat leaning against it. The ground was soaked in dark blood. Gorgon corpses and limbs were strewn about. Finn saw the body of Hemlor Nyman lying on the ground. He had been turned onto his back, his shield resting over his chest. Finn stared down at him in confusion and bewilderment.

"He has ... turned to stone," whispered Finn.

"It is our nature in death," said Dord.

"What do you mean?" asked Finn.

"Enough with your questions," said Torin, in rasped voice.

"Why did he turn to stone in death?" Finn asked Borman.

"It is the way of all Stone Giants," replied Borman.

## Chapter 24

### The Face of the North

The foothills of the Northern Realm were lush with tall grass that stretched to the horizon. The sloping lands were littered with jagged formations of rock that revealed streaks of brightly colored tiger lily and other minerals. The trees were heavyset and did not grow in clusters or groups. Instead, they grew separate from each other, like lone sentries among the grass and rock. The roots of the trees were as wide as their trunk. They started above the ground and reached out like tentacles from some great sea beast. The roots spread out and slowly descended into the ground. Their branches were thick and still full with brown and red leaves, which had only recently begun to fall to the grass or be pulled in the breeze. Luras and Matthias walked through the foothills. Their hoods were up due to the light mist in the air.

"I can smell the ocean," said Luras.

"Yes. It is still far off, but the open land lets the wind carry it through the hills," replied Matthias.

"This land is beautiful. I have never been this far

north. These trees look as if they could stand and walk."

"They can ... and they only eat Bourne, so they're quite hungry."

"What an end that would be," laughed Luras. "Make the journey north, fighting wolves and such ... only to be swallowed up by a tree."

"Don't worry. I would tell no one. I'd never admit it," laughed Matthias.

"Why are they this way?"

"The trees? I don't know. I heard that they were uprooted from another land and planted here by Granduers thousands of years ago. They left some of the roots exposed so they could make beds on them and sleep among the trees. It's just a story though. I think this is just the way the trees are."

"You were from the north ... at one time?"

"That was a long time ago."

"I would find this land worth fighting for."

"Yes, but you end up fighting for a person and not the land. You will find the Northern Realm to be inhospitable. This is why it hasn't fallen to these invaders. It is as violent as it is beautiful. And its beauty is never ending."

"What part of this realm did you live in?" asked Luras.

"I was mostly gone ... traveling across this realm and the others. Fighting. My home, though, was at the sea's edge. My wife and son lived there."

"I would like to see the ocean," said Luras.

"You also wanted to have an ale, but only had a sip. Do you now plan on looking at the sea with only one eye?"

"What happened to your family?"

"They're gone. Dead."

"What happened to them?"

"Some other time, Luras. Not today."

# A DARK TYRANNY

Luras and Matthias continued to travel the foothills. They did not stop to eat until the early evening. The light was soft in the hills; the mist mixed with a slow breeze. Tall grass revealed the wind as it swayed. They made camp by one of the trees. Its roots twisted around the camp blocking their fire from the breeze. Matthias roasted a plump field hare over the flames.

"I wonder of Wreth and the others," said Luras.

"You have to assume that they're safe," said Matthais.

"That is my hope."

"You shouldn't think of it any other way. Otherwise, it will ... do you hear that?"

Matthias reached for his sword.

"Horses," replied Luras.

They stood. Eight armed riders were in the distance. They rode towards the camp. One of the riders carried a standard with a banner of blue and white with the image of a red sword in the center. They wore plated armor over their legs and chest with leather greaves bearing steel ringlets. Their boots were coarse leather for riding, but had a plate of iron along the front for combat. Matthias pulled his hood down tightly over his brow.

"Should I put out the fire?" asked Luras.

"They have seen us. Leave it be."

Luras felt the leather straps holding his sheathed sabers.

"Remove your hood. Let them stare at you," said Matthias.

"Will they recognize you?"

"We will see."

The riders slowed as they approached the camp. They left a trampled line of grass in their wake. All but two of the riders wore helmets of leather with iron bands in the front and along the jaw. One wore no helmet at all. He was in his mid-twenties with dark hair and dull green eyes. His skin was pale, but his armor was very clean and bright. He rode upright and proper in the saddle. The other man alongside him did not wear a helmet like the others. His was of full plate. It was faded iron with silver outlying. It was not clean. There were scratches and dents in it from battle. The helmet covered his head and nose, but it did not cover his eyes or mouth. The riders stopped at the camp. They remained mounted. Their horses breathed heavily. Two of the soldiers held crossbows aimed at Luras and Matthias. The young man with no helmet was in front of the others.

"God and kings, look at that one there," said one of the soldiers.

"What business do you have in the north?" asked the young man.

"We are Acolytes. We are traveling north to meet up with more," replied Luras.

"King Tellos has declared the Northern Realm closed to travelers," said the young man.

"We did not know this. We are simply meeting with others of our kind," replied Luras.

"There are no more of your kind," snickered one of the soldiers.

"Enough," said the man with the helmet of full plate.

"Yes sir, Captain Eaves," replied the soldier.

"You will have to excuse these men. Some have seen very little battle, while one has seen too much," said the young man.

"And what of you?" asked Luras.

"The king requires noble blood to lead these men. Otherwise, they are lost to their own devices. I am Gerald Lancing, the first son of the Baron Martin Lancing. It is of no consequence to you, though. You and your friend here are not of the north, so you will be departing now," said Gerald.

"There are other Acolytes converging together in the lower hills south of here. King Tellos' declaration stands. However, they are meeting there for now with plans to travel. I suggest you meet up with your kind there ... and then leave the north," said Captain Eaves.

"That will be all, captain," said Gerald.

"How many of them are there?" Luras asked the captain.

"It appeared to be 200 – 300 hundred men the last time I checked," answered Captain Eaves.

Luras immediately desired to group with the other Acolytes.

"What have you been fighting here? What has happened to seal off an entire realm?" asked Luras.

"Wolves, Skin Merchants - our scouting parties have seen other things," answered Captain Eaves.

"I am in charge here. They will leave now ... not later," Gerald interjected, angrily. His voice was whiny and high.

"Acolytes were chosen by the Creator. Why would your king or anyone else keep them from gathering?" said Luras.

"Captain Eaves, next time you go to the south hills please look for this Creator. You see, I have seen these Acolytes you speak of ... though I have yet to see some grand Creator. I only see men full of delusion," retorted Gerald.

"What of our eyes? What of me? Have you seen a Bourne before?" asked Luras.

"I have no doubt that there is savagery and oddity to the world. You keep speaking of *we* and *us*, but I've yet to hear your companion say one word," said Gerald.

"We will leave," said Matthias.

Matthias looked at Luras. They began to gather their belongings.

"What are your names?" asked Gerald.

"We are leaving," replied Matthias.

"This I know, but you will also surrender your names," said Gerald. His voice was again high pitched.

"Remove your hood," Gerald ordered Matthias.

"I am Luras."

"Very well. I've heard enough from you. You there, remove your hood at once," ordered Gerald.

Matthias looked over the eight men. He observed their armor, weapons, and faces. He knew that two of the soldiers had seen battle, along with Captain Eaves. The remaining would be momentarily lost in a fight. They could die last. He would focus on those with experience.

*Captain Eaves first, then the soldiers. The boy has never seen battle. He will run. Strike his horse then the Captain.*

"Soldier, shoot this man if he does not remove his hood at once!" exclaimed Gerald.

"Do nothing without my lead," Matthias said to Luras.

"Clear your hands from your weapons," ordered Captain Eaves.

"I have no battle with you," said Matthias to Captain Eaves.

Matthias removed his hood. He felt the breeze through his straw colored hair and beard.

"God and kings, look at that," said one of the soldiers.

"What?" asked Gerald.

"Is that the commander?" asked a soldier.

"Commander? What commander? Who is this man?" demanded Gerald.

"Matthias Thorne?" asked Captain Eaves.

"He is an Acolyte now. Whatever he has done no longer matters," said Luras.

"This is Matthias Thorne? The great traitor of the north," said Gerald.

## A DARK TYRANNY

Luras touched the hilt of a saber with one hand.

"Easy, Luras," said Matthias.

"There is an edict for you across the four realms. Yet, here I find you ... right in our own foothills. My luck only grows by the day. Kill this man. Take his head," ordered Gerald.

Luras drew both sabers from their sheaths. Matthias could see him reviewing the men. He was picking his targets and their weak spots. Matthias felt the hilt of his greatsword.

"There is no reason to kill this man here and now. He should be brought before the king," warned Captain Eaves.

"Shoot him," ordered Gerald.

"Do you know nothing about a Bourne?" asked Matthias. "You shoot me and he will kill you all. They have a thirst for blood, the Bournes. He may not look it, but he would delight in your death. I have seen him fight. He took down a team of Storm Wolves just days ago."

"A *pack*. It is a *pack* of wolves. I'm tired of all this talk," said Gerald.

"No. A pack is a small family of wolves. This was an army of wolves ... a team of wolves. He cut them down and would easily do the same to you," said Matthias.

"Can your magical friend here dodge a bolt from a crossbow? I would truly delight in seeing that," said Gerald.

"Why can you not just let us join with the others?" asked Luras.

"Do not fire upon either of them," ordered the Captain.

"You will do so," ordered Gerald.

"We will not. Take the commander into custody. We will bring him before the king," ordered Captain Eaves.

"The king will hear of this. I will make it my business to have two men lose their heads instead of one," whined Gerald.

"Do what you must," replied Captain Eaves.

Two soldiers dismounted and approached Matthias.

"Go to the others, Luras. They are not a day's march away. I have business here," said Matthias.

"I cannot leave you here to die."

"We have no quarrel with you," said Captain Eaves. "The other Acolytes are just south of here. You should listen to your friend."

Matthias dropped his sword. The soldiers tied his arms behind his back. He sat down with his back against the large tree.

"Go Luras. Leave here and meet the others. It was never really my place to go on," said Matthias.

"What is it this man has done?" asked Luras.

"He raised arms against the king," replied Captain Eaves.

"Come now, it's more than that, Captain Eaves. Your ever so pure of heart companion here deserted his post during a time of battle. Men lost their lives in the chaos ... *innocent men* ... enlisted soldiers left without a leader or orders to follow. Please, tell me if I'm wrong. We've all heard this tale, have we not?" scoffed Gerald.

"That is a lie. I left Conlin in command," replied Matthias.

"Well, I suppose this Conlin is dead, so the king will just have to take your word for it. Of course, you used this time to track down and murder a squadron of the king's men," said Gerald.

"They killed my family," replied Matthias.

"The king ordered it. You killed men following orders. You, of all people, should know of following such ... *harsh* orders," Gerald sneered.

"They killed my family," said Matthias, almost to himself.

"Why?" asked Luras.

"A truce was made along the border of the Northern

## A DARK TYRANNY

and Eastern Realms. Part of the conditions of peace was to surrender Commander Thorne - and his line - for actions committed against the people of the eastern and surrounding realms," said Captain Eaves.

"Surrender his line?" said Luras, incredulously.

"His lineage," replied Gerald.

"Who gives out such orders and demands?" asked Luras.

"Don't act so shocked. Your companion here has carried out much worse orders," muttered Gerald.

"Any orders I carried out were in the king's name. His hands are no less bloody. I don't have to defend myself to a wicked king or some boy leader, whose only achievement is his spewing forth from the loins of a duke's spoiled wife or whore," spat Matthias.

"Well, this duke's son will still have his head in one week's time," retorted Gerald.

"Go Luras," whispered Matthias.

"No. They've no claim to you," said Luras.

"Fine, take him - just leave his head," laughed Gerald.

Luras felt the hilt of his sabers. He could feel a deep seated anger welling up inside him. Gerald continued to laugh, but the others stared at Luras. There was palpable tension that all could feel except for one.

"Calm down, Luras. You will kill mostly innocent men that are following orders," Matthias spoke softly to Luras.

"Sir, a rider," said one of the soldiers.

A lone rider galloped towards the camp. He wore a thick green cloak and leather pants and tunic. The tips of his leather boots and stirrups were stained green from the grass. The setting sun dripped a soft orange glow behind him, as it began to sink below the horizon.

"Keep your crossbows on these men," ordered Gerald.

"It looks like Helms," said another soldier.

"A scout," said Captain Eaves.

"I deducted as much. Thank you for stating the obvious," replied Gerald. "It seems this day grows more interesting by the moment."

Helms was in his mid-fifties. He was covered in dirt and dust. His hair had thinned to where only a few strains of brownish gray hair remained. His teeth were yellow and overlapped in the front. He pulled tightly on the reins causing his horse to dig its hooves into the ground.

"Captain!" exclaimed Helms.

"Calm yourself, Helms. What is it?" asked Captain Eaves.

"Address me. I am in charge here," stated Gerald.

"Yes ... yes, sir," replied Helms.

Helms looked at both Gerald and Captain Eaves. He looked at neither too long, as to not provoke anyone.

"Bandits. They're just west of here. They have captives," said Helms.

"How many?" asked Captain Eaves.

"Fifteen to twenty. I can't be sure," replied Helms.

"Twenty bandits?" asked Gerald.

"No, sir. Twenty captives. There looks to be ten or so bandits. There could be more, but that's all I seen," said Helms.

"Good work," said Captain Eaves.

"Yes. Thank you for bringing us partial information," scoffed Gerald.

"They have buckled down like they plan to meet someone," said Helms.

"Skin Merchants, probably. Selling them for their skins," said one of the soldiers.

"God and kings. Sir, some of 'em were children," said Helms.

"Well then, nine soldiers against ten vagrants. It seems I will bring the king the commander here and a lot of freed countrymen. My day only improves," said

## A DARK TYRANNY

Gerald.

"We will wait until dark. We only have eight soldiers. We will all move west towards their camp, but only eight will fight. One has to watch the commander. If it comes to battle, I would not rely on them being mere vagrants," said Captain Eaves.

Captain Eaves removed his helmet. Matthias was surprised that Captain Eaves seemed to be in his early thirties. He had a chiseled face and closely cropped black hair. His eyes were a pale blue. Captain Eaves wiped his brow with his gloved hand. He looked around him and at the setting sun. Matthias had seen that look before. It was the look of a man leading others to battle when he knew they were not ready.

*He has three men that have seen battle. The others will die or run.*

"Luras, you should help them," said Matthias.

"We need no help from him," said Gerald.

"Eaves, right? You and I both know that only three of your men have ever seen battle. The rest are just Royal Soldiers. They're not fighters. The boy will run and the others will stay and fight ... but they will die," said Matthias.

"I am not fighting with these men," said Luras.

"He is right. We could use someone that has seen battle," said Captain Eaves.

"Release him and I will help," instructed Luras.

"Never. I'd sooner let them skin all twenty than release this man," said Gerald.

"If you open your mouth to me again, come one week's time - your head would have long been buried," said Luras.

"We need your help. If not for us, for the captives. I understand your disdain. I would feel the same. There are children there. At the hands of a skin-slaver is no way to die," said Captain Eaves.

"I have seen what's left in their wake," replied Luras.

"Then you know this is the right thing to do," replied Captain Eaves.

## Chapter 25

### The Gorgon Caravan

The caravan had stopped for the night. The prisoners sat on the ground in the center of camp. A rope circled them. They knew that anyone moving beyond the roped area would be shown no mercy. More gorgons and two wagons had joined the caravan in the recent days. The wagons were pulled by three oxen a piece and were much taller than the others ones. They looked to be more like moving cabins. Each one had heavily varnished walls on the sides and a wooden ceiling on top. There was a metal latch on the outside of the back door that clanked when the wagons moved. The captives had not seen any prisoners being taken from them, so they assumed they were a type of living quarters.

Nylah sat with the other captives. She and Tilda leaned against one another, while Douglas sat behind them. The grass was damp and felt good against Nylah's skin. The valley they were in had very little breeze, but the night was still quite cool. Nylah was hungry and thirsty, as was everyone else. The gruel they were given was barely enough to sustain them. She moved her hands along the top of the grass and then rubbed what water she had collected against her face. It felt cool against her dry skin and lips.

"The nights are growing cooler, Tilda. I'm so tired, but I cannot sleep. I wish I could lay here and sleep for days. Fall asleep and when I wake no one is here but me. I should never have gone to Castle Red. I would have run if I knew this awaited me. I would have run somewhere far from here. This whole thing is like some cruel dream. Are you already asleep, Tilda?" whispered Nylah.

Nylah looked at Tilda. She rubbed the old woman's hair and face lightly.

"Tilda?"

Tilda leaned against Nylah. She stared lifelessly at the ground.

"No ... Tilda, please," whispered Nylah. "Please no."

Nylah gently laid Tilda on the ground. Her skin had grown pale. The life behind her eyes had diminished. Nylah closed Tilda's eyes with a damp hand. She straightened the woman's hair and tucked it behind her ears. Nylah rubbed her hands along the grass to gather more water. She cleaned Tilda's face as much as she could.

"Dead?" asked Douglas.

"Yes," answered Nylah. "I don't have any more tears. I can't seem to cry. Am I cruel?" asked Nylah.

"No. It's not cruel at all. We are marching to an awaiting death. You cannot care for us all," answered Douglas.

"I will not die," replied Nylah.

She felt a disdain at the resignation. She was tired and hungry. She was sick of the others' apathy.

"I will leave this place. I have to," whispered Nylah.

"I am sorry. Your friend, he will not return. He is not

coming back. He is gone. Dead," said Douglas.

"I cannot believe that Finn is dead. I refuse to," said Nylah.

"He is. He is as dead as Tilda. I'm sorry, but it is true. You need to understand the situation you find yourself in," said Douglas.

"I refuse to believe it. I understand my situation, Douglas, however, I refuse to accept it. If you feel you are walking to your death, why wait? Die now," said Nylah.

"What?" asked Douglas, incredulously.

"Kill yourself. Why walk the distance. You are dead man, are you not?" asked Nylah.

"I don't want to die. I just understand what is afoot," said Douglas.

"I don't want to die, either. I do not accept what is afoot," said Nylah.

The group of captives began to move inward, as a gorgon approached them. He did not wear a leather tunic like the other soldiers. Instead, he donned a wool shirt and pants that had been dyed a very faded brown and black. His tail was uncoiled and dragged behind him. He was flanked by four gorgon guards with spears. His black eyes looked over the prisoners. He began to speak in the guttural language of the gorgon tongue. He pointed at some captives, while speaking to the guards. They immediately grabbed those captives and pulled them from the group. Nylah stared at the ground. Her heart raced.

*If I do not see them, I won't be noticed. If I do not see them, I will not be noticed.*

Nylah heard the screams of other captives, as they were ripped from the group. She closed her eyes. Other captives bumped and slammed into her while being taken. Nylah kept her eyes closed and her head down.

*Do not look up. This will be over soon.*

Nylah felt a dry, scaly hand lock onto her arm with a

fierce grip. She was pulled to her feet.

"No!" yelled Nylah.

One of the gorgon soldiers lifted Nylah off the ground like a doll. She saw the grass passing below her. It seemed to move backwards as the gorgons approached the wagon. She caught glimpses of other captives and the group behind her. She had trouble focusing. Everything seemed to be happened in separate moments. The grass, the captives, the feet of the gorgon, the screaming, it all happened both at once and separately. She felt nauseous and dizzy.

*What are they going to do with me? The others?*

The thick door to the one of the wagons opened with a grinding thud. The gorgon soldier hoisted her inside the wagon. A few captives were already inside, while others were put in behind her. The door to the wagon shut tightly behind them. The sharp sound of a metal latch echoed throughout the wagon. A lantern hung from the ceiling giving the room a dim light. There were five other captives in the wagon with her. Two twin girls, a man of middle-age, and what appeared to be two brothers in their early twenties that both wore tattered soldier uniforms.

"They didn't kill us," said the older man.

"Are they taking us somewhere?" asked one of the twins.

"I don't think so. These wagons are part of the caravan now," said the older man.

"Look at this food!" said one of the brothers.

There was a table in the center of the room with two benches on either side. It was built into the floor and bolted to the wagon. The table was filled with food. There were two roasted hares and a pheasant at the center of the table. They were surrounded by bread, potatoes, two baskets of fruit, and jug of spiced cider. Around the table were piles of pillows with silk cases and satin sheets. The two brothers ran to the table and began to fill their mouths with strips of meat and bread. The twins looked at Nylah and the older man. They were confused and scared.

"Are they planning to eat us? Fattening us like a hog?" asked one of the twins.

"No ... no. If they planned to harvest us for food, they would have done things much differently," said the middle-aged man.

"Then, what?" asked Nylah. "We have been starving for days and now this? Why?"

"Regardless of why - we should eat. You should eat," said the older man.

"Why us?" asked Nylah.

"I don't know. Maybe they see something special in you. I do not mean that in a good manner," said the older man.

"They mean to kill us?" asked one of the twins.

"They mean to kill us all - in here or out there. You need to come to terms with that," said the older man.

"Why feed us, then?" asked Nylah.

The middle-aged man sat down at the table. He poured a glass of spiced cider for Nylah and the twins.

"I don't know. I fear we are growing closer to our destination. If I had to wager a guess, it would be to raise our spirits. Strengthen them," said the man.

"Raise our spirits?" questioned one of the twins.

"Before they take them," whispered Nylah.

"Take them?" grunted one of the brothers with a mouthful of food.

"The White Ruins," whispered Nylah.

## Chapter 26

## A Midnight Meeting

The night had set in. The clouds were scarce, so the moon was free to reflect down along the rolling hills of the Northern Realm. The night was cool with only a slight breeze that dampened the grass and trees. Four armed men sat around a campfire. Two other men leaned against a tree, whose exposed roots twisted and forked into the ground. They stood watch over a group of captives. Each prisoner had their hands tied behind their back with thick twine. There were other men that walked through the camp on their way to various sentry posts. Some of the men wore various types of armor and clothes. However, most of them wore plain clothes that were close to being considered rags. A small area had been roped off so the men could corral their horses. The animals huddled closely together eating the damp grass.

"Helms was right. They have nearly twenty captives. I count nine so far but we have to assume they have sentries posted around the camp," said Captain Eaves.

Luras, Captain Eaves, and another soldier stood a

distance from the camp. They hid among the roots of a tree. Gerald and the other soldiers were on the eastern side of the camp to flank them.

"Do your best to keep your eyes clear of the camp. I do not think Acolytes were made for stealth," said Captain Eaves.

"Is this common? Men like this setting up a camp so freely?" asked Luras.

"They would not have been so brazen in the past. Times are no longer what they were," answered Captain Eaves.

"Beg your pardon, Captain. We should move before their guests arrive," said the soldier.

"He's right," replied Luras.

"Go tell the others that Luras and I -"

"This is Gerald Lancing, son of the Baron Martin Lancing, and lieutenant of the King's Royal Soldiers," exclaimed Gerald.

"Damn him!" said Captain Eaves.

"You are surrounded by two fully armed squadrons of soldiers. Lay down your arms and you will be spared," yelled Gerald.

"They won't ever surrender, Captain. They'd be hung by the king and they know it," said the soldier to Captain Eaves and Luras.

"Stupid boy," muttered Captain Eaves.

"We need to act," said Luras.

"You go tell the others to flank from the east. Luras and I will remove the sentries here, drawing their attention. Go tell the others. Don't listen to Gerald. Leave him if you must. He will get us all killed," ordered Captain Eaves.

"Yes, sir," said the soldier.

The soldier disappeared into the night, as he ran towards the other men.

"Are you ready?" asked Luras.

"Last warning!" yelled Gerald. His voice was

beginning to rise and crack.

One of the men by the fire withdrew a dagger. It had a handle made from an elk antler. He walked towards the captives. His red hair was short and matted. Three of his teeth were cracked into jagged pieces. His throat was heavily scarred with a thick white line from ear to ear. The man's voice was a scratching rasp. As he spoke, it sounded like air was escaping from his throat. He struggled to form words.

"I think you're alone," said the man.

He grabbed a woman from the group of captives. She reached out for another woman sitting among the prisoners, but it was of no use. The man jerked the woman to her feet. She screamed as he put his knife to her throat. He pulled her hair back forcing her chin to rise. She began to sob.

"Show yourselves or I will kill each one – one right after the next," said the man with a rasp.

He pulled the blade across the woman's throat. Blood welled up and cascaded down her neck and covered her dress. The man shoved her forward. She grabbed at her open neck, as she fell to the ground. The other captives yelled out in terror.

"Cowards! You still hide in the shadows! You are alone!" yelled the man. He walked to select another prisoner.

One of the sentries stood watch just outside the safety of the camp. He wore a leather cowl that was separating at the seams and carried a bow that had begun to crack. He stood silently listening to the night. He stared blankly into the darkness. The sentry cocked his head to one side.

"Randall?" he asked into the night.

"He nervously notched an arrow and shot it into the darkness. He immediately notched another.

"Here!" yelled the sentry.

Suddenly, he saw two blue orbs pierce the darkness.

# A DARK TYRANNY

He yelled out. His arrow flew from his bow hitting the ground and breaking. The sentry felt two searing pains in his chest. He lifted slightly off the ground and then slid sideways off Luras' blades. Captain Eaves ran to them grabbing the sentry's bow from his hands. He notched an arrow.

The man with the scars put his dagger to the neck of another captive. This time it was a boy with light brown hair and soft brown eyes. He squirmed under the man's grip. The blade began to sink into the boy's skin. A large drop of blood rolled down his neck. An arrow hissed through the air. The boy cried out as the arrow nicked the top of his shoulder and sank into the man's chest. The boy fell. He grabbed the dagger from the ground and ran to the others. The boy cut at the ropes of the other captives as quickly as he could. The scarred man scrambled to his feet. The arrow jutted out from his chest. Dark red blood seeped from around the wound. His chest was swollen. He saw the boy cutting the ropes. He started to move towards him, but another arrow punched into his chest. He fell to one knee. He coughed and struggled to breathe through his mouth. He felt the shafts of the arrows sticking from his chest. The man fell over to one side and died.

Luras walked out of the shadows and into the light of the camp. Two of the men at the campfire charged at him. They both carried swords. Two other sentries left their posts and headed towards Luras. They hacked at Luras like wild savages. He parried their blows with ease. He leaned in and cleaved the man with both sabers taking off his arm and opening his chest. Luras bent down letting another man's sword swing above his head. Luras twisted and slashed him below the knee causing him to fall. He sank his other saber into the man's chest. The two sentries running towards Luras slowed to a stop, as they looked at Luras and the dead men below him. Captain Eaves appeared behind him with a sword in one hand and a short sword in the other.

"Surrender your weapons. All of you! Surrender your weapons and be spared," exclaimed Captain Eaves.

The other seven men dropped their weapons to the ground and walked to the center of the camp site. The captives continued to free each other. They did not run but stayed together in a group. One of the female captives cried over the body of the dead woman. Luras and Captain Eaves stood in front of the men with their weapons in hand. Gerald and the other soldiers slowly made their way out of the shadows. Matthias was with them. His hands were tied tightly behind his back. Gerald now had Matthias' greatsword strapped to his back.

"Who is in charge here? Was it him?" asked Captain Eaves, as he pointed to the body of the dead man with the scarred face.

"Orly was never in charge. He was always a little high strung for that," said one of the men close to the fire.

The man was of indeterminate age. He appeared to be no more than thirty years old, but he carried himself with a pretense of age and superiority. His hair was black as coal and thinning on top. Part of his right ear was missing. It was not a clean cut. The jagged bits of remaining cartilage had since scarred over with smooth skin. His eyes were tired and brown. The man was more outfitted than the others. He wore a very thin leather tunic and pants that were deeply oiled. His boots were the same as the soldiers, leather with a steel plant down the front.

"What's your name?" asked Captain Eaves.

"I'm just one of many homeless men rummaging through these hills for survival. I am actually more interested in this man's name," the man said, looking at

# A DARK TYRANNY

Luras. "But then, you are no man at all, are you?"

Luras said nothing. The men and the freed captives gawked at the Bourne Acolyte that stood before them.

"Your name?" demanded Captain Eaves.

"Call me Karl if you must," answered the man.

"Excellent work," exclaimed Gerald, as he approached. "I see you came to your senses."

Captain Eaves turned to Gerald. He was flush with anger. Just as Gerald began to speak, Captain Eaves slapped him with the open palm of his gloved hand. Gerald fell hard to the ground. He was shocked and wild-eyed, as he put a hand to his face. Blood pooled from his lip causing his teeth to be outlined in red.

"That woman's death is on your hands. You are just as responsible," said Captain Eaves.

"Ah, I recognize that voice," laughed Karl. "But I thought he had two squadrons of bloodthirsty warriors."

There was a slight laugh among the men.

"You are all dead men! All of you bastards will hang!" exclaimed Gerald, in a high pitched voice.

Gerald stood up and looked at Captain Eaves.

"You are done. You'd do yourself well to stand with them. Your fate and theirs are one in the same," hissed Gerald to Captain Eaves.

"We will see," replied Captain Eaves.

"He's right. You should kill him and come join us. It's certainly more profitable," said Karl, in a mocking yet serious tone. "Especially that one there."

Karl pointed at one of the prisoners. His hands were still tied.

"God and kings, I ain't never seen a man so white," said one of the soldiers.

"We found him in the forest south of here. Wandering around naked as the first breath of morning. His pale reed blowing and shaking in the wind," said Karl.

"Bring that man to me at once," ordered Gerald.

"Well then, at least one of you knows who he is," laughed Karl. "He is certainly worth a copper or two."

"Shut your mouth," ordered Gerald.

"Who are you?" Captain Eaves asked the man.

The man said nothing. He had a tattered blanket wrapped around his shoulders and body. His hair was almost white and hung just below his chin. The man's eyes were a pale red. There was a long wound across his arm. Blood had dried over a cut above his stomach. Both wounds were healing faster than they should. The man did not speak, nor did he look at Captain Eaves. He seemed distant in his thoughts.

"You have before you the bedeviled brother of the Seat of the Eastern Realm. The brother of the traitor king," said Karl. "A good price he will bring me."

"Come here," Luras said to the pale man. The others stared. It was the first time the Bourne had spoken.

The pale man stood and walked towards Luras. He did not seem scared. Instead, there was a resignation about him. He approached Luras and looked him in the eye.

"I am not a devil," the man said quietly, almost to himself.

"What is your name?" asked Luras, as he cut the ties from the man's hands.

"Ellison."

"I know you're not a devil," replied Luras. "No more than I."

"He is to come with me. The king will decide his fate," ordered Gerald.

"Remove your clothes," Luras ordered Karl.

"This man is worth gold," Karl said to Captain Eaves.

"I would sooner hang than sell my own people," Captain Eaves said with disgust. "I suggest you do what the Bourne says."

"He is not your people," replied Karl. He slowly began to remove his tunic.

"You can have his clothes and what supplies you need. No one will hold you here," Luras said to Ellison.

"Don't look like you can trust those slavers none, either," said one of the soldiers.

"Oh ... yes," said Karl, as he felt the remains of his ear. "My ear is now a slave in the afterlife. No, it's much less sinister. You would be amazed at what a starving child would do for food. Stealing from a dog is not different than stealing from a king, and both will scar you eventually."

Karl continued to slowly remove his clothes.

"Take care of these. I will want them back," Karl said, grinning at Ellison.

"You need to take these people to safety," said Matthias.

"Shut up. You are no more free than they are," replied Gerald.

Matthias ignored Gerald and looked directly at Luras and Captain Eaves.

"He is taking his time. He is waiting for the others. You have a group of men destined to hang from a rope, and yet they laugh at his jokes," said Matthias. "You need to take them and leave at once."

"Get them out of here," said Luras.

"Everyone gather. Stay together and keep up. We are leaving at once," said Captain Eaves.

Ellison began to feel a warmth grow over his body. His heart beat rapidly in his chest. He could smell the hot musty scent of decay and blood. The ground trembled slightly beneath his feet. He could hear the sounds of metal brushing against leather, the rhythmic breathing of beasts running and pounding against the earth. Ellison turned to look at the group of men around him. He heard the grass and dirt shuffle under their feet.

*Does no one else feel this? I can smell them. Hear them. What is this? What is happening?*

"It's too late," Ellison said.

"What do you mean?" asked Captain Eaves.

"They are already here," replied Ellison.

"I don't see anything," said one of the soldiers.

"Hurry. I would rather not stay and find out," said Matthias.

"Get the women and children on horses," said Luras.

"Everyone else go. Run. Do not wait for us," Matthias said to the other freed captives.

"Go get the horses," ordered Captain Eaves to the soldiers. "We will try to hold whatever is approaching long enough for you to have a chance at getting back."

Two of the soldiers began taking horses from the roped off area. They helped the women and children atop of them. There were more of them than there were horses. The soldiers began putting up to three riders on a horse.

"Don't wait for the others. Go as soon as you're on," ordered one of the soldiers.

"They are coming from over there," said Ellison. He pointed south into the darkness.

"Hurry," said Captain Eaves, as he began helping the soldiers.

There was only one horse remaining. The women and children were gone. The soldiers were helping an elderly man in rags atop the last horse. His hair was thinning and he was so thin that his skin appeared translucent.

"Wait. Stop," ordered Gerald.

Gerald approached the horse. It pawed at the ground in anticipation. He pulled the old man by the arm. The soldiers reacted to keep the man from falling to the ground. They held him up and looked at Gerald with confusion. Gerald pulled himself atop the horse and looked down at the men.

# A DARK TYRANNY

"Bring the commander and the other one to the king. That is an order. If you do not have them, I wouldn't bother returning," ordered Gerald.

The soldiers did not know how to react. They looked at Captain Eaves.

"Let him go," ordered Captain Eaves.

Gerald kicked the horse. Matthias' greatsword bounced on Gerald's back like a child playing with his father's things. The horse jumped forward like a bolt of lightning and galloped into the night.

"He would have left us regardless. At least this way, he did not get any of us killed in the process," said Captain Eaves.

Howls were heard to the south. The sounds of beasts running and snarling echoed in the darkness. The soldiers looked around the camp with their weapons in hand. They could hear the wolves circling them. The darkness was filled with frantic breathing and growling. The soldiers were unnerved by the howling. It was deafening.

"Stay together," said Captain Eaves.

"Cut me loose," said Matthias.

"They let the others go. They are heading back to the castle. There's another here though," Karl yelled into the night. However, his words were cut short. Luras' blades sank into the man's chest. He coughed and fell to the ground looking incredulously at Luras. Blood began to pool around him.

One of the soldiers approached Matthias. The soldier lowered his crossbow and began to fumble with the knotted twine. He kept looking back out into the night with each howl or snarl. The soldier cursed while pulling at the knots.

"Calm yourself. What are you doing? Cut it," said Matthias. The man reached to his waist for his sword.

"There!" yelled Captain Eaves.

Suddenly, two wolves charged out of the darkness.

One of the wolves leapt at a soldier that was fumbling with his crossbow. It bit down hard on the man's neck and jawline. Bone cracked, as the soldier screamed and pushed at the beast. Its teeth tore through bone and flesh with ease. The man's screams became muffled and then nothing. The beast stood on two legs and snarled at the men with a frantic savagery. It reached out for Luras with its black claws. It swung trying to rake its claws across his chest. Luras pivoted backwards causing the wolf to lean forward. Luras brought one saber down cleaving the beast's arm off. It yelled out in terror and jumped towards Luras in a frenzy. Luras had already begun to follow with his other saber. It sank deeply into the beast's leg. He twisted the blade free severing muscle and bone. The creature fell to one side. Captain Eaves struck the beast through the chest. It dropped to the ground in a lifeless heap.

The second wolf locked eyes with the soldier trying to free Matthias. It ripped at the ground with its legs, as it ran towards them. The soldier stopped trying to free Matthias and grabbed his crossbow in a panic. His breathing was loud and sounded like staccato screams. The wolf was at him before he could release the bolt. It hit him like a bull knocking him to the ground. The soldier was dazed. Everything spun around him and his stomach turned. He felt a stinging pain. A crossbow bolt jutted out from his leg. The soldier screamed reaching for his sword. The wolf sank its claws into his leg and pulled him past Matthias and towards the darkness surrounding the camp. The man scrambled and screamed. He grabbed at the grass but it tore away in his hands. The men could hear him screaming in the night, as the wolf snarled and tore at his flesh. It howled loudly in the shadows.

"Cut me free!" yelled Matthias. Captain Eaves cut Matthias' binds. Matthias quickly grabbed a sword from the dead soldier. He took another sword from the weapons surrendered by the bandits.

Ellison felt his skin growing hot. His head began to throb with pain, but he grew a clarity to his senses.

*I can hear them.*

"Skin Slavers. They're coming," Ellison said.

Ellison's body ached. His muscles felt sore and burned with fatigue. He fell to one knee holding his stomach.

*They're coming. Men and wolves.*

"Are you hurt?" asked Luras.

"I don't know," replied Ellison. "Keep them away from me. They have wolves with them. Keep them away."

"I don't see anyone," said Captain Eaves.

"These men are with them," Matthias said, motioning to the captured bandits.

Captain Eaves walked towards the bandits with his swords in hand.

"No!" yelled one of the outlaws.

"Wait!" yelled Luras.

The outlaws stood to run but they had nowhere to go. Captain Eaves struck them down quickly. He made sure each was dead. Luras looked at the dead bandits. He saw the look of shock and terror on their faces. Their bodies were contorted and spilling over each other. Luras stared at Captain Eaves with disbelief. He looked at all the men around him, Matthias, Captain Eaves, and three soldiers standing over the corpses of the men. One wolf laid dead beside them.

"They made their choice when they took those captives. The king would have killed them ... or the slavers would have taken them too. They would have drawn against us the moment they charged in here," Captain Eaves said to Luras.

"He is right, Luras," whispered Matthias. "We are already out manned."

Two more wolves emerged from the darkness. This

time they did not run towards the men. They were also not alone.

"Skin Slavers," said one of the soldiers.

"Don't give them time to plan. Any chance of survival we have is to keep them off balance," warned Matthias.

Three Skin Slavers left the shadows and began to approach the men. One of the wolves flanked them on each side. The slavers were armed with swords that were sheathed in cured skin that had been heavily oiled. Two of the slavers wore leather cuirasses that were adorned with flayed skin from their victims' hands. The skin had been dyed black, brown, and a faded purple. The slaver in the middle carried a long staff with a scalp stretched over the top. Long black matted hair draped down the staff. His teeth had been filed to points, which caused the pulp and roots to be exposed on some of his teeth. His gums and teeth had begun to rot in places. Some teeth hung from gums in thin strands. He wore a tunic woven from the chests of other men. The slavers had a putrid odor of decay that followed them. They looked at Luras with astonishment and a sick desire. The slavers spoke to one another in a garbled speech. One of the slavers motioned towards Ellison, while he spoke to the others. Luras walked towards the slavers.

The slaver with the staff looked at Luras. He spoke to the others in a garbled tone, while he turned his head like a confused dog. The slaver started to speak in the language of the realms. It was sloppy and distorted, but the words were audible. The slaver grinned and laughed, as he spoke to Luras and the others. He looked at them as if they were already dead. He did not see them; he only saw their skin.

"There is nowhere to run," the slaver said with a grin. He motioned to the darkness around the camp. "We are everywhere. You can ..."

His words were suddenly cut off. Luras sank both his blades into the slaver's neck. He crossed the blades and the slaver's head fell to the ground. The other two slavers reached for their swords, while the two wolves charged towards Matthias and the others. Luras kicked one slaver sending him to his knees. He then pivoted back twisting his sabers and slicing through the other slaver's chest and neck. The slaver grasped at the wound on his chest and fell. The slaver on the ground began to yell out to the others. Screams of rage and anger spilled out of the darkness. Other slavers ran towards the camp.

Ellison rolled on the ground in pain. His insides twisted. He felt sick to his stomach, but it was more than that. He could feel his stomach moving. His bones felt weak, while his skin burned. He gagged as if he was going to vomit, but instead his shoulders dislocated. Then his legs and arms pulled themselves out of joint. He felt his skin moving; it was stretching. Ellison yelled out in pain, but he did not hear his voice. He heard a deep roar within his gut. He saw Captain Eaves look down at him in shock.

"Matthias!" yelled Captain Eaves.

An anger brewed inside of Ellison. He needed help. He was hurting. But the wolves and slavers were trying to overtake them. Ellison thought of the lake and the slaughter of women, children, families - his friends. He thought of his brother. He thought of Malvern and the locked gate. He longed for Malvern's death. Ellison did not know if he was shaking from rage or pain. He was seering with anger. Suddenly, he could see the two wolves that had been with the slavers. They leapt at Matthias and Captain Eaves. One of the wolves hit into Captain Eaves like a galloping horse, knocking him to the ground. The other jumped towards Matthias but it darted back, out of the way of his blade. Ellison saw Luras with both his sabers in hand. He stood looking at the Skin Slavers that were gathering around them. Ellison had been unable to stop his brother, Malvern, the assault on Timball, or the massacre at the lake. Now, these Skin Slavers. Suddenly, Ellison sprung to his feet. He grabbed the wolf that was standing over Captain Eaves. He slammed it into the ground feeling its bones break. The wolf snarled and yelped. Ellison bit down hard on the wolf's neck. He could taste its blood and fur. The wolf cried out. Ellison felt the wolf's throat loosen and fill with blood. The other wolf stood in momentary confusion, as it looked at Ellison. Everyone seemed to stop. Ellison leapt at the other wolf. He dug his claws deeply into the chest of the beast. Ribs and muscle tore as he sank his claws into the wolf. It snarled and bit at Ellison in vain. Its breathing was already labored. Air escaped from its chest. Ellison stood over the wolf and cried out in anger. He heard the sound of another wolf. However, this wolf was himself.

Matthias looked at the enormous white beast that stood before him. It was a Storm Wolf. A creature of enormous size with pale red eyes. Its snow colored fur bristled and swayed in the wind like the grass below them. Its hulking frame slowly raised and lowered with each snarling breath. The wolf's breath heated the air around it. It stood on two legs. Like the others, it was capable of running on two legs or all four. Blood dripped from his mouth spilling onto white fur. Its claws were wet with blood. The wolf arched its muscled back and howled.

"Are you there, friend?" asked Matthias, looking into the eyes of the white Storm Wolf.

Nearly twenty Skin Slavers stood motionless around the perimeter of the camp. They stared at the great white wolf looming before them. They called out to each other in their garbled black speech. There were no more wolves with them. The three Storm Wolves lay

# A DARK TYRANNY

dead in the camp, along with the outlaws and Skin Slavers. Matthias helped Captain Eaves to his feet, all the while keeping Ellison in his sight. Suddenly, Ellison ran towards the shadows. He dug his claws across two slavers and slammed into another. They fell like straw men. He disappeared into the shadows. The slavers yelled to one another. Half of them pursued Ellison into the night. The remaining slavers ran towards Luras and the others. One of the soldiers hit a slaver with a bolt from a crossbow. It landed in his chest sending him backwards. Matthias cleaved one of the Skin Slavers with both blades. Luras darted from a sword and countered taking the arm from one slaver and slicing the leg open of another. Captain Eaves kicked a slaver to the ground, while a soldier shot a crossbow bolt towards another. The same soldier swung wildly with his sword. A slaver dodged his blade and it caught Matthias in his side. Matthias felt the cold sting of the blade cut through part of his hip. His tunic grew wet with blood. He turned to strike out and saw the soldier.

"Are you trying to kill me?!?! Aim away from me!" yelled Matthias.

The soldier looked at Matthias and started to speak but stopped, not knowing how to respond. Instead, he swung at an approaching skin-slaver. Luras caught the slaver as he passed with his blade. Two slavers swung wildly at Matthias. He parried their blows with ease. He sliced through one of their hands. The slaver grabbed his hand and yelled in pain. Matthias struck the slaver through the gut. The other slaver swung again, but missed Matthias. Instead, he turned and ran.

"These are not fighters. They barely know how to use their weapons," said Matthias.

"I believe their strength lies in numbers and the wolves. They split their party," replied Captain Eaves.

Luras twisted and parried two blows with both ease

and grace. He countered by slicing through one slaver's thigh and, as he fell, brought the other blade up across the slaver's neck. Luras swung both sabers at once severing another slavers arm and opening his chest. Luras' skin was a dull translucent red. He seemed oblivious to the men around him. He was aware of only himself and the slavers around him. The remaining two slavers ran back to the darkness. A soldier began to notch another bolt into his crossbow.

"Let them go," said Matthias. "We need to move before the others return."

"That man turned himself into a wolf. I seen it, just as you. He done it right in front of us," said a soldier.

"I don't think it was purposeful," replied Captain Eaves.

"I hope they don't catch him," said the soldier.

"They should hope they don't catch him. They could barely hold a sword to us. We shouldn't be here. Any decent army would have had their way with us," replied Matthias.

"His name was Ellison. Was it not?" asked Luras.

"The brother of the traitor king of the east. They say his brother lied to his people and let them die, while the army retreated to Castle Horos," said Captain Eaves.

"Come north with us," said Matthias.

"You can join with the Acolytes," said Luras.

"There is a problem there. I am not an Acolyte," replied Captain Eaves.

"The king will consider you a traitor," said Matthias.

"I do not plan on returning," said Captain Eaves. "You two may return. I do not think you will be held responsible for any of this."

"I will stay with you," replied a soldier. The other agreed.

"All of you come," said Luras.

"We aren't Acolytes, Luras. It's not our calling to journey north. I'm sure there's a resistance somewhere.

We'll find it. Don't worry yourself with us. You two go north. You can be there by morning if you walk through the night," replied Captain Eaves.

"If you change your mind, you know where to find us," said Matthias.

"I will follow the multitude of blue light," said Captain Eaves.

"Good luck," said Luras.

"What is your name?" asked Matthias.

"Xander. I am Xander Eaves," said Captain Eaves.

"Good luck, Xander," replied Matthias.

"And to you both," said Xander.

## Chapter 27

## The Land of Karth

The air had grown cooler. The dirt slowly gave way to grass covered hills. The sun was at its highest and very few clouds were in the sky. Red and brown leaves swirled and danced in the air, as a light breeze blew across the foothills. The great falcon soared high above the tops of the trees and rocks. Fin and the others made their way over the rolling hills of the Northern Realm. Finn walked beside Borman Thyn. Torin's wounds were bandaged, but he still walked carefully and held one hand over the wound. Gilnor and Dord walked with Torin. They chewed on strips of dried deer meat, while they helped their friend.

"I'm fine. Leave me be," said Torin, grumbling.

"I fear your body isn't," replied Gilnor. "Your stubbornness would keep walking long after your body is dead and stone."

"We should stop for a while. Allow him to rest," Dord said to the others.

The group stopped by a large rock that jutted from

# A DARK TYRANNY

the side of a hill. It was as if half the grass covered hill had been removed leaving a rocky skeleton in its wake. Torin sat down in the grass leaning back against the rock. He looked at his bandages; blood was soaked through and began to drip down his leg. Torin felt the wound with his fingers. It wasn't closing. He sighed angrily.

"One of you will have to sew this," said Torin. "It is not rotten ... just bleeding."

"I will do it," said Gilnor.

"Let him sew it and give me a moment to sleep. We can still walk more before nightfall," said Torin.

"We'll need a fire for this," said Gilnor.

Gilnor laid out his pack and began to sort through its contents. He removed a leather skin and opened it over the grass. He placed a needle, a pair of metal claps, and a spool of thin leather thread upon it. Dord began gathering sticks and branches for the fire. He laid them down long ways over the grass, and began to stack the others vertically making a small triangle-shaped campfire. The rock was against the wind, which kept the breeze at bay. Dord used flint and steel to start a fire. He stoked it with some dried leaves, lightly blowing and cultivating the flame. Gilnor placed the needle and the metal clamps into the edge of the fire.

"Boil some water for these," said Gilnor, as he tossed some thick woolen bandages to Dord.

"Do you want a branch or leather strap ...?" Dord asked Torin.

"How about four of your damned fingers," said Torin. "I'm no child. This isn't the first time I've been cut, clapped, or threaded. Bastard gorgon. Lizard bastard."

"Come. Let's leave them to this," Borman said to Finn.

"And you, tell your damned bird I ain't dead. Last thing I want is something pecking at my innards while he stitches them up," Torin said to Finn.

"I'm afraid he doesn't peck," retorted Finn.

"Well ... you never know," said Torin.

"You won't feel it if he does," said Finn.

"Come," said Borman.

Borman and Finn left the camp and wandered amongst the grassy foothills and rock. The breeze was cool and moist. It felt good against their skin and lifted Finn's spirit. Borman took a wooden pipe from a pouch that hung along his leather belt. It was made of bright yellow yew and was heavily polished. A water dragon was etched into the wood. Its tail started at the tip of the pipe, while its body and neck stretched along the stem and shaft. The two heads of the water dragon lifted up to the bowl of the pipe. Borman took a pinch of dried leaves from the pouch and placed it into the bowl.

"Will he die?" asked Finn.

"He might," answered Borman.

"And turn to stone ... like your earl?"

"Until the time that we are all awakened."

"When is that?"

"The last days of this world. The scattered stones of our kind will break causing the rise of those that have fallen."

"Why come back from the dead just as the world is ending?"

"To help reclaim it. The end of this world, but the beginning of the next."

"Then you are not truly dead ... just sleeping, in a way," said Finn.

"Dead as you would be or anything else. There's a reckoning coming at the end of this world. It's not just for Stone Giants," answered Borman.

"It feels as if it is already here."

"No. War and battle make it seem so, but the end is not here yet. Have you ever smoked a pipe?" asked

# A DARK TYRANNY

Borman.

"No. I haven't," replied Finn.

"Then I won't ask if you've ever had dried leaves from Tumara. I guess, even if you had smoked a pipe, you wouldn't have had those before."

"How so?"

"They don't grow here. If you smoked before you'd noticed a different texture. It keeps your wits about you. At least, that's what everyone says. It's as good a reason as any."

Borman Thyn lit the pipe by flicking a small stick against the leather of his tunic. He slowly breathed in, while putting the flame to the leaves. A rich smoke came from the pipe. It smelled of freshly cut wood with hints of cinnamon and fig. The scent mixed with the breeze. Finn couldn't explain it but it made him feel like he belonged in that very moment. He did not have a family or a home. However, he supposed coming home or visiting loved ones would feel this way. It was familiar in a sense that everyone should recognize it.

"The trees of Tumara are very old. Their leaves are rich. Here, try it. Breathe slowly. The pipe is a little larger than one from here. I suppose it will make you a quick learner," said Borman, as he gave the pipe to Finn.

The pipe was heavier than Finn had imagined. He slowly breathed in the smoke. He felt it line the walls of his throat and fill his lungs. It was a bitter smoky taste breathing in, but the rich texture of wood, cinnamon, and fig filled his nose and lungs as he breathed it out. Finn could not taste the bitterness the second the time. He enjoyed it and, for a moment, forgot Borman was even there.

"Not even a cough. Seems you were born for it. Alright ... alright. Build your own boat and sail to Tumara," said Borman, laughing.

"Do you pass Tumara ... when sailing here?" asked

Finn.

"No. Turmara is south of Stone Water. Karth is north."

"Where is Karth?"

"*Where is Karth?*" asked Borman, incredulously.

"What? Should I know?"

"Finn, you are standing on Karth. *This* is Karth," said Borman, as he motioned around him.

"What? This? This is Altaris," replied Finn.

"*Altaris* ... ha," Borman laughed and took a deep drag from his pipe. "*You* may call it Altaris ... *others here* may call it Altaris. This does not necessarily make it so. Your *Altaris* is Karth and it has been called Karth for thousands of years. The Bourne named it and lived here before the first Great War. Your kind have lived here for a few hundred and already renamed it and claim it to be the center of the world."

"I was raised in servitude. Perhaps, others know all these things," replied Finn.

"Karth is actually one of the smallest of all the lands of Ehlür. These four realms don't make a ripple in the water compared to the other lands. Most here don't know this because of the seas that surround Karth. You are isolated to the other lands. Don't misunderstand me. I like Karth. Our people lived here once before the first Great War."

"Why are they here, then? The Skin Slavers, wolves, and gorgons. Why are they here if we are so small?"

"There is a war outside your lands. It has spilled over to Karth. Gorgons and such, they are not the true enemy. They are just foot soldiers, at best. The Fire-Hain and other demon beasts of Tur. These are the true invaders. Gorgons and such – just foot soldiers."

"What are the Fire-Hain?" asked Finn.

"A demon race. Fire pumps through their veins and blackness through their hearts. They were confined to Tur for an age, but they are no longer satisfied just part of a whole."

"So they are responsible for all of this?"

"Partly, perhaps ... I don't know. Things are changing in the world. Something happened, but I don't know what," said Borman.

"What do they want here?"

"They are forging weapons for a larger war."

"It's true then. The gorgons do take your soul."

"Your lands are easier to conquer. They are split amongst realms. The White Ruins was a dark temple. It has been used before."

"They are going to kill them all. They will kill her - blacken her soul," said Finn.

"We are going there too, Finn," said Borman. "They raided one of our villages. Took children. A nephew of Gilnor and Dord, seven in total. We plan to get them back."

"Nylah is with them."

"I assumed you were coming with us," said Borman.

"I am."

"Good. We will need your bird as well."

"It's not mine. We're friends, I believe."

"A Blood Falcon will follow its companion until one of you dies."

"Have you seen others?"

"There are some in other lands, but not many. For a former slave, you have quite an impressive pet. Let's see how the others are faring."

Dord was emptying a pot of dirty water mixed with blood, as Borman and Finn returned. Gilnor was drying his hands with a rag. His needle and clamps had been cleaned and were on the leather skin. Torin slept with his back against the rock. His bandages were new. Some blood had soaked through in patches. Torin's head and hair were soaked in sweat.

"Will he live?" asked Borman.

"I believe so," answered Gilnor. "He was right. It

wasn't rotten. I had to burn the wound before threading it. I do not think he should walk anymore today. We should give it the night."

"We will lose time. He won't be able to fight if he cannot walk," said Borman.

"I can fight," said Torin, in a haze.

"Our nephew is with them too," said Dord. "I think one night will not stop us from our business."

"So be it," said Borman. "We will leave at first light. This will make as good a camp as any."

"I will fight," said Torin, as he fell back to sleep.

"I know, friend," replied Borman.

---

The evening brought a slight chill to the air. The last hint of sun still laid upon the foothills in hues of red and orange. It illuminated the trees and caused shadows to grow long and twist across the grassy foothills. The rock coming from the hill blocked the wind and kept the fire alive. It crackled and glowed an amber red. A boar slowly roasted above the fire. The air around the camp was filled with the aroma of cooking and smoke from Borman's pipe. The boar had been gutted but the falcon's talon marks remained on the skin of its belly. Finn drank a glass of spiced water while they made their plans for the White Ruins. Torin was still asleep. He had awoken for a short time to eat and drink, but soon fell back to slumber.

"We should arrive to the east of the ruins. There is a beachhead there that is close to the altar room," said Gilnor.

"Yes," said Borman.

"Why do they call it the White Ruins?" asked Finn.

"He was a slave. He has not seen it," Borman said to the others.

"It was not truly white," said Gilnor. "It was an evil

place. A great dark temple used for the wicked."

"For sacrifice - taking souls?" asked Finn.

"At times, but that was not its true purpose. It was last used by the Bourne, before they fell. They did not make the temple, but it was their undoing," said Gilnor.

"Who made it?" asked Finn.

"I don't know. Few do. It was built before our time," replied Gilnor.

"Some say Nephalis. The dark one himself built it after his exile," said Dord.

"Why has it not been destroyed?" asked Finn.

"It's cursed land. Nothing will grow. What will you put in its place?" asked Gilnor.

"Sometimes it is best to leave evil to rot and decay," said Borman.

"Over time, the sun, ocean, and sand steadily beat upon it. They slowly chipped away at the walls. They left the temple bare of color. Some of the structures have fallen; some have stayed upright. This is why it is called the White Ruins," said Gilnor.

"Did you hear that?" asked Finn.

"Yes," said Dord.

"Something is out there," said Finn, as he rose to his feet.

Borman looked out into the growing darkness. He clutched his bow. The sounds of horses could be heard in the distance. He turned to see five men on horseback riding towards them.

"Riders," said Borman.

"Humans. Appear to be soldiers," said Gilnor.

"Let them approach. We will see what they want," said Borman.

The five riders had wooden shields that hung from their saddles. The shields displayed the blue and white colors of the Northern Realm with a red sword in the center. The men wore leather cuirasses with steel ringlets. Each man wore a leather cowl and had a crossbow strapped across his back. They left a trail of broken and bent grass in their wake. One of the riders held up a hand and waved slightly. They stopped cantering the horses, as they approached the camp.

"We come only to speak with you," said one of the riders. He wore a mustache and beard that was combed to a point. His hair was black and curled out of his leather cowl. A small scar went through his lips at one side. There was a wickedness behind his pale brown eyes. "I am Devlin Molt, a warden of King Tellos. These men are, of course, with me."

"Hello to you," said Borman Thyn.

"God and kings, look at the size of 'em," said one of the soldiers.

"We can easily see that you are not from here," said Devlin.

"No," replied Gilnor.

"That one maybe," said another soldier.

"I am from the west," said Finn.

"Em. I see. You should know that an edict has been passed by the king. The Northern Realm is no longer welcome to outsiders," said Devlin.

"This may no longer be the *Northern* Realm given the condition of your neighbors. It might just be *the realm*," said Borman.

"Be that as it may, we're having issues with all manner of visitors - friend and foe alike," said Devlin.

"Gorgons raided one of our villages. They took children. Given that there is not much realm left to traverse, we should be off your king's land within a day or two, at most," said Borman.

"I am ordered to force others off the king's territory. This could be at sword point, if necessary," said Devlin.

"I am sorry for you then," replied Gilnor.

"Obviously, I do not have enough soldiers with me to do this - even if I wanted to," replied Devlin.

"No. You do not," said Borman, looking over the five

soldiers.

"So, when I leave here, I will be forced by oath to report back to the castle. Get more men. This could take a day ... to go there and return here. I trust I won't find you," said Devlin.

"You will not," said Borman.

"Good. If I may ask, where are you from? In case the king asks," inquired Devlin.

"Stone Water," said Gilnor.

"I see. Well then, one last question for you. We are also looking for a man. You would remember him - very pale skin with red eyes," said Devlin.

"What do you want with him?" asked Gilnor.

"He is the brother to a rival king," said Devlin.

"He's cursed," said one of the soldiers.

"Cursed? How so?" asked Borman.

"By the devil at birth," replied the soldier.

"Have you seen this man or not?" asked Devlin.

"So, this man is wanted because of his brother? I am glad we do not have this law in Stone Water," said Borman.

"We would all be wanted men," said Dord, grinning.

"Your answer," said Devlin, growing tired.

"No. We've not seen this man," replied Borman.

"Em. We will leave you then. I trust I will not find you here tomorrow," said Devlin.

"I hope you do not," said Gilnor.

"Good. You are large men, but I've yet to meet anyone that does not die with enough arrows. We will have plenty tomorrow," said Devlin.

Finn felt an anger welling up inside of him. He thought of Nylah as a captive. She was probably sleeping on the ground surrounded by other prisoners that were dead or dying. He was not helping her that very moment. She could be dying or worse and he was not there.

*She must think I've forgotten - or died. And this fool*

*talks ... threatens.*

"Stop with your threats," Finn was brimming with anger.

"Easy, boy," said Devlin.

"I'm no boy. The boy I see is one that is threatening to go tattle on us. You say you will gather more men. Perhaps, we should just kill you here where you stand. Why wait?" said Finn.

Two of the soldiers raised their crossbows. Their horses became nervous and pawed at the ground. Wind beat down on the camp. The soldiers looked up in shock. The Blood Falcon landed on top of the rock wall behind them. Its wings were outspread as it shrieked at the men. Part of the rock crumbled under its thick talons. Devlin stared at the beast with both fear and desire.

"God and kings, do you see that," said one of the soldiers.

"You would not even come close to hitting that bird," said Gilnor, as he motioned to the soldiers crossbows. "It will be living long after we're all dead. I would suggest you leave."

"Come. Let's go," Devlin said to his men.

"It is getting dark out. Have a safe trip back to your castle. Remember to sharpen your sticks," replied Borman.

"That we shall," said Devlin, as he turned his horse. The soldiers followed his lead. They rode back through the trampled grass and eventually disappeared into the night.

"He will be back tomorrow. I am certain. He would have fought us tonight, if he had enough men," said Gilnor.

"We will be gone before first light," said Borman. "It's no wonder the realms fall so easy."

"We should have just killed them," said Finn in anger.

# A DARK TYRANNY

The Blood Falcon lifted its wings and ascended back into the night sky.

"They are gone," said Dord, as he peered deeply into the night.

"You may show yourself, now. They're gone," said Gilnor.

"Who are you speaking to?" asked Finn.

"The noise we heard before the soldiers arrived. They came from there, but the first noise was from here," said Borman.

"It's safe. We could have told them if we wanted," said Gilnor. "We will not be able to sleep with someone prowling around out there. I'm tired. Come."

A man left the shadows and slowly walked towards the camp. He had no clothes and his skin was quite pale. In fact, it was almost white. His eyes were a dull red and his grayish white hair reached the middle of his neck. It was tucked behind his ears, but a thick strand fell curving the side of his cheek and chin. He walked towards Finn and the others, but remained wary of their intentions.

"Come," said Borman, "we have food and drink."

"Thank you," said Ellison.

"I have some wool pants. I'm wearing a linen shirt under my tunic, but I can take it off and give it to you," said Finn.

"I don't want to be of any trouble," said Ellison.

"It's no trouble," replied Finn.

"Take it," said Dord. "None of us will be able to think straight knowing that a tiny pale man is sitting by us in his bare skin."

Finn rummaged through his bag for the wool pants Imeldris had given him. He gave them to Ellison and began to unbutton his leather tunic. Ellison slipped on the woolen pants and sat by the fire. Finn removed the linen shirt. He gave it to Ellison.

"It's not washed. In fact, it's dirty," said Finn.

"I cannot be too picky, can I?" said Ellison.

"Look at that," said Borman.

"Where did you get that?" asked Gilnor.

"What?" said Finn.

"That marking. You've the seal of the First Kingdom there," said Borman.

"I've always had it. I supposed my parents had given it to me," said Finn.

"For a slave, you are a constant wellspring of mystery," said Borman, laughing. "Someone find a bard to follow this one about."

"The seal of the First Kingdom?" asked Finn.

"A coin they would use to seal decrees and such," said Gilnor.

"Who, though," asked Finn.

"Your kind - back when there was only one realm. A better time than now," said Borman.

"Do you have a treasure map on your arse, too?" asked Dord, laughing.

The men laughed. Finn put his tunic back on. Gilnor took two long leather straps from his bag. He gave them to Ellison.

"You can wrap your feet in these. They aren't boots but will do better than skin," said Gilnor.

"Thank you," said Ellison.

"I am Gilnor, this is my brother Dord, that is Borman, and this is Torin. He was wounded. I am sure he will be awake and angry as ever in the morning," said Gilnor.

"I'm Finn."

"Yes, I am sorry. This is Finn," said Gilnor.

"I'm Ellison. I am not a devil, either. Afflicted, perhaps but that is the sum of it."

Ellison began to wrap his feet with the leather straps from Gilnor. The inside of the leather was soft, while the outside was stiff and taunt. There was enough of the leather straps to cover his feet and up to the top of

# A DARK TYRANNY

his calf. He tucked the last piece of the strap back under itself and pulled it tight.

"What happened to your arm?" asked Gilnor.

"My village was attacked by Storm Wolves. We had formed a caravan to find some type of refuge. The king had locked the gates - stolen the stocks and provisions of the village. We had to do something; go somewhere. The wolves came at us. There was little to be done. They made short work of us," said Ellison.

"I'm sorry," said Finn. "Gorgons raided the castle. I was at Castle Red. We are following them, the gorgons."

"So then, Storm Wolves attack. You were bitten - but lived. Now you wander these hills in your birth clothes," said Borman.

"More or less," replied Ellison. "May I ask, do you have anything to drink that is harder than water? Something to settle the nerves ... warm the stomach."

"We did, but had to use it for this one," said Dord, as he gestured to Torin.

"It seems I am truly cursed then," said Ellison with a sarcastic grin.

"Storm Wolves have a nasty bite. Most that survive succumb to infection," said Gilnor.

"Others - a small few - well, they succumb to others things," said Borman.

"I've a knack for affliction, it seems," replied Ellison.

"You all are like wandering sages. How do you know so much," asked Finn.

"We have been alive longer," said Borman.

"Journeying over oceans and traveling from city to village ... trading and hunting. You see things, hear stories," said Gilnor.

"Like seeing a slave with a giant bird and a marking of the First Kingdom upon his chest or seeing a colorless man," said Borman, laughing.

Borman took out his pipe and sat down by the fire.

He lit it using a smoldering branch from the fire. The scents of wood, cinnamon, and fig filled the air. Finn laid with his back to the ground, as he stared up at the night sky. The fire crackled. Its heat felt good against the cool night air. Finn wished that Nylah could have been with him. He thought of her. Where she was. What she might be doing. A sense of guilt came over him. It wasn't fair. She was supposed to be free - not him. Yet, here he was. Finn did not think he would be able to sleep. He felt anxious to leave. He was ashamed that he was safe and fed, while Nylah was still a prisoner. Finn was now free, yet, all he wanted, he could not have.

"Sleep," said Borman. "I will take the first watch."

"You are welcome to travel with us," Gilnor said to Ellison. "We are going north to the White Ruins... after the gorgons."

"I've nowhere else to go," replied Ellison.

"There should be Storm Wolves, as well. Perhaps, you will feel right at home," said Borman.

## Chapter 28

### The Realm of the North

Castle Suell sat in the heart of the foot hills of the Northern Realm. The rolling hills surrounded the fortress like swells in an ocean of grass. The dips and rises of the land made claiming the castle a near impossible feat for any invading army. There was little to no line of sight for commanders and their soldiers on the ground. However, there was a perfect view from the castle walls. Archers could easily sling arrows into the valleys and hilltops. Castle Suell had lasted long enough that it was no longer a foreign structure. It was a part of the terrain, as much as the grass and rocks. It belonged.

The castle itself was made of thick granite rock that bore lines of orange tiger lily and red onyx minerals. There were four spiraling towers rising in each corner of the castle. They were connected by a wide perimeter wall that the guards used to patrol and walk from one tower to the next. Heavy iron ballistas were placed along the walls with their massive arrows aimed in different directions. In the center was the heart of the castle. A looming stone structure with a dome roof sat between the four towers. The dome was constructed from limestone. Streaks of rich marble and quartz splintered throughout it like a spider web. King Tellos lived and held court in the building. The domed ceiling was unique for the four realms. Dignitaries and builders journeyed from all corners of the four realms to see the refined structure. Very few builders were privy to the methods of domed roofs. The art had all but died out over the years. Some said that King Tellos was partially responsible. Castle Suell was a prosperous place to sell and trade, due to its many visitors. Merchants and shop owners sold their wares in the courtyard surrounding the building.

A waterway had been constructed that circled the main structure. It twisted throughout the courtyard. The bronze statue of an enormous dragon's head emptied a steady flow of water from an underground spring. The water shot out like cool wet fire from the dragon's mouth. The water ran through the canal and courtyard providing water to guards, horses and the like. Children sailed wooden ships in the water and ran along beside them. The waterway led to a statue sculptured from one monstrous piece of granite. The statue was of King Pergos who ruled many years before King Tellos. He stood aiming a javelin made of bronze and was holding a shield of black onyx. He faced the main gates of the castle. The statue served as a reminder and warning to visitors that Castle Suell had weathered attacks before and still stood ready to fight. Castle Suell would sooner fall to a plague than to a sword. The water pooled around the statue's base and swirled down an iron drain.

King Tellos stood in his war room looking down at a large table. A map of the four realms was etched upon it. Markers were placed along the table to show troop positions and the locations of scouting parties. King

## A DARK TYRANNY

Tellos was a heavy man in his late fifties. His skin was pale and fleshy, which caused the black hair on his arms and neck to stand out. His face had craters and scars from having the red fever as a child. It kept him from being able to grow a full beard, so he kept his facial hair shaved. His lips were red and had a constant pout due to the pudginess of his face. His weight, shaven skin, and pouting lips gave him an odd boy-like appearance. He compensated this with his cruelty. He wore a white linen robe with a deeply oiled leather belt with a black onyx clasp. His black hair was slicked back due to sweat. King Tellos had a propensity to sweat even in the coolest of climates. He stared down at the table in thought and rubbed his thick hands through his hair.

"If the barons cannot keep their villagers at bay, I will simply appoint new barons. This castle will not be overrun with scared farmers," said King Tellos.

"Of course. These were my words similarly, your majesty. The other barons, they insisted I broach this," said Baron Martin Lancing. Martin Lancing was a tall thin man with gray hair and a well cropped beard. His eyes were a dull green. He stood proper in a green linen tunic, while holding both of his riding gloves in one hand. His jaw was squared and his cheekbones were high and long. The baron had the appearance of one whose frame was built for muscle. Yet, he was quite thin.

"I do not have time for crying barons," said the king.

Three generals stood beside Lancing. They were all older men that had the air of authority and rank. They wore thin leather vests with sections of plated iron on their shoulders and chests. Their vests bore the insignia of the Northern Realm, blue and white with a red sword. Their woolen shirts were dyed a rich blue. Finely woven chain mail draped over their leather pants.

"What of these *Acolytes*?" asked the king with distaste.

"They have amassed here," said one of generals. His gray hair was balding, so he kept it cropped. His skin was red from the sun.

"How many?" asked the king.

"We've counted nearly one hundred, but more appear every day," said the general.

"I want an envoy sent. The north is closed," said the king. "Our armies will bring down any foreign body in the north ... *Acolyte* or not."

"Your majesty," said another general. He had brownish gray hair and a thin beard. His eyes were bright green. "If they are truly Acolytes - would that not mean the Creator of all Ehlür is sending them to fight the invaders? Why not let them? From a purely strategic position, why not join them?"

King Tellos looked at the general. He held one of the markers from the map table in his hands. He walked towards the general with a look of perplexity. In one sudden motion, King Tellos stabbed the general in the eye with the marker. The man fell backwards with his hands clasped over the stone marker protruding from his eye. Blood poured from his face and escaped between his fingers. He howled with pain. He jerked like a dying fish on the stone floor. King Tellos pulled a dagger from the table.

"Where are your Acolytes, general? This Grand Master in the sky? Where are they?" demanded King Tellos. He sank the dagger into the man's neck and twisted. The man gurgled, as blood filled his throat and pooled around him.

King Tellos walked back to the table. He placed the bloody dagger on the map table where the Acolytes were said to be forming. His fleshy hands were red with smeared blood. He stared at the remaining men in the room.

"That was one man. How can Acolytes save a realm if they cannot save one man? Real or not - if there is some Grand Master floating in the sky, he is not so powerful that invaders cannot take his lands. Some deity can make a world, but lacks the power to rule it? I will be damned if I let anyone, be it god or monster, take the Northern Realm from my grasp," said King Tellos.

"Yes, your majesty," said one of the generals.

"This realm is mine. Anyone else is an invader," hissed the king.

The king breathed heavily. He stared at the table and then looked back to the men.

"What of Commander Thorne and the other one?" asked the king.

"We have not seen Matthias Thorne since he escaped," said Martin Lancing.

"Since your son let him go."

"He was traitored by his own men. Captain Eaves and the others were working with brigands and Skin Merchants. It was a feat just for him to escape. It was Gerald that informed us about the commander and the traitor king's brother," said Martin Lancing.

"Yes ... how fortunate," said the king.

"They will be found, your grace. My son will see to it," said Martin Lancing.

"Your grace, there is also word of a Blood Falcon. It was with an outsider. He was traveling with tall men said to be out of Stone Water," said a general.

"Someone from a fallen realm. I take it these men escaped capture as well?" asked the king, angrily.

"My men were outnumbered, your grace. They came to regroup and gather more men, but the strangers were gone when they returned," said the general.

"No more small scouting parties! I want enforced squadrons patrolling the territories!" the king was searing with anger. "We are not the Western or Eastern

Realms! This does not happen in my realm. The Northern Realm. I will not allow it!"

"Yes, your grace. I will make the order," said a general.

"Bring the commander and other one to me. Find and kill the rest. It's better for someone to die than to return here crying about being outnumbered or traitored. You tell them," said the king.

"It will be done, your grace," said a general.

"Go. Take this corpse with you," ordered the king.

The two generals opened the door to the room and ordered two soldiers to remove the body. Thick lines of blood trailed behind the dead general. Martin Lancing stayed in the room, as the others left. He looked at the blood soaked floor. The king stood looking at the table with his back to the baron.

"Your grace," said Martin.

"Now what?" asked the king with a tired tone.

"You, of course, are the king. Appointed and ruling with divine knowledge."

"Get on with it."

"There is turmoil in the realm. Speaking candidly of killing barons and what not. It could cause unrest and turmoil amongst those that fill this castle's coffers and store houses."

"You are walking close to being replaced yourself," warned the king.

"Oh, I should hope not. I am the voice of reason to the other nobles. Your forces are, of course, spread out among us. I command a section, as do the others. That said, you are the king," said Martin Lancing.

"You should hold your tongue."

"You should think a little more before killing. You killed a capable man just now; a man of military strategy. We need those men if we are to repel the invaders," warned the baron in a dry tone.

"Are you sure about walking so closely to mutiny

and rebellion with the king? Was there not a dead man just where you stand?" asked King Tellos.

"This is only council," said Martin Lancing with a cold look.

"This war will not last forever," warned the king.

"I should hope not, your grace," said Martin Lancing. "I will go make your decrees to the other barons. I shall see to it that someone cleans this blood off your floor."

"I am not squeamish of blood, Martin."

"Good. We need a king of strength and cunning," replied Martin Lancing.

"No mention of honor?" mocked the king.

"Honor? This is the great and lasting Realm of the North."

## Chapter 29

The Acolytes

It was just after midday when Luras and Matthias could see the Acolyte camp. The camp was seated in a valley. Foothills loomed on all sides. The inside walls of the hills were granite and rock. They were covered with a thick moss. Mist clung to the moss causing it be a vivid green. Tents of various colors were erected throughout the camp, most were weathered and old. A section of the camp was roped off for horses and oxen. The camp itself was busy and full of life. Some of the occupants hurried through the camp with a purpose, while others sat talking. The sound of a solitary violin could be heard. It was a constant sound that hummed under the staccato clang of smiths and craftsman. Blacksmiths hovered over their iron anvils pounding smoldering steel. Wooden racks were constructed that held weapons, shields, and armor. The armor was made of both leather and plate. Bowyers leaned over their wooden shafts, sanding them with a determined precision. A group of men and women sharpened wooden arrows and laid them into a basket. The smell of food and smoke drifted through the valley.

"They've set camp in the Weeping Valley," said Matthias.

"Something bad happened here?" asked Luras.

"No. Not weeping like crying. There is a hot spring under the ground. It bleeds out of the sides of these foothills. See the rock and moss there. It's from the water that weeps from the rock," said Matthias.

"This close to the ocean?" asked Luras.

"Yes. It's an oddity. Good place to set camp. Fresh water. Walled in from the cold," said Matthias.

"There are so many of them," said Luras, as he looked down at the bustling camp.

"It seems we are not so unique after all. Were you expecting fanfare or trumpets?"

"It is just strange to see so many," replied Luras.

"I'm sure this valley is very blue and glowing at night," said Matthias, grinning. "Luras, we are here with the rest now. However, I would not descend this hill expecting a warm reception."

"I am not sure what I expect."

"Good. It's always better that way."

"Why? What are you expecting?" asked Luras.

"Questions ... problems," replied Matthias.

"I was expecting better than that."

"I suppose you could always kill the lot of them. You've grown into that role quite nicely," said Matthias, as he slapped Luras on the back. "Let's go. I need some food and fresh bandages."

"Has the bleeding not stopped?" asked Luras.

"Some. I can't believe he stabbed me," said Matthias. "I was standing right there. He wasn't even looking. Let's go."

Luras and Matthias entered the camp with stares from the other men. Some of the Acolytes were too busy to notice the newcomers. However, those that saw them took note. Luras was the only Bourne in the camp. Other Acolytes nodded at him, while some whispered amongst themselves. There were some that took note of Matthias, as well. Matthias felt the looks of scorn and condemnation from some of the other men. The moment he entered the camp, he felt that he should not have come.

*I do not belong here. I'm not like these men.*

"There," Matthias pointed towards a fire.

Several tree stumps had been cut for seats. Three were empty; two were being used. The two other Acolytes at the fire were dark skinned with deep brown eyes. They wore leather vests with steel ringlets. Their pants were dyed a light brown and made from a thin woolen fabric, which was tucked into their leather boots. Both men were wide chested and did not wear shirts under their vests. Their arms were thick and knotted with muscles. Their skin was adorned with ink etchings of sea creatures and maps. The ink was black and well faded. Matthias and Luras sat on the stumps next to the fire. The two men nodded to them a silent welcome.

"From the Western Isles?" asked Matthias.

"Aye," said one of the men. He had a healthy scar that began at this scalp and ran down along his cheek, jaw, neck, and disappeared under this tunic.

"Matthias. This is Luras," said Matthias.

"Hello," said Luras.

"Nelos. This is Tylin. We sail under Captain Dowr," said Nelos.

"Are you all Acolytes - the whole crew?" asked Matthias.

"Most turned. We went north and east after," replied Tylin.

"I hope the other man died," said Matthias, pointing to Nelos' scar.

"Ah. No," replied Nelos. "No man did this. A pod of Razor Tail."

"He was lucky," said Tylin.

"Razor Tail?" asked Luras.

"A nasty fish. Death to the lot of them. I was one of the more fortunate ones. They were able to keep my parts in and thread me back up. I only lost a foot," said Nelos. He pointed to his left leg. He wore a wooden boot that strapped just below his knee. It was well painted with the appearance of a worn leather boot. One would have to look hard to realize it was made of wood.

"Not sure I would call that luck. Maybe your bad luck was just not as bad as the others," said Matthias.

"Perhaps," replied Nelos, revealing a small grin.

"I've never looked upon a Bourne before. You are a Bourne, no?" asked Tylin.

"I am," replied Luras.

"He had not seen one himself, until recently," said Matthias.

"I understand why they look at him," said Nelos. "But they also look at you."

"I have a past here," said Matthias.

"We all have a past," replied Nelos. "We were pirating not long ago."

"Well, it seems that the Granduers are a great judge of character," said Matthias.

"Grandeurs are merely the servants of the Mighty One, the Creator of the World," said Tylin.

"I stand corrected then," replied Matthias. "Although, I wonder if there's some great misunderstanding. A Bourne, pirates, and a well-hated man ... hardly the Acolytes one would imagine."

"Who is running this camp?" asked Luras.

"A sickly old man. He was a scholar of some type," replied Nelos.

"I thought he was a farmer. His name is Heams. Ryland Heams," said Tylin.

"He wasn't a general or commander?" asked

Matthias.

"Not that I'm aware," replied Nelos.

"I would like to meet him," said Luras.

"They are discussing plans in that large tent there," said Nelos. He pointed to a large crème colored tent made from thickly woven canvas. It was stretched around wooden posts.

"We take your White Ruins back tomorrow. They've been going over the plans the last few days. Captain Dowr is with him now," said Tylin.

"Why the ruins? The land is barren and deserted," said Matthias.

"Not anymore," replied Tylin.

Two Acolytes approached the men. They wore oiled leather tunics and pants with green and brown cloaks. Each man had a quiver on his back and a sword at his belt. They each wore beards. One man's was wrapped with a leather strap at the chin. Their eyes glowed like the other Acolytes. They walked with purpose and had a pensive look. Matthias had seen the look before. It was the look men had before battle. It was one thing to die, but another to send men to their deaths.

"You there," said one of the men. "The general would like a word."

"I didn't think there was a general in charge," said Matthias. He looked at Nelos and Tylin.

"There is and he would like a word," said the other man.

"We should see what he wants," said Luras, rising to stand.

"Only him," said the man.

"Am I now being detained by this group?" asked Matthias, incredulously.

"I've no orders to detain you. The general only said he wanted to speak with you," replied the man.

"He can wait here until you return," said the other man.

# A DARK TYRANNY

"Of course, he can. He is an Acolyte just like the rest of you," said Matthias.

"Go. I will be here," said Luras.

"You've no reason not to trust him," said Matthias, as he stood.

Matthias followed the two men towards the large canvas tent in the center of the camp. The grass had already been trampled in areas making dirt pathways throughout the camp. The wound on his waist began to grow warm and throb again. There was a dampness against his skin; he felt the slight trickle of blood. Matthias walked slowly behind the men. The pain in his waist was more intense with each step. He noticed the stares and whispers from others as he past. Other Acolytes looked at him and then spoke to one another in hushed tones. Matthias could smell the general's tent with each approaching step. Mint and lavender drifted from the tent. It was not a natural scent. Instead, it was heavy and medicinal. It lingered around the tent like warmth from a fire. Matthias followed the men inside.

There was a table in the center of the room. It was made from wagon boards. They were laid across a series of wide tree stumps. The stumps had been flattened with precision. The boards laid perfectly flat across them. A cured leather skin made from oxen was draped over the table. A map of the four realms was etched in the leather skin with meticulous detail. Painted stones were strewn across the map. They represented various armies and fortresses. Matthias saw a blue stone that sat upon their location on the map. A black stone sat upon the White Ruins. Three wooden chests were in one corner of the room. They were aged. The red stain on the wood had long worn off. The metal latches were covered with rust and oxidation. They were the size a family would use to put clothes and valuables in when traveling. However, these were open and filled with books, maps, candles, and glass vials filled with medicine and oils. A lantern hung from the center beam of the tent. It had a small tin bowl attached above it. Scented oil and medicine were poured in the tin to heat over the flame. A small stream of translucent gray and purple smoke drifted up from the bowl. It was the source of the mint and lavender that encased the tent both inside and out. Matthias had smelled it outside, but, once inside, it made his eyes water and his throat feel slightly numb.

   A frail man stood over the table peering down at the various stones. He was tall and thin and looked to be in his mid-seventies. His hair was gray and cut short; the skin on his face was closely shaved. He was ordinary in his appearance. His clothes were plain wool like that of a farmer or laborer. The wrinkles on his face were more pronounced around his eyes and brow. He had a tired looked about him. His movements were both purposeful and deliberate, due to his waning strength. The only vibrance about him was the blue glow around his faded brown eyes. A man with skin as dark as coal stood beside him. He had muscled arms and an imposing frame. He appeared to be in his early forties, as his hair was just beginning to show some gray. He had a thick curly beard. His hair was very short and stubbly, as if he had been bald just days prior. His eyes were a soft hazel but now glowed blue like an Acolyte. He wore a thick leather vest that was worn and faded from the sun. It had been heavily oiled, but sun damage could still be seen. It flaked and bent at the seams. The vest had a bronze circle attached to the chest. A map of the Western Isles had been etched upon it. He wore wool pants with stripes of brown and faded maroon. His boots were black and had a buckle on one side. The man's muscled arms were adorned with ink drawings, like the other men from the Western Isles.

   "Commander Thorne, sir," one of the men said to the old man.

"Thank you both. Rest. Get some food," the old man replied.

The two men had a hesitant look.

"It's quite all right," said the old man.

The two men nodded and left the tent. Matthias stood putting his weight on the side that was not wounded. He could feel a steady trickle of blood.

"I take it you are Ryland Heams, the general here. You must be Captain Dowr," said Matthias.

"I am hardly a general. I was a teacher of military strategy and, of course, history. A few months ago, I was on my farm. I was in bed thinking that my time here was coming to a close," said Ryland Heams, coughing. "Now, here I stand."

"There you stand," said Matthias. "So, you aim to lead the Acolytes to victory?"

"There is no victory for us. The Acolytes are to bide time. We keep the enemy at bay, giving honorable men a chance to rally."

"And if they do not rise to the cause?" asked Matthias.

"We hold the enemy back as long as we can. I believe some will rise to the occasion, Commander Thorne," replied Captain Dowr.

"I am no longer a commander. You may call me Matthias, but not commander."

"Captain Dowr and I were going over the plans for tomorrow."

"The White Ruins. I heard. We were just speaking with some of Captain Dowr's men."

"You and the other one - the Bourne," said Captain Dowr, in a deep voice accented with the tongue of the Western Isles.

"His name is Luras. He is an Acolyte just like the both of you," replied Matthias.

"No one denies this," said Ryland Heams. "Nor, though, can we deny that the Bourne nearly enslaved the world. Now, one walks into our camp. Surely, you understand our basic concern."

"There's no foul motive to Luras. He was selected by a Grandeur the same as you," replied Matthias.

"Nephalis was a Grandeur," said Captain Dowr.

"Not all Grandeurs revel in good. There has always been a war. Sometimes, it comes to the surface. It did a thousand years ago and it does today," said Ryland Heams.

"I don't speak for all Bourne or for Grandeurs. This, I do know - the Bourne in your camp has fought alongside me for days now. If anything, he has a childlike notion of right and wrong."

"That's why, when a Bourne decides to be evil, the world reaps their wrath," said Ryland Heams.

"Here, I thought I was to be detained yet again. Instead, there is only talk of Bournes and deeds done a thousand years ago," said Matthias.

"The Bourne is an Acolyte, as far as we know. We simply have questions - concerns like any rational person would. We only ask that you keep watch. We are not sending him away," replied Ryland Heams.

"Good. Because, otherwise, you would be acting against the wishes of those that chose you - all of you."

"And you," said Captain Dowr. "You are an Acolyte yourself. You are not including yourself in your speaking."

"I am here, am I not?" replied Matthias.

"Yes. There you stand ... bleeding it seems," said Ryland Heams.

"We were attacked a day ago. Skin Slavers and wolves," said Matthais.

"You were cut by a Skin Merchant? Has the wound gone green?" asked Captain Dowr.

"No. A northern soldier cut me. Scared and hacking away. There's no rot to the wound. I just need it sewn."

"We haven't a healing table or proper apothecary,

but Captain Dowr and his men are quite proficient at fixing wounds," said Ryland Heams.

"I would prefer to keep my foot," replied Matthias.

"Ah, Nelos would agree with you. Sadly, his foot was gone before he left the water," said Captain Dowr.

"Good. Thank you, Captain," said Ryland Heams. "Do you think you will be able to fight tomorrow?"

"Depending on how well they sew. I plan on going with Luras," replied Matthias.

"You are both welcome on the Lisbeth," said Captain Dowr.

"So you are taking boats to the ruins. Then what? Walk the bar?" asked Matthias.

"There is no good strategy for the White Ruins. It will rely on force and numbers. A sandbar surrounds the island, two hundred yards all around. We have to strike before they fortify their defenses," said Ryland Heams.

"My ships will go as far as they can. Then it will be skiffs and ladders to the bars," said Captain Dowr.

"The men will be running the bars to the ruins. Perfect targets for arrows," said Matthias.

"The first men out will hold back to fire arrows," replied Captain Dowr.

"Their arrows won't reach the ruins, only the beach, possibly the old village," said Matthias.

"It is enough pressure to send out any foot soldiers or scouts hiding in outskirts," said Ryland Heams. "There is no real strategy to the White Ruins. It's how they were designed. You take it by force and numbers ... or not at all."

"And if you take it? What then?" asked Matthias.

"It's cursed ground," replied Ryland Heams. "For us, it does not serve as much purpose. For our enemy, it is a perfect staging area before entering the realms. Nothing will grow there and we do not need another port, especially one with a sandbar like the ruins."

"Then what?" asked Matthias.

"Claim it. Burn what we can. Leave a scouting party behind to warn us of the first sight of others," replied Ryland Heams. "More importantly, marking the entry of the Acolytes into the war, at least, the war here."

"Are other Acolytes already fighting elsewhere?" asked Matthias.

"You are one step ahead," said Ryland Heams, smiling. "Get sewn and bandaged. Rest. The war for a new age is upon us. Nothing will be the same after tomorrow."

"And Luras?" asked Matthias.

"Keep him close," replied Ryland Heams.

"You will find that the closer he is to you, the better your chances of living," said Matthias.

"Understood," replied Ryland Heams.

Matthias turned to leave but stopped. He paused for a moment and turned back to Ryland Heams and Captain Dowr.

"I will only say this once. You appear to be a decent man. I understand that his being a Bourne is of concern. However, if you cross him - Acolyte or not - there will be a reckoning. I will see to it," said Matthias.

"Matthias, history is full of reckonings. It is what ultimately awaits all of us. Now, rest. A much larger reckoning begins tomorrow," said Ryland Heams.

## Chapter 30

## The White Ruins

Nylah stared out the window of the wagon. It was a thin slit in the wood. There were no bars. The opening was too small for even an arm to stick out and climbing through it would be impossible. The smell of salt and moist air drifted through the window with each gust of wind. There was a wooden bench built into the wall covered with silk and linen pillows. Nylah stood with her knees on the bench. She held onto the window with her fingers to brace herself while peering out. The ocean swells caused the ship to rise and fall at the will of the water. The gorgon caravan had reached the end of the northern territory two days prior. Their ships were waiting for them. The fleet had anchored safely in the ocean during the invasion. The gorgon armada returned from the ocean to take the caravan to the ruins. The captives were herded into long black warships. The masts held large sails dyed yellow and black. The ships cut through the restless ocean, as they sailed towards the White Ruins.

The wheels had been removed from the two large one-room wagons that held Nylah and the other prisoners. They were now simply wooden rooms, a mobile cell. They were both put onto a supply ship. It dwarfed the smaller gorgon warships. Oxen, provisions, and weapons were loaded along with the two wooden cells. Nylah could see the other warships. The other captives held onto one another, as the warship cut through the swells. They were no longer roped together. There was nowhere for them to run.

The other captives with Nylah were sleeping, except for one of the twins named Desa. She had thick curls of red hair that were twisted into a thick braid. Freckles laced her pale cheeks and nose. Desa was seventeen but looked much younger. She lacked the curves of other girls her age. She had followed Nylah's lead and was staring out the small window on the other side of the cell. Like Nylah, Desa was unable to eat or sleep as much as the other captives. She had a constant feeling of dread.

"Nylah, come look. I can see them," whispered Desa.

"The ruins?" asked Nylah, as she got down and walked towards Desa. She stepped over and around the other sleeping captives.

"Yes. There it is," replied Desa. Nylah stood on the bench beside her.

The White Ruins drifted within the small framework of the window. They stood looming in the distance, relics from another age that refused to be forgotten. There was a massive cathedral made of chiseled stone in the center of the island. The stone looked to be quartz or alabaster. The roof was a dome that was twisted into a spiral. Although, a wide section of it had long since split and fallen. Gulls sat along the fractured framework of the dome. They cried out into the expanse of sky around them. Three towers extended

# A DARK TYRANNY

from the cathedral. They were of varying heights, but even the smallest one stretched high above the cathedral. The wooden storm windows for the towers had rotted off leaving gaping holes scattered throughout the stonework. Two of the towers had broken and crumbled apart. A patchwork of stone and sun-burnt timber jutted out from the severed towers like a broken bone. One of the towers was still standing. It was the smaller tower. Like the cathedral, it had a domed roof that twisted at the top. It was constructed of bronze, which was somewhat clean, but heavily scratched from the onslaught of wind and sand. The bottom borders of the dome were coated a tarnished green and brown. Rocks and debris littered the ground around the ruins. A statue of a grandeur was erected near the rows of cracked steps in front of the cathedral. It held a sword in one hand and a piece of parchment in the other. The bust of the statue had long ago split and fallen. The head and pieces of the wings laid in different places around the base of the statue. The coastal village that wrapped around the cathedral was a now dilapidated mess of stone and exposed timber. The rotten wood had faded and turned gray from the sun. The bones of the dead villagers had long ago turned to dust and blown into the sea.

"Other gorgons are already there," whispered Desa.

"Preparing for our arrival," replied Nylah, quietly.

"I don't want to go. They mean to take our souls. I'll kill myself first. I will," said Desa.

"I know," replied Nylah. She put her arm around Desa's back. "Maybe, there will be a chance for us yet."

"How? They are everywhere," whispered Desa. Her eyes welled with tears.

"I don't know, Desa. I don't know."

## Chapter 31

### An Entrance at Dawn

The three boats cut through the dark water with a quiet precision. They were skiffs that villagers of Gist used for day trips. They traveled along the coast hauling Dill root to the neighboring villages. Finn and the others had only taken three of them. They planned to return them if they could. The majority of villages were deserted anyway, as it was dangerous to travel. The boats did not have a cabin, only a long narrow hull. They were meant for swift travel, rather than a voyage of any significant amount of time. The boats had one square sail that caught the wind with ease. Borman, Gilnor, and Dord each manned one of the boats. They had lived much of their lives traveling on the water. They maneuvered the boats for stealth and speed. Gilnor had Torin in his boat. Dord had a boat to himself. The extra room would be needed for those they took back from the gorgons. Finn and Ellison rode with Borman.

# A DARK TYRANNY

The clouds were very dark and moved quickly in the night sky. There was still some time before the first hints of dawn spread over the horizon. The moon was radiant and hung low in the darkness. It reflected strips of light across the black water. Finn looked up at the sky. His cloak was pulled tightly around him. Small swells and waves beat rhythmically against the boat, splashing water onto Finn and the others. The closer Finn was to the ruins the more angst he felt. It was hard to know that Nylah was so close yet still a captive.

"It shouldn't be long now," said Borman.

"I can see torches but not the ruins," said Ellison.

"I doubt we will see much beyond torches until we're there," replied Borman.

"It is like they're guiding us in," said Ellison.

"There must be quite a few of them ... to feel secure enough to light their presence," said Borman.

"The caravan alone had many gorgons," said Finn.

"We don't plan to fight them all or announce our presence, if possible," said Borman.

"They will have sentries patrolling," said Ellison.

"Yes. Those we will fight and kill quickly," said Borman.

"Are you sure about this, Ellison?" asked Finn.

"Where would I go? If there are people that can be freed, we should try," said Ellison.

"Your help is appreciated," replied Finn. He looked into the distance at the torches.

"We will find her. I hope we find them all," said Ellison.

"As do I," replied Finn.

"If someone had told me last year that I would be where I am now," said Ellison.

"Should we live, there is no guess to where you will be next,'" said Borman.

"In a warm tavern with a jug of spiced ale and room full of songs and laughter," said Ellison. "That would be nice."

"Brace yourselves. We should be close to the sandbar. It's too dark to see. I will slow our speed as much as I can," said Borman. The three boats continued to slice through the water towards the looming shadows in the distance.

A light fog drifted over the island. Two gorgons patrolled the coastline. They walked the ground between the cathedral and the outpost on the southern tip of the island. Each one carried a lit torch and a spear. A sword hung from their waists. One gorgon had a warhorn buckled to his leather belt. Their tunics were dyed black but were faded from the sun. Both gorgons were tall and thickly muscled. Their scaled skin wrapped tightly around their apish frames. One of the gorgons stopped walking. He spoke to the other in a dark guttural tone. The other gorgon began to reply but an arrow whistled out of the darkness. It cut through the gorgon's throat and cracked through its neck. The gorgon twisted and fell to the sand and rock. The other gorgon reacted quickly, reaching for the warhorn on his belt. He put it to his lips, but two more arrows pierced through the shadows. One hit the gorgon in the stomach, while the other split open the front side of his face. The gorgon dropped the warhorn and fell to his side. He reached again for his horn. He tried to yell out. The gorgon could see Gilnor approaching out of darkness. He was wet from the knees down. Others were behind him. Borman let loose an arrow. It cut through the night with a low whistle. The arrow hit the gorgon in the chest with a dull thud. It fell lifelessly to the sand.

"Put out those torches," said Borman. "And it's best to retrieve those arrows. We will need all of them."

Gilnor buried the torches in the sand. He took one of the swords from the dead gorgons and gave it to the Ellison. Dord and Borman pulled the corpses into the water. It was not deep, but it was able to conceal. Torin marked the sand and rock with his sword. It was a faint circle with a line crossing through it.

"To find our way back," said Torin, holding his side. "They will not see it until first light. If we are not gone by then, our stealth is lost regardless."

"There were more lights gathered around the main structure," said Gilnor.

"We saw them from the water. They did not move. It is like a camp," said Dord.

"I saw them as well. The captives are probably close to the ruins, if not in the ruins themselves," said Torin.

"Let us hope they're not. We need to move. Wolves will not be carrying torches," said Borman.

The group went further inland off the beach and walked along the edge of the village. It was mostly rubble but a few buildings were partially intact. They moved slowly and tried to stay out of the sight of the other patrols. The smell of dust and decay was prevalent. It blended with the salt air and it pushed throughout the island. It proved difficult to move through quietly. The ground was a mixture of fragmented rock, dead wood and sand. There were no bushes or vegetation. The ground thirsted for water and life, but all around it was death and dust. The slowness bothered and ate at Finn. Everything was drawn out. He was tired of waiting. The misery of the island pulled at his core. Nylah was there somewhere. She was alone. A prisoner on the most cursed ground in all the realms. Nothing about this was right. Finn filled with anger at his entire life up to that moment. It burned inside him.

"Are you all right," Ellison whispered to Finn.

*How can I know this? I can almost hear ... sense his blood running. He is hot with anger.*

"It is hard to be so close," replied Finn, quietly.

"Keep on your target," said Borman. "Rashness will

ensure our defeat."

The group continued to move forward. The looming presence of the White Ruins grew more visible. The gorgons had made a camp outside of the cathedral. It did not appear to be a main camp. It was encircled with torches planted within the rock and sand. Captives were huddled together in the center. They were once again roped together. Gorgons patrolled the camp, while others ate or slept against rocks. Larger groups of gorgons could be seen in the distance, as they entered or left the cathedral. A pile of dead prisoners was made just outside the ring of torches. Some of the corpses looked to have died from the journey, while others were ripped and gutted. Gulls set atop the heap of dead bodies pecking at the flesh and each other. It was a rancid smell that cried out to all the scavengers of the island.

The group approached the outskirts of the camp. They crouched behind a wall of white stone that used be part of a stable or house. There were other shelters around the cathedral that had partial roofs and walls intact. They could see the pile of bodies and the camp behind it. The majority of the island was still asleep or milling about.

"They will all wake soon," said Torin.

"Those bodies," said Finn.

"I don't think they would have killed her, Finn ...or Stone Giants for that matter. They are here for weapons not food," said Gilnor.

"They ate them?" asked Ellison.

"More likely than not," said Borman. "There is nothing kind about the gorgons or who they serve."

"I don't see her down there," said Finn. "I can't see them all, but I don't see her," said Finn.

"Hause and Kiev are there," said Dord.

"Yes. There," said Gilnor, excitedly.

"There are so many. Gorgons and captives," said

Ellison.

"We kill the sleeping ones first. Quickly and quietly," said Torin.

"We will then have a short time to kill the others and move the captives back to the boats," said Borman.

"There isn't enough room for them all," said Ellison.

"We will take all we can. The rest can wait on the edge of the bars. We can try to come back," said Borman.

"They will drown," said Ellison.

"Better to drown free," said Torin.

"I don't see Nylah," said Finn. "What of Nylah? I'm not leaving without her."

"I know. We have to get our people too. They are why we came," replied Borman.

"I will stay and help you," Ellison said to Finn.

"We can speak to the other captives. They will know more. We are to start here, though," said Gilnor.

"Do you see any Storm Wolves?" asked Ellison.

"I don't but I am sure they're here," replied Dord.

"Is that a problem?" asked Borman.

"No," said Ellison.

"Conserve your arrows. Fire at what you know you can strike and kill. We will need all of them. Sleepers first. Then, we kill the rest," said Torin.

"Are you all right for this?" Borman asked Torin.

"Ask me that again and I will kill you first," said Torin.

The first to notice anything was one of the captives. The arrow whistled through the camp with precision. It lodged into the skull of a sleeping gorgon. It did not cry out. Instead, it simply laid heavier against the ground. The dry and brittle ground took in all the dark blood. Three more arrows crossed through the camp. This time one of the gorgons tried to move. He reached and grabbed wildly at the arrow in his throat. Another arrow followed, striking him through the eye. His hands fell, as he dropped lifelessly. Other captives saw the dead gorgons. They looked around into the darkness. One of the gorgons saw the captives looking in different directions. He approached the center of the camp. Something was off. The captives did not look at him. They stared forward or at the ground. He looked to the other gorgons. The sleeping gorgons did not move. Then, he saw it. An arrow jutting from the eye of a gorgon. It was suddenly clear. He could see the other arrows. The dead gorgons. He looked around the camp, while at the same time grabbing for his warhorn. He breathed in but felt something hit him from behind. He fell to the ground with a searing pain across his back. Blood pooled around him. He reached for the horn but his arms did not work. He looked up and saw Gilnor standing over him. Gilnor's sword dripped black blood. The gorgon heard rustling and noise in the camp and the clanging of swords before he faded to his death.

Finn quickly notched arrows and picked targets. He picked gorgons that Gilnor and Torin had engaged in combat. The quicker the gorgons fell, the less chance there was to alert the entire island. Gilnor and Torin hacked wildly at the gorgons. They pounded them back with their shields crushing bone and tearing muscle. They felt arrows from Finn and Borman whisk by them. The gorgons at the camp fell hard and fast. They had no tactical advantage and were taken unaware. The gorgons lashed out at Gilnor and Torin with spears and swords. However, when a gorgon would strike at them, they were met with arrows. The arrows dug deeply through leather and scale breaking bone and spilling blood. The gorgons that did not fall felt the stinging bite of the stone giant's sword. It was an easy victory.

Dord ran to the prisoners. The seven children taken from Stone Water were huddled together. One of them had a thick head of blonde hair. The boy's eyes welled with tears, as did Dord's. Dord pulled the boy into his chest and rubbed his hair. The young stone giant sobbed uncontrollably.

"You're safe, Kiev. We are here to take you home," whispered Dord. He wiped the tears running down Kiev's cheeks.

"They killed Mora," said Kiev.

"Come, we need to get you out of here, all of you," Dord said to the other children.

Ellison took his sword and began to free the rest of the prisoners. They stared in bewilderment at the pale man with red eyes that was cutting them free. Finn began to walk through the captives looking at each one. Borman pulled arrows from the gorgon corpses. Torin walked the camp and looked into the surrounding village. He kept one of his hands on his wound.

"Do you see anymore?" asked Borman.

"No. I did not hear any horns, either," replied Torin.

"We need to hurry. Someone must have heard this," said Gilnor.

"I don't see her," said Finn, as he continued to look through the captives.

"Take Kiev and the others to the boats," said Borman. "The rest of you listen - we have another boat. Follow these men."

"Nylah," Finn called out. "I am not leaving without her."

"You are alive," said Douglas. His soldier's tunic was almost completely gone. His gray hair was thin; his face was tired and stressed. The journey had nearly proved too much. "I thought you were dead."

"Nylah?" asked Finn. "You are talking about Nylah? Is she here?"

"Yes, Nylah. I told her you were dead," said Douglas.

"Where is she?" asked Finn.

"Before the ships, they put her and some others into wagons," said Douglas.

"Where are they now? These wagons?" asked Finn.

"There are more in the ruins," replied Douglas. "There are more."

"She is in the ruins?" asked Finn.

"We must hurry," said Gilnor.

"Go with them. There's another boat," Finn told Douglas. "I am going to the ruins."

"We are taking them back to the boats," said Dord.

"Hurry," said Borman.

Dord and Gilnor took Kiev and the others from the camp. The remaining captives followed them. They ran towards the shoreline and down the beach. Borman watched them until they disappeared into the night. He listened for the sound of a horn but it never came. He turned back to Finn and others.

"There are too many of them for two boats. They will panic and take the third one - our way off the island," said Ellison.

"I am sure of it," replied Borman.

"Go. There's no use in all of us being stuck here," said Finn.

"I'm staying," said Ellison.

"Torin and I didn't run back to the boats, did we?" said Borman.

"We need to leave this camp. More will come and see what's happened," said Finn.

The sound of a horn broke the silence of the night. It came from a distant part of the island. Another horn sounded. This one was closer to the ruins. The dull baritone hum of warhorns began to blast throughout the island. The gorgons began to stir. The sounds of yelling and dark speech could be heard. Ellison looked around the camp and further inland.

"That is too many for this. It can't be for us," said Ellison.

"No, they would be on us already. This is something else," said Borman.

"There. Do you see that?" asked Finn.

# A DARK TYRANNY

"God and kings. I see it. The blue lights in the water. It's all around us," said Ellison.

The White Ruins erupted with commotion and activity. Gorgons spilled out of the ruins and its surrounding camps. They were armed for battle. Storm Wolves ran alongside howling and snarling with rage. Some ran on all fours, while others charged forward on two. The gorgons wore black and yellow tunics. They carried spears and large square shields that had the image of a twisted snaked etched into the wood. Others carried large swords or bows. Their warhorns continued to hum with the anticipation of battle. A squad of gorgons saw Finn and the others. They charged towards the camp yelling. Three gorgons notched their steel tipped arrows and fired.

"Move!" yelled Finn, pointing to the stone wall behind them.

They ran towards the rubble of the village. Arrows fell behind them, while others whistled past. One of the buildings had a partially covered roof. Two broken walls supported it. They were made of stone. Rotten wooden beams crossed over the walls and helped support the roof. Finn and Borman turned firing arrows at their pursuers.

"Do you hear that?" yelled Ellison.

"Get down!" yelled Torin.

Arrows began to fall all over the coastline and village like rain from the sky. The gorgons chasing Finn and the others were littered with arrows. Arrows hit the roof of the stone structure and broke or rolled to the ground. Screams and cries were heard throughout the island. Borman pushed a stone loose from the wall. It fell leaving a trail of dust floating in the air. He could see the shoreline. A ring of blue darted over the water like fireflies at night. The first hints of morning began to crest the horizon. The shadowy outlines of Captain Dowr's ships could be seen in the distance. Men poured out of them on ropes and ladders. Flickers of blue glowed and radiated, as they moved closer to the island.

"We picked the right day," said Torin, as arrows continued to fall around them.

"Who are they?" asked Finn.

"Acolytes," replied Borman Thyn.

## Chapter 32

### The Battle of the White Ruins

The ships surrounded the island. They were silhouetted against the first orange and red hints of morning. The fog of night was slowly dissipating. Acolytes climbed off the ships in droves. They used ladders and ropes to reach the sandbars. Squadrons of Acolytes were already on the bars firing arrows towards the island. The arrows hissed and streamed through the air, momentarily getting lost in the dark sky. They arched downward and fell to the ground like hawks darting for prey. The other Acolytes gathered on the bars waiting to invade. The glow from their eyes flickered on the water. The wet breeze dampened the men and everything in its path.

Matthias and Luras stood on the deck of the Lisbeth, watching the arrows announce their arrival. Nelos and Tylin stood nearby speaking with Captain Dowr. Matthias wore his leather vest with steel ringlets over a maroon woolen tunic. His yellow hair and beard were wet from the breeze. He checked his armor and weapons. He had a sword and a shield. The shield was round and made of reinforced planked wood with an iron center. A short sword and dagger hung from his waist. Luras wore his black leather tunic with steel ringlets and brown leather pants. The hood of his dark green cloak was pushed back. His two sabers were sheathed across his back.

"Are you ready?" asked Matthias.

"Yes. How is your back?"

"Better. Nelos did a good job."

"Good," replied Luras.

"It will be chaos soon ... when we reach the island," said Matthias.

"I suspect as much."

"Stay close. There will be a push to move forward. It sometimes fails and falls back. Make sure you are not too far forward. Men often find themselves closed in, isolated. They get lost in the fight and find themselves surrounded. Know where you are and where others plan to be. If we stay close and keep our wits, we will live and make it to the ruins," said Matthias.

"Good luck to you," said Captain Dowr, as he approached them.

"And to you," replied Matthias.

"I will be here; you will be there. You can have my luck. You'll need it," said Captain Dowr, grinning.

"The other ships are taking the captives," Nelos said to Captain Dowr.

"What captives?" asked Luras.

"There are others on the island as well. They freed a group of prisoners," said Nelos.

"It's time," said Captain Dowr.

"I'll see you below," said Matthias. He took hold of a rope and began to lower himself to the sandbar.

The invasion had begun before Matthias and Luras touched down on the sandbar. The Acolytes had ceased their barrage of arrows and descended upon the island. They were met by armies of gorgons and Storm Wolves.

They clashed along the shore and inland towards the ruins. Some of the Acolytes never reached the shore. They floated lifelessly in the water, pierced by gorgon arrows. Packs of Storm Wolves ran along the shoreline ripping and tearing at the Acolytes. The Acolytes continued to press forward. Some of them had fought before. They formed small squads and repelled the wolves and gorgons the best they could. The sounds of screaming, fighting, and dying filled the air. Wounded were already scattered throughout the island calling for help. Their cries were met by snarling teeth. A group of Acolytes stood upon the rubble of the village firing arrows at the wolves and gorgons charging the shoreline. The faint silver glow of Luras' skin had already begun to emanate a red hue. He drew his sabers, as he neared land. Matthias held his sword and shield ready for battle.

"Remember, stay close and keep your rage at bay," said Matthias.

A pack of Storm Wolves ran the coastline devouring the wounded Acolytes. One of the wolves caught Luras in its sights, as Matthias and Luras left the water. It broke from the pack and ran towards him in a mad rage. It alternated between running on two legs and four. Two other wolves followed behind it. Luras did not charge the wolf. He stood motionless, both sabers in hand. The hulking beast snarled and breathed rapidly, as it barreled forward. It sprung into the air, lunging itself at Luras. Its claws were outstretched. Saliva poured from its jaws. Luras twisted to one side, while bringing one blade down. It severed the beast's arms. He followed by dragging the second blade across the wolf's exposed belly. It erupted in blood. The wolf cried out and fell to the sand. It jerked and convulsed. Luras brought down both blades, piercing the neck of the beast.

A second wolf leapt towards Luras. Matthias

slammed his shield into the wolf's snout, crushing bone and teeth. The wolf yelped and snarled, as blood dripped from its mouth. Half its jagged teeth remained intact. The rest stuck in Matthias' shield or fell to the ground. One of its eyes was already swelling shut from the blow. Matthias swung his sword cleaving the broken snout. The wolf ran but bled to death a few paces from them. The third wolf continued to charge towards them. Matthias put up his shield and braced himself. An arrow whistled past them and lodged behind the beast's shoulders. It rolled to the ground and snapped at the arrow, which was out of reach. A second arrow thudded into its throat. The wolf fell to the sand. It coughed and choked on its own blood. Matthias pierced the wolf's chest with his blade. It died instantly. Matthias saw a squad of Acolytes continuing to fire arrows at the wolves and gorgons.

"Let's move inland," said Matthias.

The island had erupted into turmoil. Matthias and Luras joined with the main wave of Acolytes. Gorgons and men were strewn across the island. Wolves continued to attack the Acolytes from all sides. There was no form to the battle. There was chaos from all sides. It was savagery at its purest. Gorgon armies charged from the cathedral. Their raw strength was overpowering. They could sever two men with the single swing of a blade. Shields could barely take one blow from a gorgon before splintering. Matthias considered the disarray.

*These men have fought, but not in battle. We won't last this way. They're too strong. Historians ... read about battles but they've never fought in one. We will lose. This is random butchery.*

"Together!" cried Matthias. "Move together! Fight as one or die alone!"

"Move in!" yelled Luras.

The other Acolytes seemed to welcome a

# A DARK TYRANNY

commanding voice on the field of battle. They fought and did their best to move into one unit.

"Shields in front! Three men deep! Archers behind! Guard our flanks with arrow and sword! No gorgon gets behind our lines! Stay together!" ordered Matthias.

*This feels too natural. Instinctive. Damn them all for this.*

Matthias and Luras fought their way towards the ruins alongside the other Acolytes. They continued to press forward as a formed unit. Men with shields took blows from the gorgons. Shields split knocking the men to the ground. Some did not get back up. Arrows were fired at will. Luras did not strike at the torso of the massive gorgon soldiers. Instead, he parried or dodged their blows. He followed digging his blades into their legs and thighs.

"Their legs! Their strength means nothing if they cannot stand!" yelled Luras.

Matthias felt his skin pull at his stitches with every blow. He used his shield both as a weapon and armor. He broke bones and spears as he slammed into the gorgons. He followed with long cleaves with his sword. Matthias had stood in a shield wall many times. He knew how to pivot his shield to break a spear shaft. This shield wall was not the best, but it would due. He made standing in front of him a very dangerous proposition. Gorgons fell around him. The Acolytes continued their press forward at a great cost. A trail of fallen men and gorgons was left with each push forward. Fallen Acolytes cried out in pain. Luras looked at the carnage around him. He moved towards a fallen Acolyte that had a jagged spear extending from his stomach. The man was crying as he held the spear shaft in his hands.

"Steel yourself, Luras. We haven't time for him now. We must keep moving forward or we will all die," warned Matthias.

"Please!" the man pleaded in a whisper.

"Luras!" yelled Matthias.

"I'm sorry," Luras said to the man, as he turned back to the fight.

It was the first time that Luras saw Matthias how the realms once knew him. A pragmatic commander that was bent on killing the enemy. His concern was the army and not the soldier. Violent men were needed in violent times. It was times of peace that were most dangerous to men like Matthias. He was comfortable in battle. He was at home.

Matthias could see the massive steps of the cathedral. His blonde hair was wet with sweat. Black blood coated his leather gloves and shield. The fight raged around him like a wildfire. The ringing sound of steel on steel mixed with the cries of men. It was almost deafening. He grabbed fallen men by the shoulder to help them back to their feet. If they could not rise, he let them stay. The Acolytes around him had finally fallen into a rhythm. They were pushing forward over the gorgons. These men were experienced fighters, but they were accustomed to small melees. They were beginning to understand the shield wall and fighting as a unit. It was still sloppy, but it was no longer a one-sided fight. Blood spilt on both sides.

The Acolytes stabbed and chopped at the gorgons legs. When they fell, they were encased in the wall like water wrapping a stone. The men inside cut down the wounded gorgons. Storm Wolves leapt over the shield wall, lashing out at the Acolytes inside. They raked their claws wildly over the men. Cries of pain caused the men in front to turn back. It gave the gorgons a chance to cut down the men in front.

"Stay forward!" yelled Matthias. "Do not break!"

The Acolytes hacked at the wolves. Luras saw that the other men had control of the wolves behind him. He continued to fight the gorgons. His skin radiated a deep red hue. He was angry but his rage seemed to hone his balance and strikes. The gorgons were strong but slow.

"When I say, open long enough for me to get through," Luras said to the two Acolytes in front of him. They both held shields and were in the front of wall.

"You want into that mess?" asked one of the men.

"Just for a while," replied Luras.

"Now," said Luras.

The two men moved their shields apart long enough for Luras to move through. He held his sabers outstretched slicing two gorgons across the waist. The blades cut through leather opening their scales and spilling out all their skin held inside. Luras bent down as a gorgon's spear struck over his head. He thrust both blades out front. They sliced the knees of two gorgons. They fell. The shield wall continued to move forward. It swallowed the fallen gorgons. Luras stood parrying strikes. He followed each one with an arch of sabers. They sliced any gorgon that stood close. Luras then fell back and let the shield wall move past him.

Matthias could see the cathedral.

*We are winning.*

A small figure in gray woolen clothes ran to the steps. It caught Matthias' attention. He backed up behind the other Acolytes to see what it was. The figure had a head of short blonde hair. It was a young boy. He ran up the steps and stopped. The boy momentarily turned around to look back at the battle. He appeared frightened by the fighting. Matthias' gaze met the boy's. He yelled out at Matthias, but the battle was too loud. It did not matter. Matthias knew the words the boy was yelling. He could see it in his eyes. Any father knows those words without hearing them. He was calling for help. The boy ran up the stairs and disappeared in the darkness of the cathedral. Matthias ran behind the men that were fighting. The shield wall continued to move forward. Luras saw Matthias running and followed.

"Matthias!" yelled Luras.

Matthias flanked the large mass of men and gorgons. He ran towards the broken steps of the cathedral. Luras followed behind.

"We are separating ourselves from the group," yelled Luras.

"I saw him," said Matthias. He was out of breath. "He ran inside."

"Who?" asked Matthias.

"He saw me. He ran inside," said Matthias.

"Who? Who did you see?" asked Luras.

"My son."

## Chapter 33

Dark Tyranny

The stairs to the cathedral were wide and long. They were deeply fractured and cracked. Some of the stones had crumbled long ago. The stairs led up to the front room of the cathedral. The roof was still whole over the room but the walls had gaping holes. The mortar had crumbled between the stones leaving splintered lines along the walls. They allowed the first rays of morning to cascade into the room. Golden beams of light crossed the room and illuminated the shadows. Dust floated through the shafts of light. A statue stood in the center of the room. It was another grandeur. However, this one was much larger than the one in the courtyard. It had no hair and its body was heavily muscled. Its strength did not appear stocky, but rather lean and agile. The green moss stones over its eyes had been heated and smoothed to a mirror like texture. The grandeur's wings were outspread, as if it would soon take flight. Its chest and legs were covered in strips of bone. The base of the statue was constructed from moonstone. Skulls of men, dogs, and other animals were carved throughout the base. The grandeur looked to be standing victoriously over the bones of the world. A dark grime had begun to cover the base. It cloaked the statue in its grip.

The chaos of battle ensued outside the cathedral. Finn and the others entered the front room of the ruins at the onset of the fight. The room was empty, as the gorgon armies battled the Acolytes. They stood close to the walls, in order to not be seen by the gorgons or any enemies that may be guarding the ruins.

"Nephalis," said Torin, as he pointed to the statue.

"Careful. The floor is crumbling," said Finn.

"Do not let down your guard," said Borman. "This place is not empty."

"Stop," said Ellison.

"What is it?" asked Finn.

"Do you not hear that?" asked Ellison.

"What do you hear," asked Torin.

"Wolves."

Looming shadows prowled along the walls outside. They blocked the beams of light as they passed. The shadows snarled and let out rumbling growls. Others approached and began to sniff and dig at the ground. Borman motioned for the group to slowly walk forward, leaving the room. Ellison started to move but felt his body growing hot. He began to lose control of his legs. Ellison fell to one knee and toppled over. The stone floor was cracked and coated in dust. It floated around him and stuck to his hair and clothes.

"Ellison," whispered Finn. He reached down to help.

"No," said Ellison. His heart beat rapidly.

"Those wolves will hear him," said Torin.

"I'm not leaving him here," declared Finn. "Help me move him."

Borman and Finn grabbed Ellison by his arms. As they raised him, Finn could feel the muscles of Ellison's arm constrict and expand.

"Something is happening to him," said Finn.

"Go," said Ellison.

Snarling and howls were heard outside the room. They grew in number. The wolves ran by the walls causing the rays of light to flicker. They suddenly erupted into a rage. Wolves dug deeper at the walls, while others raced up the steps and into the front room of the cathedral. Their red eyes glowed in the shadows. Eight Storm Wolves entered the room. They stared at Finn and the others with hatred and madness. Saliva dripped from their jaws. The wolves' teeth were stained with blood. Some of them stood on two legs, while others remained on all fours. They bared their teeth. The fur on their hides raised. Ellison fell to the ground with his hands over his stomach. Borman and Finn slowly notched arrows.

"Each one on target," Borman said to Finn. "We will not get more than one shot."

"I've the one on the far right," said Finn.

"Middle," replied Borman.

The wolf in the center darted forward charging at Finn. Borman let his arrow sail through the room. It crossed the shafts of light and dug into the wolf. It hit the wolf below the neck. The wolf cried out but continued to charge. Finn's arrow whistled through the room. It caught another wolf below the eye. The wolf grabbed at the arrow, breaking it off. Blood streamed down its face. The wolves ran at them. The first one ran on two legs. Borman's arrow still protruding from its neck. It lunged into the air exposing its claws and teeth. Borman braced himself and reached for his sword. Suddenly, a massive white Storm Wolf rose between them. It stood on two legs and breathed rapidly. Its hulking shoulders moved rhythmically with each breath. Its eyes were a dull red. They were full of anger. It struck the wolf before it hit Borman, sending it flying to the ground. The white wolf barreled into it, slicing and digging its claws into the other wolf's face and snout. There was a whimper and a snap. The white wolf turned back to the pack of wolves. It snarled and growled. Its white fur was already dampened with blood. The white wolf stared down at the other wolves. Its hulking frame rising and lowering with each breath. Borman notched another arrow and released. It sank into the chest of another wolf. Finn followed his lead. The white wolf sprang towards the pack. It raked its claws against one wolf, while sinking its jaws into another. The wolves charged the white wolf knocking it back. It rolled across the floor, slamming into the base of the statue. The white wolf rose, blood dripping from its teeth. It roared and snarled at the wolves. It charged through the wolves, knocking them aside. The white wolf kept running. It left the room and sprinted down the stairs of the cathedral. The other wolves shot after it with a mad rage.

"Go," Borman said to the others.

"What of Ellison?" asked Finn.

"He took them with him, but they could return," said Borman.

"This way," said Torin.

Torin led Finn and Borman from the room. They ran down a short stone hallway. Large sections of the walls had fallen to the floor. They had to climb over the downed stones and jagged rocks. They entered the main hall of the cathedral. It was a tremendous oval shaped room. Half of the roof had fallen. Large sections of the domed ceiling laid in chunks along the stone floor. The fallen dome had crushed some of the chiseled columns that formed a circle around the center of the room. Altars were made from the stone work of the floor. Some of them were crumbling or broken. Rotten timber and rocks spilled over them. Gulls cried and flew over the exposed roof of the cathedral. The morning sun laid heavy rays of light through the tears in the ceiling. Gulls crossed through them, as they landed upon the stones and exposed timber. Statues of grandeurs laced the round walls of the room. They were twenty feet high and were made to look down on the various altars on the floor. Gray stonework was erected in the center of the room. It was a large circle that looked like a massive well. Streams of swirling smoke drifted from it. There was a flicker of red and orange from below it. The colors laid their hues on the inside of the gray stones.

"Where are they?" said Finn, impatiently.

"They have to be close," said Borman.

"They're not here?" said Finn, as he looked over the room. "Perhaps, they've moved them."

"No. The entire purpose they brought them - the reason - would keep them in the ruins," said Borman.

"There, that stonework is new," said Torin, pointing to the gray stonework. "Smoke. Something is under the floor."

Finn ran to the center of the room. There was a circle where the floor had been chipped away. Gray stonework had been built around it like a border to keep others from falling through the floor. Finn leaned against the stone and looked down. Smoke and heat enveloped his face. The heat burned his eyes. Below the floor was another room. Fire coated the floor of the room below. There were three small stone paths that went over the fire. They met in a circle in the middle. The fire seemed to spill over the stone paths in places, leaving steam and smoke in its wake. A black altar stood in the center of the circle. Two gorgons stood by it. They wore leather armor and carried spears. Then, Finn saw the cages. Three charred metal cages were suspended from the ceiling. They hung directly over the fire. They were full of prisoners. Steam and smoke rose up from under them, heating the metal and those inside. They did not scream or cry out. They had the look of defeated resignation, as if their only hope was that they were not chosen next. Chains from the cages wound over pulleys from the ceiling. They connected to a wrought iron lever on the center landing. Finn's heart raced. He looked at the cages, but they were too full. The captives were packed too tightly together. He could not see everyone inside.

"She's down there. We have to move right now," whispered Finn.

"There must thirty or forty captives in those cages," said Torin.

"It's too far to climb. We need another way down," said Borman.

"I can jump to one of the cages. We can use clothes to make a rope. There has to be something," said Finn.

"Look at the floor," said Torin. "That is liquid fire. It's like a pool. See it drift over the stones. If you fell, you would drown - that is if your body was not burnt at once."

"What flies over the fire?" asked Borman. "Look there."

Shadows descended and flew over the fire. The burning light from the flames was lost in the black void of their form. They appeared like patches of black fog circling above the fire and under the cages. Dark bones moved within each shadow. They appeared like translucent skeletons that were more vapor than bone. They reached out at the cages with their thin boney fingers. They circled the room like starving animals.

"Ghuls," said Torin.

"What are they? Are they with the gorgons?" asked Finn.

"They are what you see. They're after scraps from the dead or worse," answered Torin.

"How do we kill them?" asked Finn.

"I don't have an answer for that. There's dark magic

# A DARK TYRANNY

here. They might have been here before the gorgons even arrived. This is cursed ground," said Borman.

"Nylah is in one of those cages. Dark magic or not, I have to try," said Finn. He was hot with anger. He felt rage welling in his heart.

"Look," said Torin. The Ghuls darted from the fire and disappeared into the walls like frightened birds. "There's something else."

Two figures entered the room. They walked along the burning path towards the circular stone landing. They were equal, if not slightly taller, than the Stone Giants. Thick red skin wrapped tightly around their stocky muscular frames. The bulging veins in their arms and legs glowed a fiery red like molten iron. Each one had thick horns protruding from the front side of their heads. They curved down, almost in a circle like the dense horns of a ram. They were dented and scratched. Their faces were thick and angular; their jaws were heavyset. They wore plated armor over their chest and legs. It glowed red like melting steel. However, it stayed intact. Their greaves were charred black iron and wrapped tightly around their thick forearms. Brown smoldering scales covered their taloned feet. Each one had a long two-handed scimitar against their back.

"Fire-Hain," said Torin.

"There lies some of your true enemies," Borman told Finn.

"Can we kill them?" asked Finn.

"Yes, but not like gorgons - not as easy," said Borman.

"But they die," said Finn.

"Yes. They die," said Borman.

"How do we kill them?" asked Finn.

"Shoot and stab them till they're dead," said Torin.

"Then a well-placed arrow would suffice," said Finn.

The dark speech of gorgons yelled behind them. Two

gorgons dressed for battle called out, as they drew their swords. One of the gorgons was already wounded. Three more rushed to meet them. They charged towards Finn and the others. Borman fumbled for his bow, as he was taken by surprise. Finn notched an arrow and sent it flying towards the gorgons. It landed below the throat of one of them. It stumbled but continued to charge. Torin drew his axes. He looked down below and saw the gorgons and Fire-Hain looking up at him. The Fire-Hain gave orders to the gorgons and turned to leave.

"The Fire-Hain are coming," warned Torin.

Borman was able to release one arrow before the gorgons reached them. He hit the same gorgon as Finn. However, his arrow rested in its skull. The gorgon jolted backwards, as it fell to the floor. Torin blocked the blade of one gorgon with his axe. He countered and dug his other axe into the gorgon's shoulder. The axe sank down through its arm and into its chest, cutting armor and scales. The gorgon fell with the axe lodged in the side of its chest. Torin pulled on the axe twice before it broke free. Borman drew his sword. He parried the wild hacks by the gorgons. Finn hit one with the shaft of his bow, breaking its teeth and drew his sword. Torin kicked one gorgon to the ground and followed with his axe. Borman felt the sting of iron pierce his forearm. His skin felt wet and warm. Finn sank his blade into the gorgon's gut. Borman followed sending his blade through its chest. Blood dripped from Borman's forearm. He wiped it against his tunic. Torin buried his axes into the chest of the last gorgon. He twisted and threw the gorgon over the side of the pit. The gorgon's body detached from the blades and fell to the liquid fire below. It thrashed and burned instantly. Finn notched an arrow. He leaned over the side of the pit. The two gorgons were still below. He released and his arrow whistled past the cages. It dug into the side of one of the gorgon's chest. It stumbled and fell to the floor. Part of its leg and arm dipped in the liquid fire. It melted the muscle and bone. The gorgon cried out and jerked to one side. The other gorgon moved out of sight from the opening above. The burnt gorgon bled profusely on the stone floor. The blood dripped over the side of the floor. It boiled before it hit the fire and burned. Ghuls suddenly descended upon the dying gorgon like ravenous beasts. They pulled at him from all directions. He was lifted into the air twisting and jerking, as they fought over him. Flesh and bone cracked and ripped. His tunic and sword fell to the liquid fire. It was all that was left.

"I need to get down there," yelled Finn.

"There must be another way down," said Borman.

"Hurry. We don't know when they will be here," said Torin, as he looked around the room.

"There!" yelled Finn.

In the back of the main hall, a broken column pierced the floor like a spear. The floor around it had crumbled and fallen, leaving a gaping hole around the column. Finn ran to it and looked down. The column was nearly six feet in diameter. It went through the floor, crossed over the room below and continued through the next wall. The section of the column passing over the alter room was charred black from the heat.

"I can crawl down on this and jump to the floor," said Finn.

"We don't know where the Fire-Hain are? There could be more," said Torin.

"You said they were coming here," replied Finn.

"We need to move or prepare to fight," said Borman.

"It looks as if we fight," replied Torin, as he turned from the column and looked at the Fire-Hain approaching them. "Go, Finn. Hurry."

Finn grabbed hold of the column and hoisted

himself atop it. It was warm to the touch. He turned to see the Fire-Hain. There was only one of them. Finn slowly made his way down the column. It was steeply slanted, so he was forced to crawl on his hands and knees. The stones of the column grew warmer with each step.

"The other could still be down there. Be careful," said Borman.

"I came for Acolytes - yet, I find Stone Giants," rasped the Fire-Hain with a deep growling tone.

"Your plans are not what you thought, then," said Borman.

"You'll find no fear amongst us. We have fought and killed your kind before," said Torin.

"A new age has dawned," said the Fire-Hain.

"So everyone says before they realize they're wrong," replied Borman.

The Fire-Hain drew his massive scimitar from behind his back. It sang as he pulled it from its iron sheath. With both hands, it swung in a wide arch. The blade hissed as it cut through the air. Torin pivoted to one side. He hit the scimitar with his axe. The sound of metal on metal screeched through the main hall. Borman had two arrows left. He notched one and sent it sailing at the Fire-Hain. The fiery beast turned as the arrow flew by. Borman quickly notched a second arrow. Torin moved in swinging one axe to parry the scimitar. He followed with his second axe to the Fire-Hain's chest. His axe sparked and scraped against the red beast's armor. Borman released his second arrow. It sped through the air, hitting the Fire-Hain in the base of the neck. The Fire-Hain stumbled backwards but caught his footing. Searing red blood dripped from its neck. It lit the arrow aflame. Torin attacked again. He lunged forward at the Fire-Hain, swinging both axes. The red beast twisted from his blows. It brought the scimitar down on Torin as he passed. Torin felt a white

# A DARK TYRANNY

searing heat slice across his back. He fell to the stone floor. His head hit against the stones, causing his nose and lips to spill blood. The Fire-Hain lifted its scimitar for a final blow. Borman charged. He barreled into the red beast knocking it off balance. The scimitar missed Torin and echoed against the stones. Borman drew his sword.

Finn was further down the column. He was over the altar room, but not yet over the stone path. He could hear the fighting but could not see them. The column was beginning to slowly burn his hands. He could not keep them against the stone for long. His eyes burned from the heat and smoke rising up from the fire. Finn searched the cages for any sign of Nylah. There was no way to see her. There were too many people in each cage. The gorgon by the altar stared up at the hole above him.

Borman parried the blows of the Fire-Hain the best he could. The scimitar was solid and heavy. The strength of the Fire-Hain showed in each blow. Torin tried to stand, but the wound on his back was grave. Blood pooled under him. His legs shook and felt weak. His vision wanted to fade. He fought hard to stay conscious. The Fire-Hain unleashed a flurry of strikes at Borman. Its scimitar hummed through the air. Borman held tightly to his sword. The swings from the scimitar nearly knocked the sword from Borman's hand with each hit. The Fire-Hain swung wide at Borman. He dodged but part of the blade ripped across his chest, knocking him to his feet. The top of his tunic split revealed an open wound across his chest. Borman could tell the blow did not hit bone, but it was deep. Blood flowed down his chest and onto his pants. He started to rise but the fiery beast was over him. Its scimitar was raised to strike him down. Borman looked at the beast with resignation. He knew it was over. He had no time to move, nor counter the blow. He looked over to Torin, but he was no longer there.

The Fire-Hain swung down with his sword. Torin slammed into the back of the fiery beast. The scimitar sparked against the stone floor, as it whisked by Borman. Torin wrapped his arms tightly around the Fire-Hain. He clasped his hands together to keep the creature from pulling him off. Torin felt his arms burn against the smoldering armor and blood from the fiery beast. The creature tried to reach behind to grasp at Torin, but its arms were pinned down. Borman gathered his strength to stand. The Fire-Hain roared with anger. It stumbled back, as it wrestled with Torin's grasp.

"It may be a new dawn, but your days of dark tyranny are over!" shouted Torin with his last breath.

The Fire-Hain felt a massive weight crush down on him. His arms snapped. Bones crushed and splintered from its fiery skin. Torin's body crackled, as it turned to heavy stone. His arms still locked tightly around the Fire-Hain. The creature could not hold the weight. It fell backwards into the fallen column and slid down. It fell through the hole in the floor. The stone body of Torin encased the creature like a cage, as they sank through the air. They crashed sideways into one of the stone paths above the fire. Molten blood dripped from the creature's eyes, nose, and ears. Its broken legs were gnarled and twisted. The weight of Torin's stone body teetered on the pathway. It dipped slightly into the liquid fire. The beast cried out with a searing rage. Its legs dissolved in the flames. Finn held tightly to the column. The impact from Torin and the Fire-Hain had almost sent him over the edge. His hands were red and burning. He steadied himself. Finn was close to the path. He was close to being able to jump to the stones below. Finn tried to keep looking at the iron cages hanging above the flames.

*They're too many. Stay calm. She is here ... in one*

*of these cages. Steady yourself.*

The Fire-Hain saw him. Finn ignored it. It would soon fall into the flames from the weight of its stone prison. Finn reached for an arrow. He would need it for the gorgon when he hit the pathway. The column was too hot for steady aim. The Fire-Hain looked towards the gorgon. It began screaming at it in the black guttural speech of the gorgons.

*What is saying?*

The gorgon turned back towards the altar. The weight of Torin's stone body continued to dip into the flames. This time it did not stop. The Fire-Hain screamed and wrestled with the stone. It was no use. They drifted over the side and sank into the flames. The Fire-Hain burned and melted, as the stone sank deeper. Finn started to lower his legs over the pathway. He was straight over the stones. The gorgon stood by the altar and placed one hand over the lever. Finn hung from the column. His heart raced. He could not draw an arrow until his legs hit the ground.

"Stop!" yelled Finn, frantically. He dropped from the column and ran towards the gorgon.

The gorgon released the lever. The cages spun loose. A loud clang echoed the room. The cages dropped. Finn raced towards the gorgon. He notched an arrow and sent it sailing forward. It hit the gorgon in the stomach, rocking it backwards against the altar. The gorgon fell to the stone floor. One of its hands hit the liquid fire and dissolved in a patch of red flame. The steel cages splashed into the fire. Liquid flames shot up from the impact. They fell down on the stone walls, the iron cages, and those inside them. The prisoners yelled in panic and terror. The cages slowly sank. The prisoners climbed the bars of the cage but they sank too fast. Captives fell screaming into the fire. They were devoured by the flames. The room echoed with horror.

"No! No!" screamed Finn. He grabbed the lever but

the last of the chain slipped through the pulley and fell to the fire below. The cages were completely submerged - engulfed in the liquid fire. Finn shook. He fell to his knees. His heart raced; his hands trembled. Tears streamed from his eyes, as the liquid fire began to steady itself.

*Nylah ...*

## Chapter 34

A Dark Council

Luras entered the front room of the cathedral. The acrid stench of blood penetrated the room. Two Storm Wolves lay dead on the stone floor. Blood pooled around them, as the dry stones drank it though their cracks and crevices. The sun cast beams of light through the tears in the walls. The metallic ring of swords clashing could be heard in the main room of the cathedral. Matthias studied the room. The statue of a grandeur loomed in the center with dead wolves below it. He heard the sound of the boy's sandals flapping against the stones.

"This way," said Matthias, running to the hallway.

"Wait. Slow down, Matthias," said Luras.

They ran down the hallway and over the fallen stones. The figure of the boy kept running in the distance. Matthias continued his pursuit. They entered the main room of the cathedral. Light cascaded down from the broken roof above. The room was circled with statues of grandeurs. Columns had fallen throughout the room, breaking altars and cracking the floor. Gulls flew around the gaping tear in the domed roof. The boy ran along the wall. He passed by the many statues. Behind one of them was a darkened hallway. The boy did not look back. He turned down the hallway and disappeared into darkness.

"There," said Luras. "We can help them."

Torin, Borman, and Finn fought with the gorgons at the center of the room. There appeared to be a circular pit or hole in the floor. Gray stonework was built up around it. The Fire-Hain had not arrived. Finn had not yet descended down the column. Luras grabbed Matthias by the arm. He pointed to the others with one of his sabers.

"We need to help them."

"You help them. Go, if you must. I cannot," said Matthias, pulling his arm away.

"Matthias! This is some of type dark magic. Those men are *real* and they need our help."

"I have to know," whispered Matthias. He turned away from Luras.

Matthias walked past the statue and entered the darkened hallway. Luras hesitated, looking back at Finn and the others. He turned and followed after Matthias. The walls of the hallway were intact. There was little light. Dust and a pungent smell of decay filled the air. The blue glow from their eyes cut through the darkness. There was a staircase at the end of the hallway. The stones had begun to crumble and split. It twisted down in a tight pattern. The acrid air grew warmer, as they descended the staircase. It began to irritate and sting their eyes. The stairs emptied into a bare room. It was dark and hot. The only things in the room were two lanterns that hung from the walls. They gave off a dull flickering light. The yellow light from the flame mixed with the icy blue of their eyes. The walls caught the light in patches. Shadows still filled parts of the room. There was a wooden door at one side. It was shut but not locked. The wooden crossbeam that locked inside the iron latches leaned against the stone wall. Luras sheathed one of his sabers. He removed one of the lanterns and held it by its rusted handle. The light sobbing of a child echoed the room like a fleeting whisper.

"Where are you?" asked Matthias.

Light flickered across the walls in hues of yellow and blue. In a darkened corner of the room stood the boy. He stared at Matthias with tears in his eyes. Light danced across his face. He appeared nervous and apprehensive. Luras walked closer to the boy, holding his lantern outstretched. Matthias stared at the boy. Tears slowly filled his eyes. They rolled down his cheeks and into his yellow beard. He slowly reached a hand out for the boy. Matthias took hold of the boy's forearm and gently pulled him close. The child wrapped his arms tightly around Matthias' neck. Matthias hugged him. Tears streamed from his eyes.

"I've missed you so much," he whispered. His voice cracked with emotion.

"Don't leave," said the boy, sobbing.

"I'm not going anywhere without you," replied Matthias.

"Matthias, your son is dead," whispered Luras. "This is dark magic."

"This is my son. This is Wylin," said Matthias.

"No," said Luras.

The light in the room became fainter. Luras looked around the room. The flame from his lantern still burned, but the light did not break the shadows. The glow from his eyes still illuminated sections of the walls, but the shadows remained. There was a coldness to them, an arrogant disdain for the light. Luras backed away to the center of the room.

"These are not shadows," said Luras.

"Matthias," hissed a voice in a low murmur. It sounded like hundreds of small voices whispering as one.

The shadows on the walls began to ripple, as they crossed over the stones. They slowly detached from the walls. They were no longer shadows. They appeared like drifting voids of darkness. They slowly prowled through the air around them. Luras raised one of his sabers, while still holding the lantern. One of the shadows floated past the sword. The blade split it in two sections but it easily regained its form.

"Don't leave me," said the boy.

"No," replied Matthias. "I'm here."

The shadows converged together to form a large void in the room. The darkness slowly pulsed and swelled. It molded into the shape of man. His face flowed in out of the void like black water. The form flickered, causing multiple shadowy figures to briefly appear. They would flicker and dissolve back into one body. The shadowy figure put his hand on the boy's shoulder. Its hand lacked structure. It dissolved like smoke, as it rolled across the boy's shoulder.

"Matthias," said Luras, "we must go."

"I can't leave him," replied Matthias. "Not again."

"That is not Wylin. This is sorcery - not your son."

"Yet, there he stands before you," hissed the figure.

"Mama is there," said the boy. "Please, come with me."

"They will only take you to darkness," said Luras.

"Have these Acolytes taken you in?" hissed the dark figure. "Have you been embraced by the realms? What has been given to you, Matthias - that has not been stripped away?"

"These are lies," said Luras.

*I have nothing. No trust from the Acolytes, nor the realms. Wylin ...*

"This boy is an illusion," said Luras.

"How can an illusion feel so real?" asked Matthias.

"Come with him. To her. There is much to be done," said the dark figure.

"Do you think they mean to let you be? You will be a slave to them - to darkness," Luras pleaded with Matthias.

Matthias stood. He walked to Luras and put one hand on the Bourne's shoulder.

"You have been a better friend than I deserved," whispered Matthias.

"You will be in league with the enemy. Matthias, think about this. You don't know what they will demand of you."

"I can't leave them, not again. I'm sorry," said Matthias, as he embraced Luras. "I didn't think this was possible. I thought they were lies."

"What do you mean? Have they spoken to you before? Matthias, they are lies. They are confusing you. Wylin is dead. This is not him. Your wife is dead. She isn't waiting for you. Think about this," said Luras.

"There is one thing they demand of me," said Matthias.

"What?" asked Luras. He felt a slow searing pain just below his chest. His legs became weak. He dropped the lantern. Glass broke against the stone floor. The oil spilled bringing a small lake of flames with it.

"I'm so sorry, Luras," whispered Matthias. He stepped away from Luras.

Luras was confused. He looked down at Matthias' dagger pushed deeply into his body. Blood began to flow from the wound. It stained his tunic and dripped down his leg. Luras dropped his saber, as he fell to one knee. He pulled the blade out. It fell against the stones with a high pitched raddle. Luras fell backwards hitting his back against the wall. He leaned against the stones starring up at Matthias in shock.

"Matthias," said Luras, as he put his hand over the

wound. Blood began to seep through his crossed fingers.

The dark figure behind them flicked and pulsed. The shadows lit with a dark energy. There was a depth to the shadows. The boy took Matthias by his hand. They turned back to the dark void behind them. The boy walked into the void. Matthias followed. Luras watched, as the darkness engulfed them. The blue aura of Matthias' eyes dimmed. It was replaced with a blackness that subdued the blue glow, like oil dripping into water. The void faded and dissolved. It took Matthias and the boy with it. The room was empty except for Luras. The blade had cut deep. He felt weak and tired.

*If I close my eyes ... I will die.*

Luras grabbed hold of the saber beside him. He kept one hand on his wound, as he gathered his strength. He did his best to stand.

## Chapter 35

Fury

Finn was on his knees in the circular landing of the altar room. He stared at the cracked stone floor, oblivious to the world around him. His tears had dried. They left streaks of clean skin under his eyes and along his cheeks. Ghuls slowly picked and tore at the dying gorgon that laid on the edge of the landing. They pulled and fought over him like jackals. Some of the Ghuls circled Finn. They reached at him with their spiny fingers of black bone. They hissed and rumbled at each other with greed and anticipation. Finn was lost in himself; he only thought of Nylah. He felt sick and his head ached. He thought of every action that led to that very moment. His hands began to tremble.

*I failed her. It should never have come to this ...there is nothing left.*

"I am so sorry," Finn spoke aloud.

"Finn!" Borman called out from the hole in the ceiling above. He stood over the gray stonework looking down from the main hall above.

Finn remained silent.

"Finn! Behind you!" yelled Borman.

Finn could hear the deep rasping breathing of the second Fire-Hain. The Ghuls scurried back into the walls. It entered the far end of the room. It walked along the center pathway towards Finn. A massive two-handed scimitar was in its hand. The fiery beast's armor glowed a molten red. Its scaled talon's gripped the stones with each step. Finn remained on his knees with his back to the approaching beast.

Borman had no more arrows. He struggled to his feet, holding the wound on his chest. Blood ran down his tunic and over his hands. The hole in the floor was too high for him to jump. He slowly staggered towards the far corner of the room. He could descend to the floor the same as Finn. He would use the column that pierced through the room.

"What is this?" rasped the creature.

The deep bellow of the Fire-Hain's voice ate at Finn. The tone and authority of its voice planted a seed of rage within him. He thought of Nylah. He thought of his life as a slave and then a captive. He had loved her. Finn thought of her last moments before the fire. Tears began to well again. However, they were the product of blind fury and anger. Finn felt beads of sweat forming on his brow. His face was flush. Finn stood. He took hold of a sword that leaned against the altar. He gripped it tightly and turned to face the Fire-Hain.

"Have I upset you, little one?" it growled.

"I am no child," said Finn.

"All humans are children," said the Fire-Hain. "Drop your sword."

"I may die today, but it will not come without a fight. This is not your land. They were not your people, you seething bastard," said Finn.

"You will claim no death today. Your soul - I will make claim against it. I might imbue it in the very sword you hold. You will live out your days at the hip of a gorgon or buried in the flesh of your own kind."

Finn lunged at the Fire-Hain. He swung his blade wildly. The Fire-Hain stepped out of the way of his blows. It blocked and parried each strike with ease. Finn grew angrier with each failed strike. He breathed heavily. The heat from the fire burned his lungs. The Fire-Hain had not even swung at him. The red beast looked down with amusement.

"Is this your first time wielding a sword, boy?" laughed the Fire-Hain.

Finn swung at the fiery beast in a rage. His lungs ached; his muscles were tired. The Fire-Hain again parried the blows with its scimitar. Finn feinted a strike at the beast. It moved to block the blade. Finn then swung at the beast with all his strength. His blade tore through the top of its shoulder. Molten blood spilled down the beasts arm. The Fire-Hain roared in anger. It thrust its scimitar at Finn. He tried to parry the blow, but the blade was swung with an overwhelming force. His sword flew from his hands, rattling against the ground. Finn turned to get another weapon from the altar. However, the Fire-Hain grabbed him by the back of his head. It was too strong for Finn to escape. Finn felt the beasts steaming blood drip off its hand and down his neck. The beast threw Finn forward. He hit the stone altar and fell to the ground. He did not move. The Fire-Hain towered over him.

"Stop!" yelled a voice from behind the red beast.

The Fire-Hain turned to see Luras standing on the center pathway at the back of the room. He held his wound with one hand and a saber in the other. Blood soaked his tunic and dripped down his pant leg. He struggled to keep himself afoot. The Fire-Hain left Finn and walked towards the Bourne. The beast stared in bewilderment.

"Leave him be," said Luras. "If you require a fight,

you need look no further."

"A Bourne?" rasped the Fire-Hain. "It seems you are not in the position to make such demands."

"I do not need an ample body to strike you down," said Luras, as he fell to one knee.

"Are you an *Acolyte*? We were allies - the Fire-Hain and the Bourne. You disgrace your people," said the red beast.

"There is but one Bourne walking this world and he is not in league with you," replied Luras. He struggled to his feet.

"You're a traitor to your own kind," growled the Fire-Hain.

"I'm tired of talking. I haven't the patience. What you have to say means nothing to me. I don't care. Leave him be. If you want a death, come closer," said Luras.

The Fire-Hain raised its giant scimitar. The blade's razor-sharp edge reflected the fire that burned around them. Luras drew his other saber. He stood motionless waiting for the beast to attack. The Fire-Hain swung hard at Luras. Its blade cut the air. Luras pivoted to one side, missing the blow. Luras then erupted in a flurry of blades. Sparks flew as their swords clashed. The Fire-Hain tried frantically to block and parry the blows. The Bourne used his blades with deadly precision. The red beast was overwhelmed by Luras' onslaught. Luras' blades caught the Fire-Hain on the arm and leg. They shaved skin and muscle. Blood flowed from the wounds. It steamed and dripped like molten iron. The Fire-Hain let out a frustrated roar. It sliced back at Luras with its scimitar. The large blade ripped through the air. The Fire-Hain continued to swing in a tantrum like flurry. Luras moved from the blade. He parried the blows. However, he did not block them. The Fire-Hain was too strong. Instead, Luras used the force of the blows to his advantage. He directed the scimitar with each parry. It hit the stones with a line of sparks. Luras slashed his sabers along the Fire-Hain with each parry. The red beast grew hot with rage. Molten blood dripped over its arms, legs and hands.

Luras' wound began to sear with pain. His legs grew weak and unsteady. He fell to one knee. The Fire-Hain swung at the Bourne. Luras stood again. He parried the blow while dragging a blade across the beast's fiery skin. The Fire-Hain stumbled backwards. Luras again fell to one knee. He could feel his wound pulsing. A steady flow of blood streamed from it. Matthias' dagger had cut him deeply. The Fire-Hain walked back towards Luras, leaving a trail of smoking blood in its wake. The beast raised its sword to strike. Luras tried to stand, but he was too weak. He fell back to one knee. He dropped one saber to the stone floor and held his wound. He kept the other saber pointing at the Fire-Hain. The red beast was riddled with the effects of Luras' blades. It started to bring its scimitar down to end Luras. The Bourne slid his saber into the knee of the Fire-Hain. It easily cut through skin and bone. Steaming blood erupted from the beast's knee. Luras pulled his saber out sideways cutting more skin and tendons. The Fire-Hain cried out in pain. It was seething with rage. The beast did not even look at its knee. Instead, it raised its scimitar high above its head. Luras tried to use his saber to push himself back up. However, he had lost too much blood. He lacked the strength and fell back to one knee. He used his saber to keep his balance. He stared up at the Fire-Hain.

*I die from betrayal ... not this blade.*

There was a shriek from above. Stones fell from the ceiling. They crashed into the fire below causing splashes of flame and smoke. The hole above the landing cracked and crumbled, as the great falcon soared down into the room. Stones and dust were left in its wake. Sunlight spilled in from the gaping hole.

Each stroke of the falcon's wings sent swells of liquid fire rocketing against the stone walls. The falcon dived towards the Fire-Hain with its razor talons outstretched. The red beast turned from Luras, bracing itself for the falcon's attack. It was too late. The Fire-Hain jerked up, as the great bird's talons cut through his armor and sank deeply into his chest. Molten blood erupted from this torso. He dropped the scimitar. It hit the stone pathway and slid into the fire, melting as it sank. The Blood Falcon lifted the red beast off the ground. Its wings sent the liquid fire pummeling against the walls. It dripped off the stones, leaving charred rock and smoke. The Fire-Hain struggled to free himself from the bird's grasp. The great falcon closed its talons. The red beast's chest imploded with a snapping of bone. The Fire-Hain went limp. It slid off the falcon's talons. Its head hit the stone pathway, as it fell into the fire. Flames consumed the red beast. The flames ran across the its body melting skin and armor. The Fire-Hain slowly sank away into the fiery depths.

Luras leaned back against the stone pathway. He struggled to keep his eyes open. The world around him wanted to fade to darkness.

*I want to sleep.*

He saw Borman jump down from the column above. He ran towards Luras. The Blood Falcon perched itself upon the altar above Finn. Luras could no longer fight it. He closed his eyes to sleep.

## Chapter 36

### The War Begins

A cool wind drifted through the tent. It took the stench of blood and sweat from the room. Men laid on straw mats. Others laid on bunks hastily made from wood and canvas. Most of the men slept. Others quietly moaned, as they were too scared to sleep. They worried they might not wake. The sun was still up. It came in through the openings of the tent and illuminated the canvas walls. Luras laid on a bunk in the corner of the room. A coarse canvas bandage wrapped his chest. It was stained with blood. He drifted in and out of sleep. Luras strained to keep his eyes opens. His vision was tired and blurry, but it slowly sharpened. He turned his head to take in his surroundings. His wound stung with every movement. He heard footsteps approaching him.

"Easy," said Nelos.

"Where am I?" asked Luras.

"Back at the camp. You are lucky you lived. You were cut deep."

"Matthias?"

"He is not here. You spoke of him in your sleep," replied Nelos.

"How did I get here?"

"A stone giant. He and another man brought you here."

"Water," said Luras.

"Go tell the commander that he is awake," Nelos said to another Acolyte. "Of course, let me get you some."

Nelos poured water into a wooden cup and held it to Luras' lips.

"Slow," said Nelos. "You were cut deeply."

Ryland Heams entered the tent with Captain Dowr. The commander looked much older and tired than the day before. He looked at the other wounded men, as he walked towards Luras. He had the look of personal responsibility and sorrow for each man. Captain Dowr nodded to Nelos as they approached. Nelos retrieved a wooden stool and placed it by Luras. Ryland Heams slowly sat on the it with the caution of an elderly man.

"Thank you, Nelos," said Ryland Heams.

"His wound is healing. It is serious. Cauterized and stitched. He needs to rest but he'll recover," said Nelos.

"Good," replied Ryland Heams. "I would ask you how you feel, but I fear I already know the answer."

"I have been better," replied Luras.

"And what of Commander Thorne?" asked Ryland Heams.

"He's gone," replied Luras.

"Gone? Gone where?" asked Ryland Heams.

"Some type of illusion. I don't know. His son was there or a version of him. He left with them both," said Luras.

"Them both?" asked Captain Dowr.

"A man made of shadows or shadows appearing to be a man. They left through some type of portal. It was made of darkness. Blackness. He left with them, but not before this," said Luras, putting a hand upon his bandages.

"So, Commander Thorne is now with the enemy," said Ryland Heams. "This is not good at all."

"I do not think he is with them. He is confused," said Luras.

"Regardless, he is with them now," said Ryland Heams.

"Most likely further north. Across the sea," said Captain Dowr.

"Then that is where I will go," said Luras.

"This isn't about Commander Thorne. This was just a battle. Our entry into the war. There is a much larger war afoot. We need everyone. Chasing after the man that betrayed you does not help the cause," said Ryland Heams.

"I would not be pursuing him out of betrayal. He's lost."

"I have different plans for you, Luras. I ask that you hear me out," said Ryland Heams.

"You may find they coincide," said Captain Dowr.

"We are moving. I am breaking the Acolytes into squads. I am sending them to different parts of the realms. We are to keep the lands safe enough for others to rise up. It will not happen here. King Tellos has amassed his armies to shut off the north. He had planned to start with us. It seems our camp is somewhat of an oddity of late. His villagers have come in droves to see those that were freed. Some of them had family taken. Then, there's the Stone Giants. One brought you here," said Ryland Heams.

"There is also a Blood Falcon," said Nelos.

"Yes. All these things have brought many villagers to our camp. King Tellos is cruel but smart enough to not kill the hands that feed him. I sent word to him that we are leaving. I plan to go with a group east to speak with King Welthorn. They are calling him a traitor king. He may be open to us ... given his situation," said Ryland Heams.

"What of me?" asked Luras.

"I would like you to travel north with Captain Dowr. We need to know what is actually happening outside the realms. We need to know the true picture of our enemy. Sail with Captain Dowr north. Bring back answers. There are other Acolytes in the world. Let them know of the Acolytes in Altaris," said Ryland Heams.

"You have many men here already. Why me?" asked Luras.

"Any man I select could ask the same question. Why you? Why not you? In the end, does it matter?" replied Ryland Heams.

"It does for me," said Luras.

"Mainly, because you are a Bourne Acolyte. You demand attention," replied Ryland Heams.

"We will take two ships north - the Lisbeth and the Tigress. My guess is that Commander Thorne is further north in the lands of Tur," said Captain Dowr.

"Or the surrounding islands," said Nelos.

"He is not your goal, but if you find him, so be it," said Ryland Heams.

"I need to have a message sent to the Greenling Woods," said Luras.

"To whom?" asked Ryland Heams.

"I have some friends there. Matthias knows the location to something of value to them. I need to make them aware, until things can get sorted out," said Luras.

"I can have someone bring the letter, but how will they find them?" asked Ryland Heams.

"Your messenger need only spend one night in the forest. They will come to him. A small parcel of pipe leaves would be nice as well," said Luras.

"I can help there," said Nelos.

"Then, I head north with you Captain," said Luras.
"Indeed it does," replied Captain Dowr.

---

Borman walked through the Acolyte camp with a canvas bag full of food and supplies. The Acolytes and villagers stared at him in wonder. He was proof to some that the world was larger than the realms. There was life and mystery across the oceans. Part of it now walked among them. Borman's wound had been bandaged. It was beginning to heal nicely. Gilnor and Dord stood with their nephew and the other children. They were packed and ready. The children wore cloaks with their hoods pulled low. Gilnor nodded at Borman as he approached.

"It will be a good day for travel," said Borman. "The air is cool. You can smell the sea."

"It will be a good start," said Gilnor.

"There is food, water, and such," said Borman. He handed the canvas bag to Gilnor. "I've also put in some Tumara leaf, as well. Don't waste it."

"You are sure about staying?" asked Dord.

"For now, I've grown fond of his temper," replied Borman.

"If you are worried for him, bring him to Stone Water," said Gilnor.

"His place is here. Anyhow, I would like to see more of Karth. It was ours," said Borman.

"We will bring them back and return," said Gilnor.

"Make sure Stone Water is fortified first," said Borman.

"We will," replied Gilnor.

"Stay alive," said Dord.

"Tell your sister I'll return soon," said Borman.

"Of course. She won't be pleased," said Dord.

"I expect as much," replied Borman. "Now, go before

it gets too late to travel."

"Be safe," said Gilnor. He put his hands on Borman's shoulders.

"You as well," said Borman. "Kiev, you and the others stay close to your uncles."

Borman watched as Gilnor and Dord led the children from the camp. They walked in a line with Gilnor in front and Dord in the back. They ascended the grassy foothills and disappeared behind the hills. Borman stared at the horizon line. The grass moved in waves with the breeze. It felt good to breathe in the cool air. For a brief moment, Borman wanted to run to them. He felt alone. He watched the grass dance along the horizon in hopes to see them again. They did not reappear. Borman took out his pipe.

---

Finn kneeled down by a wagon in the Acolyte camp. He packed his satchel with strips of salted beef, apples, and other provisions. The Blood Falcon perched on the wagon behind him. Its maroon feathers slowly moved in the breeze. It picked at its talons with its beak. The villagers gathered around the wagon to look at the massive bird. They were in awe over it. Some whispered and pointed to Finn. They discussed how he obtained such a creature. Others stared at the pale man with red eyes that stood by him. Ellison had been given clothes by some of the Acolytes. He wore a black wool tunic under a leather vest, boots, and pants. A sword hung from his waist and a curved dagger was buckled to his belt. He wore a hooded leather cloak that was brown and deeply oiled.

"I was told there is a man forming an army. They are in the east," Finn said to Ellison.

"I will be a wanted man in the east," replied Ellison.

"We all will," said Finn.

"Who is this man?" asked Ellison.

"Someone named Xander Eaves. There is revenge to be found in the east, especially for you."

"Timball was a good village. People say that about their home - but this time - it's true. It had the best tavern. I wish you could have seen it," said Ellison.

"I still can," said Finn.

Finn closed the satchel and stood. He looked at the villagers that had gathered around the wagon. He saw able men that stood with their families. Others stood alone. Finn grew indignant at how they could stand back and watch as others were taken. Their lands and loved ones were stolen, yet they stood and let it happen. They walked the Acolyte camp like it was a carnival, each one trying to get a glimpse of the Blood Falcon, Acolytes, or Stone Giants. Finn was sickened that this all happened while enemies raided their lands and imprisoned their people. Finn stood.

"Yes, there is a falcon here and giants there. But know that while we stare upon them, our lands are burning while able men stand back and watch," Finn said to the crowd. "I'm not standing idle. Some of us are going east to meet with others that choose to fight. I have no more alliance to kings or realms. My only desire is to kill as many enemies as I can before I fall. Gorgons, wolves, kings - it makes no difference. Our enemies will come to you, whether you fight or not. I'd prefer to meet them in battle than in the dark of night."

"The king, his barons, they will claim our lands if we leave," said one of the villagers.

"If you're of the same mind, than come with us and fight," replied Finn. "If some king or baron takes your lands, then we will return - and take it back."

# Epilogue

## The Lisbeth

The Lisbeth cut through the foaming swells with deft efficiency. The ship was built for speed and distance. It was not a freighter or supply ship. It was meant to outrun other ships. It was made from ironbark wood from the euclid trees in the Western Isles. It was oiled a deep brown. The sails were maroon and crème. On the front of the Lisbeth, there was the figurehead of a woman with flowing yellow hair that covered the intimate parts of her body. She held a small child in her arms. The woman held it tightly, as the ship chopped its way over the swells and waves. There was a strong wind so Captain Dowr was able to push the ship to its limits. The wind whistled and hissed, as it blew past the ship. The Lisbeth keeled slightly to one side. The ropes pulled tight with the dull hum of stretching twine. The sun was out. It heated the wood on the ship and glared over the water. It was a day to make great headway. The last few days had been slow and full of rain. Captain Dowr barked out orders to his crew. They would use the day to make up for lost time. The Tigress followed behind with Tylin at the helm. He knew that

# A DARK TYRANNY

Captain Dowr would push the ships until the wind broke or the sun went down. Both ships pushed through the ocean with determination.

The captain's quarters in the Lisbeth were small. The ship was not built for comfort. There was a desk, a bed, and rows of bookshelves built into the walls. The wood was old but heavily polished. A lantern hung from the ceiling. However, there was enough light from the portholes during the day. It cast through the round windows in beams of yellow and gold. The room smelled of wax and dust. The ship was old. No matter how clean the room, dust still floated through the light. Luras shared the captain's quarters with Captain Dowr. A bunk was put in the corner of the room for him. Luras spent most of his time below resting and recovering from his wound. He read the many books that littered the shelves. He read about the Western Isles and its surrounding lands. He studied maps of Tur and its islands. It was only within the last few days that he felt strong enough to walk freely throughout the ship. Nelos still checked his bandages twice a day. Luras had gotten to know Nelos and Captain Dowr quite well. He liked them, especially their direct manner of speaking.

Luras laid in his bunk. He watched the lantern slowly rock back and forth, swaying with the boat. He drifted in and out of sleep. Luras heard a bell ring. For a moment, he could not tell if he was dreaming it or not. It was real. Luras jolted up. There was commotion on deck. He heard feet running above him. The watchman on the mast was calling out and ringing the bronze bell. Luras rose out of the bunk and adjusted himself to standing. He left the room for the deck above.

The crew lowered the front sails, as the ship slowly turned into the wind. It glided by the wreckage. Large chunks of black wood floated in the water. A yellow and black sail coated the surface of the swells. It moved rhythmically with the water. Debris littered the water around the wreckage. Bottles, paper, clothes, baskets, and other items drifted with the current. There were also bodies.

"Gorgons," Nelos said to Luras, as he looked over the railing. "A supply ship."

"What happened to it?" asked Luras.

"Something didn't like it," answered Nelos.

"Razor Tails," said one of the men.

"No. Something much larger than Razor Tails," said Nelos. "We don't want to be here long enough to find out."

"There!" yelled a crew member from the other side of the ship.

"They've found someone," said Nelos, as he and Luras ran to the other side.

Luras watched as the crew of the Lisbeth pulled three women from the sea. They were burnt from the sun and nearly unconscious. One of them did not move. Luras walked closer to them. One of the women was clearly dead. Her eyes were rolled back and she had begun to bloat. She looked similar to another girl they took from the water. She was alive, but unconscious. The third woman had black hair that curled in ringlets. Her eyes were a vivid green. She was scared. Luras approached her. He kneeled down beside her.

"Someone get some fresh water," said Luras.

"Help me," said the woman.

"You are safe," replied Luras.

"Don't let them take me again," she said.

"The gorgons are gone. You're with us now. You are safe," said Luras.

The woman began to cry. Luras put his arm around her.

"What is your name?"

"Nylah."

# Appendix I

List of Names in

Of Darkness and the Light

## **The Southern Realm**

~ Finn: born into servitude to the King of the Southern Realm, falconer at Castle Red.

~ Nylah: daughter of a noblewoman, lives in the Southern Isles, niece to Lady Tanda.

~ Margery: born into servitude to the King of the Southern Realm, baker at Castle Red.

~ The Baron of Moor: head of Castle Red.

~ Lord Hartley: a nobleman of the Southern Realm, friend to Lady Tanda.

~ Lady Tanda: a noblewoman of the Southern Realm, aunt to Nylah.

~ Lilith: the daughter of Lady Tanda and cousin to Nylah.

~ Tilda: merchant of the Southern Realm, friend to Nylah.

~ Waltur: the butcher of Castle Red.

## The Eastern Realm

~ Easton Welthorn: King of the Eastern Realm, resides in Castle Horos.

~ Ellison Welthorn: brother of Easton Welthorn.
~ Malvern: adviser to King Welthorn.

~ Jon Leland: Royal Treasurer of the Eastern Realm, adviser to King Welthorn.

~ Riley Moore: Minister of Land of the Eastern Realm, adviser to King Welthorn.

~ Haurice Marlon: Captain of the Guard of the Eastern Realm, adviser to King Welthorn.

~ The Council Elect: two villagers elected to the king's Council to speak for the villagers, a largely ceremonial position.

~ Jon Lince: copier of books, scrolls, and maps for the village of Timball.

~ Jared Horn: merchant in Timball.

~ Cal Mossy: logger and lumber merchant in Timball.

## **The Village of Reddington**
(Outskirts of the Eastern Realm)

~ Thorson: alderman of Reddington.

~ Wreth: villager of Reddington, a bowman.

~ Norris: villager of Reddington, husband to Lindy.

~ Lindy: villager of Reddington, wife to Norris.

~ Robert: villager of Reddington, a child.

~ Imeldris: lives outside the village of Reddington, friend of Finn.

## **The Northern Realm**

~ Matthias Thorne: exiled commander of the Northern Realm, a wanted man by all realms.

~ King Tellos: king of the Northern Realm, resides in Castle Suell.

~ Martin Lancing: nobleman and baron of the Northern Realm, adviser to the king.

~ Gerald Lancing: lieutenant of the King's Royal Soldiers, son of Martin Lancing.

~ Devlin Molt: Warden of the Northern Realm.
~ Xander Eaves: a captain in the Army of the Northern Realm.

~ Helms: scout and soldier of the army, reports to Xander Eaves.

~ Denthas: mercenary of the Northern Realm.

~ Jarren: mercenary of the Northern Realm.

## **The Western Realm**

~ King Uthan: King of the Western Realm.

~ Henri: villager of Wyndale, husband of Mary and father of Finn.

~ Mary: villager of Wyndale, wife of Henri and mother of Finn.

~ Noble of the Western Realm: known as the child monger, handles matters for the king, collects children born during the king's season of birth.

## **The Stone Giants (Stone Water clan)**

~ Hemlor Nyman: Stone Giant, the Earl of the Stone Water clan.

~ Borman Thyn: Stone Giant of Stone Water, friend to Finn.

~ Dord Kynd: Stone Giant of Stone Water, friend to Finn, brother of Gilnor.

~ Gilnor Kynd: Stone Giant of Stone Water, friend to Finn, brother of Dord.

~ Torin: Stone Giant of Stone Water, friend to Finn.

~ Kiev: nephew to Dord and Gilnor, a child, captive by gorgons.

~ Hause: nephew to Dord and Gilnor, a child, captive by gorgons.

## **Woodlanders of the Greenling Woods**

~ Watsy: Woodlander of the Greenling Woods, hotheaded, scout.

~ Locke: Woodlander of the Greenling Woods, scout.

~ Hermie: Woodlander of the Greenling Woods, scout.

~ Weyton: head of the Woodlanders.

## **The Acolytes**

~ Luras: formerly a Nighteye named Mirkus, now a Bourne, last of his kind.

~ Ryland Heams: leader of the Acolytes in the four realms.

~ Captain Dowr: former pirate from the Western Isles, captain of the Lisbeth and the Tigress.

~ Nelos: former pirate, shipmate under Captain Dowr.

~ Tylin: former pirate, shipmate under Captain Dowr, helms the Tigress.

# Appendix II

## Map of Altaris

## (Smallest continent of Ehlür)

# Altaris

*formerly Karth*
*(smallest continent of Ehlür)*

## ~ ABOUT THE AUTHOR ~

C. M. Pendleton is the author of the epic fantasy series Of Darkness & the Light. He holds a bachelor's degree in science and attended Gordon-Conwell Theological Seminary. He lives in North Carolina with his wife and four children.

Visit www.cmpendleton.com for more information about C.M. Pendleton and this series. Register to receive updates about forthcoming books and stories pertaining to the Of Darkness & the Light series.

Made in the USA
Middletown, DE
18 December 2016